IN ENEMY HANDS

★★★★★ "IN ENEMY HANDS is an exhilarating romantic suspense tale . . ."

—H. Klausner, Independent Reviewer

"IN ENEMY HANDS is an exciting suspense that will force you to read it in one sitting. Heart-stopping action, rapid-fire dialogue, and adventure in every chapter propel IN ENEMY HANDS forward in a race to the finish."

—*Romance Junkies*

★★★★ "IN ENEMY HANDS is a well-written, non-stop, action-filled story of good versus evil. The characters are well defined, and there are some excellent, imaginative scenarios that will leave you breathless. The interaction between Dante and Nadia is sizzling and based on love and trust. If you enjoy a good romantic thriller, this is the book for you."

—*Affaire de Coeur*

"IN ENEMY HANDS is **fantastic**! It is action packed and deeply sensual and I was on the edge of my seat from the first page to the last. . . Michelle Perry has written a truly captivating and thrilling book with IN ENEMY HANDS. It's a must read for any romantic suspense fan. I can't wait to read it again!"

—*www.joyfullyreviewed.com*

"Ms. Perry delivers another impressive romantic suspense with IN ENEMY HANDS. The action is almost non-stop and both characters are more than sufficiently developed in order for us to understand why they feel and act the way they do. If you are in the mood for a thrilling romance with characters you can't help but adore, then this book is a must read. I'm certainly hoping some of the secondary characters will get their own book in the future."

—*Romance Reviews Today*

THE THREE MOTIVES FOR MURDER

★★★★ "Perry pens a suspenseful mystery that will keep readers guessing and on the edge of their seats."

—*Romantic Times*

"I absolutely loved Natasha and Brady. Natasha has lost herself since the horrible deaths of her friends. She is stubborn, passionate and strong-willed. She thinks Brady is sexy and too stubborn to listen to the truth of what happened years ago. But she loves him and is not willing to give up on him. Brady is sexy and charming. He is disgusted with himself for still having feelings for Natasha after the pain she caused him. Brady thinks Natasha is selfish, stubborn and he can not deny the love he still feels in his heart for her. The secondary characters in THE THREE MOTIVES FOR MURDER are fun, sexy and vibrant. I had to keep reading to see how they would play out in the story."

—*Billie Jo, Romance Junkies*

"THE THREE MOTIVES FOR MURDER is a fast action intense suspense with twist and turns that keeps readers guessing until the very end.

Perry creates a complex mystery with just enough romance, mystery and suspense to bring readers to the edge of their seats and keep them glued to the pages. THE THREE MOTIVES FOR MURDER moves readers along on a roller coaster ride taking them from high points to low and never letting up until the mystery is revealed."

—*Tara & Deb, Review Coordinators, Suspense Romance Writers*

DEDICATION:

For Patricia Yarworth Myers

Published 2008 by Medallion Press, Inc.

The MEDALLION PRESS LOGO
is a registered tradmark of Medallion Press, Inc.

Copyright © 2008 by Michelle Perry
Cover Model: Melissa Noble
Cover Illustration by Adam Mock

Printed in the United States of America
Typeset in Adobe Garamond Pro

ISBN# 1933836008
ISBN# 978-193383600-3

10 9 8 7 6 5 4 3 2 1
First Edition

ACKNOWLEDGEMENTS:

Rebecca Miller, Ronnie Wayne Scissom, Rebecca Coleman, Cat Walker, Lori Saltis, Theresa Gaus, Karla Bran, Patsy Phillips, Nicole Service, Gladys Brady, the Perrys, the Yarworths, the RWG gang: Angie, JAC, Sky, Kristen and Judith.

CHAPTER 1

On Thanksgiving morning, we gathered in darkness in an abandoned Sears parking lot. When I exited my ancient Pontiac, I didn't bother to lock it. Hey, if a thief wanted it, more power to him. My defroster had stopped working last week, so—after scratching a clear patch on my iced-over windshield with the edge of a CD case because I couldn't find the scraper—I'd spent the twenty-minute drive scrubbing the fog off the inside windshield with my sleeve, squinting at the road, and trying not to breathe.

Rubbing my hands together, I moved toward the black van. Other agents drifted from the shadows like ghosts. In the predawn hours, the cold November sky cast everything in a strange, monochrome gray tint, making me feel like I was caught in a black-and-white

1

movie. Our dark clothing only added to the effect. We entered the van in a somber procession that made my throat ache, because this wasn't like any raid I'd ever been on.

There was no AC/DC *Back in Black* blasting from the speakers, none of the pumped-up, adrenaline-laced chatter. No Johnny Angel asking if I wanted to sit on his lap.

"Hey, Chief, I'm askin', not harassin'," he'd joke when Bill shot him a stern look.

Today, the inside of the van was utterly silent. Pale, worried faces gazed at me and nodded in greeting, all except one. With his head in his hands, Cougar hunched forward on the edge of the bench that lined the sides of the van. His unruly brown hair peeked from beneath the edge of his black knit cap. I slid in beside him and squeezed his arm.

He glanced at me with bloodshot blue eyes, then leaned back. His gloved hand grasped mine, a gesture that would've normally inspired any number of rude comments and catcalls. But not today.

Instead, Luke Jacobi, the agent on my right, took my other hand and reached for the man on his right. In a show of solidarity that made my eyes burn, agent after agent linked hands with the man on either side, until at last Bill clasped Cougar's and completed the circle.

Tucker Fitzgerald cleared his throat. "Our Father,

please extend your protection over the men . . ." He glanced at me. "—and woman—assembled here today, and most especially protect our brother, Angel. Guide us in our mission, and deliver him unto us unharmed in body and spirit."

We all echoed his amen and the circle broke. When I attempted to release Cougar's hand, he gripped my fingers and refused to let go. That was okay. He and Angel were like brothers, and I knew he was taking this harder than anyone. If holding his hand gave him some comfort, I was glad to do it, because I damn sure couldn't think of anything reassuring to say. Angel had vanished yesterday in the middle of an undercover operation, and I think we all assumed the worst. Even the DA had finally stopped dragging his feet and drafted a search warrant for the estate of Frank Barnes, a suspected class one drug dealer.

Usually, riding in the van didn't bother me, but today my stomach lurched when we took the curves. This was the fulfillment of a dream for me, a lifelong quest for revenge, but suddenly Frank Barnes didn't matter. Seeing him punished didn't matter; I only wanted my friend to be alive.

"Almost there," the driver said.

We threw on tactical gear and checked our weapons. Our badges hung on cords around our necks, and I pulled Cougar's from beneath his shirt. When the van braked to a stop, Bill barked, "Go, go, go!" and threw open the door. We hit the ground running.

ATF agents spilled from another van and surged in front of us with a battering ram. They splintered the front door while we raced around back. For a few seconds, it was chaos. Agents shouted "ATF!" or "DEA!" or simply "Police!" when we stormed inside. Someone was screaming "Down! Down! Down!" but there was no one inside to get down.

The mansion seemed utterly vacant, but we didn't slow down until we'd searched every room, every closet. Cougar and I swept the last room together.

Nothing.

Cougar kicked the bedroom door. It cracked against the wall hard enough to knock a hole in the plaster. He turned and stalked out of the room.

"Cougar, no!" I yelled, not really knowing what I was telling him not to do, but alarmed by the fury on his face. I raced back down the stairs on his heels. He stopped on the landing, yanked his helmet off, and hurled it across the room. It bounced off the paneled wall with a loud thwack, and he turned his stormy eyes on me. "Barnes *knew*, Necie. He knew we were coming, just like he knew Angel was a cop." He pointed over my shoulder and shouted, "Which one of you bastards is working for him?"

Pressing my hands against Cougar's chest, I glanced behind me at the cluster of men. Karl and the ATF agent beside him glared back. Not knowing what else to do, I grabbed Cougar's arm and dragged him outside. He let me, or otherwise I couldn't have budged him.

Snow fluttered from the sky, and the cold wind shrieked around us, whipping my hair in my face. We stood on the back deck facing each other while the tiny white flakes swirled around us.

"Cougar, listen to me," I said, but he was staring over my shoulder, through the patio doors. Grabbing his chin, I forced him to look at me. The despair in his eyes made my stomach clench. "Listen," I repeated, softer this time. "You can't throw accusations like that around. I know—"

"I know, too," he said, his face reddening. "Angel didn't mess up. Someone sold him out."

The words hung between us, and I had to admit, I believed it, too.

Cougar shook his head, the muscle in his jaw working furiously. "There's no way Barnes could've known unless there was a mole."

The whine of a motorcycle interrupted our conversation. A hooded rider exploded around the corner on a yellow Yamaha and raced toward the woods. Cougar and I vaulted the railing and took off after him.

Cougar entered the forest a few steps ahead of me. When he lurched to a stop, I collided into his back and knocked us both down on the slippery leaves.

Scrambling to his feet, he never even looked at me. I peered around him to see what had his attention.

Angel sat on the ground, tied to a tree, with his long legs splayed out in front of him. Snow dusted his black jeans like powdered sugar, and his chin rested against his chest. Blood streaked the front of his white T-shirt.

Half-running, half-stumbling, Cougar raced toward him, the motorcyclist forgotten. He grabbed a fistful of Angel's black hair and jerked his head up.

A tiny black hole burned in the middle of his forehead.

"No!" I screamed—or at least I think I did.

The howling wind abruptly died, leaving behind a moment of utter stillness and silence.

Angel's eyes fluttered open, and he stared at Cougar.

"Hey, man," he said. "I'm freezing. Get me up from here."

CHAPTER 2

Cougar gaped at him, then shot me a disbelieving look. He still clutched a handful of Angel's hair. "Y-you," he stammered.

"What's the problem?" Angel said, and winced, though I think he was trying for a smile.

Somehow that broke my paralysis, and I scrambled toward them. "Angel, you've been shot."

He frowned. "No. Barnes knocked me out or something. I can taste blood. I think he hit me with the gun . . ."

I slid next to him, and couldn't resist the urge to check his pulse. Cougar stared at me, and I noticed he was clutching Angel's other wrist.

I heard a commotion behind me, and turned to see Ubi and Tucker burst through the tree line. Like us, they stared dumbfounded at Angel.

"Would you all quit gawking and get me up?" Angel said.

"You've been shot," I repeated, and yelled over my shoulder, "Call 911!"

"Necie, I'm fine," he protested. "Let me up."

He struggled against the ropes, and I pressed a hand on his shoulder to still him.

"You have a hole in the middle of your forehead, handsome," I said shakily.

It was small caliber, probably a .22. The sickly sweet stench of his charred flesh made my stomach knot.

"What?" Angel's brown eyes widened. His usual bravado disappeared. Suddenly, he looked very young and confused.

Gently, Cougar tilted Angel's head forward, then he turned his own face away. "And you've got an exit wound the size of a half dollar," he whispered.

Angel blinked. "I've really been shot?" He squeezed his eyes shut. "I-I remember Barnes holding the gun to my head, but I thought it misfired or something. I thought he hit me with it. Am I gonna . . . can you see . . ."

"Just hang on, man," Cougar said. "I'm not moving you until the EMTs get here."

A tear slipped from the corner of Angel's eye and stalled halfway down his cheek. "Coug, I'm scared," he said.

Though his face was nearly as white as the snow

falling around us, Cougar tried to smile. "Ah, man . . . you think he'd know better than to shoot a Red Sox fan in the head."

Angel snorted. He leaned his head against Cougar's, and they both laughed. Then they cried.

"Just hang on," Cougar said.

The ambulance arrived seven minutes later. The EMTs didn't seem to know what to do with him any more than we did. Afraid to lay him down, they managed to transfer him to a gurney while keeping him sitting up straight. Cougar insisted on riding with them to the hospital.

Angel was in surgery for three hours. Cougar paced the waiting room, then finally the hallways, hounding the nurses for information every few minutes. I tried to calm him down before they threw him out. Most of my attempts at conversation garnered only a grunt in reply, but when I asked how Angel had seemed on the way to the hospital, Cougar stopped pacing and sagged against the wall. The tightness around his mouth vanished for a moment, and he almost smiled.

"He asked the driver to find out the Notre Dame score. The poor EMT was so flipped out that he did it. When Angel heard they were down by seven, he said, 'Bummer.' Then he closed his eyes. I tried to keep him talking, because, you know, my mama used to wake me up every two hours after I'd taken a helmet to the head in a game. Sometimes I'd wake up and find her hovering

9

right over me. I'd yell, she'd yell . . . it scared the hell out of both of us. She was checking to see if I was still breathing. That's what I was doing to him."

Ubi nudged Cougar and pointed to the ticker on the silent television screen mounted in the corner of the room. Notre Dame had come back to win by three.

"Good," Cougar said, rubbing his forehead. "Good."

I squeezed his hand.

The OR doors swung open, and we ran to meet the surgeon. He pulled his blue-green cap off and squinted at us.

"So, how is he?" Cougar said. "When can we see him?"

"Are any of you family?"

Cougar threw open his arms. "C'mon, man! We're all family. Just tell us how he's doing."

"I'm sorry to tell you this, but Mr. Angelino is in a coma."

"What?" Cougar exploded, and the surgeon took a step backward. "Man, what did you do to him? He was doing great! He was talking and everything."

The surgeon's mouth tightened, and he turned to leave. I pushed between them and clutched the doctor's sleeve.

"Please," I said. "He didn't mean anything. We're all upset. We were hoping for better news, with the way Angel was acting . . ."

The man's frown softened. "The damage done by a head injury is not only the result of the first impact. Swelling can prevent blood from coming into the brain, causing damage. That's what's happening to Mr. Angelino. We drained a hematoma, and have him on medication to reduce the swelling. Right now, we're monitoring the pressure."

"What about brain damage?" Tucker asked.

"Well, he's lucky the bullet was small caliber. A bullet entering the skull sets up sonic vibrations within the cranial vault, which sends shock waves slamming through gelatinous brain matter. A powerful shot can vibrate the whole brain to a pulp even if it barely passes through the brain's substance. With a .22, you don't have as much of that vibration."

"Then why do they say a .22 is a hit man's gun of choice?" Ubi asked.

"Well, with a .22, sometimes the bullet gets in and can't get out. It ping-pongs around in the skull until it levels everything. To be honest with you, I don't know how Mr. Angelino got so lucky. Someone up there must be watching out for him, because . . ." The corner of his mouth twitched. ". . . he, ah, has an unusually thick skull."

Cougar snorted behind me, and I smiled.

"Sometimes bullets take weird paths," the doctor continued. "The shot passed through the prefrontal lobe and followed the curve of his skull to exit out the back of his head. I was actually expecting more extensive damage than I found. If we can get the swelling down,

I have great expectations for him."

"What do you mean, 'great expectations'?" Cougar asked. "Will he be. . .normal?"

"He'll probably have to spend a while in therapy to relearn some skills—the frontal lobe affects cognitive ability. For example, he may remember what a toothbrush is, but not how to use it. He might have trouble sequencing—following the steps to make a pot of coffee, for example. You might also see a change in temperament. Someone who was previously outgoing might seem suddenly shy."

He paused, and we fell silent. I thought about Angel, and how impossible it was to imagine him being shy, or not even knowing how to brush his teeth.

The surgeon cleared his throat. "But let's take it one step at a time. Our main worry right now is swelling. If we can control that, we've won most of the battle." He glanced at Cougar. "I promise, I'll do everything I can to help your friend."

Cougar wrapped his arm around my shoulder and leaned into me as he extended his other hand to the surgeon. "Thanks, Doc."

The surgeon shook his hand before slipping away.

Cougar turned from me and scrubbed his face with his hands. "Aah," he said. "Shit."

I pasted on a smile and moved in front of him. He looked up, but his eyes stared straight through me.

"Angel's tough," I said. "He proved that today. He's going to be okay."

Cougar blinked and finally focused on me. "I told his mother the same thing on the telephone. I promised her he was okay." He exhaled. "Now I have to tell her he isn't."

Not knowing what to say, I wrapped my arms around his waist and hugged him tight. He squeezed me briefly and kissed the top of my head. Then he pushed me away.

"Go home," he said. "Spend what's left of Thanksgiving with your husband and kid."

Glancing at my watch, I realized dinner at my mother-in-law's was already over. Elizabeth Bramhall suffered neither fools nor tardy daughters-in-law lightly. The headache throbbing behind my eyes seemed to intensify when I imagined walking into her house an hour and a half late and having her and the rest of Grady's entire extended family stare down their aristocratic noses at me. To say I didn't fit in with them was an understatement. Maybe if I hung out a little longer, some of them would be gone by the time I got there. Besides, it felt wrong to leave before they brought Angel out of recovery.

"I'll leave in a few minutes."

Without waiting on a reply, I flopped down in one of the waiting room chairs and closed my eyes. I didn't mind blowing off Grady's snooty family—or even

Grady, for that matter—because Elizabeth and his uncles always monopolized him at these things anyway. At the last family gathering, the only Bramhall who'd actually spoken to me without being spoken to first was Grady's crazy Aunt Mary. I hated that I'd missed Thanksgiving dinner with Abby, however, even though I figured she was too busy playing with the other kids to notice.

I didn't mean to drift off, but I found myself dreaming of the beach, of sweet-scented tanning lotion and frozen daiquiris—something that was explained when I awoke to find Cougar's jacket tugged up under my chin. The smell of his tangy, coconut-lime aftershave clung to it, and won him my vote for the best-smelling man on the planet.

I rose and folded the jacket over my arm. Tucker dozed a couple of chairs down, but Cougar stood at the window, staring down into the parking lot with his arms hugged to his chest. The rest of our team seemed to have cleared out. With a start, I realized it was growing dark outside.

Grady was going to be so pissed.

"Hey," I said, and Cougar turned to face me. "Any word?"

"He's out of recovery, but he'll be in the critical-care unit until tomorrow. No visitors, so you might as well go home. Tucker's staying with me."

He cupped his hands over his mouth and blew into them. "Is it just me, or is it friggin' cold in here?"

I tossed him his jacket. "This might help. Want me to find some blankets?"

"No, I'll be okay. Just go home and eat a piece of pumpkin pie for me. I'll call you if anything changes . . ." Cougar grimaced. ". . . either way."

With a nod, I left. After another twenty-minute bout with my windshield, I pulled into my driveway. The house was completely dark. I frowned at the glowing green numerals on my dash. Ten minutes after six. Why weren't Grady and Abby home yet?

Using the remote clipped on my visor, I opened the garage door. Grady's gleaming Porsche sat in one of the bays.

Strange.

After parking, I climbed out and put my hand on the Porsche's hood. Cool to the touch. I fished my house key out of my pocket and entered through the side door. Moving through the dark kitchen, I wandered into the living room to search for the phone. I reached for the light switch, but my hand—and my heart—stilled when I saw the silhouette of the man sitting on my sofa.

Maybe Barnes had come to settle the score between us once and for all. With my hand on my gun, I flipped on the light.

"Oh, geez," Grady snapped, shielding his eyes. "Cut that off!"

I was so relieved that I did what he asked, despite his tone. "Grady, what are you doing? Where's Abby?"

"She's spending the night with Mom. They're going shopping tomorrow, to get those shoes Abby wants."

"The Tahoes? I told Abby she couldn't have them."

Grady gave a theatrical sigh. I was glad the light was off, because if I'd seen him roll his eyes, I would've probably thrown something at him.

"Mom wants to buy them for her. I don't see what the big deal is."

I yanked off my coat, threw it at the chair, and missed. "The big deal is, I said she couldn't have them. No six-year-old should own a pair of $120 shoes."

"Mom can afford them. Hell, *we* can afford them. The way you act, you'd think we were on welfare or something."

"Just because you have money doesn't mean you should throw it away. Do you think it helps Abby to cater to her every whim?"

"She's my kid. If I can give her what she wants, I will. You've got to get rid of that chip on your shoulder about money, Necie. Did the irony escape you that you just parked a two-thousand-dollar car in the garage of a half-million-dollar home? I thought about just having that piece of crap towed and buying you a new one, but I know you're so damn pigheaded you'd probably send it back."

I gritted my teeth. Nobody gave me anything. If I didn't earn it, I didn't want it. Period.

"Look," he said. "I know you had things rough

growing up, but things aren't like that now—"

"I'd advise you to drop this line of conversation, Grady."

He laughed, and the soft clink of ice cubes distracted me. "Are you drinking?"

He held the glass up and rattled it in response. "No. You want one?"

I hated when he drank, because that usually meant he was looking for a fight. His next words seemed to prove it.

"Where the hell have you been all day?"

I moved toward the couch. Despite my nap, I was exhausted. I didn't feel like fighting, so I made an effort to control my temper. "The raid went bad. We found Angel, but he'd been shot. We've been at the hospital waiting on him to get out of surgery."

"You missed Thanksgiving dinner."

"What?" I stood in front of him. "Hel-*lo*. Did you hear me? Angel was shot. He's in a coma."

"I don't know Angel. All I know is, you told me you'd be home early. What good did you do him by sitting at the hospital?"

Pressing my hand to my forehead, I replied, "He's one of us. I had to be there."

Grady stood. Nose to nose, we glared at each other in the faint glow of the streetlight streaming through the window. He threw his glass against the fireplace, and I flinched when it shattered.

"Who is 'us,' Necie? When I say 'us,' I mean me, you, and Abby. I thought when we married you would eventually settle down and forget this, be the kind of wife you should be—"

I stiffened. "I am not your mother, Grady."

"Then be Abby's," he shot back. "She kept looking at the clock and asking when Mommy was coming. Do you know how embarrassing it was, to sit there with my entire family and know that my wife was too busy to spend the holiday with me?"

"Unlike most of your family, I have a job."

I started to walk away, but he grabbed my arm. "Let go of me, Grady," I warned.

"Or you'll what, shoot me? Arrest me? Ms. Badass with a badge. You think you're something, don't you?"

When he was drinking, he didn't bother to conceal the bitterness he felt about my job. Though I knew I shouldn't even try to talk to him when he was like this, I couldn't stop the defensive words that burst from my mouth. "You knew what I was when you married me. You knew my job was important to me."

"No, revenge is important to you. Did you even get him?"

I exhaled. "No."

"No," he repeated. "So this goes on, right? Can't you see it will never end?"

I jerked my arm free. "It will. And he'll pay for what he's done."

"At what cost, Necie? Abby will never understand this obsession. She'll hate you one day. To get revenge on Barnes, would you lose your own daughter?"

His words stunned me. It was a moment before I could even answer him.

"I won't lose Abby. I love her, and I'm a good mother."

"Hey, if you say so." He grabbed the Scotch from the end table and took a swig straight from the bottle.

I spun on my heel and stalked upstairs to the bathroom. Slamming the door, I locked it behind me, then sat on the edge of the tub for a moment to get my bearings.

It wasn't true.

Yes, I worked, but lots of women did. I loved my daughter and spent a lot of time with her, at least as much as Grady did. How dare he accuse me of neglecting her? I thought of my own mother. She'd worked two jobs to support us, and I'd spent a lot of time alone, but I'd always known she loved me. Abby knew I loved her, too.

Didn't she?

My thoughts were troubled while I showered. I took my time, wanting to postpone the conclusion to our fight. As luck would have it, Grady's snores echoed from the couch when I made my way back downstairs.

Drifting into the living room, I stared down at him for a moment, wondering when things between us had gone so wrong. He'd changed so much. . .but maybe I had, too.

Dressed in a robe with a towel swathed around my head, I wandered into the kitchen. I hadn't eaten all day, and my stomach rumbled. Neat rows of Tupperware lined the first shelf of the refrigerator, leftovers from Elizabeth's catered Thanksgiving meal. When I withdrew them, I thought of Cougar and Tucker sitting in that waiting room with nothing but vending-machine fare.

That decided it. I shut the refrigerator door and hurried upstairs to change clothes.

Moving stealthily back to the kitchen, I snatched a plastic grocery bag from the dispenser by the sink and shoved the containers inside, even the one that held the slab of Grady's favorite chocolate pie.

After a moment's hesitation, I grabbed Grady's keys off the peg over the counter. I felt vaguely hypocritical, but from the looks of him, he wouldn't be going anywhere anytime soon, and I was too tired to fight the fogged-windshield battle again tonight.

I made a pit stop at the 7-Eleven to get myself some fresh coffee—neither Cougar nor Tucker drank the stuff—then drove to the hospital. I found Cougar sitting alone in the waiting room. His eyes were closed, and his head leaned back against the wall. Stubble darkened his jaw, making him look like a Calvin Klein model.

Swallowing hard, I pushed the thought from my

mind and crossed over to him.

One pale blue eye fluttered open and squinted at me. "What the hell are you doing back here?"

Dropping into the chair next to him, I said, "Thanks for making a girl feel welcome. Where's Tuck?"

"I sent him home."

"What about Angel's mother? Is she here?"

"Not yet. She hasn't been able to get a flight out." Cougar yawned and sat up. "You didn't answer my question. What are you doing here?"

"Which answer do you want?" I ticked them off on my fingers. "One, Abby isn't home. She's going shopping with her grandmother tomorrow to get some shoes I told her she couldn't have. Two, I was worried about you. I know how you are, Mr. Hot Bod. You probably haven't eaten anything as lowly and unhealthy as a candy bar since seventh grade. I'd hate for you to have to choose between eating a Snickers and chewing your own arm off."

Cougar smiled and reached for my coffee cup. "How much of this stuff have you had already? I don't know if I've ever seen you so . . . chatty."

"Three," I said, ignoring him. "Grady's furious with me. He thinks I'm a bad wife and a bad mother because I missed Thanksgiving with the Bramhalls, a bunch of his snooty relatives who barely speak to me anyway. He got tanked and passed out on the sofa."

Cougar lifted an eyebrow and took a sip of my coffee. He made a face and handed it back to me. "Did you tell him about Angel?"

"Yes, I told him about Angel, but Grady lives in a parallel universe where carving turkey is more important than pals. Hey . . ." I dangled the sack in front of him. "Speaking of which . . . if you're through playing twenty questions, I'm starving."

"Me, too," he admitted, and we stood. He took the bag from me and brushed a hand against my lower back. Together, we walked into the hall. A young nurse leaned against a cart, scribbling something on a clipboard. Cougar released me and touched her arm.

"Miss . . . Melody," he corrected with a smile, scanning the name tag on her scrubs.

She flushed and smiled back. "Can I help you?"

"My friend and I are going downstairs to eat. If anything changes with John Angelino, could you page me? My name is Jason Stratton."

"Jason Stratton," she repeated slowly, as if savoring the taste of his name on her lips. "I sure will."

Cougar favored her with a wide grin, and I thought she was going to swoon.

Cougar at close range was some powerful mojo, a fact I acknowledged and tried to ignore. Hard to do when he smelled as good as he looked. I caught a whiff of his aftershave when we stepped inside the elevator and smiled.

"What?" he asked, but he was smiling, too.

I rolled my eyes. "You have more groupies than Mick Jagger."

He winked. "It's the accent. City girls have a thing for Southern accents." He opened the bag and peered inside. "What do you have in here? Please say you have dressing."

"I have stuffing."

He wrinkled his nose.

"What? Isn't that the same thing?"

"Nope. You guys use croutons or something. My mother makes cornbread dressing. I've never found anything like it here in Philly."

We walked into the empty dining area and took a table by the Coke machine. Cougar laid out the containers on a chipped table while I dug through my purse for change.

"Cornbread dressing, huh?"

"Best-tasting stuff in the world. I'd give a week's pay for a big bowl of it right now."

The wistfulness in his voice made me look up. I remembered the wonderful holiday meals I'd shared with my mother. I'd give anything for just one more Thanksgiving with her.

"I'm sorry you didn't make it home for Thanksgiving," I said.

Cougar's shoulder gave a funny little jerk, and he started ripping the lids off the containers. "Ah, I haven't been home in a few years. My mother will probably visit in a couple weeks. She usually does. Maybe my little brother."

"What about your dad?"

Cougar's ears reddened, and he turned toward the microwave. "My old man and I . . . don't talk." He jabbed at the buttons. "What's the matter with this damn thing?"

"Why don't you talk to your dad?" I asked, caught off guard by the sudden tightness in his voice.

Cougar gave up on the microwave. He opened his mouth, shut it again, and sat in one of the chairs.

"I'm sorry," I said. "That was a seriously nosy question."

He looked up and gave me a crooked half smile. "You really want to know?"

"Sure." Feeling suddenly flustered and not knowing why, I fed a dollar into one of the machines. I bought a bottle of Aquafina and handed it to him, then tried the microwave before taking a seat. Definitely broken.

"We're friends," I said. "You can tell me anything."

It struck me how little I knew about his past. It seemed strange, considering all the things I *did* know about him.

He studied me for a moment, then muttered, "Football."

"What?"

"We don't talk because of football. Did you bring plates?"

"No, I forgot. We can eat out of the containers."

"You sure?"

I waved him off. "I don't mind if you don't. Now, what do you mean, you don't talk because of football?"

"Grab a couple of those plastic forks by the— thanks," Cougar said as I snatched one off the table and tossed it to him. He opened the packet, speared a piece of turkey, and gulped it down while I waited impatiently. Pointing his fork at me, he asked, "Do you know why everyone calls me Cougar?"

I hadn't really thought about it, but it seemed much more fitting than the "Potter" nickname Barry Lavene had tried to tag him with during our rookie season because of the scar on his forehead. I shook my head.

"If you're a boy in Texas, when someone asks who you are, what they really mean is who do you play for? Big football state. I was a Macaw Cougar. You know Lane Brentwood in Personnel? He's from Houston, and his boy played against me in the state championship game my junior year. When I first came here, he started call-ing me 'that Cougar kid.' It stuck." He shook his head and took a bite of green bean casserole. "Fifteen hundred miles from home, and I'm still a friggin' Cougar."

I dug into the stuffing. "State championship. Wow. Did you win?"

He shrugged. "Yeah, we won. My dad was our coach. We were down by seven with two minutes to go in the first half, and I threw an interception. Their player ran it all the way back for a touchdown. When we went into the locker room at the half, my dad dislocated my jaw."

I swallowed hard over a forkful of stuffing. "Oh, Cougar . . . what did you do?"

He laughed, and rubbed his chin. "I picked myself up off the floor, spat out a couple of teeth, and went back out there. I think the guys felt sorry for me. I overheard Bucky James telling the others, 'Whatever he throws, you catch.' They did. We came back and scored twenty-four unanswered points. People still talk about that game. I avoided the press and climbed in Dad's truck afterward. I was expecting him to say something . . . I mean, he wasn't big on either praise or apologies, but I thought I'd at least get an 'attaboy.' All he did was bitch about the interception and the fact that I'd caused him to lose his cool in front of the team. Something changed inside me that night. He put me in pads when I was a runty four-year-old, and it took thirteen years of busting my ass trying to please that man before I realized it couldn't be done."

"Why wasn't that good enough? You won."

Cougar savagely chewed another piece of turkey before answering. Waving his fork, he said, "See, he was a state championship quarterback, too. Plus, he had an undefeated season. That's all I ever heard, how good he was, what he could've been . . . He didn't get to play in college. His father got killed in an accident at the mill, and Daddy had to quit high school before graduation to support his mom. He never got over it. From the day I was born, he had all these plans for me. I would play for the University of Texas. I would be just like him . . . but I never could measure up to the image he had in his head of what I was supposed to be. I was never fast enough, or accurate enough, or determined enough. At least until that night. I was only a junior that year. I had one more shot at it, but this time I wasn't playing to please him; I was playing for spite. I didn't date, didn't hang out with friends—didn't do anything except football. I got my undefeated season. I got my back-to-back championship. And one day, I got a visit from a University of Texas recruiter. You should've seen my father's face . . ."

His mouth set in a grim line, and I knew whatever he was about to tell me wouldn't be pretty.

"I told the recruiter I wasn't interested. My old man and I had a knock-down, drag-out in front of everyone, then he kicked me out. I went to live with my grandmother, attended the University of Tennessee. Got a little financial aid and worked out the rest. I was scared to death, but I felt free. It may sound cliché, but that day, I started living for me."

He laughed and took a swig of his water. "Man, I don't know why I told you all that. I bet you're sorry you asked." He said it jokingly, but there was a vulnerability in his eyes I'd never seen before.

"Not at all."

He smiled and chugged the rest of his water. Leaning back in his chair, he said, "So, that's me. What about you? I'm going to feel like a jackass if your family isn't as dysfunctional as mine."

"Oh." I exhaled. My past wasn't something I talked about much, even with Grady. It was awkward, but after everything Cougar had told me, I felt obligated. "Well, there's not much to tell, really. My father left before I was born. My mother worked two, sometimes three jobs, to support us. She died when I was a senior in high school."

"I'm sorry," he said quietly. "What happened?"

"Um, lung cancer. She was a smoker. She'd been feeling bad for awhile. I'd tried to get her to go to the doctor, but she wouldn't do it because she didn't have insurance. By the time she finally went, it was too late."

"That must have been tough. Did you have any family to help?"

I shook my head. "Just the two of us. I did like you, worked and put myself through college."

"What about your father? Have you ever had any contact with him?"

I nodded. "He came to see me after my mother's funeral. Said he wanted to help me. I told him to go to hell. I'd managed without him for the past seventeen years, and couldn't imagine why he'd think I needed him now."

"Kinda harsh, don't you think?" Cougar asked

around a mouthful of roll.

"Was it?" I asked, and didn't realize how sharp I sounded until Cougar held his palms up in surrender. Clearing my throat, I said, "My mother worked herself to death. He left her when she needed him most. He left me, and started a new family. You know how you resented your father for foisting this whole other life on you? Well, I resented him for the same reason. It didn't have to be like that between us. He made his choice, and it wasn't me."

I forced a smile. "But it worked out okay. Made me stronger. I learned I didn't have to depend on anybody."

"Even Grady?" Cougar waved his hand. "Never mind, I retract that question. But I admit, I've always been a little curious about how the two of you ever hooked up. You meet him at college?"

The chirp of my cell phone saved me from replying. I frowned down at the caller ID. "Ubi," I told Cougar, and answered it.

"Necie! We've got a tip on Barnes. ATF is chasing him on I-676 East. They think he's heading to a private airstrip in Medford."

My heartbeat began to gallop.

Medford. Cougar and I were close. Maybe we could cut him off.

"I'll stop by and grab Cougar—"

"I've got Cougar." I rummaged in my purse for a

pen. "Do you have the location of that airstrip?"

"Hang on a sec."

Cougar jumped up and began closing containers. I waved to get his attention. "Leave them," I said.

Ubi came back on the line with the address, which I scribbled on my hand. Clicking the phone shut, I said, "Let's go. I'll explain on the way."

I relayed Ubi's information to him while we sprinted down the corridor and outside to the parking lot.

"Where's your car?" Cougar asked. "We'll have to take it. Tuck's supposed to pick up mine."

I panicked for a moment when I didn't see it, then remembered I was in Grady's car. "That one," I said, and pointed at the black Porsche in the corner.

Cougar laughed as we ran to it. "I don't think we should steal doctors' cars."

Hitting the door locks, I muttered, "Shut up. My defroster's broken and I haven't had time to get it fixed yet."

"Hey, I ain't complaining. It's a nice ride."

I made a face at him, then threw the car in gear and squealed the tires when I roared toward the exit of the lot. When I rounded the corner of short-term parking, I had to hit the brakes hard to keep from mowing down a maintenance man. Cougar bounced off the dash, smacking his arm into Grady's cell phone.

"Can I use that thing?" he asked.

"Sure."

He lifted it from the holder and squinted at the tiny buttons. "These things get smaller and smaller. How the hell do they expect you to dial out?"

He stole one of Grady's plastic-wrapped toothpicks from the visor to punch the number in.

"Hey, Kim, it's Jason," he said. "Look, can you do me a favor? You heard about Angel. Yeah. No. I don't know. The thing is, we've been called out and I hate to leave him alone, in case he wakes up or something. His mom's coming in soon, but—you will?" He exhaled. "That'd be great. Thanks. I owe you one." He laughed. "Okay, so more than one, but you're not supposed to be keeping track."

I tried not to listen, but couldn't help myself. Cougar's relationship with the beautiful DEA computer tech had been the topic of water-cooler conversation for weeks. Were they a couple, or weren't they? Inquiring minds wanted to know. Listening to his easy conversation, I guessed rumors of their breakup had been greatly exaggerated.

Dating Cougar had to be like dating Brad Pitt. How much self-confidence would a woman have to have to go out with a man that good-looking? But this was Kimberly Lausen we were talking about. Runner-up for Miss New Jersey. For all I knew, she *had* dated Brad Pitt.

Cougar hung up with her and called Ubi. For the next ten minutes, they relayed locations back and forth.

"Necie!" Cougar shouted. "He's coming right at us.

He just turned off Kaighn Avenue and onto Route 70."

My stomach flip-flopped. All of a sudden, it hit me—really hit me. Only a couple of miles separated us.

We were going to get Frank Barnes.

He was the reason I was there, the reason I'd joined the DEA in the first place. I should've been excited. I should've been happy. But I simply felt numb.

"What?" Cougar barked. "Okay, okay . . . we're there. Necie, turn around."

"What? I thought we were going to beat him to the airstrip."

"Turn around, turn around. He's spotted the tail and took a right. He's about to hit Union Street. We need to get him before he hits 541. They're setting up a roadblock, but I don't know if they can get there fast enough."

Checking the rearview mirror, I jerked the wheel and slid the Porsche into a U-turn. Horns blared as I raced west on the eastbound shoulder. Cougar clutched the dash until we finally made it back to a median ramp. He exhaled when we crossed over into the correct lane. Adrenaline shot through my veins, and I laughed at his wide-eyed expression.

I was beginning to like Grady's car.

"Country boy," I teased. "You've never driven the wrong way down a four-lane?"

"Where I grew up, we didn't even have four-lanes," he replied shakily. "I learned to drive in my daddy's cow pasture."

I turned onto Jones Street and rocketed past a semi and a taxi. "How many are with Barnes and what are they driving?"

"Just him and a driver. They're in a silver Jag."

Shifting gears, I said, "Let's see if Grady's toy can live up to its spec sheet."

Cougar groaned when I floored it. He kept shooting worried looks at the speedometer.

"There they are," I said. "So, what are we going to do now? I don't have a strobe in here."

Cougar grinned and checked the clip in his Glock. He did the same for my gun and laid it in my lap. "Pull up beside them. I'll flash my badge. Maybe they'll pull over when they see they're dealing with some crazy chick in a Porsche."

We laughed, but I did what he said. Ahead, the Jag veered into the right lane, blowing by a Mustang on its left like it was standing still. I swung around the Mustang, too, and took the left lane. When we drew alongside the Jag, I blew my horn. The driver shot us a shocked glance. Cougar flashed his badge and motioned for him to pull over.

Barnes leaned forward in the passenger seat. For an instant, our gazes connected, and I saw the startled recognition dawn on his face.

I hadn't expected the driver to obey, but I didn't expect him to ram us, either.

The wheel nearly wrenched itself from my hands when the Jag slammed into us.

"Shit!" Cougar yelled as his window shattered and the side air bag deployed. "I can't see!"

We skidded toward the shoulder. He twisted in the seat and kicked at the spidered glass while I fought for control.

One more hit would've sent us off the embankment, but for some reason, the driver didn't take it. The Jag accelerated. Cougar ducked under the air bag curtain and peppered the back of the Jag with bullets.

A shot hit its mark and the right rear tire exploded. The Jag fishtailed and bounced off the back of a tractor trailer. Horrified, I watched it fly into the air. It tumbled over and over and landed on its top in the median.

I slammed on the brakes, and we screeched to a stop on the shoulder. Cougar's door wouldn't open.

"Wait, Necie, wait!" he yelled, but I was already out and sliding down the snowy hill.

Barnes was running up the opposite hill.

"DEA, freeze!" I screamed, but he kept moving. He sprinted up the bank like a man half his age and ran into the traffic. Brakes shrieked and a horn blared when a minivan swerved to miss him.

Behind me, I heard the blast of gunfire.

Darting across the road, I charged into the patch of forest behind him. I caught a glimpse of his tan coat before he disappeared into the pines. I tried to listen for him, but the roar of my pulse in my ears drowned out all other sound. Carefully, I crept through the thicket. Although I couldn't see him, I *felt* him.

"Denise," he gasped, and I whirled to face him.

Barnes squatted against a tree, his gun dangling between his knees. He made no attempt to point it at me. Blood streamed down his face, and his skin was an awful, mottled gray color.

"Drop it!" I shouted.

"Please—"

"Drop it," I repeated, advancing toward him with my Glock centered on his chest. "Don't make me kill you."

Our eyes met, and I remembered the last time I'd seen him, on the worst day of my life. I'd hated him then. I hated him now.

"You would shoot your own father?" he asked, but his fingers went slack.

The gun sank into the snow at his feet.

CHAPTER 3

My heart froze.

"You are not my father," I spat. "You are nothing to me. You should've killed me when you had the chance. Frank Barnes, you are under arrest—"

"It doesn't have to be like this," he said. "There's so much you don't know."

Advancing, I continued, "You have the right to remain silent and refuse to answer questions. Do you understand?"

"I never meant to hurt you."

"Do you understand?" I yelled, hating the angry, bitter tears that sprang to my eyes.

"I never meant to hurt Gail."

"Shut up!" I hissed. "Don't say her name. Don't you dare. Anything you say may be used against you in a court of law. Do you understand?"

"I'm so, so sorry, but you have to know . . . it wasn't all my fault."

"You bastard!" I cried, and jabbed the gun against his forehead. Fear flashed in his eyes—eyes that were the same shade of green as mine. "Is this what you did to Angel?" I asked. "Did he beg for his life? Will you?"

"You won't shoot me," he said. "You can't. We're family."

"If you say that one more time, you're going to find out differently. You have the right to consult an attorney before speaking to the police and to have an attorney present during questioning now or in the future. Do you understand?"

"I tried to be part of your life. I tried to support you. Gail wouldn't let me."

"Liar!" I shrieked, and my finger tightened on the trigger. "You walked away from us, and you never looked back. Why can't you be man enough to admit it?"

"There's a picture in my wallet, of you and me when you were about three. I came to see you. Gail's mother let me take you to the carnival once. Do you remember?" He reached for his pocket, and I poked him so hard with the gun that he fell backward in the snow.

His mention of my grandmother jolted me. I vaguely remembered her. She would show up sometimes at our house, and my mother would always turn her away. I never knew what had happened between them, because she died when I was ten.

Dimly, I heard Cougar yelling my name.

"Over here," I shouted, and swiped at the tears on my cheeks. "If you cannot afford an attorney, one will be appointed for you before any questioning if you wish. Do you understand?"

"I understand," he said heavily, as Cougar burst into the clearing.

Woodenly, I recited the last two verses of his Miranda rights. Cougar cuffed him and hauled him roughly to his feet. More officers materialized through the trees, and the ATF took command of Barnes. They peppered him with questions, but he said nothing. He merely stared at me with sad eyes. I didn't want to look at him, but somehow I couldn't look away.

"Are you okay?" Cougar asked, and I forced my attention to him while they dragged Barnes away.

My heart leapt when I noticed Cougar was clutching his arm. Blood painted his fingers. "What happened?" I gasped. "Were you shot?"

"It grazed me. No big deal." He took a deep breath. "When you started up that hill, I thought the driver was going to shoot you in the back. I didn't have an angle on him, but I saw him crouched behind the back bumper, watching you. I don't know why he didn't shoot you. I've never felt so helpless in my life."

He surprised me by pulling me into his arms and

hugging me tight. "I don't know what I'd do if I lost you and Angel both."

I pulled back and touched his face. "It's over. We got him. And Hardhead's going to be all right, too. You won't lose either of us."

Cougar laughed and lifted an eyebrow. "I wouldn't be too sure of that. Wait till Grady sees his Porsche."

I groaned. "I'm dead meat, huh?"

He knelt to scrub his bloody fingers with a handful of snow. "Just keep looking all cute and pitiful," he advised.

I smiled, despite the sense of impending doom I felt. But Grady wasn't the one I was worried about—not yet, anyway. Would Barnes tell everyone about us?

When I'd first started work with the DEA, I'd made Grady ask one of his law school professors about the legal ramifications of my working Barnes's case. He'd said that since Barnes and I'd had virtually no contact in my entire life, our connection should neither endanger the investigation nor get me fired. But that was little consolation, because I knew if the truth came out—*when* it came out—my career would be ruined. My team would never trust me again.

I could pretend I didn't know—his name wasn't even on my birth certificate—but lying was Barnes's thing, not mine. If the truth came out, it came out. I had no control over it now, but that knowledge didn't ease the worry twisting my stomach. I already felt awful about keeping it from my teammates, but what choice did I have? If I'd admitted who I was, they wouldn't have let me near the case, and I'd wanted—I'd *needed*—to be a part of bringing Barnes down.

"It'll be all right," Cougar said gently.

Confused, I watched him stand and brush his hands on his pant legs. Then it dawned on me he was still talking about the car.

He grinned, pinched my cheek, and cooed, "Now who could stay mad at a sad widdle face like this?"

"Jerk," I muttered, and aimed a halfhearted kick at his behind. He dodged it, then veered toward me and slung his good arm around my shoulders. He kept it there while we trudged back to the road. I wondered if all men from Texas were like him, always touching, always teasing. Although it had unnerved me at first, I was getting used to it.

We reached the highway just in time to see the wrecker pull away with Grady's Porsche. I groaned again, and Cougar laughed.

Ubi offered us a ride to the police station. The three of us wedged in the cab of his little Toyota pickup like sardines. I was going to have a bruise on the inside of my knee where he shifted gears and he had the heater on full blast. I felt a little queasy with the hot air battering my face, and Ubi's jerky "speed up and brake" driving wasn't helping things any.

"Hey, can we stop by my apartment on the way?" Cougar asked, and I stifled a groan.

While he ran inside, my mind kept flashing to what Barnes had said. My mother had told me he'd left when she was pregnant and never looked back. Why would he lie about that now? Did he think I'd feel sorry for him? Surely he hadn't expected me to let him go.

Cougar reappeared ten minutes later, stuffing something into his jacket pocket, and we lurched on our way.

Pandemonium reigned outside the police station. Cougar shoved a path through the throng of reporters, and Ubi and I followed in his wake.

Bill stood in the doorway of a glassed-in office like a kid watching his parents fight, not wanting to go in but unable to look away. He glanced at us as we crowded around him, then turned his attention back to the three men inside. The precinct captain faced down Barnes and a red-faced man in a gray suit who I assumed was Barnes's lawyer. I saw enough lawyers on a daily basis that I could pretty well pick them out of a crowd.

"What do you mean, you're holding him for attempted murder?" the lawyer sputtered. "Attempted murder of whom? The agents who arrested him were in an unmarked car. My client didn't know they were DEA. He was only trying to defend himself."

The captain shifted the toothpick in his mouth. "We're arresting him for the attempted murder of Agent

John Angelino, who was shot on Mr. Barnes's premises this morning."

Barnes's hands were still cuffed behind him, and I noticed him popping his fingers one by one with his thumb. The simple movement chilled me, because it was a habit I shared. I'd done it all my life, much to my mother's—and later Grady's—annoyance.

Barnes leaned to whisper something to his lawyer, then rocked back on his heels. He rolled his neck and seemed to notice me for the first time. For an instant our eyes met, and my telltale heart threatened to beat out of my chest in the sudden terror that everyone else would see what I was only now seeing myself. We looked alike. We really did. I'd stared at his pictures a million times, but I'd never noticed it before.

The fat lawyer braced his hands on the edge of the desk. "My client wasn't even home this morning. You say the victim is in a coma. What evidence could you possibly have to connect Mr. Barnes to the shooting?"

The captain nodded at Bill, who took a hesitant step inside and gestured at us. "Angelino was conscious when they found him. They heard him say—"

"I've got better than that," Cougar interrupted. He fished a tiny cassette from his pocket and handed it to Bill. "This is Angel's statement. I took it on the way to the hospital, and it was witnessed by two ambulance attendants."

Fear sparked in Barnes's eyes.

Good, I thought.

The captain punched a button on his phone. "Marty, find me something to play one of those little tapes on."

Bill fingered the tape, his brows furrowed. "How?" he asked. "We were on a raid. I know you didn't have a recorder with you."

Cougar tugged his earlobe and gave a bitter smile. "I was afraid . . . I don't know . . . I was afraid Angel's luck wouldn't hold out. That maybe he wouldn't remember later. And I wanted to catch him fresh, so I borrowed the EMT's cell phone, called my answering machine, and got him to give his statement into it. We had to call it three times, because it kept cutting us off, but it worked."

Awed, I shook my head. "Cougar, that was brilliant."

I glimpsed the pain in his eyes before he looked away. "I wish it was unnecessary. That Angel could speak for himself." He glared at Barnes. "You smug bastard. If he dies, you'll wish you'd used that bullet on yourself."

"Captain!" the lawyer barked. "I won't allow my client to be threatened."

The captain sighed. "Bill, please control your agent."

Bill opened his mouth, and Cougar held up his hands. "Okay," he said, and walked toward the window.

"Excuse me," a redheaded deputy mumbled, and I twisted to let him by. He handed a small tape player to his boss and retreated.

In a moment, Cougar's breezy recorded voice filled

the room. "This is Jason. You know what to do." A long beep followed, then a different version of his voice, this one tight and stilted, announced the time and date. "Please state your name and badge number for the record."

"John Angelino, Special Agent. Badge number BA7803655."

"Where are you?"

"Um, the back of an ambulance."

"What are your injuries?"

"I've, uh, been shot."

"Jason Stratton, Special Agent. Badge number AS0514198. I, along with Special Agent Denise Bramhall, found Agent Angelino in the forest behind Frank Barnes's house as we conducted an early morning raid. He was tied to a tree and unconscious from a small caliber shot to his forehead. Do you remember what occurred just prior to our finding you?"

Angel's voice cracked. "I, um . . . I was working undercover in a sting to net Frank Barnes. I'm not sure what happened exactly. I met him at his house for dinner Wednesday night. We had some mahimahi, and I guess it was drugged, because next thing I knew, I was sitting in the snow. I was messed up, couldn't talk, couldn't move. Barnes stood over me. He said, 'Whatever the DEA paid you, son, it wasn't enough.' Then he pointed a gun at me and pulled the trigger. I sort of remember my head snapping back, but I didn't feel anything yet. I guess I passed out, because the next thing I remember is you and Necie showing up."

Cougar led him through another series of questions that I realized were meant to show cognizance. Cougar's voice sounded dull and heavy, perhaps toneless to a stranger, but it was stark to the ears of someone who knew him. My admiration for him swelled when I realized how smart he'd been, and how much strength it must've taken. He'd all but wrapped Barnes up with a bow and hand delivered him to the DA.

A deputy led Barnes away to be fingerprinted. He gave me a searching look when he passed, but I turned my head. We briefed the captain and talked among ourselves for a moment.

Finally, I spotted an empty desk and sat behind it to write out my report.

I was nearly done fifteen minutes later when the squad room door burst open and a disheveled, wild-eyed Grady barreled inside.

"Necie!" he cried, and I think every cop in the building reached for his piece.

"It's okay," I said, jumping up to intercept him. Grabbing his arm, I dragged Grady to a corner. I dreaded the scene to come, but saw no way to avoid it. I didn't want my co-workers to see us fight.

"I called the office when I woke up and found you gone," he said. "They told me you were here. Something about a wreck, so I called a cab—"

Taking his hands, I launched into a feverish explanation. "Grady, let me tell you what happened. My defroster was broken, so I took your car. I'm sorry. I'll pay for the damages—"

"Necie—"

"We got Barnes, but his driver rammed the Porsche when we were chasing them. I think—"

"Necie!" he said, louder.

Heads turned in our direction and Grady flushed. He ran a hand through his rumpled blond hair, then surprised me by taking my face in his hands. In a hushed voice, he said, "Baby, I don't care about the car. I care about you. Are you okay?"

The concern in his eyes was so unexpected . . . for a moment, I simply gaped at him, my explanation dying on my lips. Then I smiled.

It was Grady's turn to look startled. He grinned and stroked my cheek with his thumb. "It's been a long time since you smiled at me like that," he said softly. "It still makes my heart go crazy."

Who are you, and what have you done with my husband? I thought, but I remembered this guy. He was the frat boy I'd fallen in love with. I thought he was gone for good, but he was still there, hidden somewhere deep inside the lawyer I barely knew.

I found myself thinking of the night we'd met. I

was working as a waitress in a little off-campus dive when he'd strolled in one night wearing a white T-shirt that read "Sotally Tober" and an easy grin. He'd asked me out that night, and probably the next forty nights straight, ignoring my insistence that I didn't date frat boys. Actually, I didn't date anybody. Didn't have time. But nothing I said fazed him. He'd come in, take a table in my section, then make me laugh by ordering some crazy drink, like Screaming Chocolate Monkeys, Alien Urine, and memorably, Passed Out Naked on the Bathroom Floor. We'd laugh again when I had to call it out to the bartender. Things got to the point where Grady would hang out until closing and then help clean the place up. He even tutored me in chemistry when business was slow.

Finally, I accepted his invitation. We went to the movies, which turned out to be a big mistake. Between work and school, I was averaging around four hours of sleep a night. I fell asleep on his arm almost as soon as the lights went down. Bless his heart, he didn't move during the next two hours, though his arm must've been killing him. I woke during the big action scene and was mortified, but he simply kissed my forehead and told me how beautiful I looked sleeping.

"What?" Grady asked again, his smile widening. "Now you're just making me nervous."

"I was thinking of our first date." I wrapped my

47

arms around his waist and pressed my face against his chest. I could still smell the Scotch on him, but I let it go. He stroked my hair and kissed the top of my head.

"I'm sorry," he said. "I acted like a jerk tonight. It scared me when I woke up and you weren't there. I don't know what I'd do if you left me for good." He squeezed me, then pulled back to look at my face. "So, you got him? You really got him?"

"Yeah." I glanced across the room at Cougar, who watched us while he talked on his cell phone. Our eyes met and he looked away. "We got him."

"Are you okay?" Grady asked.

I nodded and smiled up at him. "I am now."

"Hey, you know Mom's got Abby all night. You want to go out or anything? We could see a movie that's not rated G."

I laughed. "I'd probably crash on you for sure tonight."

"That'd be okay." Grady winked. "I still like to watch you sleep."

Winding my fingers in his, I said, "I've got a better idea. It involves you, me . . . the hot tub. What do you think?"

He grinned. "I think I'm glad I told that taxi driver to wait."

Grady surprised me by brushing a kiss on my lips. While I was still recovering from that, I felt a blast of cold air when the front door crashed open.

"Where is he?" a woman's voice demanded. "What have you done with my father?"

I think I realized who she was before I even turned around. With my breath caught in my throat, I twisted to stare at the exotic brunette in the black fur coat.

My half sister.

When the young cop at the door merely gawked at her, she shoved past him and stalked to the front desk. Slapping her hands on the wooden surface, she leaned forward until she was nearly nose to nose with the startled man behind it. "Frank Barnes!" she said. "Where is he?"

The phone hung slack in the sergeant's hands and he, too, could only stare. The whole room seemed to freeze in her wake. She snapped her fingers in his face. "You speak English? Anybody?"

Jerking her chin around, she scanned the room. Time seemed to stop when our gazes met. Her eyes narrowed, and her lovely face flushed.

Though we'd never met, never spoken, I knew what she was. She was an apocalyptic blend of our father and the crazed Latina junkie he'd left my mother for. All the snitches gave the same report: Since her teenage years, Maria had been primed to run the family business, and she was far deadlier than her father. It chilled me to the bone to think we were related.

She apparently knew who I was, too. The malevolence in her stare struck me like a physical blow, and involuntarily, my grip tightened on Grady's fingers.

"Where is he?" she repeated, her dark eyes glittering.

My stomach sank.

This is it. It's all over.

Cougar's deep voice shattered the silence. "He's in a cell, where he belongs. I hope he rots there."

Maria's head snapped around, and I felt almost limp when she released me from her glare. The string of obscenities she directed at Cougar seemed doubly damning and shocking, spewing from such a beautiful creature.

Cougar merely smiled and cracked his gum.

"C'mon," Grady whispered, grasping my forearm. "Let's go."

Numbly, I nodded, but I was terrified Maria would hurl my secrets at my retreating back.

We slipped outside, leaving Maria and Cougar arguing. Grady slung his arm around my shoulder. Gratefully, I leaned into him, looping my arm around his waist. He felt warm and solid, and I clung to him a little tighter than normal.

"Are you sure you're okay?" he asked, and we ducked to protect our faces from the buffeting wind.

"Yeah." I felt a rush of tenderness for him then, something I hadn't experienced in a while. When he opened the cab door, I said, "Hey, Grady. I've got some vacation time coming. Maybe we could—"

"Necie, hold up!"

Grady's smile faded when my supervisor jogged over to us.

"Glad I caught you!" Bill's breath came in bright, white puffs. "Hiya, Grady."

"Hey," Grady muttered.

"I left my statement with Cougar," I said quickly, hoping to get out of there and salvage Grady's good mood.

"There's something else. Can I talk to you for a sec?" Bill nodded toward the building. "Inside?"

"Um, sure," I said, and ignored Grady's sigh. I gave him a quick kiss on the cheek and whispered, "I'll be right back."

"Meter's running," he said tersely.

"I know. I'll hurry."

Grady nodded and yanked open the cab door. I sprinted toward the building.

Inside the double doors, Bill said, "Hey, you want a trip this weekend? I've got a Jersey job, one of those undercover details you like."

I glanced outside. A stony-faced Grady stared back at me through the cab window. "Ah, can you get someone else for this one, Bill?"

Bill's eyebrows shot up. "Sure. Just wanted to give you first dibs. That was good work tonight."

He gave me a quick clap on the shoulder, which was about as touchy-feely as it got with Bill. I kissed his cheek, thinking of how this man had been more of a father to me than Frank Barnes ever could be. He'd taken me under his wing from day one and always seemed to be looking out for me. I had another pang when I thought about Barnes and what he could do to my career and friendships. If he wanted to, he could make me lose everything.

Bill waved good-bye and walked down the hall. I turned and nearly smacked into Maria Barnes when she exited the restroom. She swiped her reddened eyes with a tissue and gave me a bitter smile. "One day soon, I want you to look back to this night and realize you started this."

I blinked. "Are you threatening me?"

"What?" she asked mockingly. "Threaten my own sister?"

She laughed when I glanced around to see if anyone was listening, but her eyes were hard when she said, "Don't delude yourself into thinking you're better than me. I see it in your eyes. You're ashamed of him. You're ashamed of me. I've always hated you, did you know that? No matter what you did to refuse him, he always talked about you. Well, maybe now he'll realize that I'm the only daughter who gives a damn about him."

She bumped her shoulder into mine and started down the hall.

"I'll see you around, Denise," she called over her shoulder. Cougar emerged from one of the doorways, and she shot him a bird when they passed.

He grinned at me and circled his index finger by his temple. I had to force myself to return his smile. My hands were shaking.

Glancing back down the hall, he said, "Did she threaten you? I heard her say she'd see you around."

"It's nothing," I said. "Just trash talk."

Cougar grunted. "She's a psycho, that's for sure. But what chance did she have, really? I mean, look at her father. Evil begets evil—"

"I have to go," I blurted. I really couldn't stand to contemplate that line of reasoning at that moment. "Grady's probably left me by now."

Cougar laughed. "Go, then. You're probably on thin ice as it is tonight."

I rolled my eyes and started backing away. "Call me if there's any word on Angel."

"Will do."

"And get someone to look at that arm."

"Yes, Mother," he said with a wink.

I ran back outside. Grady leaned across the seat to push open the cab door.

"What did Bill want?" he asked with a frown.

I slid in beside him, and the cab lurched into motion. "He wanted me to work this weekend."

Grady threw up his hands. "Of course, he did. Damn it, Necie—"

"I told him no."

Grady paused in midrant and stared at me. "You did? Why?"

I resumed my position under his arm. "Well, this is a holiday weekend. I want to spend time with you and Abby. I know I missed the big dinner, but we could still go somewhere together."

"That sounds nice," he said, and hugged me close. "And we can still have dinner. Mom sent us some leftovers."

Uh-oh . . . I wondered if I could blame the disappearance on refrigerator trolls. Grady was talking about the weekend, though, so I didn't interrupt. He sounded so happy and excited. Maybe I had been neglecting him. Neglecting him and Abby both.

When we got home, Grady poured me a drink, but he didn't drink any more himself. We stripped and climbed into the hot tub.

"Hey, Necie," he said, while he kneaded my shoulders. "I'm not trying to start anything, I swear. But you said something about vacation. I was thinking, now that you've captured Barnes—how would you feel about a leave of absence?" He nuzzled my neck. "We could spend more time together, maybe even have another baby, a perfect little boy to go with our perfect little girl?"

His words chilled me. I wasn't sure I was a good enough mother for one, much less two. Abby's conception had been an accident, but one I'd never regretted, even though at times the responsibility scared me to death. I loved her more than anything. I only hoped I could give her what she needed from me.

And giving up my job? My main goal had always been Barnes, but his arrest didn't change who I was. I loved my job, and I loved the people I worked with. It scared me to think of walking away from it all.

"Relax." Grady slid his hands down my bare arms. "You don't have to give me an answer right now. Just promise me you'll think about it."

"Okay," I whispered, and leaned my head back against his chest.

For the next couple of days, I thought of little else. Grady, Abby, and I spent a nice weekend together as a family. We played board games and baked cookies and even had a pillow fight. No television or Playstation for Abby; no calls to the office for Grady and me. I had to call and check on Angel, though, but in an effort to keep the peace, I'd slip into the bathroom to do it. For the first time, I considered leaving the DEA for good.

But on Sunday evening, I got a call from Cougar.

Angel was dying.

CHAPTER 4

With a quick apology to Grady, I raced to the hospital. With the exception of Ubi and Linda, who were on assignment, my whole team waited there with Angel's mother and teenage sister, Tori.

We spent a restless night in the intensive-care waiting room with a dozen other families before a nurse told us Angel's condition had stabilized. It was the most emotional experience I'd ever had except for the birth of my daughter. Looking at the tired, anxious faces around me, I knew I couldn't quit my job. Grady would never understand . . . but these people were my family, too. They needed me. I needed them.

Though he still hadn't regained consciousness, we celebrated when Angel was transferred out of intensive care and into a regular room. Then we drew up a schedule to make sure he was never alone. Though I spent as much time as possible with my family, Grady made no secret of the resentment he felt when I took my turn sitting up with Angel.

One night, I was playing checkers with Tori when Tucker showed up to relieve me. I stood and glanced at the clock, thinking that maybe I could make it home in time to read Abby a story before she went to sleep.

When I looked at Angel, I was startled, as always, to see his dark eyes open and staring through me. He'd only recently started doing that, opening and closing his eyes randomly and in response to pain. Cougar had been so excited about it, but for some reason, I could hardly stand to look into those blank, black eyes that had once been so sparkling and alive.

I had no sense of him inside there. Still, like everyone else, I talked to him and hoped for the best. Crossing over to him, I pulled the cover up under his chin and bent to kiss the pale cheek his mother shaved every day. "Later, handsome. Tuck is here, and he's carrying the sports page."

Tuck's beeper went off while I was slipping on my shoes.

"It's Bill," he said, staring at the numbers. "Hang on a sec."

"Take your time," I assured him, and he went outside to use the phone.

He reappeared a moment later. "Hey, Necie. Can you stay a little longer? I've gotta run. It's the case I've been working on. Ubi said he'll be here as soon as he gets off his shift, but it'll be three or four hours."

"I can stay by myself," Tori said, but we ignored her. No way was I leaving a fifteen-year-old alone, even if it was at the hospital.

"No problem. I've got to finish kicking Tori's butt at checkers anyway," I said with a wink, and she stuck out her tongue.

After Tucker left, I called Grady to tell him I'd be late.

"What? Necie, this shit has got to give. You can't stay out all night and work tomorrow. Tell them to find somebody else. Doesn't he have family?"

Afraid Tori could hear him yelling over the phone, I clamped it to my ear and turned my back. "Tuck was called in," I said softly. "I'll be home around eleven or twelve. I'll get some sleep before I take Abby to school. You'll just have to pick her up tomorrow afternoon."

"What about Tiger or Panther or whatever the hell you call him? What about Bill?"

"Cougar's sitting with him tomorrow, and Bill is with Tucker. I really have to go."

I hung up the phone before he could say anything else. Tori kept her head down, pretending to study her next move, but I could tell by her reddened face that she'd heard enough.

"I really can stay by myself," she said.

"I know that, honey," I said. "But I don't want you to."

"I don't want you to get in trouble with your husband."

"Don't worry about him," I said with a wink. "His bark is worse than his bite."

Or so I thought, until Angel's door burst open an hour later. A glassy-eyed Grady barreled inside, with a nurse clutching at the back of his jacket. Tori screamed and scampered toward the corner. Angel jumped, but stared sightlessly ahead.

"Sir, *sir!*" the nurse shouted. "Visiting hours are over. If you don't leave, I'll have to call security."

"I'll leave, but first I want to know the truth" he slurred. Pointing at Angel's bed, he said, "Necie, were you sleepin' with this guy? Is that why you spend so much time here?"

"Grady!" I gasped, mortified.

I pushed past Tori and seized Grady from the nurse's grasp. "I'll handle this," I told her.

"He has to—"

"I'll *handle* it," I snapped, and pushed Grady out into the hall.

He stank of sour sweat and Scotch.

"Where's Abby?" I demanded. "You'd better not have left her alone."

"What kind of father do you think I am?" he said, his green eyes hurt. "I took her to Mom's."

"You took her to your mother's? On a school night? Were you drunk then? So help me, Grady, if I ever catch you driving with her—"

"I'm not drunk now."

"Oh, really?"

He gave a defensive shrug. "Well, you weren't there. Mom doesn't mind taking her."

"I mind, Grady. She's our kid. We're responsible for her, not your mother."

"Then act like it." He seized my throat in his hand and held my head against the wall. "I asked you a question. Are you sleeping with this guy?"

I kicked him hard on the shin and he let go of me. "Don't be stupid! Angel is a friend. That's all."

"Something's wrong with our marriage," he said, and I laughed, my fury kindled like a forest fire.

Not even caring that the nurse was watching, I grabbed the front of his shirt and pushed him backward. He stumbled and nearly fell. "This is what's wrong with our marriage. Your drinking."

"I drink because my wife is never home."

"That's not true."

"Your work gets most of your time, then Abby. Then some vegetable in a hospital bed who doesn't even know you're there. When's my time, Denise?"

"I'm calling security," the nurse said, and stalked off.

"Go home, Grady. We'll talk about this later. You

don't want to go to jail. Are you driving?"

"No. I got a cab."

"Is he waiting?"

"I think so."

I rode the elevator with him to the lobby, nearly sick with anger and frustration, but helpless to do anything about it. Grady's drinking was getting steadily worse. I didn't know if it carried over to his work or not, but I didn't see how he was going to try a case in the court-room tomorrow. I loaded him into a cab and paid the driver to take him back home.

"I love you, Necie," Grady said. "But I hate the way you make me feel."

He slammed the door and left me staring after him when the cab pulled away.

I tried so hard not to cry while I took the elevator back up, but I couldn't stop the tear that slipped out when Tori rushed over to hug me.

"Necie, are you okay?" she asked. "Was that your husband?"

"I'm okay," I said. "Look, Tori, please . . . don't tell the others about this. I'll keep him away from here."

She stared at me with big, solemn eyes, then nodded. "Would you like a Coke or something?"

I forced a smile. "That would be great."

She scampered away, and I dragged my chair close to Angel's bed. Those sad, vacant eyes seemed to reflect the despair I felt inside. I dropped my head into my hands and sobbed.

When I felt a hand in my hair, I thought it was Tori, but it wasn't.

It was Angel.

CHAPTER 5

Angel?" I said, and he blinked.

My tears forgotten, I gripped his cool hand. "Angel, can you hear me?"

He blinked again, and his fingers twitched in mine. I sensed movement in the doorway and glanced up to see Tori shove the door open with her hip. She backed into the room, clutching a soft drink in each hand and a bag of chips between her teeth.

She dropped the chips on the tray. "Hey, I hope diet is okay. They were out of regular Coke."

My heart pounding, I ignored her and stood over Angel. "Blink twice if you understand me."

Angel's dark lashes fluttered closed once. Twice.

Tori dropped one of the soft drinks. The can clattered against the floor and rolled under the bed. With a squeal,

63

she grabbed his other hand. "Angel, this is Tori."

We both squealed when his head turned toward her and he blinked twice.

"We should call Mama."

"We should call Cougar," I said simultaneously, and we laughed. "Go!" I shooed her toward the phone.

In moments, I heard Mrs. Angelino's excited chatter over the line. Tori grinned and held the phone away from her ear. When she got off the phone, I tried to call Cougar's cell twice. I got an out-of-area message both times and thought about having the central office page him, but decided to wait. In a couple of hours, he would see for himself.

I was getting off the phone with Ubi when Angel's mother arrived. It finally occurred to me that maybe I should page a nurse.

A male nurse came in a hurry when I told him over the speaker what was going on. "Move over a sec, ladies," he said, and I tried. Angel gripped my hand with a strength that surprised me. From the look on Tori's face, he had hold of her, too.

The nurse laughed. "Be that way, then. If I had a hold of two pretty ladies like this, I guess I'd hang on, too. So, let's do this like the movies. Blink once for yes, twice for no. Do you understand?"

One blink.

"Are you in pain?"

Two blinks.

Angel's mother jumped up and down and crossed herself.

The next few hours passed like minutes as we peppered him with questions. The most we got in response was a strained "uhhh" or a blink, but he was trying. Better than that, he understood.

When Cougar walked through the door at midnight, Mrs. Angelino, Tori, and I grinned at him like idiots.

I laughed when he looked down to check his fly. Giddily, I stood and launched myself at him. He staggered backward under my momentum, but managed to keep us from falling.

"Whoa!" he said, clutching me. "You been hitting the caffeine again, Neese?"

I grabbed his hand and dragged him to Angel's bedside. Angel lay flat on his back, staring at the ceiling. I placed Angel's hand in Cougar's and snapped my fingers. "Hey, Beavis, Butthead's here."

Cougar sucked in a breath when Angel squeezed his hand and turned to face him.

"H-hey there, buddy! Can you hear me?"

Angel blinked, and Cougar gave a loud war whoop.

"We need to call your grandmother," Mrs. Angelino told Tori. "Help me dial out on this thing."

While they hovered over the phone, Cougar asked, "Well, what happened? Why didn't you call me?"

"I tried. And I don't know. I was crying, and he—" I paused, embarrassed I'd let that slip. Cougar frowned. "—he patted my head."

Cougar stared at him, then back at me. I felt pinned by his gaze, much as I had Maria's. Then he asked the question I didn't want to answer.

"Why were you crying?"

I flushed and looked at Mrs. Angelino. She was yelling and laughing into the phone receiver.

"It's nothing," I said quietly, so she wouldn't hear. "Grady was here, drunk, making an ass out of himself. He asked if I was having an affair with Angel."

Cougar stared at me for a long moment, then gave me what looked like a forced smile. He clucked his tongue at Angel. "Look at you, man. Lying here in the hospital and still having jealous husbands bust down your door."

I appreciated his attempt to make light of it, but the mood in the room suddenly seemed tense. I hung around until Mrs. Angelino got off the phone, then made my escape.

"Wait!" Cougar said. "I'll walk you to the parking lot."

"That's not necessary—" I began, but he was already moving toward the door.

We walked side by side down the hall. Cougar kept his head down, his hands jammed in his pockets. I wondered what he was thinking.

When we stepped onto the elevator, he said, "So, ah

. . . this thing with Grady . . . you okay to go home?"

"What? Oh, yeah." I shook my head. "He's probably sleeping it off by now."

"Are you sure? Because you know you and Abby can stay at my place—"

Touched and feeling wildly emotional, I kissed his cheek. "Don't you ever get tired of being such a hero?"

He grinned and pressed his hand to his cheek. "Nah. The hours are long, but the fringe benefits are outta sight."

We laughed and he said, "But seriously . . . you know I'm here for you. If you need somebody to talk to. If you just want me to whup his ass."

I giggled. "Whup his ass? Let me guess . . . another Southern thing?"

He snapped his gum and winked. "You betcha. A good one, too. We do that when we see people we care about getting hurt." Slanting his eyes, he said, "Besides, I can't talk Boston thug like Angel . . . or wait, maybe I can." He cleared his throat, and in a voice that sounded more Rocky Balboa than John Angelino, he said, "Hey, Neese, you want I should throw tha' guy a beatin'?"

I snickered behind my hand. "That was terrible."

He rolled his eyes. "Yeah, okay . . . it was. I'll stick with whup his ass. Sounds manlier, anyway." His eyes shone when he said, "Angel's really coming back to us, isn't he?"

"Yeah, he is."

"Look, Necie . . . If staying at the hospital is causing you trouble at home—"

"No."

"—we could do something else."

"No," I said, louder this time. "I won't abandon my friends. Grady will have to get over it."

"And if he doesn't?"

I shrugged. "Then he'll have to get out. I can't live like that, under someone's thumb. I won't."

He walked me to my car. For a moment, we simply stared at each other in the amber glow of the security lights. Being this close to him, seeing the concern in his eyes, made my heart do this crazy little jitterbug it had no business doing. I swallowed hard and reached for the door handle. He grabbed my wrist. Only inches separated us. I felt a funny pain in my chest and realized I was holding my breath.

He squinted at me. "Man, I hate to let you go like this. Are you sure you're gonna be all right?"

I nodded, not trusting myself to speak. Our whole team was tight, but whether it was because of our ages, our poor upbringings, or simply the fact that we got thrown on more assignments together, I'd always felt particularly close to Cougar and Angel. Now something was changing between Cougar and me, at least on my part. I tried to tell myself it was nothing, that I was only imagining things because of my troubles with Grady, but lately, every time I was with Cougar, I found myself thinking of how *easy* it was to be with him. Maybe it was some kind of safety mechanism. After all, only an idiot would fall for a guy like Cougar, a handsome charmer who had his pick of women. But I couldn't help but wonder what it would be like to be involved with a man who accepted me for what I was. Somebody who not only accepted me, but maybe even admired me a little, too. Grady didn't even respect me anymore.

"Necie?"

I shook my head, clearing the cobwebs. Cougar folded me in his arms, and for a moment, I lay my head on his chest and listened to the steady beat of his heart.

Finally, I pulled away. "I gotta go," I whispered, and he nodded.

"Do you promise you'll call if you need me? If he starts any crap—"

"I promise." I climbed inside the car, expecting him to walk away, but he simply stood there. When I pulled away, I dared a glance in the rearview mirror. He hadn't moved.

"Get it together," I said, and flipped on the radio.

While scanning the stations, I became annoyed by the inane banter of the evening DJs and switched it off again. My thoughts returned to Grady and his humiliating accusation. In place of the anger I'd first felt, I was consumed by an unrelenting sadness.

Was my marriage over? Did I want it to be? Was he

too greedy, too needy, or was I the selfish one? I could no longer be sure.

When I got home, I found a fully clothed Grady sitting on the toilet seat with his face in his hands. I walked into the bathroom and propped against the bathroom sink. "We need to talk."

"Not now," he mumbled.

"Yes, Grady, now."

For some reason, I found myself staring at our reflections in the mirrored shower door. This wasn't love. Not anymore. This was something scary and angry and bitter and heartbreaking. I was tired of walking a minefield every time I stepped through my front door. Still, the words jolted me when I spoke them out loud. "Grady, I'm leaving."

His blond head snapped up. "What? Necie, no!" Tears filled his eyes, and I twisted around, unable to look at him.

"I can't live like this anymore. It's killing me."

"Necie—"

I hugged myself and faced him. I felt like I was outside myself. This couldn't be me. This cool, flat voice didn't even sound like me. "Grady, you had no right. I've never cheated on you, and I've never given you reason to think I have."

His face reddened, whether from embarrassment or anger, I couldn't tell. I could no longer read him.

"You're never here," he said. "What was I supposed to think?"

That was pretty weak. He sounded like a petulant child, and that snapped me out of the numbness that enveloped me. I threw my arms wide. "Never here? We've spent more time together in the past few days than we ever have."

He glared at me. "There's a difference between spending time with me and killing time until you have an excuse to leave again. Do you think I don't know that? Do you think I don't *feel* that?"

"That's not true," I said, battling to speak over the lump in my throat. "I want to be with you, but . . ."

"But what?"

"You're suffocating me."

"You're abandoning me!" he yelled.

I rubbed my forehead. Neither of us said anything for a long moment. How could this have happened to us? I felt almost desperate to understand. "It didn't use to be like this, not as bad. Why now, Grady? Why do you need me so much after all these years?"

He gave a bitter laugh. "You make me feel so pathetic. What am I supposed to say, Denise? Maybe the real question is why you don't need me anymore. How do you think it makes me feel, knowing that if Bill or any of those other people you work with called you right now, you'd be out the door, and I can't even get you to sit down to a family meal with me?"

His words tore at me. I walked over and knelt in front of him. "Grady, you know what that was about. One of my friends was missing, and the person responsible was my own father. I had to be there."

"Okay, fine. Forget all that. Barnes is in jail. You've told me all this time that's what you wanted, that's what you were working toward, but I can't even get you to take a leave of absence."

"I never said I wouldn't."

"You didn't have to say it. When I suggested we have another baby, you went as rigid as a wall."

"That wasn't because of my job," I said softly. "It was because of your drinking. You have a problem, Grady. Can't you see it's getting worse?"

He stared at the floor. With a sigh, I turned to leave.

"What if I quit drinking?" he said. "Would you stay? I don't want to split up our family, Necie. If I quit drinking, will you take a few months off, let us see if we can fix this thing?"

A million thoughts ran through my head, most of them concerning Abby. Shouldn't I do everything in my power to keep us together, for her?

Turning back to Grady, I said, "Yes."

"What?"

I cleared my throat. "If you promise to quit drinking, I'll turn in my request for leave tomorrow. It'll probably take it a couple of weeks to process, but if you're willing to fight for us, I am, too."

"Are you serious?" He lurched to his feet and gave me a faltering smile. "You would do that for me?"

"Yes," I said, but as he took me in his arms, I felt like part of me was dying.

CHAPTER 6

The next day, I left home half an hour early so I could speak to Bill in private before our team's Monday morning meeting. As expected, he was already in the boardroom, scribbling notes on a dry-erase board.

"Hey, Denise!" he said, and checked his watch.

"I'm early. I need to talk."

He turned and gave me a quizzical look, then motioned me forward. "What's on your mind?"

I put my request for leave in his hands before I could change my mind. He glanced down at it, then peered at me over the top of his eyeglasses. "Is something wrong?"

The fatherly concern in his eyes was too much. I pinched the bridge of my nose and said, "I don't know what else to do."

"Honey, what is it?" He prodded me toward a chair. "Is it the team? Has somebody done something—"

"No, it's—". I pushed a wave of hair out of my face and fought to speak over the lump in my throat. "This is so damn hard."

"Let me guess . . . Grady," Bill muttered. He squinted at the paper again. "Six months? Denise, I don't know what's going on with you, but are you sure this is the answer? Six months is a lifetime in the DEA."

I chewed my already ragged thumbnail. "It's my job or my marriage, Bill. I don't think I can have both anymore. At least not for awhile."

"Why not?"

When I didn't answer, Bill cursed and leaned back in the metal chair. "You shouldn't have to choose, Necie. You're a damn good DEA agent."

I forced a smile, but my heart was breaking. "But apparently I'm a piss-poor wife."

Bill's face reddened. "Who says it's you? What if I said Grady was a clingy, selfish little—"

"Don't," I said, and took his hand. "Please, just . . . don't. I have to think about Abby and what's best for her."

Loud laughter from the hallway made us both look up. I heard Cougar's voice and knew I was almost out of time.

"Please, Bill," I said. "Don't tell the others yet. Let me do it."

He nodded and tugged at his beard. "This is a mistake, Necie. Don't lose yourself trying to please someone else, even if he is your husband."

The door burst open, and Cougar dragged Tucker through it in a headlock.

"Who is she?" Cougar asked, and skinned his knuckles over Tuck's head.

"Let . . . go," Tucker gasped.

The pair stumbled against the table. I winced when it screeched across the floor.

Bill stood and stepped toward them. "Boys, cool it."

Cougar released him. Tucker staggered away from him and flopped into the chair beside me.

Cougar pointed at Tucker. "This ain't over. You're gonna tell me."

"Tell him what?" I asked, as Ubi and Linda walked through the door.

"The name of the woman who sent him all those cookies to Angel's room." Cougar grinned and ruffled Tuck's sweaty brown hair. In a singsong voice, he said, "Tucker's got a girlfriend."

Tucker shot him a dirty look before he noticed we were all gaping at him.

"What?" he demanded.

This was big news. Our terminally shy Tuck had a girlfriend?

I smiled, the cloud hanging over my head momentarily dissipating. "What? Tell me, Tuck. Whisper in my ear."

I didn't really expect him to, but he leaned over and cupped his hand to my head.

"Anne Marie," he whispered. "Angel's physical therapist."

"Oh!" I leaned back and punched his shoulder. "Hey, I know her. She's cute!"

"Who?" Cougar asked, dropping into the chair on the other side of me.

I mimed zipping my lips, and Cougar snorted. He pushed me aside to wink at Tucker. "Man, did you ever screw up. You know Necie can be bought. A Big Mac, a Snickers bar. . .she'll sell you out."

"Nuh-uh!" I said, but Tuck looked worried. Cougar grabbed my shoulders and pulled me backward against him. "Who is it, Necie? Tell me." He started tickling me. "Tell me!"

"Stop it!" I gasped, slapping at his hands. "Tuck, help me."

Bill banged his fist on the table. "Kids, kids . . . man, I feel like a kindergarten teacher. Settle down. We've got work to do."

Cougar smiled and leaned back. He made one last feint at my ribs, and laughed when I flinched.

Bill rolled his eyes, and turned to Linda, who occupied the seat on the end. "You start."

We went through our routine, giving him a brief update on the cases we were working, then he threw out the new business.

"Okay," he said. "I need a husband/wife for an undercover op this weekend. Any takers?"

"Timeline?" Cougar asked.

"At best, a couple days. Could turn into a couple weeks though, depending on how twitchy our host is. We probably won't get it kicked off until the weekend."

Cougar leaned back in his chair and scratched his chin. "How 'bout it, Neese? Will you marry me?"

I thought about the paper on Bill's clipboard and wondered how long it would take it to be processed. "Ah, I'd better pass on this one."

The room fell silent. We had a pretty clean system for stuff like this: Cougar, Angel, and I loved the undercover assignments. Linda, Ubi, and Tucker preferred to stay behind the scenes. I could only imagine what they were thinking.

"O-kay," Cougar said slowly. "Well, what do *you* say, Linda? I swear it's not a rebound thing."

Linda winked. "You're not exactly my type, hon, but what the hell?"

That got a laugh, because we all knew Linda's type ran petite, blond, and decidedly female.

I felt Cougar's gaze on me as Bill talked, but I couldn't meet his eyes. I spent the rest of the meeting wondering how I was going to tell him I was leaving.

I didn't want to leave him. I didn't want to leave any of them.

Bill marked something on his clipboard and said, "That's all I've got. See you guys later."

Ubi and Tucker headed for the door, announcing that they had to be in court by ten. I pushed away from the table. With nothing pressing on my agenda, I thought about asking Cougar if he wanted to grab breakfast. Before I could get the words out, Kimberly Lausen edged inside the open door. Her beautiful face lit in a smile when her gaze landed on Cougar. "Hey, Jason. Got a sec?"

"Sure." Cougar stood and brushed my shoulder when he moved past. I felt a twinge of jealousy while I watched him hurry to her. They stood close together. She was nearly as tall as Cougar, and every hair of her stunning auburn hair fell neatly in place. I had to admit, they looked good together. He smiled when she tucked a piece of paper in the front pocket of his shirt.

Forcing my attention away from them, I glanced at Linda. She was watching them, too.

"Thanks for taking the assignment," I said. "I've got a lot of things going on right now."

She wrinkled her nose and smiled. "Ah, pretend marriage to Cougar doesn't sound too traumatizing, even to me." With a wink, she added, "That boy's almost sexy enough to make a woman change her mind."

I chuckled, thinking of how I hadn't met a woman yet who seemed immune to Cougar's charms.

Because of our different assignments, I didn't get to see Cougar again until Wednesday night, when we shared a shift at the hospital. Thankfully, Grady had let up a little about the visits since I'd agreed to take the time off. I waited until I got Abby tucked in before I headed to the hospital.

The guys were watching a basketball game. Angel's bed was cranked in an upright position, and he looked almost normal sitting there, though he still couldn't talk or grasp a pen for very long. Cougar sat eating pretzels, his feet propped on Angel's bed. His socks were so white I found myself wondering if he did his own laundry.

"Hey, Neese," he said around a mouthful of chips. "Celtics and Knicks. Who you got?"

"Knicks."

"That's my girl!" He winked at Angel. "Two against one. You gotta get better, pal. This ain't any fun without you yelling at the TV."

I sat on the other side of the bed and squeezed Angel's foot. "Aside from your misguided hoops alliances, you doing all right today?"

Angel blinked. I kicked off my shoes and stretched out on the bed beside him, careful not to disturb his IV lines. A blanket of sadness fell over me, nearly crushing me when I thought of all the time I'd spent with these two men, of how deeply I cared for them both. We'd started in the DEA as kids, and had done a lot of growing up together in the past eight years. The thought of spending the next six months without them left me feeling miserable and afraid. I told myself that I'd still see them, that they'd still be around, but I knew it wouldn't be the same. It would never be the same again.

"Spill it," Cougar said. "You look like you lost your best squirrel dog."

I fingered the edge of Angel's cotton blanket, unable to muster a smile. "I, uh, put in for some time off."

Cougar was silent for a moment. Then he nodded. "That's good. Take a couple weeks off, go somewhere warm. Take Abby to Disney World—"

"I put in for six months."

It hurt me to see the shock on his face. In some twisted way, this was harder than when I told Grady I was leaving. Cougar had never wronged me, never hurt me. I felt like I was betraying him. Abandoning him at a time when he needed me most.

"Necie, no!" he said, and the ragged tone of his voice twisted the knife a little deeper. He dropped his feet to the floor and leaned forward. Then he stood and walked over to the window, staring down at the lights below. "Why?" he asked without turning around.

"I'm trying to save my marriage. Grady said he'd

stop drinking if I took some time off."

Angel's slack, handsome face turned toward mine, and the compassion I found in his dark eyes was more than I could bear. A tear slid down my nose, then another.

Cougar whirled. "You mean, you're giving up your career so he'll give up a *habit*? You think that's fair?"

"I'm not giving up my career. It's only a few months." Even as I said it, the words felt hollow and false.

"Bullshit. C'mon, Denise . . . if Grady gets you out that long, do you really think he'll let you come back?"

"What can I do, Cougar? I have a little girl to think about."

"Yeah, you have a little girl to think about. Do you think it's setting a good example for her to see her mother give up a job she loves just to please some jealous asshole?"

I rose from the bed and took his place at the window, staring down at the twinkling lights of North Broad Street. My shoulders shook from the force of the tears I'd sworn I wasn't going to cry.

Cougar slipped up behind me and draped an arm around my neck. He pulled me to him in a gentle headlock, and buried his face in my hair. Somehow this was harder to take than his yelling at me.

"Don't leave me," he said. "Please don't leave me. I've got two people in this world that I can depend on, and they're both in this room. I don't want to lose you."

The door opened, and I pulled away from him. The

nurse did a double take at my tearstained face, then hurriedly checked Angel's vitals and left.

I sat in the chair Cougar had abandoned and leaned my head against the wall. "I don't want to leave—"

"Then don't." Cougar sat on the bed in front of me.

"It's not that easy—"

"Yes, it is. Just tell the bastard to grow a spine. If he really loved you, he wouldn't be so threatened by you."

I shook my head. "You don't have kids, Cougar. You don't know what it's like. If it was only Grady—"

Cougar caught the hesitation in my voice and pounced. "If it was only Grady, would you leave the DEA?"

"No," I admitted.

"Then don't do it. Abby's not the one who's asking you to quit."

"But Abby's the one who would benefit if I did."

Cougar pushed a hand through his hair. "Are you sure about that? Or is that something Grady's fed you? What are you going to do all day while she's at school? Do laundry and grocery shop like a good little mommy?"

I couldn't take this. I was dodging blows from every side now.

"Is there something wrong with that?" I snapped.

"There is if that's not what you want to be doing." Cougar scrubbed his eyes with the back of his hand. "My mother . . . my mother used to paint. She was good, too. I remember how happy she was in the summer, when she'd set up her easel in the backyard and paint while I played. A guy from the electric co-op saw one of her paintings one day while he was checking the meter. He offered her fifty dollars for it on the spot. She was so happy about that little bit of money, because she'd earned it herself doing something she loved. She told Daddy about it as soon as he got home from work. I don't know what it was, whether he was threatened by the fact that she found happiness in something he didn't have anything to do with or even understand, or he didn't like that she'd gotten any attention, but he hounded her about it after that. Every time she picked up a brush, he harped about something. 'Quit wasting my money on that foolishness,' or 'Quit wasting your time, ain't you got something better to do?' Eventually, it was easier for her to just give it up. I bought an easel and set it up at my place for when she visits, but she never touches it. I think she's afraid to even dream about it anymore. He did that to her, because of his insecurities. Grady's going to do the same thing to you, and one day you'll hate him for it."

We stayed up half the night talking, and when I left the next morning, I felt more torn and confused than ever. But things seemed to be going so much better between Grady and me. It was like a cloud had lifted off our home. When I looked into my daughter's smiling face, I figured that whatever I had to give up would be worth it.

Two days later, I sat in the conference room with Cougar and Bill, going over our files on Barnes. With all the things going on at home, I hadn't even had time to think about him. Funny how priorities could change in an instant. His preliminary trial date was approaching, so we were going over everything from top to bottom. When I realized we would probably run late, I excused myself to call Grady.

"Hey, babe," he said. "What's going on?"

"I'll probably be running a little late. Do you think you could pick up Abby this afternoon?"

"Yeah, sure. I'm about to head out. I left some files at home that I need, so I figured I could prep the case as easy from there as I could here. How late do you think you'll be?"

I glanced at my watch and mentally gauged the paperwork remaining on the conference table. "About an hour."

"Okay. Well, don't worry about supper. Abby and I will pick up some Chinese on the way home."

"Sounds good. I'll see you then."

"I love you, Denise," he said.

"Love you, too," I said, and clicked the phone shut.

I made it out of the office fifteen minutes ahead of schedule. When I drove by the movie theater, I saw the name of a cartoon Abby had been asking to see on the marquee. Maybe we could take her to the seven o'clock show after we ate.

But when I walked in the door, the house was too quiet. No TV blaring in the living room, no takeout cartons on the kitchen counter. I walked down the hall to Grady's office and threw open the door.

He was sipping something and reading over a file. His startled eyes flew to me and then his watch. "Shit!" he said, and slammed the glass onto the desk.

My pulse spiked. "Grady . . . you *forgot* her?"

"I was working and lost track of time . . ."

Something in his eyes clued me in, some minute shift. I stalked over to his desk and snatched up the glass of cola.

"Necie, wait!"

But I'd already turned it up to take a sip. Jack and Coke. I spat it out and hurled the glass at the wall behind him.

"Hey!" he cried as it shattered, splashing him and his precious papers.

I ran out the door to get my daughter. I was seething when I threw the car in reverse and hurtled down the driveway. I hit the mailbox and nearly the ditch as I shot onto the main road.

How could he have forgotten her? My pulse thudded in my ears when I thought of Abby standing there searching for us. I was going to kill him.

It was nearly twenty minutes after dismissal when I wheeled into the school parking lot.

The place looked deserted.

My tires bumped against the sidewalk when I slid into a parking space. I jumped out of the car and ran up the wheelchair ramp. The front doors were locked.

I raced around the building. My desperation grew with every door I tried and found locked.

Where was Abby?

I yanked hard on the gymnasium door and stumbled backward when it flew open. The girls' basketball team was running sprints. A few of them gave me curious looks as they raced to the foul line. I didn't see the coach, so I crossed the floor and entered the main building.

Abby's classroom was empty. Fear gripped my heart like a cold fist. I could barely breathe as I staggered down the hall and rounded the corner. A gray-haired custodian pushed a dust mop in front of the principal's office. She clutched her heart when she glanced up to see me barreling toward her.

"Please," I gasped. "My little girl . . ."

"Mrs. Bramhall, is that you?" a crisp voice called from inside the office. I sidestepped the janitor's dust pile and entered.

Abby's principal, Ms. Defries, gave me a frosty smile. "If you're looking for Abigail, she called her grandmother to pick her up."

Tension hissed out of me like air from a tire. I grabbed the doorknob to steady myself. "Oh, thank God. I was so scared. Thank you, Ms. Defries. Her father and I . . . we had a little scheduling mix-up. It won't happen again."

Her cool voice stopped me when I turned to leave. "That's what Mr. Bramhall said last time."

Slowly, I faced her. "Excuse me?"

"Mrs. Bramhall, I realize that sometimes scheduling is difficult when both parents work outside the home, but this is the third time this has happened this semester. It's not good for Abigail. She was very upset. Perhaps you and Mr. Bramhall should consider making other arrangements for Abby's transportation to and from school. I notice that she's also been tardy twice in the past month."

I was too shocked and furious to speak. This had happened to my baby more than once? I was going to kill Grady. I forgot to say good-bye. I forgot to say anything as I stalked out of the office.

Elizabeth's gray Cadillac sat waiting by the curb when I pulled into my driveway. I slammed the car in park and sprinted up the yard. I could hear her and Grady yelling at each other before I even opened the door.

They stood nose to nose in the living room, waving their hands and shouting at each other. Abby hunkered on the sofa, hugging her knees to her chest. I took one look at the tears rolling down her face and my temper skyrocketed. She looked terrified.

I ignored Grady and Elizabeth and crossed over to her. She threw her arms around my neck with a desperation that made me want to throttle her father and grandmother. I hugged her and smoothed my hand over her hair. "It's okay, baby," I said, glaring at them over her shoulder. They took the hint and shut up. "Go upstairs and do your homework. I'll be up in a minute."

"I-I don't have any homework."

I wiped her cheeks. "Then go play your Playstation. I need to talk to Daddy and Grandma."

She nodded and scampered up the stairs. I listened until I heard her bedroom door shut, then turned to Grady. He wouldn't meet my eyes.

"Thank you, Elizabeth, for picking her up, but if you'll excuse us, I really need to talk to Grady about this."

She gave me a wide-eyed, indignant look that was so much like Grady's I might've laughed under different circumstances. "No, I will not leave. Not until I've said what I came here to say."

Trying to keep my voice even, I said, "And what is that?"

She twisted her pearl necklace. "I'm tired of the two of you taking this child for granted. It's time for the both of you to grow up and stop being so selfish. Can't you see you're hurting her?"

"Elizabeth—"

"You're parents now. It's time you started acting like it."

I was in no mood for a parenting lecture from anyone, much less the woman who'd turned Grady into such a spoiled brat. I took a step toward her, and Grady moved between us.

"Mom, just go," he said. "I said I was sorry. Let that be enough."

She took a deep breath and smoothed a wave of blond hair from her forehead before peering over his shoulder at me. "Denise, I think you need to decide what's more important to you, your job or your family. I don't think you can have both."

Even though I was about to take time off from work, her words provoked me. I shot Grady a baleful glance and wondered what he'd told her. Today was his fault, not mine. I'd be damned if I let him pin the blame on me. "What about Grady? Why is it me who has to decide between career and family? Why not him?"

She gave me an exasperated look. "Because he's a man, dear. Women are different. *Mothers* are different. Once you have children, you can't carry on like you did before. You have responsibilities."

"What about Grady's responsibilities?"

"Grady's job puts him under a lot of pressure—"

I folded my arms across my chest and laughed. "And mine doesn't?"

"Don't twist my words. I know you're under pressure, too—that's what I'm saying. You don't have to be! You don't have to work. Grady can support you both. None of this would be happening if you didn't spend half your time at work—"

Anger flashed over me like a lightning strike. "No, Elizabeth. None of this would be happening if your son didn't spend half his time in the bottle."

Elizabeth blinked at me, then stared up at Grady. "You've been drinking?"

Grady scowled at me. "No, I—it's nothing, okay? I had one drink today, and Necie flipped out. I'm not drunk." He spun in a slow circle. "You can see I'm not drunk."

"Whatever," I said, and shoved past him.

"Necie, wait," he called, but I ignored him while I hustled up the stairs to Abby's room.

She lay on her pink bedspread, staring at the ceiling. I stretched out beside her and wrapped my arm around her waist.

She covered my hand with hers. "Are they still fighting?"

"I think they're winding down," I said. "What do you say we get out of here for awhile? I'll take you out to eat, anywhere you want."

Her eyes brightened. "Anywhere?"

"Yup."

She giggled and sat up. "Let's go!"

Grady and Elizabeth were starting round two when we snuck downstairs. They didn't even see us when we slipped through the kitchen. Abby slowed, but I tugged her along.

91

In my car, I got her belted in, then popped in one of her Disney sound tracks. Soon she was singing along, the shadows in her eyes vanquished.

I was halfway into the city before I realized I'd left my purse at home. I didn't have my driver's license, and I didn't have a dime on me.

"Fantastic," I muttered. What was I going to do now?

Then I remembered I had forty dollars in my locker from where Tucker had paid me back for some auto parts I'd picked up for him. I'd chance the driver's license and simply hope I wasn't pulled over. I turned around in a bank parking lot and headed toward the office.

"Hey, kiddo. I need to run by the office a sec. That okay with you?"

She smiled at me in the rearview mirror. "Will Uncle Bill be there?"

"I don't know. Maybe."

It was snowing again by the time we reached the DEA headquarters. Abby raced up the sidewalk with her head tilted back, catching snowflakes on her tongue. Ubi strode out the door, but caught it on the backswing and held it open for us.

He stooped to peer at Abby. "Necie, you've shrunk!"

She giggled and covered her mouth with her hand.

He winked up at me. "Oh, there you are. This must be Abby." He held out his hand. "Nice to meet you."

She yanked his arm violently up and down.

He laughed. "Hey, hey! You're a rough little thing like your mother, huh?"

"Learned from the best," I said. "I didn't realize you two hadn't met."

Ubi was the most recent addition to our team, but he'd fit right in. Sometimes I forgot he hadn't always been around.

"I would've known her anywhere." He ruffled her hair. "I'm Ubi."

Abby giggled again. "Scooby?"

He pretended to be offended. "Do I look like a Great Dane to you? Ubi."

Abby caught the teasing in his voice and said, "Hey, Scooby. Is my Uncle Bill up there?"

Ubi rolled his eyes. "Oh, yeah. He and Cougar are hashing it out."

I snagged the back of Abby's coat to keep her from rushing inside without me. "Hashing what out?"

"I don't know, and I don't wanna know. I took one look at Cougar's face and headed in the other direction, you know what I mean?"

"Yeah," I said, thinking of the argument I'd be facing when I went home.

When we reached the fifth floor, Bill's office door was closed. I hustled Abby past it and down the hall to the locker room. I extracted the forty bucks from my locker and stuffed it in my pocket.

"I want to see Uncle Bill," Abby protested when I herded her past his office again.

"Honey, I think he's busy—"

Bill's door swung open, and Cougar collided with me when he charged out of the office. He grabbed my shoulders to steady me. His face was red, his brow furrowed.

"Hey!" I said. "You okay?"

"No, I'm not okay. I'm piss-tachio!" he said, when he saw Abby behind me.

Abby lifted an eyebrow and I laughed. "He's from Texas, honey. They talk funny there."

"Watch it!" he reprimanded, and knelt beside her. "Hey, Princess Abby. How's it going? Long time, no see."

"Hi," she said. Then she spied Bill through the doorway and darted around Cougar. "Uncle Bill! Uncle Bill!"

"Abby!" he said, and held out his arms. She launched herself at him.

"I've been dumped," Cougar said, and stood.

While Abby chattered at Bill, I elbowed Cougar and said, "So what are you pistachioed about?"

The corner of his mouth quirked, then he shook his head. "Not here. What are you guys doing?"

"Now? We were going out to dinner."

"Just you and Abby?"

"Yeah."

Cougar glanced around the office and then back at me. "Mind if I tag along? I need to talk to you about something."

"Um, sure. I'll give you fair warning, though. I already told Abby she could pick where we ate, and I can tell you right now it won't be Subway."

Cougar scoffed. "Can't be worse than any of the places you and Angel drag me into."

Half an hour later, he changed his tune.

"Fat Daddy's?" He squinted up at the neon sign. "You actually eat at a place called Fat Daddy's?"

I grinned and pocketed my keys. "You were warned."

A giant eagle in a green jersey greeted us at the door. Cougar winced, from the bright lights or the booming pop music, I wasn't sure.

"How many?" the eagle yelled.

"Three," I yelled back, and he motioned us forward with a giant wing. Children bounced around like popcorn in a popper. As we wandered deeper inside, the whiny boy-band voices were replaced by the ping and sirens of video games.

Cougar clutched my elbow and pulled me backward against him. "Is this hell?" he asked pitifully.

I laughed and tugged him toward the booth. Abby made me get in our side first. Cougar slid in across from us.

Our teenage waitress gave him the eye while she handed out menus. Cougar shoved his toward me. "You order," he said.

I almost felt sorry for him. Glancing at Abby, I said,

"The usual?"

She nodded.

"We'll take a large pig, pineapple and sweet pepper. Pan, with a pitcher of Pepsi. Give him a water."

Cougar grinned despite himself. "Oh, my God," he said, and covered his face with his hands.

"What?" I asked when the waitress walked away. "I don't know what you're whining about. We've got the five basic food groups covered. What more do you want?"

"Tokens!" Abby screeched. "Can I have tokens, Mama?"

"I'll have to get change." I waved my hands to get her to let me out.

"Wait," Cougar said. "I got it." He pulled out his wallet and handed her a five.

"Thanks!" Abby said, and ran toward the token machine.

I watched her settle into a race-car seat, then leaned across the table. "So what's going on?"

Cougar frowned and toyed with the jar of parmesan. "The tape. The tape of Angel's statement is missing from evidence."

"What! Oh, no. How did that happen?"

"How do you think it happened? I'm telling you, Denise. Barnes has someone inside. But I kind of figured that might happen. I made an extra copy before I left my apartment that day. Tonight, I'm gonna make a dozen of them. I'll send them to the DA, the feds . . . the

Daily Fucking Herald."

The eagle paused as he walked by our table to shake his wing at Cougar.

Cougar rolled his eyes, then leaned toward me and lowered his voice. "What gets me is the person who did this is someone we know. It has to be. And he doesn't give a damn about Angel. With no tape, what do you think Barnes would do next? He'd get one of his thugs to take out the only witness."

My stomach twisted at the thought of Angel lying there helpless. Even though one of us was always with him, how hard would it be for someone to get to him?

Cougar sighed. "I told Bill to pass around the word that there are extra copies. I don't know what else to do."

Abby bounced over to the table and grabbed my hand. "Play with me, Mama."

"Just a sec, honey. Cougar and I are talking—"

Cougar smiled and ruffled Abby's hair. "It's okay. Let's play."

Moments later, I found myself sitting in a race-car simulator that nearly gave me whiplash when Abby's car slammed mine into the wall. Cougar laughed behind me. "Drives like her mother."

After getting annihilated in a Space Invaders game, I begged for mercy and something I could actually play. Abby and I challenged Cougar to a game of foosball.

"You girls don't know who you're messing with."

He slipped his leather jacket off his broad shoulders and tossed it in our booth. "I had one of these babies in my basement when I was a kid."

"Is that right?" I winked. "Well, let's see what you got, big boy."

Cougar opened his mouth like he wanted to say something more, then clamped it shut again and grinned. We scored the first point, but then he scored the next two.

"Time-out," Abby said, then moved around the table to stand by Cougar.

"Hey!" I protested. "You're abandoning me?"

"Sorry, Mom." She shrugged. "Your defense stinks."

Cougar snickered while I pouted. They finished trouncing me and gave each other a high five. Our pizza still hadn't arrived, so we drifted through the crowd to the Skee Ball lanes. Skee Ball, I could handle, but even here, Cougar showed me up. He found the sweet spot and sank four 100-pointers in a row. The winner light flashed above the machine, and it spat out a row of tickets that he gave to Abby to redeem. She returned with two pink plastic leis.

Cougar took them from her. She giggled when he dropped one over her head and planted a resounding kiss on each of her cheeks. When he draped mine over my head, he grabbed my waist and pulled me close to whisper, "Wait'll I go to the hospital tonight. I'm gonna tell Angel I lei'd Necie. If that doesn't get him talking, nothing will."

I laughed and pushed him away. "You're awful!"

He wagged his eyebrows and flashed those perfect white teeth.

Our waitress nodded at me while she moved through the crowd, holding a pizza tray near her ear. Cougar squeezed the nape of my neck and helped me hustle Abby back to the table to eat. She ate most of two pieces, then begged to be excused. For the first time, I thought about Grady sitting at home, probably drunk and angry. Might as well let her have fun while she could.

I motioned her on. She smacked a kiss on my cheek before heading back to the Skee Ball lanes.

Cougar grabbed his third slice of pizza, cast it another dubious look, then took a big bite. "You know," he said. "The scary thing is, I'm thinking this ain't half-bad."

"Told ya."

He watched Abby while he chewed, then swallowed and sipped his water. He surprised me by saying, "I used to think I didn't want kids, but they're kinda nice, huh?"

It took me a moment to manage a reply. "What's nice about them? They abandon their mothers for stinking at foosball."

He smiled, and suddenly I was very conscious of the knee that brushed mine beneath the table. "You know what I mean." He nodded at Abby. "Look at her. She's beautiful, and so damn smart, just like her mother. It must be nice to look at some little person like that and see yourself."

Speechless, and more than a little flustered, I sipped my Pepsi without comment.

He stole one of Abby's abandoned crusts and munched on it while he stared into space. "Of course, that kind of thing can bite you in the ass, too. I think my dad looked so hard for himself in me that he didn't want to see anything else. I think my worst fear in life is turning into my father."

Ha! Tell me about it, I thought. It occurred to me how very little I'd thought about Barnes in the past few days. When Barnes looked at me, what did he see?

Cougar insisted on buying. He handed his Visa to the girl behind the register, then placed his hand on my hip when he reached around me to scrawl his name on the slip and snag a peppermint. When the girl said, "Have a nice night, Mr. and Mrs. Stratton," he smiled and said, "You, too," without bothering to correct her.

Abby held his hand while we walked to the car, and it gave my heart a funny little twinge to see them like that. Again, I wondered if I was reading more into the situation than there really was. Cougar was a flirt— everyone knew it—just a harmless flirt. But lately he didn't feel so harmless at all.

He fastened Abby's seat belt, and she chattered to him all the way back to the DEA office. It was snowing again. I felt like I was back in the asteroid game again and had to struggle to keep my eyes from straying to the dizzying pattern of flurries striking the windshield.

"You getting out?" he asked when I slid into a space in short-term parking. "I was going to give you one of those tapes if you're not in a hurry."

"Sure." I threw the car in park and again thought of the scene that was probably waiting for me at home. "No hurry at all."

Again, Abby ran ahead. She threw her arms wide and pirouetted in the drifting banks.

"Watch this," Cougar said, and stooped to grab a handful of snow. He packed it between his hands and hurled it at her.

"Hey!" she yelled when it struck her in the back. "Who did that?"

Cougar pointed at me, but Abby took one look at his face and knelt to make her own snowball. She lobbed it at him and missed by a foot. "Mama, help me!" she cried.

Together, we converged on him. He batted off my attempt, but one of Abby's missiles hit him full in the face.

"Hey, this isn't fair," he said, dodging the snowballs we hurled at him.

"Tuck, help me!" he yelled, and I turned just in time to catch one between the eyes. I heard them laughing while I sputtered and brushed the snow from my eyes.

The war was on.

Drawn by the commotion, Linda and another agent joined the fray, providing Abby and me with some much-needed assistance. I hurled a one-two at Tucker and turned to find Cougar grinning at me. He hefted a cantaloupe-sized snowball in his hands. I feinted left, then right, and ducked when he lobbed it at my head. With a screech, Abby charged, flinging snowballs as fast as her little hands could form them. I turned to run and Cougar grabbed me around the waist. As if I weighed nothing, he picked me up and ran, using me as a shield. Both Abby and Tucker pelted me until I couldn't see. I was laughing too hard to breathe.

Cougar's iron grasp around my waist loosened for a second and I wriggled free. He chased me around the side of the building. My Keds slipped on the grass, and he launched himself at me. We went down in a flurry of arms and legs and rolled in the wet snow, trying to rub the slushy mess in each other's faces. Cougar pinned me in seconds flat. His eyes twinkled in the glow of the streetlight, and he flashed me a triumphant grin.

I was conscious of so many things in that instant: the cold, wet snow beneath me; his warm, hard thigh between mine. The sweet, coconut-lime scent of his aftershave. His smile faded while he stared down at me. My pulse leapfrogged when his fingers tightened around my wrists, and he lowered his head.

He stopped just shy of kissing me, his mouth

hovering above mine. His peppermint-scented breath came in warm, tantalizing puffs against my face.

"Grady is a lucky son of a bitch," he said, an instant before Abby and Tucker raced around the corner.

"Get them!" Benedict Abby shrieked, and suddenly I found my face shoved against the warm skin of Cougar's neck. He clasped his hands around his head and shielded us from their attack.

Snowballs struck his back with a dull whup-whup-whup, but I was barely conscious of the sound while I breathed in the heated scent of him. My lips pressed against the throbbing pulse in his neck, but I couldn't pull away, couldn't move at all from the crush of his big body. Then the laughter faded. Abruptly, Cougar rolled off me and sat on the ground. He stared at Abby's retreating back while I struggled to sit up.

My knees wobbled when I stood. Feeling suddenly awkward, I stretched a hand down to help him.

He shook his head. "Go," he said with a wave. "I'll be around in a minute."

"But it's cold."

"Not cold enough," he mumbled, refusing to meet my eyes.

His brusque tone disturbed me. Unsure of what I'd done to annoy him, I grabbed his arm.

He shook off my grasp. "In a minute."

"But—"

Finally he looked at me. The corner of his mouth quirked. "Geez, Neese. Give a guy a break."

I stood there, frozen by the bitter wind and the strange expression on his face.

He gave me a pointed look that was part exasperation, part pure mischief. "I'm afraid I might embarrass myself."

"Oh." Like a dummy, I stared blankly at him for a moment before it sank in. Of their own volition, my eyes flew to his crotch, and my breath caught when I saw the bulge there. "*Oh!*"

He laughed when I jerked my gaze away.

"Well, there go my hero points." In a deep, grave baritone, he said, "I am but a man."

I forced a chuckle, though I was too shell-shocked to do much more. I was glad for the biting wind, another excuse for my red cheeks. I gestured toward the front. "I'm just going to . . ."

He laughed again when I fled.

A truce had apparently been called around front. Abby sat between Linda and Tucker on the front steps. The other agent was gone. The slight lift of Tucker's eyebrow made my face burn. He grinned at Linda, and she ducked her head, taking a sudden interest in her boots.

"Where's Cougar?" he asked.

I avoided his eyes by pretending to dust snow off my jacket. "He'll be around in a minute." Glancing at Abby, I said, "You ready to go, kiddo?"

She kicked at the snow in front of her. "Aww, do we have to?"

"Yes, ma'am. You have to take a bath and get in bed."

She sighed and used Tucker's leg to push herself to her feet. "Bye, guys."

"Bye, sweetie," Linda said.

Tucker stood and ruffled Abby's hair. "Make your mom bring you back to play again."

Abby took my hand, and we walked toward the car.

"Hey, you guys leaving?"

I turned toward the sound of Cougar's voice. His face was half-hidden in the shadows as he leaned against the brick building.

"Yeah." I plucked a strand of damp hair off my cheek. "Abby has school tomorrow. But thanks for dinner."

"You're welcome. I guess I should be getting to the hospital anyway. Talk to you tomorrow. And see *you* later, brat."

Abby waved, and I hurried her along to the car.

She fell asleep in no time. I sighed, thinking of how grouchy she'd be when I woke her to give her a bath.

A few minutes later, I pulled into the garage and went around to get her out. A light winked on, and Grady opened the back door. I didn't know what to expect when he started toward us.

"Here." He took her from my arms. "I've got her."

He carried her up the steps. I took it as a good sign

when he didn't stagger. Maybe there was hope for a calm discussion yet. I didn't smell liquor on him.

"Hey, baby," he said, when she stirred in his arms. "You're wet." He glanced at me. "You're wet, too. Where have you been, besides Fat Daddy's?"

I was about to ask him how he knew that when I realized I was still wearing the pink lei.

Abby blinked up at him and yawned. "We had a snowball fight, Daddy. It was so cool. Cougar hit me, but I got him back."

Grady looked at me again with narrowed eyes. "Cougar? You've been with Cougar?"

I shrugged off my coat. "I had to go by the office. We ran into him."

"We beat Mama playing foosball," Abby said, and I did a mental wince.

Grady stood Abby on the kitchen floor. The muscle in his jaw twitched, and his hands balled into fists at his side. "So you had dinner with him, too?"

"Don't even start," I said, and patted Abby's behind. "Get upstairs, honey. Mama will be up in a minute to help you with your bath."

She nodded and kissed us both before moping up the stairs. I could almost see the tension rolling off Grady's back before he turned to face me.

"So I read it wrong?" He cocked his head. "It's not the vegetable, then. All this time, you've been sleeping around with Cougar."

I threw my keys on the kitchen counter. "Don't be stupid, and don't try to make this about me. You've got a problem, Grady."

He laughed. "Damn straight, I've got a problem. It's you. It's always been you. Sometimes I wonder what my life would've been like if I'd never met you."

"Oh, so you wonder that, too," I said, and shouldered past him. He grabbed my arm and spun me around.

"Don't walk away from me." Before I could react, he seized the pink lei around my neck and twisted his fist around it. He steamrolled me backward and slammed me into the wall hard enough to knock the air from my lungs.

CHAPTER 7

Inexplicably, he kissed me, even as he tightened the cord around my throat. His tongue invaded my mouth as I fought for my next breath.

I balled my hand into a fist and swung. The blow landed solid on the side of the head. He staggered, loosening his grip, but he didn't let go. He pressed his shoulder into me to block my arm. "What's the matter? Are my kisses not as good as Cougar's? In what other areas am I lacking?"

Spots danced before my eyes, and self-preservation took over. I rammed my knee as hard as I could into his groin.

Grady screamed and fell to the floor, curling into a fetal position. I stood over him, gasping for breath and massaging my burning neck.

"Mama!"

I glanced up to see Abby standing at the top of the stairs. Grady scuttled back and leaned against the wall.

"Get in your room," I said. "I'm coming."

"But, Daddy—"

"Daddy's fine," Grady rasped. "I just fell."

"Abby, go!" I said in my don't-mess-with-Mom voice. She turned and ran back to her room.

"Necie—" Grady said, and I whirled.

Angry tears stung my eyes. I pointed at him. "Stay the fuck away from me."

Without waiting on a reply, I ran upstairs to check on my daughter.

I paused outside Abby's bedroom door, trying to compose my face into some mask of neutrality, but inside I raged. How dare he treat me that way? He wasn't even drunk!

I plastered on a smile and twisted the knob. Abby had stripped to her underpants. She stood at the foot of her bed, gazing at me with huge, sad eyes. My smile faltered, and I hurried across the room to take her in my arms. As I held her small, warm body close, I knew that something had to give. Things between her father and I had grown steadily worse. I couldn't live like this. I couldn't let her live like this.

"Is Daddy okay?" she asked in a small, quiet voice.

"Yeah, baby. He's okay. Let's get you in the tub."

She moved toward the adjoining bathroom. I glanced at her bedroom door, then doubled back to lock it behind us. I felt a little annoyed with myself for the apprehension I felt, but I could no longer predict what Grady might do.

After shampooing Abby's hair, I left her to do the rest herself. I thought about packing our clothes and leaving, but where was I supposed to go, a motel? Besides, why should I be the one to leave? Let Grady go home to his mother. She'd welcome him with open arms.

I pressed my ear to her bedroom door, but heard nothing in the hall beyond. I eased open the door and peered into the hallway. No Grady jumping from the shadows. Feeling stupid, I hurried down the hall to our bedroom.

He probably was sitting in some bar somewhere.

My heart thudded while I snatched some clothes from my dresser and closet. This was how far we'd come. I couldn't believe I actually feared Grady, but here I was, worrying about the gun in my purse downstairs.

Back in Abby's room, I locked her door behind me again and sat on her bed until she came out of the bathroom. I thought about telling her not to open the door if Grady knocked, but how could I tell her that?

I popped in one of her favorite movies and kissed her cheek.

"Hey, babe. I'm going to take a shower and then I'll come watch with you, okay?"

She nodded, and made no comment when I picked up my shirt and shorts and headed to her bathroom. I washed myself with bubblegum-scented soap and thought about my next move. Tomorrow, after I took Abby to school, I'd tell Grady to pack his things. Tomorrow I'd tell him I wanted a divorce.

A divorce.

I stood under the pulsing hot spray and wondered why the thought didn't upset me as it once had. I wanted to care. I wanted to feel something, but it was like I was hollow inside. Dead. My only concern was how to explain it to Abby. Whatever Grady and I did or said to each other, I didn't want her caught in the cross fire.

I toweled my hair dry and dressed, then joined Abby beneath her Strawberry Shortcake comforter. She scooted over to make room for me, and I saw the questions in her eyes, but still she made no comment. I set the clock and cut off the television and lights. She was asleep in minutes, but rest proved more elusive for me.

The next morning, I pulled on a pair of jeans and kept on the same shirt I'd slept in. Abby got out of bed without her customary protest and dressed quickly, as if she sensed my anxiety.

When I opened her bedroom door, my heart skittered when I found Grady lying in the hallway in front of it. He was snoring. I pressed a finger to my lips and lifted Abby to my hip. Cautiously, I stepped over him.

I nearly screamed when he grabbed my ankle.

"Necie." He propped up on an elbow and rubbed his eyes with his free hand. "Wait."

"Let go of me," I said, and tried to shake off his grasp.

"Baby, I'm sorry—"

I shot him an angry glance. "Not in front of her."

Immediately, he released me. I moved toward the stairs.

"But when—"

I paused on the first step. Our eyes met. Tears glistened in his, but still I felt nothing. I kept walking.

"Will you come home for lunch, so we can talk?" he called.

"I don't know."

He followed me all the way to the garage and waited until I set Abby down to thrust a piece of paper in my hand. I stared down at the name Marty and a phone number I didn't recognize.

"What's this?" I asked.

"He's a coordinator for the local AA meetings. I'm going to one tomorrow night." Grady clasped my hand. "Please, Necie, don't give up on me. You're right, I need help. I need you, too, and Abby."

What about me, and what I need? I thought, but didn't say it out loud. If Grady was ready to admit he had a problem, I wanted him to get help. He was the father of my child; I didn't want to see him destroy himself.

"Will you come home for lunch?" he asked again.

His green eyes pleaded with me. It shocked me how haggard he looked. When had he lost so much weight?

"I'll be here at noon." I shut Abby's door and faced him. "But I'm not promising anything."

"That's okay," he said. "I understand."

When I walked through the double glass doors of the DEA building, I spotted Cougar standing by the elevators. He gave me a little wave in greeting and pressed the up button. His brown hair was damp, and he wore no coat. I tried not to notice the way his navy T-shirt stretched over his chest, or the rocky cleft of his bicep peeking from beneath his sleeve.

"Morning," he said when I drew near.

"Morning." My face heated when I thought about our encounter in the snow, and some of the things he'd said to me last night.

Oh grow up, I thought. *This is Cougar. He probably says the same sort of thing to the waitress who brings his morning bagel.*

I jumped when he leaned in to sniff my hair, then felt a flash of irritation at myself. This school crush thing I had going had to stop.

"That's different," he said. "Cotton candy?"

Did the man notice everything? Maybe that was the magic of Cougar. He had a gift for making every woman around him feel like the only one who existed.

"Bubblegum. I used Abby's shampoo."

He nodded, unscrewed the cap from his Dasani bottled water, took a swig, then closed it back. He looked troubled—maybe even a little nervous. It wasn't something I was used to seeing in Cougar.

"Look, Necie," he said. "About what happened last night . . . I'm sorry. I didn't mean to embarrass you or anything."

He frowned and uncapped his water again when the elevator lurched to a stop and the fifth-floor button lit.

"That's okay," I said when he turned the bottle up. "No, ah, hard feelings."

Cougar dribbled water down the front of his shirt. I giggled as he coughed and laughed.

My smile faded when Kimberly glided into the elevator in all her auburn-haired glory. I felt downright schlumpy in my jeans and wrinkled T-shirt.

She grinned at Cougar, who was dabbing at the front of his shirt. "How did you miss a mouth like that?" she asked.

"Ha, ha," he said. "This pick-on-Jason day or something? Necie's already been poking fun at my expense."

"Poor baby," she cooed, and winked at me.

I tried not to hate her and her perfect genes. It wasn't her fault she was five foot eleven, curvy, and brilliant. Okay, so maybe I would try not to hate her tomorrow. I'd had a bad night.

Still, I consoled myself, it couldn't be easy to love a guy like Cougar. At least with Grady, I knew where I stood. Quicksand. But Cougar was too smooth, too charming. The kind of guy who could lull you into thinking everything was perfect right until the day he wanted to be perfect with someone else.

Kim got off on the next floor. "See you, Necie. See you, Cougar."

"See you," I said.

Cougar caught the door. "Hey, I'll be over to change your oil tonight."

"Okay." She waved. "See you then."

I studied my ragged nails as the door shut. "Is that some kind of code for kinky stuff?"

He gave me that funny half smile again. "Nah, just a favor for a friend."

I leaned against the wall, thoughts of Grady replaced by thoughts of Cougar's "friends."

We had a short meeting, and I felt a pang when Cougar and Linda left to do some legwork on their undercover operation. That should've been my job.

Tucker and I, since we had no immediate assignment, were delegated to cleaning up our messy conference room.

"So, how are things going with Anne Marie?" I asked when we were alone.

Tucker glanced up from the haphazard stack of files beside the copy machine and smiled. "Perfect. Think she's the one, Necie."

I paused swiping on the dry-erase board. "Oh, wow! You think that already?"

"More like something I know." Tucker leaned against the table, his brown eyes animated. "I think I knew it from our first kiss. Was it like that with you and Grady?"

I laughed, and realized how bitter it sounded. "No," I said quietly, and turned back to the board.

Five minutes later, Tucker said, "Hey, what's this?"

I twisted to see him holding up a videotape.

"It says Barnes Surveillance, but there are no ID numbers, no log-in stickers."

"Oh, God." I crossed the room and took it from him. "What's it doing here? All these are supposed to be with the prosecutor's office."

Tucker shrugged. "Maybe it's a scrap. That could be why it's not coded."

"One way to find out." We walked over to the TV/VCR combo, and I punched it in. Tucker pressed the TV's power button, and we moved back to watch.

Unease stole over me when the empty room flashed on-screen. It was a conference room much like this one, but the tables were nicer. Real wood. I stared at the picture of migrating geese on the wall. Where had I seen this room before? It wasn't part of the Barnes estate.

The sound of her laughter preceded Maria Barnes into the shot. She backed into the frame, wearing a long black coat and clutching a man's tie. She reeled him toward her. My heart stilled when I saw the back of his head.

"Hurry!" Maria said, and Grady pressed a finger to

her lips to shush her. He disappeared from the screen for an instant, then charged back to her, seizing her in a hungry kiss.

CHAPTER 8

I sensed Tucker's head whip around. Though we stood inches from each other, his voice sounded like it was coming through a tunnel. "Is that—?"

He reached for the power button. Unable to voice my "no" or even tear my eyes from the couple on the screen, I slapped at Tucker's hand.

The walls of my own conference room seemed to swell and pulse while I watched Grady yank the coat from her shoulders.

She wore nothing beneath.

He backed her to the table and lifted her up on it, kissing her with a fervor he hadn't shown me in years. He fumbled with his belt and dropped his pants. Her long legs locked around his waist.

Sweat beaded my forehead though my body had

turned to ice. I couldn't breathe.

The room started to sparkle, little flashes of color like the glitter from Abby's dance shoes.

The next thing I knew, I was hanging halfway out the eighth-story window.

"Breathe, honey," Tucker was saying. "Breathe."

A gust of cold air slapped me in the face, and the bands around my chest loosened a bit. I took a hard gulp that burned my lungs, then another. I don't know how long we stood there like that before I told him I was okay.

Tucker hauled me back inside. Moans and shrieks echoed from the TV, but I couldn't look at them anymore. This time I didn't try to stop Tucker when he jabbed the power button.

He let loose a stream of obscenities that would've been funny under other circumstances. Mild-mannered Tucker swearing like Cougar. He pushed me into a chair and wiped a hand down his flushed face.

"Okay," he said, like he was trying to devise a plan. "Okay . . . so what are you going to do?"

I cracked my knuckles. "I'm going to throw his ass out."

"Fine. I'll help. So will Cougar and Ubi. We'll make sure he doesn't give you any trouble."

"No, Tuck . . ." I stood, and he did, too. "Please don't tell anyone."

"But—"

"Please."

Tucker stared at the darkened television. "What if the tape's a fake? Just something to rattle your cage? I can get Eric in the lab to look it over. He won't say anything."

"I don't need the lab to look at it," I said, and moved to extract the tape from the player.

All I needed to see was my husband's face.

"Necie . . ." Tucker grimaced, then folded me into his arms. I hugged him back.

Someone coughed behind us. Cougar frowned from the doorway. "Am I interrupting something?" he asked, his blue eyes flashing.

I pulled away from Tucker. "Uh, no. You're not interrupting." Unable to think of an explanation, I grabbed my purse, shoved the videotape inside, and headed toward the door. "See you guys later. I need to run home."

Cougar wordlessly stepped aside.

"Necie, wait!" Tucker said, but I pretended like I didn't hear. I needed to talk to Grady alone.

Bill was in the elevator. He smiled and glanced at his watch. "Lunchtime already?"

"No, I . . . something came up. I have to run home."

He squinted at me. "Everything okay?"

I took a deep breath. "No. And I need to talk to you about my leave."

"I put it on Sandra's desk. It should go through sometime this week."

"Can you tear it up?"

Bill lifted his eyebrows, then he grinned. "You bet I can. But what changed your mind?"

"Most single moms can't afford to take a leave like that, especially working for the DEA."

His smile faded. "Oh, honey . . . I'm sorry."

"Me, too. Sorry for myself . . . mostly, sorry for Abby."

The elevator stopped, and Bill glanced at the light. "My floor. Listen, is there anything I can do?"

"Just tear up that request." I waved before the door slid shut.

In the parking lot, I was fumbling for my keys when someone grabbed my shoulder. I turned, half-expecting to see Cougar, but it was a panting Tucker.

"Necie . . . I was afraid . . . I wouldn't catch you."

I gaped at his red face. "Did you just run eight flights of stairs?"

Tucker leaned against my car. "Yeah. I don't want you to go alone. Damn, when did I get this old?"

I punched his arm. "I'll be okay. I'm armed and dangerous, remember?

Tucker studied me with grave eyes. "Anne Marie told me what Grady did at the hospital."

"How did she—never mind. I bet we were the talk of the hospital."

Tucker grinned. "I think maybe Anne Marie and I are, but you were second." He sobered. "She only told me because she was worried about you."

"He won't hurt me. I won't let him."

Tucker held up his palms. "At least let me take you home. I'll get Anne Marie to come get me. You can call the school and give us permission to pick up Abby. We'll take her to a movie or something so you can do what you need to do."

I sighed. That *would* make things easier. I handed him my keys. "Okay. Thanks."

We didn't talk much on the way home. I kept replaying the image of Grady and Maria in my mind. In my heart, I knew the tape was real, but I wanted him to have to look me in the eye and tell me himself.

Tucker hugged me before he left, and Anne Marie did, too, though we barely knew one another. Tucker told me he'd call before they headed back with Abby, but looking into his worried face, I figured he'd call before that. I waved good-bye to them and sat on the couch to wait on Grady. He walked in at half past twelve, carrying a sack of burgers. The smell of grease and onions made me queasy. I turned on the TV.

"I was hoping I'd beat you here," he said. "Are you hungry?"

"No."

"C'mon." He waved the bag in front of me. "Let's eat, then we'll talk."

"I'd rather watch a movie." My eyes never left Grady's face while I pressed the play button. I hadn't rewound it. The room filled with the sound of Maria's shrieks and Grady's grunts. The color drained from his face. His eyes darted from the screen to me, and his Adam's apple bobbed while he swallowed.

"You bastard," I said, and pitched the remote as hard as I could at his head. He threw up his arms to protect his face, and I heard a loud crack when the remote struck his watch.

All the things I'd wanted to say to him flew from my mind. I couldn't even stand to look at him. My sneakers thudded against the steps as I raced upstairs.

I yanked a suitcase from beneath the bed and unlatched it with a shaking hand. Grady filled the doorway while I moved toward the closet.

"Necie, you can't leave."

"I'm not leaving, you are." I jerked an armful of his suits from the closet and threw them at the suitcase. Some of them fell to the floor, but I didn't slow.

"Necie . . ."

"What?" I turned on him. "It's not what I think? Come on, Grady. Surely you can do better than that."

"It was only sex," he said softly. He walked inside the room, and I shot him a warning glance. "I've regretted it since the day it happened."

I swiped my nose with the back of my hand. "Somehow I missed that part on the tape." I strode toward his sock drawer.

"Necie, just . . ." Before I realized what he was doing, Grady was beside me. He seized my wrists. "Stop and listen to me!"

I yanked free of him. "Listen to what? There is *nothing* you can say to make this okay." The tears I'd sworn I wouldn't cry stung my eyes. "She's my half sister, Grady. You knew who she was."

"She came to me, wanting to talk about you . . . It wasn't something I planned, Necie."

I sneered and shoved him out of my way.

His eyes narrowed. "How did you get that tape anyway? Were you having me followed?"

"Oh, please. How do you think I got that tape? She set you up, Grady. I found it at work. I'm just glad I found it before the whole place saw it." He rubbed his hands over his face, and I resumed packing. "You've suspected me of sleeping with Angel and Cougar and God knows who else, but all this time it's been you. How did you get the gall to do that?"

"Necie, I'm sorry. Sorry for everything."

I stiffened my spine and stared him down. "There's nothing you can say."

He sat on the edge of the bed and covered his face with his hands. When I saw his shoulders shake, I felt nothing except contempt.

I shoved everything I could into the suitcase and the rest into a duffel bag.

Finally he lifted his head. "What about the AA meeting tomorrow night? I can't do this without you."

I was through letting him guilt-trip me. "You can if you love your daughter."

"What about Abby?" he said.

"You can see her all you like as long as you stay sober."

"What do you think this will do to her?"

I gritted my teeth. "Don't try to use her against me, not with this. She's the only reason I've stayed this long."

Anger flashed in Grady's eyes. "I get it. You don't give a damn about me." He shook his head. "And you wonder why I looked somewhere else . . . You don't care about me, and I love you so much it hurts."

I laughed. "Huh, that's another thing I missed on that tape. Maybe I should've paid more attention." I picked up the duffel bag and threw it in his lap. "Get the hell out of my house."

He gave me another long, sad look, then he did.

I locked the door behind him and called Tucker to check on Abby. I realized I mostly felt relieved that Grady was gone, then felt guilty for that.

Explaining to Abby that her daddy wouldn't be living with us anymore was the hardest thing I'd ever done in my life. I tried to explain that he would always love her and would always be part of her life, but I saw the fear in her eyes. I let her sleep in my bed that night, and tried to reassure her that everything would be all right. As I stared at the ceiling, I wondered if that were true.

I awoke the next morning to a pounding head and a stiff shoulder from sleeping on my side all night. Abby barely spoke on the way to school. Her little face looked strained and grim, and all I could think of were the words I'd said to Grady.

There is nothing you can say to make this okay.

My daughter's life would be changed forever. When I'd found out I was pregnant with her, I'd vowed that she'd have a better childhood than mine. She'd have the things she needed, including a stable home with both parents. Looking at her slumped shoulders, I felt like a failure.

I was halfway to work when I realized today was Barnes's preliminary hearing. Dismayed, I glanced down at my jeans and rumpled T-shirt. Not exactly the sort of garb that would impress a judge. Bill might shoot me on the spot. I made an illegal turn in a fire lane and raced back home to change.

Twenty minutes later, I jockeyed for a position in the overcrowded elevator between two smelly vice cops and a cleaning crew. My shoes pinched my toes, and I'd poked a fingernail through my only pair of hose in my haste to get them on. Not wanting to go bare-legged in November, I'd twisted them around so the run was in the back. At least I could pretend I didn't know if someone pointed it out.

My surly mood didn't improve when I found the note

on my locker announcing one of Bill's special meetings, attendance mandatory. I clacked down the hall in my heels toward the conference room. Cougar and Linda were already inside, but at least I'd beat Bill there.

"Hey, guys," I said breathlessly and plopped down next to Linda.

"Hey," Linda replied, but Cougar never glanced around. He slouched in his chair and stared straight ahead at the blank dry-erase board.

"What's this about?" I was looking at Cougar when I said it, but he didn't answer.

"I don't know," Linda said.

Cougar checked his watch and grumbled, "He'd better fuckin' hurry."

I elbowed Linda. "Who peed in his Cheerios?"

Cougar twisted to glare at me, and my jaw dropped when I saw the shiner on his left eye. "Whoa! What happened to you?"

He turned back to the board and bounced his pen on the table in a hard rat-a-tat-tat. "None of your business."

I held up my hands. "Fine, then. Sorry I asked."

Bill wandered in, scribbling notes on his clipboard as he walked. He bumped into the podium, readjusted it, then smiled at us. He blinked when he looked at Cougar, but all he said was, "Where's Tucker?"

Cougar leaned back in his chair and crossed his arms over his chest. "Yeah, Necie, where's Tucker?"

I frowned at his tone. "How am I supposed to know?"

"I'm right here."

I turned to look at Tucker, who sounded as grouchy as Cougar, and got my second surprise of the day. His lip was swollen and an ugly red scrape colored his cheekbone.

"Is something going on here I need to know about?" Bill asked.

"No," they said in unison.

Tucker took the seat farthest from Cougar, which happened to be the one to my immediate right. Cougar grunted and shifted in the other direction.

"Okay," Bill said. "Ubi's at the hospital, so you guys can fill him in. Necie and Tucker, he'll be with you two backing up John David's unit at the warehouse next week."

"Wait." Linda turned to me. "Thought you were taking a leave?"

"Not anymore."

"Whoo hooo!" Linda pumped a fist in the air, and both Tucker and Bill smiled. I didn't look around to see Cougar's reaction.

"Hey." Linda leaned forward, her gray eyes animated. "So, do you want to swap assignments? This undercover stuff makes me nervous. I can brief you."

"When's it going down?" I asked.

"Tomorrow night."

I felt trapped. On the one hand, I didn't want to be away from Abby right now, but on the other, I didn't want to give them the impression that I thought I could pick and choose my assignments.

As if reading my mind, Bill said, "It's just a meet and greet right now. I don't think it will be a long assignment."

"Okay," I said. "Sounds great."

Bill gave Tucker and Linda their files and a quick summary before dismissing them. "Go on. I'll catch Necie up."

After Linda shut the door behind them, Bill said, "I'm glad it worked out like this. Nothing against Linda—she's a fine agent—but this is more your speed, Necie. If Massey got a nervous read off her, the whole thing would be blown."

I cracked my knuckles. "So what's the job? Routine buy?"

Bill took his glasses off and rubbed them on his shirttail. "Not exactly. Aaron Massey is hawking a cure for cocaine addiction. Fast, no withdrawals, no major side effects. The hell of it is, we think it lives up to its promise for about 40 percent of his clientele."

"And the other 60 percent?"

Bill shook his head. "Dead. We think he's piled up five bodies from Fort Lauderdale to here, but we don't have enough to prove it."

"What's the plan?" I asked.

"Massey's wife died four years ago from an overdose. That's what started his obsession with finding a cure. As far as we know, Massey himself has never used. He's been pretty selective about his customers, too, but I think he'll strike at the right bait. You're going to give him a situation that mirrors his own. Necie, you're the addict; Cougar's the despairing husband. Keep it subtle; let him overhear just enough to piece it together."

"Where's this going to happen?"

"Whenever he's in town, he eats at a French joint called Paradis. He's due back tomorrow, according to our snitch. I've got some notes in the file. Go over it and talk tonight, figure out your game plan." Bill glanced at his watch. "But right now, we need to get to court."

The federal courthouse was only a mile away, but the cold, blustery Philadelphia day didn't exactly invite a stroll. Bill collected the rest of our crew and announced he was driving. I found myself in the back of his sedan between Tucker and Cougar while Linda rode shotgun.

I couldn't figure out Cougar. He deflected another attempt at conversation and stared out the window. Like a third grader, he jerked his leg away from mine when our knees brushed. Whatever. I didn't have time to worry about it. I had enough drama going on in my life without his little tantrums. We followed Bill inside and took the row of seats behind the prosecutor's table. Any minute now, they'd be bringing Barnes in.

My stomach twisted when Maria Barnes walked into the courtroom. I was expecting a smirk, a comment—something—but she never even glanced at me. Visions of her and Grady exploded behind my eyes.

"Papa!" she said, and began to run.

A bailiff escorted Frank Barnes through the side door. Maria shoved the officer aside and threw her arms around Barnes's neck. His hands were cuffed behind his back, but he placed an awkward kiss on her cheek before the bailiff pulled her back. Then he glanced at me.

All the noise in the courtroom faded while we stared at each other. His dark eyes seemed to plead for—what, mercy, understanding? I could give him neither, so I looked away.

The prosecutor leaned back to whisper to Bill. "We turned down another plea bargain. This guy knows he's going down. The only thing that will save him now is if he decides to roll on his suppliers."

"All rise for the Honorable Judge Forrester," the bailiff called, and we stood.

I'd been in Matt Forrester's court many times and knew him to be both fair and stern. Although I didn't expect any surprises at the preliminary, I felt reassured by Forrester's presence.

The prosecutor's summary of the case was clear and concise. With the judge's permission, he played the tape of Angel's testimony, then called Cougar to the stand to verify how it had been obtained. I was up next, and the prosecutor asked me to give my assessment of Angel's lucidity at the time we found him.

My heart fluttered when Barnes leaned to whisper something to his lawyer. I hadn't really thought he'd reveal our relationship yet—that was a big card best saved for a jury—but in that instant I froze.

"No questions for this witness, Your Honor," the lawyer said.

"Any other witnesses?" the judge asked.

"No, Your Honor," the prosecutor replied.

The judge cracked his gavel and proclaimed that there was sufficient evidence to bind Barnes over to the grand jury. In the interim, he would be returned to jail to await trial. This motion didn't seem to surprise anyone except for Maria Barnes. When the bailiff took Barnes's arm to lead him away, she shrieked and grabbed the back of his shirt.

"Papa, no!" she cried, and I felt a sudden, unexpected stab of sympathy for her. She'd lost her mother a few years ago in an auto crash, and it seemed somehow sad and telling about Maria's life that she could be so despondent over a miserable excuse for a man like Frank Barnes. I felt a sense of shared destiny as I stared at her. If Barnes had stayed with my mother, would I be on the other side of the courtroom crying for my father? Maybe abandoning me had been the biggest favor he'd ever done me. I'd wanted revenge on him for so long, but now that I tasted it, it was bitter and unsatisfying.

We filed out of the courtroom, and my team gathered by the water fountain. I didn't have the heart to join in their excited chatter. I found myself watching the courtroom doors. When Maria slipped through them and rushed into the bathroom, I excused myself from the group and followed her.

When I pushed open the door, I found her clutching the edge of a sink, crying.

"Are you okay?" I asked softly.

She looked at me and growled before snatching a swath of paper towels to dab at her raccooned eyes. With her smeared, blotched makeup, she looked like a kid playing dress up.

"I hope you're satisfied," she snapped, then gave a short bark of a laugh. "Oh, wait, I know better. You're married to Grady."

My sympathy shimmered and dissolved a little as her dark eyes met mine in the mirror.

"Geez, Denise. You must really make him beg for it. I haven't seen a guy that eager since junior high."

Though her face was hard, I glimpsed a hurt, angry child beneath her tough facade.

"Does it make you happy," I asked, "to destroy my marriage?"

"About as happy as it makes you to destroy our father." She checked her makeup in the mirror, then strode up to me. "This isn't over. Grady was only the

133

start. By the time I finish with you, you won't have anything left."

"Do you think I don't know about loss?"

"Oh, please." She tossed the wadded-up paper towels at the garbage can and missed. "Don't start that 'poor little Denise' crap with me. So you grew up without a father. Well, guess what? You had him." She threw her hands out. "Even now, he protects you. He never got over leaving you behind, you know. Growing up, he called me your name more often than he called me mine." Her eyes narrowed to slits, and she gave me a coy grin. "But Grady wasn't calling your name, was he? I don't think he was thinking of you at all."

The door opened, and a couple of women walked in. I felt their curious looks and took a step away from Maria.

"See you around, Maria," I muttered, and turned away.

"You bet you will," she replied as I pushed open the door.

Cougar was gone by the time I rejoined my team, and Bill and the others were planning on lunch. I didn't think I could handle a big meal at the moment, so I begged off and called a cab. I was in assignment limbo until tomorrow night, so there was no reason to go back to the office and I had some time to kill before picking up Abby. I walked to the little deli on the corner, picked up a pint of Ben & Jerry's, hailed a cab, and headed to the hospital.

Mrs. Angelino and Tori smiled when I walked into the room.

"Hey, guys," I said, and Angel opened his eyes. He smiled, too. I patted his sheet-covered foot. "Hiya, good-lookin'. I brought you something." I dug the carton of ice cream from the bag and wagged it in front of him. "They were out of Chunky Monkey, so I got Karamel Sutra. You want some?"

Angel nodded so vigorously I laughed.

"I'd rather have a cheeseburger," Tori said. "I'm starving."

Mrs. Angelino frowned. "Karamel Sutra? What kind of name is that for ice cream?"

Angel winked and I suppressed a smile. "Okay." I sat on the edge of his bed. "You two go grab some lunch. I'll take care of our boy here."

"You sure?" Mrs. Angelino asked, but Tori was already on her feet. I waved them away with a plastic spoon. "Take your time."

Angel and I watched them leave, then I tugged the top off the container. "So . . ." I shucked the spoon from its plastic sleeve. "Barnes was in court today. They bound his case over to the grand jury. We were only there for about half an hour. Cougar saved the day with his tape."

Angel nodded, but his brown eyes tracked the spoon while it skimmed across the chocolate ice cream. He was as big a junk-food freak as me. I lifted a bite to his lips.

"Oh, ah." He closed his eyes and groaned. "So . . . good."

I laughed. The first real words I'd heard him say since his surgery, and they were inspired by Ben & Jerry's. I chattered aimlessly to him about our new assignments while I fed him and stole a bite for myself when I reached the gooey caramel center.

The door opened.

"Hey, what are you doing ba—oh, hey," I said, when I realized it wasn't Mrs. Angelino and Tori, but Cougar. "I was just telling Angel about our new assignment." Twisting back to Angel, I said, "So anyway, Cougar's my new husband. We meet up with Massey tomorrow night. Sounds like fun, huh?"

I glanced over my shoulder at Cougar, who sat rigid in one of the chairs. When our eyes met, he blurted, "Are you sleeping with Tucker?"

Startled, I gaped at him before deliberately turning back to Angel. He looked shocked, too. I caught a sliver of ice cream that dribbled from the corner of his mouth and gently spooned it back. I attempted to joke, but I heard the edge in my voice when I asked Angel, "Why is it, when I marry a guy, he instantly turns from Prince Charming to possessive asshole?"

Cougar grunted, then his chair scraped against the floor. I didn't look up when he stalked from the room, but my hand shook when I lifted the next spoonful to

Angel's mouth. "I swear you're gonna have to come back to work soon," I told him, fighting tears I didn't understand. "Everyone's gone crazy since you've been in here."

What was wrong with Cougar? Even if I *was* sleeping with Tucker, what was it to him?

Angel's face reddened as he struggled to speak.

"Shhh," I said, alarmed by the effort he was exerting. "It's okay. I shouldn't have said anything. You've got enough on your plate without worrying about my problems." I forced a smile. "And for the record . . . no, I'm not sleeping with Tucker."

"Cou-gar," he said.

"Him, either. Now finish this ice cream before it melts."

Angel accepted a couple more bites before turning his face away. He'd just dozed off when a nurse came in to take him to physical therapy. Together, we managed to get him into the wheelchair. I checked my watch after she wheeled him away, then moved to the chair Cougar had abandoned. Bright winter sunlight streamed through the windows, making me drowsy. I leaned my head back and closed my eyes.

I dreamed of Cougar.

We were outside, somewhere. Snow swirled around us, and my hair whipped in my face. For a moment, we simply stared at one another. Frustration darkened Cougar's face before he turned away.

"What do you want from me?" I yelled over the howling wind then touched his shoulder.

He spun and grabbed my hand. "You know what I want."

His words made my stomach flutter, but I said, "I don't."

"You do." He yanked me toward him and I half-fell into his arms. "I want everything," he said, then he kissed me.

I awoke with his name on my lips and my pulse pounding in my ears.

Cougar stood at the foot of Angel's bed, watching me. His mouth opened in surprise, and in that instant, his face was completely open and unguarded. It spooked me to see him look so vulnerable.

"I'm not sleeping with Tucker," I said, before I even realized I was going to.

Cougar's eyebrows shot up, and the hard lines in his face softened. I stood on wobbly legs, still disoriented from the dream kiss. The air crackled with some strange undercurrent. My chest hurt, and I realized I was holding my breath.

Cougar took a step toward me and held out his hand. "Necie . . ."

Angel's door opened. Cougar dropped his arm and turned away when Tori entered. She held the door for her mother, who pushed a pale Angel inside.

"Look what we found in the hall," she said with a

wink. The nurse followed behind her, scribbling something on a bag of IV fluid with a marker.

Cougar moved quickly to help them get Angel back into bed, then he faced me. "Hey, we need to talk," he said, and my stomach flip-flopped.

"Massey's hit town a day early. Bill thinks he'll be at Paradis tonight. Do you think you can make it?"

"Oh." I shook my head to clear it of the strange, stupid thoughts it seemed filled with. "Yeah. Let me call Elizabeth to see if she can keep Abby."

"What about Grady?" Cougar asked, and I rolled my eyes.

"Long story. I'll tell you later."

I moved to the desk phone and tried to call Grady's mother. No answer. I hung up and stared at the wall, trying to think of anyone else I could trust to take care of her for a few hours.

"I can watch your little girl, Necie," Tori said. "I babysit a lot back home."

"We could both go," Mrs. Angelino added. "As soon as Linda gets here to stay with John."

"That would be great," I said. "Are you sure you don't mind?"

Mrs. Angelino made a face. "After all you've done for John? Don't be silly."

"Are you going home now?" Tori asked. "Because I could ride with you, let Abby have a chance to get used to me before you leave."

Cougar glanced at his watch. "I can go home, get ready, swing back by here to pick up Mrs. Angelino, then bring her by your house." A funny look crossed his face. "That is, if you want me to pick you up. If it will cause problems, we could meet somewhere—"

"Grady's not there," I said. "Yeah, that sounds great. Tori, you ready to ride?"

"Yup!" She kissed her brother on the cheek before bouncing toward the door.

Cougar followed us into the hall. He grabbed my hand as we walked toward the elevator. It felt so much like my dream that my breath caught, but when I turned, he let my fingers slip through his.

"So, we know what needs to go down with Massey?" he said.

"Oops, forgot my purse," Tori said. "Be right back."

I nodded, then looked up at Cougar. "Yeah. We'll make a little conversation. I'll go take a hit as soon as we get there . . . we'll fight." I forced a smile. "We're getting pretty good at that."

Cougar blinked and stared down at his shoes. "I'm sorry, Necie." He shuffled his feet and wouldn't meet my eyes. "Guess I owe Tucker an apology, too."

Finally it dawned at me. I gaped at him. "Your fight . . . it was over me?"

Cougar shot me a fierce look. "I don't want to see

you get hurt. Not by Tucker, not by anyone."

For a moment, I couldn't think of a single thing to say. Then I laughed. The whole situation was so crazy. "But surely Tucker told you we weren't seeing each other . . .?"

Cougar gave me a sheepish grin. "After I called him what I did, he wasn't telling me much of anything."

Again, he left me speechless.

"Okay," Tori said behind me, and I jumped.

"See you around seven." Cougar kissed my forehead and ruffled Tori's hair before reentering Angel's room.

I don't know how long I stood there, staring after him, before Tori coughed.

"Ready?" she asked, and I nodded.

Tori kept me entertained all the way to the courthouse. She was a great kid, possessing the same innate goodness and goofy sense of humor as her brother. I'd felt an instant connection to her and hoped Abby would, too. Abby had never really stayed with anyone besides Elizabeth, and I wasn't sure how she'd react to the babysitting plan.

My worries proved unfounded. Abby seemed thrilled at the prospect of spending the evening with the bubbly teenager. We stopped by the grocery store to pick up some snacks, and Tori laughed when I tossed a couple boxes of cheap pantyhose in the cart.

"What?" I asked, checking to make sure I'd gotten the right size.

"No offense," she said, her dark eyes twinkling. "But that's the same brand Mom wears."

I made a face, and Abby giggled. "So?"

"So you're supposed to be this cool spy—"

I snorted. "Honey, I am *not* a spy."

"Undercover agent. Whatever. Either way, it's gotta rank more glamour than dollar pantyhose."

"Tori, I think you have this huge misconception of what my job is like," I said, but when I got to thinking about it, she was probably right. My character for tonight would never wear $1 pantyhose. "Okay," I said, and tossed a box of Fruit Loops into the cart. "We'll stop by the mall."

"Yay!" Abby cheered, and clapped her hands.

We made it home an hour and a half later, after making stops at Frederick's, Blockbuster, and KB Toys. I put the groceries away and left the girls coloring at the kitchen table while I went to get dressed.

When I threw open my closet door, I was relieved that—unlike the Kimberly Lausens of the world—I didn't have to spend a lot of time debating what I was going to wear. My "fancy" wardrobe consisted of two court dresses, a silver floor-length gown, and a basic black number that made most of its appearances at the funeral home. The slinky silver gown was a present from Grady, something to wear to his firm's Christmas ball last year. I figured it was shimmery and high-end enough to pass muster at Paradis.

The answering-machine light blinked furiously at me, so I pressed the button to listen to my messages while I applied some makeup. Two hang-ups and three messages from Grady. The first two were pleading; the third, pissed. I erased them and sat on the edge of the bed to dig out my address book.

On the second trip through my haphazard filing system, I found Jimmy Milano's number. Jimmy was a divorce lawyer from the Bronx who looked like a young Alan Alda. We'd officially met five years ago, though I'd seen him many times at the courthouse before that. He was standing in the pouring rain beside a Lexus with a raised hood. When he kicked the fender and pitched his cell phone over the Betsy Ross Bridge, I took pity on him and offered him a ride. We both had court, so it wasn't out of my way, but he was so grateful he hung around after his case to buy my lunch. I liked his wry humor and threw business his way whenever I could. Now he was going to get mine.

"Milano," he answered grumpily after the third ring.

"Hey, Milano. This is Denise Bramhall."

His voice brightened instantly. "Necie! Hey, hon, what's up?"

I peered into the mirror and winced when I plucked a stray eyebrow. "Got some business for you. How much you charging these days?"

"All I can get away with. What's the matter, that boss of yours gone through another blonde?"

"Nope, this one's me."

"Ah, sweetie. . .I knew you were too good to be married to a lawyer. What did the schmuck do?"

"Irreconcilable differences. I'm a Virgo, and he's an asshole."

Jimmy laughed.

"But seriously, I want the house and I want the kid."

"How old's your kid now?" he asked.

"Six."

"Hmm." I heard ruffling pages. "Okay, what grounds?"

"He drinks too much, he's been physically abusive, and he's cheated on me, but I'm willing to keep that off the record if he agrees to alcohol counseling and supervised visitation until I'm sure he won't drink around her."

"Sounds fair to me. He won't want that to go public. Do you have any proof?"

"I've got videotape of the cheating and witnesses who saw him try to choke me at the hospital."

Milano whistled the chorus from "We're in the Money."

I smiled. "All kidding aside, how much are you going to need up front? I just spent all my money on panty-hose."

"For you, doll, no up-front charges. When the dust settles, it'll work out to the usual . . . I get half, his lawyer gets half."

I laughed. "That's what I figured. Why is divorce so expensive?"

"Because, my love, it is *worth* it. Drop by my office in the morning and I'll get this thing rolling."

I hung up and went in the bathroom to finish my makeup. In the bottom of my bag, I found a couple of little red capsules. I smiled and stuck one in my purse.

Cougar and Mrs. Angelino arrived promptly at seven. Cougar stayed in the car, so I hurriedly showed Mrs. Angelino the list of emergency numbers and grabbed my coat. Abby was so busy playing Monopoly with Tori that she barely glanced up when I kissed her good-bye.

It was raining. So much for the time I'd spent on my hair. Cougar reached across to open the door for me. I slid into the seat and inhaled the masculine scent of leather and cherry air freshener. Cougar was more gorgeous than ever in his black suit. I shivered a little and tried not to stare.

"You cold?" he asked, and shoved a stick of Dentyne in his mouth.

As he offered me the pack, I shook my head no, but he turned up the heat anyway. Then he slung his arm across the back of the seat and backed out of my driveway.

I didn't recall ever feeling this tense before an assignment. Cougar's lack of conversation wasn't helping any. The only sounds were the swish of the windshield wipers and the snap of his gum. I turned down the heat.

"Thank you," he said, and tugged at his collar.

We pulled up at Paradis fifteen minutes later, and he handed the valet the keys. Inside, he helped me out of my coat, and my face heated when he scanned me from head to toe.

"You look beautiful," he murmured. "Shall we?" He held out his arm and I took it, leaning into him as we approached the maître d'. Cougar nudged me.

Through the glassed-in front, I spotted Massey. Cougar slipped the maître d' a bill to give us a table by the bar. He showed us to a table directly behind Massey.

"I got it," Cougar said when the waiter reached to pull out my chair. Cougar kissed my bare shoulder as I sat, sending a spark racing through me.

After the waiter took our wine order, Cougar stood. "Let's dance," he said.

I smiled. "Nobody else is dancing."

He winked and gave me one of those sexy half smiles. "Then we'll get it started."

"In a minute," I said. "I need to, ah, freshen up. I'll be right back."

"Here?" Cougar said, loudly and angrily enough to draw a glance from Massey. "Denise, you said this weekend was for us. Can't you even make it a whole day without that shit?"

"Shhh." I pressed a finger to his lips, then kissed his cheek. "Don't be like that. It's only a little pick-me-up.

Don't make a big deal about it."

I headed toward the bathroom. At the door, I looked back at Cougar. He'd stood, jamming his hands in his pockets. He signaled the bartender with a jerk of his head and took the bar stool next to Massey.

I killed nearly fifteen minutes in the bathroom, giving Cougar time to work. While I waited, I fished out the red capsule and shoved it up my nose. The special effects would be a new one on Cougar. I grinned when I imagined his reaction. Finally, I decided enough time had passed. I squirted a couple drops of Visine in each eye to make them all bright and shiny, then went back to the bar.

Cougar had his head down, deep in conversation with Massey. I fixed on my most dazzling smile and tapped Cougar's shoulder. He gave me a wary glance.

"Hey, baby." I sniffed loudly and swiped at my nose. "I'm ready for that dance now."

Cougar leaned back and sighed. Gesturing at Massey, he said, "Honey, this is Jack. Jack, this is my wife, Denise."

"Hey!" I said. "Nice to meet you, Jack. Are you from Philadelphia? It's a fantastic city. Jason and I are having a blast here, aren't we, honey?" I spoke rapidly and shifted from foot to foot like a hyperactive kid. I'd seen enough junkies in my career that I had a pretty good handle on their mannerisms. I wiggled my nose like Samantha on

Bewitched, and Massey gave me a sad smile.

"A pleasure, my dear. No, I'm not from Philadelphia, but I agree. It's a lovely city."

Cougar stood and took my elbow, a resigned look on his face. "Let's go, honey. Leave the man to his drink. The waiter's come by twice to take our order. Any idea what you want yet?"

"You know, I'm not really hungry. I want to dance."

Cougar frowned. "I'm not in the mood anymore."

"Oh, please." I slid in next to him and brushed a tiny kiss on his neck. "Please, for me. Just one little dance?"

Cougar sighed. "Okay." He nodded at Massey. "Nice to meet you, man."

Massey smiled and lifted his glass. Cougar whirled me away. I reached up to wind a lock of his hair around my finger. Leaning close to his ear, I whispered, "How's it going?"

Cougar waited until his back was to Massey to reply, "Pretty good. He's asking a lot of questions." He smiled. "You're so good at this it's scary."

I stroked his face and kept my face lowered so Massey couldn't read my lips. "What do you need me to do now?"

Cougar pulled me a little closer. I tried to ignore how nice his chest felt, hard and warm beneath the crisp white shirt. "We need to fight," he said. "Leave me here."

"Okay." I rested my cheek on his shoulder. "Get ready for some special effects."

With Cougar's big body shielding me from Massey, I pressed the side of my nose and felt the capsule break. I smiled up at Cougar and watched the shock register in his eyes as the fake blood trickled out of my nostril.

"Baby, you're . . . bleeding," he said, and the corner of his mouth twitched. He ran to the bar and yelled at the bartender to get him some napkins. I touched the liquid under my nose, then pulled my hand away, staring at my red-slicked fingers in bewilderment.

"Is she okay?" Massey asked while Cougar shoved a fistful of napkins at me.

"No," Cougar snapped, and grabbed my arm. He jerked me to the side, but made sure we were still within Massey's earshot. "I can't do this anymore."

"Can't do what?" I reached for his arm, and he brushed my hand away. I wadded the tissues up and pressed them to my nose. "Can't do what, Jason?"

He balled his fists and jammed them in his pockets. "This. I can't do this. It's over. If you won't get help, I want a divorce."

Even though we were acting, the words struck me. The tears that welled in my eyes were real. "Jason . . . no."

"I love you too much to watch you kill yourself." He paused, then grabbed my shoulders. "Say you'll leave with me tonight. We'll fly back to Houston. Your daddy will help us."

I pushed him away. "Don't involve my father. I

don't *need* help. You're overreacting, as usual."

"Overreacting? Can't you see this stuff is eating you alive?"

The waiter approached us. "Sir . . . madam . . . is there a problem?"

"No!" I yelled. Shooting Cougar a pointed look, I said, "I'm going back to the hotel. Are you coming?"

He blinked and stared at his shoes. "No."

I stalked out of the restaurant. Outside, it was pouring. The cold, gray rain pelted my bare shoulders and I wished I'd grabbed my coat. I peered in the window when I passed. Massey was staring openly, but I didn't see Cougar anywhere. Not seeing the valet, I lifted my arm to hail a cab and someone grabbed my shoulder. Cougar spun me around.

"What are you—" Before I could process what was happening, he kissed me.

His hot, demanding mouth was a sharp contrast to the icy rain beating against my back. Never, not in seven years of marriage, not in my entire life, had I been kissed like that. By the time he released me, I felt as liquid as the winter rain running off the sidewalk.

We stared at each other. Cougar wiped a hand down his face, then flagged a cab. He opened the door, handed the cabbie some money, and helped me inside.

"I'll call you," he said, then shut the door. He slapped the roof of the cab and we pulled away from the curb.

I sagged against the ripped vinyl seat and pressed a trembling hand to my lips. Like trying to slip back into a dream from which I didn't want to awaken, I closed my eyes and tried to recapture the sensation of being in his arms, of feeling his heart thundering beneath my palm as he electrified me with that kiss. Damn it, it wasn't fair. I'd never felt passion like that, and the moment had been so fleeting, over before my stunned brain could process what was happening.

The heat that enveloped me slowly ebbed. I shivered and stared sightlessly out a window fogged by my breath. A sense of loss fell over me when I remembered it was only make-believe.

How could a kiss like that have meant nothing?

Cougar had flirted with me in the past, but so had Angel and Tucker. It was harmless, a way to pass the time and blow off steam on a stressful job. They had even flirted with Linda. But things had felt different between Cougar and me lately. More intense, more personal. What would Cougar do when he found out I was getting divorced? What would *I* do if he wanted to take our flirtation further? Of course, I wanted him. I wasn't too deep in denial to admit that. But I wasn't sure if I could handle sex without love, though I'd loved Grady at one time and look how that had turned out. Besides, Cougar was a co-worker—

Dear God, what was I thinking?

I opened my eyes and found the cabbie staring at me in the rearview mirror. "You okay, miss?"

No. I wasn't anywhere near okay. My life was out of control. This situation with Grady was messing with my head. I shouldn't be entertaining thoughts like this—about Cougar of all people. The man who was dating Miss Almost New Jersey.

"Lover's quarrel?" he asked, and I blinked.

"Huh?"

He gave me a knowing smile. "It'll be okay. I see lots of folks in this line of work. That guy back there's crazy about you. I bet the phone will be ringing when you walk in the door."

Well, it was, but it wasn't Cougar on the other end. I stared down at my mother-in-law's number on the caller ID and waited for the answering machine to pick up.

"Denise, it's me—" Elizabeth's cool voice began, and I picked up the receiver.

"Hold on a sec." I removed my shoes and accepted a towel from Mrs. Angelino. "Okay. What can I do for you, Elizabeth?"

"I'm calling about the wedding."

"Wedding?" I paused toweling my hair.

"My niece . . . in Baltimore? I asked you a month ago if Abby could go with me."

"Oh, yeah." I barely remembered the conversation. "When is it again?"

I caught the trace of exasperation in Elizabeth's voice. "Tomorrow night. Are you still going to let her go? We'll probably stay at my sister's overnight."

"She can go if she wants to. I don't have a problem with it."

"I spoke with her earlier. She wants to go, but I told her we'd have to see what you said."

"Elizabeth, what happens between Grady and me doesn't have to affect your relationship with Abby. I know you love her. She loves you. I don't intend to keep her from you."

"Well, I didn't think you would, but then I called this evening and found out you'd left her with strangers. Is there some reason you didn't ask me to babysit?"

I bristled at her tone, but lowered my voice so Tori and Mrs. Angelino wouldn't hear. "They're not strangers to me. I tried to call you first, but I couldn't reach you." I peeked in at Abby, who was sleeping soundly. "Now, what time do you want to pick her up tomorrow?"

"Four."

"Fine. I'll have her ready." I hung up and went to talk to Mrs. Angelino and Tori. They assured me all had gone well. Tori tried to refuse her pay, but I insisted and asked them if they wanted to spend the night, since it was so late. After I got Mrs. Angelino settled in the guest room and Tori on the couch, I went upstairs to grab a shower. Afterward, I pulled on a robe and flopped across the bed to paint my fingernails.

When the phone rang, I glanced at the caller ID and snatched it up. "Hey, you."

"And the Academy Award goes to . . ." Cougar laughed. "You were amazing! Where did you get the fake blood?"

"Abby was a vampire last Halloween. I saw the capsules in my makeup bag and thought I'd get creative."

"It worked. How could Massey not buy that? You even had me freaked out."

I thought about the kiss. I wanted to ask him about it, but I didn't know what to say.

"What did Massey do?"

"He mentioned his wife and said that maybe he could help us. He told me about the drug. I'm supposed to meet him day after tomorrow."

I leaned back against the pillows. "Doesn't it make you a little sad, that this time we're busting someone who's actually trying to *help* people?"

"A dealer's a dealer, whether he's selling drugs or the cure. You gotta realize . . . he's killing people, too."

I blew on my nails. "People who are already killing themselves."

"That doesn't make it okay."

"I know it doesn't, but don't you feel somewhat sorry for him?"

"Sure. Your performance this evening brought that home for me. I thought about you, and how it would kill me to watch someone I love destroy herself like that."

We lapsed into silence. I felt as nervous as a teenager talking to the captain of the football team and cursed myself for reading more into his words than he intended. But that was the second time tonight I'd heard him mention "love" and me in the same sentence. Make-believe or not, it made me jumpy. I smeared my thumb polish twice, and finally put the nail polish away.

Cougar cleared his throat. "I guess I'd better let you—oh, wait! I knew there was something else I was supposed to tell you. I ran into Bill's wife at the station. She's throwing Bill a surprise birthday party tomorrow night at the Sizzler and wanted me to pass the word."

I laughed. "He'll kill her." Bill didn't like surprises, but maybe his latest wife hadn't figured that out yet.

"Yeah, I know, but hey, it's free food, and it's not Fat Daddy's."

"Hey, you admitted it was good."

He chuckled. "Yeah, it was good. That whole night was pretty good."

There he went again. My cheeks burned when I remembered our snowball fight. Maybe I'd have the snow dream again. That was probably as close as I'd ever dare get to him again.

"What time are we supposed to be there tomorrow?" I asked, and was mortified to hear the squeak in my voice.

"Six."

"I'll see you there." I started to hang up when I heard him call my name. "Yeah?"

"My birthday's in a couple months. Will you wear the silver gown to my party? That was just . . . hot."

"That would look real sharp at the Sizzler."

He laughed and I said, "Good night, Cougar."

"Well, we don't have to have it at the Sizzler. There's always my apart—"

"Good *night,* Cougar." I hung up and stared at the phone. Then I laughed. "Get a grip," I muttered. That was typical Cougar. He talked to me like that all the time. I had to stop taking it personally. I had to stop thinking of him.

But I thought of nothing else while I drifted off to sleep.

The next afternoon, I kissed Abby good-bye and went back inside to finish loading the dishwasher. Then I started getting ready, because I had to stop by the gun shop before they closed at five thirty to pick up Bill's present. I'd ordered the antique Colt .38 for him a few weeks ago, but hadn't had time to pick it up yet.

I slipped on my funeral dress, flats, and $18 stockings and headed for the mall. The owner of the gun shop already had the Colt in a gift box for me, so I had some time to kill before heading to the Sizzler. I thought about going early to see if Bill's wife, Ellen, needed help decorating, but I'd gotten the distinct impression she didn't like me much. I opted for a little window-shopping instead.

A swingy red dress in a display case caught my eye. I liked it enough that I went inside for a closer look, but then walked back out when I saw the price tag. I wandered past Bath & Body Works and Spencer's and drew up short when I caught my reflection in the mirrored wall.

Wow, I wasn't looking too hot tonight. The funeral dress had been so named for a reason. It was plain, dull, and dowdy—the kind of thing I'd worn to keep Grady from pitching a jealous fit when I went somewhere without him.

I'd stopped by to see Milano on my way to work. I'd signed the papers and he promised me he'd take care of things. I didn't have to worry about what Grady thought anymore. On impulse, I hurried back to the store with the red dress. I paid for it and a pair of matching red pumps, then slipped it all on in the dressing room. I stuffed my funeral dress and flats into the bag and left.

A lady hawking Merle Norman called to me when I headed toward the mall exit. "Free makeover?"

I glanced at my watch. "What can you do in ten minutes?"

Eight minutes later, I was on my way with ruby lips and smoky eyes and a bag of cosmetics I'd probably never use again. I hardly recognized myself and wasn't sure if that was a good or bad thing.

My cell started ringing the moment I walked inside the Sizzler. I grabbed it out of my purse and glanced down at Elizabeth's cell number.

"Davidson party," I said to the girl behind the register. She pointed me toward the banquet room. I nodded my thanks and answered the phone.

"I hope you're happy," she shrieked, and I pulled the phone back from my ear. "How could you do this to him?"

"What are you talking about?" I asked.

"Grady told me he was served with divorce papers. He's devastated."

Whoa, Milano moved fast. I never dreamed he'd get the papers out today. I missed part of what Elizabeth was yelling at me while I processed this.

"—that you're asking for supervised visitation. How dare you! You know he'd never hurt Abby."

"I don't think he'd hurt her on purpose, but he's been drinking so much lately—"

"I don't want to hear that," she snapped.

"Whether you want to hear it or not, it's true." I leaned against the wall and nodded as someone from the office passed by.

I heard a sobbing sound in the background, and my grip tightened on the phone. "Elizabeth," I said, as calmly as I could force myself, "where's Abby?"

"She's right here."

I exploded. "What do you mean, she's right there?"

"She needs to know all these things you're slandering her father with aren't true."

"Which part, Elizabeth? The drinking, the abuse, the other woman? Put my daughter on the line."

"You won't blame all of this on him. You're a horrible mother, Necie. You've neglected your family over and over again for your job. If you think you can take her from us, you're sadly mistaken."

"Put my daughter on the line NOW."

"If it takes every dime—"

I gritted my teeth. "If you don't put my daughter on the line this instant, I'm going to call the state police and have an APB put out on your ass for kidnapping."

For a moment, I thought she'd hung up on me, then I heard Abby's timid voice say, "Mama?"

She sounded so frightened. I swiped at a tear and tried to keep my voice steady. "Hey, baby. Listen, your grandma's upset right now. I don't want you to pay any attention to what she's saying—"

"She says you're trying to take me away from her and Daddy forever and ever. You wouldn't do that, would you, Mama?"

I swallowed over the lump in my throat. Furious, helpless tears streamed down my cheeks. How could she do this in front of that child? "No, baby. I wouldn't do that. Like I said, Grandma's upset. She doesn't know what she's saying. Your daddy and I love you. We'll—"

"She doesn't want to talk to you anymore," Elizabeth interrupted.

Anger bubbled inside me, hot and black. "You listen to me and listen good. If Abby's not home in three hours, I'm calling the police."

"See, Abby," she said. "It's started already. Your mother says you can't stay for the wedding—"

"You bitch!" I snarled. "Are you out of your mind?"

"Go ahead, curse me all you like. Just more for me to tell the judge."

"Get her home and get her home now. You have three hours." I clicked the phone shut and leaned against the wall, stunned by what had just happened.

I didn't know what to do. Maybe I should call the police now—but no, that would only frighten Abby worse. She had three hours to get her back and then—

And then what?

I covered my face and sobbed.

"Are you okay?" someone asked, and I could only nod. People were staring. I headed toward the restroom, needing a few minutes to compose myself before I tried to drive.

I kept my head down, and just when I thought I was going to make it to the restroom without being caught by someone I knew, the men's room door swung open and Cougar stepped into the hallway.

His smile vanished with one look at my face. I ducked my head and pushed past him into the ladies' room. To my horror, he followed.

"What are you doing?" I shrieked, glancing behind me to see if anyone else was inside. Both stall doors hung open.

Cougar acted like he didn't hear me. "What's wrong?"

"Everything," I whispered, and twisted away from him to stare at my reflection in the mirror. I looked washed-out and pale, except for the reddened tip of my nose and the black smudges beneath my eyes. Yanking a paper towel from the dispenser, I tried to do some damage control and only succeeded in smearing the mascara further.

"Damn it!" I cried.

Cougar ripped off another sheet, dampened it, and caught my chin in his hand. Too miserable to protest, I stood there like a child while he cleaned my face. "There," he said, and tossed the soiled paper towel in the trash. "Now talk to me. What's the matter? You and Grady fighting?"

"Please, Cougar . . . not now. I don't feel like talking."

He gave me a crooked grin. "Then how about dancing?"

I couldn't return his smile. "I've got to go."

"Go? You just got here." A tear-dampened twig of hair stuck to my jaw, and I shivered when he brushed it away with his thumb. His blue eyes darkened, and my breath caught in my throat when he leaned toward me.

The restroom door burst open, and we jerked apart. The giggling pair who entered fell silent when they saw us. I didn't know one of the women, but the smirk on the other's face made my stomach lurch. I swallowed hard and stared at Andrea Jacobs, Kimberly's best friend.

"Are we interrupting something?" she asked.

"No." I hurried around them and yanked open the door. I'd explain things to Bill later.

Cougar followed on my heels. He darted around me to block my exit.

"Necie, talk to me. What's wrong?" he said.

I forced a smile. "Look, I'm fine. I was upset but now I'm over it. Go back to the party. You're in enough trouble already."

He shot me a perplexed look. "In trouble with whom?"

"Kimberly. Andrea will tell her . . ." I flushed, and finished lamely, "Who knows what Andrea will tell her."

"About what?" He looked genuinely confused, and I was beginning to feel stupid.

"Never mind."

"Oh!" Cougar smiled. "I get it. You thought she'd be jealous. You don't have to worry about Kim."

My ears burned. What he really meant was Kim didn't have to worry about me. Duh. It *was* stupid, to imagine the leggy redhead spending even a moment being jealous of me. Whatever. I didn't need this right now. I was worried sick about my little girl.

I shoved the gift box at Cougar. "I've really got to go. Will you give this to Bill when he gets here?"

"He's already here." Cougar accepted the box and glanced toward the banquet room. "Somewhere. So much for the surprise."

"Give this to him. Tell him I'm sorry, but something came up. I'll talk to him tomorrow."

Cougar frowned. "Okay, but . . . are you sure you're all right?"

"Positive. Now I mean it. Go," I said, and left him standing there.

I slipped through the gathering crowd. A teenage boy held the door open for me, and I half-staggered outside, gulping in the cold night air and fighting the queasiness that pitched my stomach. I fumbled for my keys and tried to remember where I'd parked.

Footsteps slapped the pavement behind me, closing in fast. Exasperated, I whirled. "Cougar, I said—"

Grady snarled at me in the glow of the streetlight. "Cougar? Is that who you're all dressed up for?"

"What are you—how did you know I was here?" I asked.

"I followed you. I knew that with Abby out of the way, you'd make plans with whoever you're sleeping around with—"

"Me?" I took a step toward him, but changed my

mind when I caught a whiff of Jack Daniels. Jack made Grady mean. I turned to leave.

"Don't walk away from me!" he screamed.

CHAPTER 9

He shoved me hard in the back. Caught off guard, I pitched forward. Asphalt bit into my palms and knees as I skidded forward and smacked headfirst into a car.

I think I blacked out for a second, because the next thing I knew, someone was yelling and I was mostly on my feet, leaning against a dirty Taurus. I opened my eyes in time to see Grady take a swing at my head.

Due more to the dizziness than reflex, I fell again and he missed. He seized a fistful of my hair and tried to haul me back up, but I'd curled into a fetal position. He didn't have the leverage to move me.

With a howl, he launched a kick at my ribs. Color exploded behind my eyes, and I gasped for breath. I couldn't find my purse, and I had the horrible thought

165

that I was going to die right there, in the parking lot of a building filled with armed officers.

"Here's what I think about your divorce." He hurled something at my head, and I watched the paper wad bounce off the tire. Then I saw a black Stamford loafer rear back for another shot at my ribs.

Grady slammed into the Taurus. Bill wretched Grady's arm behind his back and smacked him into the car again. "You're under arrest for assault of a federal officer!" he yelled. "Necie, are you okay? Linda, check on Necie. You have the right to remain silent—"

While Linda scrambled toward me, I heard a commotion behind her and looked up. Tucker, Ubi, and some guy I didn't know had their arms locked around Cougar, trying to hold him back. He was dragging them all, shouting curses at Grady.

"Bill, get him out of here," Tucker pleaded, his face red with exertion. Cougar surged forward and nearly broke free.

Bill handcuffed Grady and shoved him toward his Expedition. Sirens screamed around the corner, and Bill reversed directions, prodding Grady toward the sound. I watched them load Grady into a squad car.

I jumped when Cougar fell on his knees beside me. He grasped my face in his hands.

"Necie, are you okay?"

His eyes were wide and glassy, his face pale even in

the amber glow of the streetlight. I nodded, then burst into tears.

He hugged me. "Shhh, it's all right. It's all right." He tilted my face toward the light and scowled. "I'm going to kill that son of a bitch."

"Get back, get back," Linda told the crowd, and moved to stand in front of us. To Cougar she said, "An ambulance is on the way. They're caught in traffic."

"No!" I said, and tried to push myself upright. "No ambulance."

The crowd seemed to edge closer. I couldn't take the whispering and staring anymore. "Get me out of here," I begged Cougar.

Instantly, he stood. "Kim!" he yelled. "Kim!"

She materialized through the crowd, and he tossed her his keys. "I'm taking Necie to the hospital."

She snagged the keys in midair. "Go. Take care of her."

Instead of helping me stand, Cougar scooped me up in his arms. I wrapped my arms around his neck and buried my face against his shoulder. I heard Linda cancel the ambulance on the radio. Tucker hurried ahead of us to open the car door, and Cougar gently deposited me in the seat.

"Where are your keys?" he asked.

"My purse . . ."

"I'll get it. Tuck, stay with her."

Linda had already started our way with it. She handed it to him, and he passed it to me. The crumpled divorce papers poked out of the side pocket. Tucker squeezed my hand and kissed my forehead.

"It's going to be okay," he said. "We won't let him hurt you again."

He shut the door. Cougar climbed into the driver's seat and cranked the engine. He said nothing as we roared away, merely stared straight ahead with a grim expression on his face and clutched the wheel with white-knuckled hands.

"I'm okay," I said, though my head was pounding. "I don't want to go to the hospital. Abby's coming home—"

"Necie, he *assaulted* you. We need to make sure you don't have a concussion or something." He glanced at me. "What the hell happened, anyway?"

"I filed for divorce."

Cougar's gaze snapped back to me, his lips parting in surprise. A horn blared and he nearly clipped a Trans Am before jerking back into the correct lane.

"I need to go home, Cougar."

He flipped on the turn signal and swerved into a BP parking lot. He twisted in the seat and motioned me forward. I winced when he pressed around the lump on my head.

"How many fingers am I holding up?"

"Two."

He snatched a pen from the dash and made me track it as he moved it in front of my face.

"Where else do you hurt?"

"My knees. My ribs."

He gave my knees a cursory examination, then reached for my sides. I'd be lying if I said my body didn't jolt to awareness when his hands gently pressed and prodded below my breasts. I might've had the crap beaten out of me, but I wasn't dead yet.

"Please," I said. "I need to go home. Abby will be there soon."

Cougar shot me another long, hard look, then he sighed. We pulled back onto the road, this time heading in the opposite direction.

We arrived at my house fifteen minutes later. Cougar offered to carry me inside, but I didn't want the neighbors to see that. I might as well have taken him up on his offer, though, because I found I couldn't put weight on my left ankle. Cougar stooped, allowing me to wrap an arm around his shoulder, and I hopped to the front door like a wounded crow.

"You got a first-aid kit?" Cougar asked when I hobbled inside.

"Bathroom." He glanced past me, and I realized he'd never been inside my house. Without asking my permission this time, he swept me in his arms and carried me upstairs.

"There," I pointed him toward the master bath.

Cougar kicked the lid to the commode shut and plopped me atop it.

"First-aid kit is under the sink."

Cougar popped open the kit and began laying supplies on the sink. "Do you have a camera? We need to document your injuries."

"Uh, yeah. Three doors down, on the left. There's a digital camera on the computer desk."

He retrieved it and snapped probably a dozen shots. He lowered the camera, pausing long enough to shove a stick of gum in his mouth. "Take off your dress."

I gave a startled laugh. "*Excuse* me?"

Cougar frowned and tossed me the short white robe hanging on the linen closet door. "I'm serious here. Need to get a shot of your ribs, too. You're bound to have a bruise there, as hard as that bastard kicked you."

When I hesitated, he said, "Come on. Leave your underwear on. I've seen you in a bikini before. Same difference. I'll think professional thoughts . . ." He smiled and cracked his gum. "Mostly."

I laughed, mostly out of pure panic, and he turned his back to give me some privacy. Whether it was because my hands were shaking, or where they were stiffening, I couldn't grasp the back zipper.

"Cougar, could you . . . help?"

I lifted my hair and hopped around to present him

with my back. The floor creaked when he took a step toward me, then his warm breath tickled my neck. My heart seemed to thump with every click of the zipper.

"Okay," he said, releasing me. "Not looking."

I shrugged the dress from my shoulders and let it fall to the floor. I slipped on the robe, thankful that, at least, I had on my good underwear. "You can turn around now."

"Let's see what we've got." He carefully peeled open one side of the robe. When he saw the ugly purple and red welt, he let loose a stream of obscenities and trailed his fingers over it. I shivered.

"Necie, we probably need to get this x-rayed."

"Um-hmm," I said, then snapped back from la-la land. "No. It's not broken or anything."

"Could be cracked."

"Could be, but what could they do for that anyway?"

Cougar took one more picture and laid the camera on the back of the toilet. Then he pulled my robe closed and tied it. I sat back down, and he knelt in front of me. The troubled look on his face made my chest constrict.

"Look," he said. "I need to know one thing. The reason you're divorcing Grady . . ." He grazed his thumb across my swollen lip. "Is it because of this? If I find out he's been hitting you—"

"No." I gave a mortified laugh. "This is only the icing on the cake. First, it was his drinking, then I found

171

out he'd been unfaithful . . . all this OJ stuff is new."

Cougar winced. "Why didn't you tell me what was going on?"

"So much has been going on. And it's just . . . humiliating."

"You have nothing to be ashamed of. He does." Cougar shook his head. "But I'll tell you one thing. He'll never hurt you again. Now . . ." He gave me a strained smile. "Let's check out those knees."

I held my breath when his long, tan fingers slipped beneath the lacy edge of my stocking and rolled it down. I flinched when he tried to pull it past my knee. Dried blood stuck the nylon to the raw wound, and it felt like he took another strip of flesh when he gave it another tug. He pulled it free and pitched it at the wastebasket.

I sighed. "Huh. Shows what Tori knows. Eighteen-dollar hose doesn't last any longer than a pair of dollar ones."

"*What?*" Cougar grinned.

"Never mind. Ow. Ouch!" I said when he pulled the other stocking free. It looked like a sad, raggedy snake hanging over the side of the trash can. Cougar placed my bare feet on his thighs and began cleaning my wounds.

After taping the last piece of gauze in place, he rested his hands on top of my feet and waggled his eyebrows. "You got any place else that needs fixing? I'm kinda getting into this playing doctor thing."

I giggled and he winked. Then he grabbed the

windowsill to pull himself up. The cell phone clipped to his pocket played "Save a Horse, Ride a Cowboy."

"Excuse me." He flipped it open and wandered to the hallway. "Hello? Yeah. She's okay. No, we're at her place. She didn't want to go to the hospital. Bunch of scrapes and bruises, but—"

I left him talking and hopped my way to the bedroom to pull on some clothes. No way I wanted Elizabeth to pull up and catch me half-naked with Cougar.

He rapped on the door while I tugged a T-shirt over my head.

"You okay in there?"

"Yeah." I tightened the drawstring on my shorts and hopped back to open the door.

"That was Linda," he said, eyeing me. "They're all worried about you, and cussing me for not taking you to the doctor."

"I need to be here. My mother-in-law is supposed to be bringing Abby."

He frowned. "I forgot to check that ankle."

"Ah, it's okay." I wrinkled my nose. "But the next time I get in a fight, I'm wearing my Keds."

Cougar gave me a sad smile, then leaned to kiss my forehead. I closed my eyes, suddenly very conscious of his proximity and the fact that we were standing about three yards from my bed.

He cleared his throat. Embarrassed at the route my

thoughts were taking, I limped past him to the safety of the hallway. Or so I thought. Once again, Cougar lifted me off my feet.

"You don't have to carry me," I said, jolted by the feel of his big, warm hands on the back of my bare legs.

"And you don't have to act so tough all the time. Not around me."

Touched, I rested my cheek against his shoulder. That was nice to hear tonight. Cougar had seen me at my best and my worst, and he liked me anyway. Like I'd been looking at it through the wrong end of the telescope, I suddenly saw just how guarded my marriage had been. I'd never really felt free to be myself with Grady, not even in the beginning. He always made me feel like I was lacking somehow, and his attempts to take care of me came off as attempts to control me. I didn't get that vibe from Cougar.

When I was with him, I felt safe from everything and everyone except myself.

After placing me on the couch, Cougar flopped down beside me and pulled my feet into his lap. He inspected my ankle with the same diligence he had my ribs. "Well, it's not swollen, but it probably wouldn't hurt to get some ice on it."

I opened my mouth to protest, but he silenced me with a finger shake and a frown, propped my foot on a throw pillow, and wandered into the kitchen. Closing my eyes, I tilted my head back on the sofa arm and listened to him rattle around in my freezer.

He startled me when he touched my face. "Hey," he said. "You okay?"

I blinked at him. He leaned over me, close enough to kiss, and for a moment, I thought about doing just that. Then a long, auburn hair brought me crashing back to reality. Casually, I peeled it off his shirt and let it fall to the floor. Grady must've hit me harder than I thought. I'd forgotten that the second prettiest girl in New Jersey was waiting for Cougar at home.

"I'm fine," I said, a little louder than I intended.

Cougar backed off and held up his palms. "Sorry." With a sheepish grin, he said, "You and Angel have made me a nervous wreck. I'm turning into my mother."

I smiled despite myself. He winked, lifted my foot, and resumed his seat.

The ice pack felt good against my ankle, but not as good as the fingers that kneaded my instep. "Thanks . . . for everything," I said. "But you don't have to babysit. I know you have to get back. You can take my car."

He lifted an eyebrow. "You trying to get rid of me?"

"Of course not, but I—" I rolled my eyes. "I don't want you to get in trouble with Kim."

He gave me a patient look. "That's the second time you've said that tonight. I told you, Kim and I aren't dating anymore."

Did not, I wanted to say, but my mouth was too dry. I would've remembered that.

"We're friends."

Like we were friends? I wondered, then decided I didn't want to know. My ego was as bruised as my body tonight, and right now, I wanted to think the connection Cougar and I shared was special.

Call me Cleopatra, Queen of Denial.

My silence seemed to make Cougar nervous. He leaned forward and talked faster. "Kim's dating a marine. He's stationed in Pensacola right now. She hates to go to work functions alone, says the chemist geeks won't leave her alone—"

We jumped at the pounding on the door.

"Denise!" Elizabeth yelled. "Denise, are you in there?"

I started to stand, but Cougar moved my foot back to the pillow.

"I'll get it," he said.

I pushed myself up on the couch and watched him stride toward the door. I caught a glimpse of Elizabeth's flushed face when he opened the door.

"Who are you?" she demanded. "Where's my daughter-in-law?"

"She's on the couch," he replied, ignoring her first question. "Hiya, Abby."

"Hi." Abby peeked at him from behind her grandmother. She wouldn't look in my direction at all.

Elizabeth stalked toward me. "Denise, I want you to know how much you've inconvenienced—dear God, what happened to you?"

I glanced at Cougar and he nodded. Pasting on a smile, he scooped Abby up in his arms. "Hey, kiddo. Why don't you show me your room while your mom and grandma talk?"

"Okay," she said, and they headed up the stairs.

I waited until they were out of sight, then turned to face Grady's mother.

"Your son happened to me. He assaulted me tonight. He was drunk, again."

Elizabeth blanched and took a step backward. Her hand fluttered to the pearls at her throat. "I-I don't believe you."

"You don't have to believe me. He did it in front of a couple dozen witnesses in the parking lot of a restaurant."

Elizabeth's face washed even paler. She staggered toward me, nearly falling over an end table. "Grady . . . where is he now?"

Alarmed, I tried to stand. "Elizabeth? Elizabeth, are you okay?"

"Where is he?" she shouted.

"Jail. He's in jail," I said. "Unless he's posted bond—"

Elizabeth shot me a horrified look, then grimaced. She grabbed her chest.

Helplessly, I watched her fall to the carpet.

CHAPTER 10

"ougar!" I screamed. "Cougar, help me!"

Footsteps thundered down the stairs while I scrambled around the couch to Elizabeth and flipped her onto her back. She blinked up at me with dazed eyes.

"Grandma!" Abby shrieked.

I glanced at Cougar. "Her heart, I think it's her heart."

"Call 911," he said, and knelt beside Elizabeth. Abby scurried to her other side.

While I gave the operator directions, Cougar eased Elizabeth into a sitting position, propping her against the couch. "Mrs. Bramhall, can you hear me? Everything's going to be all right. Help is on the way."

She gave Cougar a weak nod and awkwardly patted Abby's head. Elizabeth's color scared me, a waxy, deathly gray. Sweat beaded her upper lip. Her eyelids fluttered closed.

Abby twisted to glare at me. The hostility on her face took my breath away. "What did you do to her?" she cried.

Tears blurred my eyes. I reached for her and she flinched away.

"Don't *touch* me!"

"Abby," I managed, but she'd already turned back to Elizabeth.

"Grandma, please open your eyes."

Though I could tell it taxed her, Elizabeth did what she asked. I knelt beside Abby, but didn't try to touch her again. For the next seven minutes, we sat in silence. I knew exactly how long it was because I watched each second tick off the mantel clock.

At the faint sound of sirens, I shifted and grabbed the back of the couch. Cougar moved quickly to help me to my feet. Abby shot me another contemptuous look over her shoulder, and I wondered if something had been irreparably broken between my daughter and me tonight.

Cougar, Abby, and I followed the ambulance to the hospital. Abby would have nothing to do with me, choosing to cling to Cougar instead. He let me out at the emergency-room entrance before going to hunt a parking space and Abby insisted on staying with him.

Shivering, I stepped inside the automatic doors to

wait for them. I'd grabbed a long coat while heading out to the car, but I still wore my shorts and T-shirt beneath. When a cell phone began to ring, I reached for it automatically before I remembered it wasn't my purse that I held, but Elizabeth's. Not knowing what else to do with it, I'd brought it along. She would need her insurance card, I was sure. Now I stared at the little black phone hanging out of the side pocket and wondered if I should answer it. It might be one of her brothers . . .

I snatched it out and flipped it open before I could change my mind. "Hello?"

Silence on the other end.

"Hello?" I repeated. "Elizabeth Bramhall's phone. May I help you?"

"Necie?" Grady said. "What are you doing with Mom's phone?"

I fumbled the cell and nearly dropped it. Oh, hell, why had I answered it? What was I supposed to do now? In the glow of the streetlights, I watched Abby and Cougar walk down the line of cars. For my little girl, I could be civil. For her, I'd do the right thing.

"Uh, listen, Grady . . . we're at the hospital."

"Who is? You are? God, Necie, I didn't mean to hurt you that bad. I was upset, but you know I'd never intentionally—"

"It's Elizabeth," I interrupted. "She was having chest pains, but I think she's going to be okay. She's responsive and at the hospital now."

He lapsed into silence, then sighed. "Man, could this night get any worse?"

Yeah, I thought. *Try it with a couple of cracked ribs.* Nothing like a size ten in the side to put things in perspective.

"You got three minutes," I heard someone say in the background.

"Okay," Grady said. "Look, Necie. I know it's a lot to ask, but could you call my uncle Morty? This is my one phone call, and—"

"Sure."

Before I could hang up, Grady started talking faster. "Babe, I'm so sorry. I love you. I don't know—"

I snapped the phone shut and would've banged my head against the glass if I thought I could've withstood one more ache tonight. Pinching the bridge of my nose, I laughed. How screwed up was my life?

The double doors swung open, and Cougar shot me a curious glance. "Necie?"

I waved him off. "I'm fine. I need to make a couple of phone calls. Would you mind—"

He nodded. "No problem. Abby and I will wait in there. Come on, squirt," he said, and tugged her inside.

I took a deep breath and called Grady's uncle. He answered on the fourth ring, sounding sleepy and annoyed. His tone didn't improve much when I identified myself.

"What can I do for you, Denise?"

"I'm at the hospital. Elizabeth's been admitted with chest pains."

"Where's Grady?"

I hesitated. "In jail. He assaulted me tonight."

"*What?* What are you talking about, assault? That's the stupidest thing I've ever heard—"

"No, Mort. The stupidest thing is me calling his lawyer for him. Elizabeth and I are okay, thanks for asking. Now I gotta go."

"Denise, wait!" His voice turned sugary in an instant, reminding me of why I disliked him so much. "Honey, I'm sorry. You call me out of the blue, telling me all these things . . . *are* you okay?"

I leaned against the glass entryway and stared inside at Cougar and Abby. Cougar hunched forward in a waiting room chair, watching me. "Just . . . don't bother, okay, Morty? I want to make a deal."

That brought his sharp lawyer voice back. "What kind of deal?"

"I want a divorce. My terms. If Grady agrees, I won't press charges."

"Now wait a minute—"

"I'm not asking much. Grady already knows what I want. I'm calling my lawyer now. We'll meet you at the jail."

I pressed END without waiting on a reply and called Milano's house.

"Milano," he said through what sounded like a mouthful of chips.

"Hey, Milano. You busy?"

"Hey, doll. Never too busy for my cutest client. What's up?"

When I heard sirens approaching, I stepped outside to clear the way for the ambulance. My ankle and ribs throbbed. If it wouldn't have caused Cougar to rush to my aid, I would've sat down right there on the sidewalk. "The most embarrassing thing happened tonight. I got beat up by a lawyer."

"What?"

I gave Milano the CliffsNotes version of the attack.

"So, where are you now? Are you okay?"

"I'm at the hospital, but not for me. My mother-in-law might be having a heart attack. She—never mind, I'll tell you later. Well, what do you think? Should we meet with them tonight, or wait till morning or what?"

"As much as I'd like to see him spend the night in jail, we should probably move tonight. Our main leverage is not letting the press find out about his arrest. The longer he stays there, the more likely they will. But, Necie . . . are you sure you want to do this? I guarantee you, I can get you anything you want at this point, without your handing him a Get Out of Jail Free card."

"I want this to be over." Glancing inside at Abby, I said, "He's the father of my child. I don't want to destroy his life. I want him to get help."

"Okay, I think we can work something on that end, too. Are you at Jefferson?"

"Yeah."

"I'll pick you up in fifteen. It's on my way."

Clicking the phone shut, I shoved it back in Elizabeth's bag and limped through the automatic doors. Cougar waited on the other side to help me.

"What's going on?" he said. "Are you all right?"

With a glance over his shoulder to make sure Abby was out of earshot, I said, "I called my lawyer. We're going to the jail to see if we can make a deal with Grady and his lawyer."

Cougar tensed and narrowed his eyes. Keeping his voice low, he said, "I don't get it. Why would you do that for him? Look what he did to you."

"I'm not doing it for him. I'm doing it for Abby. You see how angry she is at me. I don't want her to hate me. No telling what Elizabeth has told her already. I want out of this marriage, and this is the quickest way to accomplish that. Grady's Uncle Mort will make him agree to whatever I want to save Grady's law career."

"I still don't like it. He does this—" he made a sweeping gesture at my body, "—and gets off scot-free? I don't think so. I'm going to thump his—"

I silenced him with a finger to his lips. "No, you're not." I smiled and kissed his cheek. "But thanks for wanting to. You're a good friend."

He frowned, his eyes stormy. He looked like he wanted to say more, but then he exhaled and stared out into the night.

"Milano's picking me up—"

His gaze snapped back to me. "I'll drive you. I want to be there."

"We both know that's not a good idea. You know what Grady thinks about us already. And I was hoping you'd take Abby to Mrs. Angelino's for me. I'll give her a call to make sure it's okay."

Cougar scrubbed a hand over his face. "She's with Angel tonight. I'll take care of Abby. She told me she was hungry. We'll grab a bite to eat or something, then go up to Angel's room to wait for you. Your lawyer will bring you back here, right?"

"I'm sure he will." I squeezed his forearm. "Thank you. Thanks for everything."

He kissed my forehead and glanced down at my foot. "How's that ankle?"

"Okay. I can put a little weight on it now."

"Why don't you get it checked out while we're here?"

"Not necessary."

He shook his head and gave me a little smile. "You're the most hardheaded person—"

"No, that would be Angel."

Cougar laughed and scratched the back of his head. The tension between us evaporated in a rush. He wrapped his arm around my shoulder and guided me toward the sitting area. "Yeah, hard to dispute that now, huh? I don't know what I did to get stuck with the two of you—"

"You love us both and you know it."

"I do, but you still drive me nuts." He helped me into the chair beside Abby, who jumped up and walked to the window.

"She'll get over it," he whispered. "Be right back."

He strode over to the nurses' desk and said something to the middle-aged woman behind it. Then he pointed at me and flashed his badge. He leaned halfway over the counter to speak to her, and I could tell by the flushed look on her face that the old Cougar mojo was working its magic. She disappeared through a door marked STAFF ONLY and returned a moment later with a pair of battered crutches, which she passed over the counter to him. Cougar thanked her and signed a form. He carried them back to me with a triumphant smile and plopped in the seat beside me to adjust them.

"They aren't the best-looking things in the world, but they should get you by a day or two and keep you from doing more damage to that ankle. You have to have a prescription for new ones—"

"They're great, thank you."

"Abby, honey, come here," he said, and she grudgingly faced us. Cougar patted the chair beside him, and to my surprise, she wandered over, taking care not to touch me as she passed.

"Your mom has to leave for a little while. Would you like to go grab something to eat with me? Then we'll go see what Tori is up to."

"Okay." She smiled. "Can we eat pizza?"

Cougar rolled his eyes and made a grab for her. He tickled her and asked, "Is that all you're made of? Pizza?"

"Yup," she said with a gasp when he released her. Her smile faded. "But what about Grandma? Is she going to be okay?"

Cougar made a trip back to the desk and talked with the same nurse. She told him that if the doctor didn't come out to speak to us in a moment, she'd get an update.

Five minutes later, she came over to report that Elizabeth was doing fine, but would be admitted overnight for observation and tests.

A crowd of teenagers entered the waiting room, talking loudly among themselves about a car wreck. Abby crawled up into Cougar's lap.

"Why don't you two go on?" I said. "Milano should be here any time."

"I'm not leaving you," Cougar replied at the same

time I spotted Milano walking through the entrance. He gave us a smile and a little wave and sauntered over.

"That's him," I said, and stood to greet him. Cougar hoisted Abby on his hip and stood, too.

I introduced them. Cougar extended his free hand to Milano to shake, then glanced at me. "Be careful."

"I will."

He nodded and walked toward the exit.

Milano gave me a cheerful grin and made a karate chop in the air. "Don't worry, I'll protect you. I know Tai Chi Nygun."

"You do?" I smiled, anticipating the punch line.

"Oh, yeah. He's my proctologist. He sees assholes like Grady every day."

I snorted.

Milano nodded toward the exit. "So, this Jason . . . is he someone I need to know about, for the case?"

"He's a member of my team."

"You're not sleeping with him?" Milano held up his palms. "Sorry I have to ask, but I need to be prepared for anything."

"It's okay. No, we're not sleeping together. I've got enough problems without throwing that in the mix. But his name might come up. Grady's jealous of him, and every other guy I work with."

"He seems like a nice guy. Very concerned for you."

"Cougar's a friend. My best friend."

"Cougar, Cougar . . ." Milano snapped his fingers and his eyes lit up. "Now I remember where I know this guy from. He's the one all the court reporters talk about. They swoon when he walks by."

"Even Henry?"

Milano winked. "Oh, Henry's the first to hit the floor."

I giggled at the image, then clutched my ribs. "Ow, don't make me laugh."

He handed the crutches to me. "I could give you my bill, and make you cry."

"Give it to Grady," I said, while we headed toward the door.

Milano rubbed his hands together. "Oh, don't you worry about that. He's going to get the full Milano treatment. So . . . how's your mother-in-law?"

"They say she'll be fine. Back to hating my guts in no time."

"My mother-in-law's mad at me, too. I made a Freudian slip at the dinner table last night."

"What . . ." I gulped when we stepped into the cold night air. "What did you say?"

Milano giggled behind his hand like a kid. "Well, I . . . what I meant to say was, 'Please pass the butter,' but what slipped out was, 'You ruined my life, you overbearing shrew.'"

He kept me laughing all the way to the jail. I almost forgot the grim task that lay ahead of me. That is, until we pulled up at the police district.

Milano patted my hand. "Chin up, kiddo. I promise, this is going to work out."

We found Grady and Mort waiting for us in a conference room. A stone-faced Mort sat back, while Grady propped his elbows on the table, resting his face in his hands. It hurt me to see the handcuffs on his wrists, and the reddened eyes that stared up at me, but I steeled myself. He had done this, not me. I was through feeling guilty for other people's actions.

Grady winced when I hobbled inside, and tears filled his eyes. I looked away from him, choosing to stare at Mort instead.

"I trust Grady's told you what I want?"

"He has." Mort sighed. "And he agrees to your terms."

"We have a few additional requests in light of your client's recent actions," Milano said, and pulled out a chair for him.

Mort shot Grady an *I told you so* look and snorted. "And what would those be?"

"Surely you agree that there is sufficient evidence to suggest your client has a drinking problem." He paused, but Mort merely blinked at him. "So, as part of the agreement—in the best interest of your client's minor child—we insist that he attend an alcohol treatment program and meetings with LCL for a period of no less than six months."

"LCL?" Grady said. "What is LCL?"

"Lawyers Concerned for Lawyers," Milano replied. "They're a private, nonprofit corporation that assists lawyers, judges, and law students who are experiencing any level of impairment in their ability to function as a result of personal, mental health, addiction, or medical problems. LCL provides assistance with problems such as career and family difficulties, depression, and stress, as well as alcoholism, substance abuse, gambling, and all other forms of addiction. They are very discreet."

"What about money?" Mort asked. "I assume Denise wants alimony?"

"No, just the standard child support under Pennsylvania law and that your client continues to cover Abby under his medical insurance. Your client pays my fees."

"About Abby . . ." Grady looked at me. "I want to see my daughter."

"And you will," Milano answered. "But under supervision until you've completed your alcohol program. That supervisor doesn't have to be court appointed. It can be your mother, but if at any time we find that Abby has been left alone in your care, all visitation will be suspended."

Grady slapped the desk. "I don't believe this . . . you talk about me like I'm some kind of . . ." He rubbed his hands over his rumpled blond hair. "I could take you to court and get joint custody. I've never hurt Abby."

"If you take us to court, you lose your license. Is

that a trade off you're willing to make?" Milano's hard, unflinching expression betrayed none of the affable joker he'd been outside this room. It made me think of people and the many masks they wore.

Grady leaned to whisper to Mort. They conferred for a few minutes, then Mort shifted.

"We agree to your terms. It'll take us a few days to get it all drawn up—"

"I've got it right here." Milano removed a folder from his briefcase. "The first four pages are the original terms; the last page contains the addenda."

Mort scanned the papers, then scanned them again. He shoved them over to Grady and handed him a pen.

Grady hesitated, the pen between his fingers, and gave me another long look. I stared at the crutches beside me. He scrawled his name on the last two pages.

"I'm sorry, Denise," he said. "I'm so sorry."

"Thank you." Milano retrieved the papers and helped me stand. "I'll leave you a copy of these outside at the desk. We'll go tell them she's dropping the charges."

Like Lot's wife, I couldn't resist one last look over my shoulder. Grady sat up, a flicker of hope in his eyes. I stared at him, for some reason recalling the night Abby was born, the joyous expression on his face when he'd held her for the first time. I'd loved him then. He'd loved me. But those people were gone now. That love was gone. Our marriage had been reduced to a few typed pages, and when I walked out the door, I'd be lying if I said I wasn't relieved.

Milano insisted on walking me back inside the hospital. He checked with the desk to see where they'd moved Elizabeth, then waited for an elevator with me.

"They said she's doing fine, but I'm a little worried about you, kiddo. You don't look so hot."

"I'm fine." I forced a smile. "Just very, very tired."

"No wonder. You've had a heck of a day. I had one of those yesterday." He sighed. "I put on a shirt, and a button fell off. I picked up my briefcase, and the handle fell off. I was afraid to go to the bathroom."

I laughed despite all the aches and gloom and chaotic thoughts that plagued me. "You're way too laid-back to be a lawyer, Milano."

"Tell me about it. An alarming number of lawyers suffer from seriousness, like that Mort fellow. Do you think he stuffs his own shirts, or has to send them out?"

The elevator slid open, and he held the door while I hobbled inside. He pressed the button for the fourth floor and closed his eyes, humming along with the piped-in music.

"Is it a sign of old age, when the song you danced to at your high-school prom becomes elevator music?" He opened an eye and squinted at me. "That reminds me. Guess what the DEA agent's favorite song is?"

"Um . . ." I rubbed my aching forehead. "Let's see . . .

'Amazing Grass'?"

He winced. "Boo, hiss. No, but 'Don't Sell It on the Mountain' did come in second."

I leaned against the elevator wall. "Give me a break, would ya . . . I can't match wits with you on a good day, much less on an amazingly bad one."

"'Yakkety Yak, Don't Smoke Crack.'"

"That's terrible," I said, but I was smiling when the elevator opened.

We walked down the hall in silence until I found Elizabeth's door. "This is my stop. Thanks for everything, Milano."

"No problem." He surprised me by giving me a quick hug. "You take care of yourself, doll. And not to sound mushy or anything, but don't let this sour you on love. There are still some decent men out there."

"Yeah, but they've been hunted to extinction."

"Ah, you'd be surprised. Just stay away from lawyer types. You're too good for us. Find yourself a nice doctor, a podiatrist maybe . . ." He winked. "Or maybe a freakishly handsome DEA agent with a weird nickname who looks at you with big goo-goo eyes."

"Uh-huh, that's exactly what I need, to be one of the women dropping like flies around his feet."

Milano started walking away. "Don't rule out your own bug-zapping abilities. You're not too shabby, for a steenkin' fed."

"Gee, thanks."

"Don't mention it." He stopped and snapped his fingers. "This Cougar guy . . . does he wear an earring?"

I snorted. "You kidding? He's from Texas."

Milano shrugged. "Ah, too bad. Ben Franklin said, 'Men who have pierced ears are better prepared for marriage. They've experienced pain and bought jewelry.'"

"Ben Franklin said that?"

"Nah, but people will believe anything you say if you tell them Ben Franklin said it first. Later, kid."

I waved good-bye and took a deep breath before opening Elizabeth's door.

Mort's wife, Jane, sat in the chair beside her bed. They both gave me the same stony look when I walked in.

"What are you doing here, Denise?" Jane asked.

Ignoring her, I approached the bed and spoke to Elizabeth. "How are you doing?"

"How do you think she's doing? You just had her son arrested—"

"I dropped the charges. He's probably on his way here now."

Jane's eyes glittered. "How nice of you, after he gave you everything you wanted. Mort called us from the jail. We know what you did."

Although I'd sworn I wouldn't let any of them provoke me, I couldn't control the anger that flashed over me. "Excuse me? What I did? Look at me. Do you realize what I could've done?"

"Jane . . . Denise, please. Not here." Elizabeth closed her eyes. "I'm fine, Denise. Where's Abby?"

"She's on the next floor, with my friends."

Elizabeth and Jane exchanged a knowing look, and I bristled. "Look, I only wanted to see how you were doing. I'd better go before . . ." I almost said "before Grady gets here," but stopped myself. Elizabeth knew what I meant anyway.

"Yes, I think that would be best. Please tell Abby I'm okay and I'd like to call her tomorrow night, with your permission."

"Of course."

I was still seething by the time I made it to Angel's room, but my bad mood evaporated when I stepped inside. Cougar, Tucker, and Angel abandoned the ball game they were watching and turned their attention to me.

This is my family, I thought. *These are the people I love.*

Abby lay curled in Cougar's lap, asleep. The sight made my chest tighten, and I thought about Milano and his bug analogy. It was one thing to know I was about to get zapped, but an entirely different one to turn away from the light.

"How'd it go?" Cougar asked. I didn't realize how tense he looked until his face relaxed. Abby stirred, and he absently stroked her hair.

"Well, she's smiling, so it must not have been too

bad." Tucker stood, vacating the chair beside Cougar, and helped me into it before taking a seat at the foot of Angel's bed.

"Grady agreed to my demands, signed the papers. In about a month, it'll be official."

Cougar nodded, his eyes thoughtful. "Now that he's signed the papers, can we kick his ass?"

I couldn't tell if he was kidding or not. Brushing a piece of hair from Abby's cheek, I said lightly, "No, because he's still her father." Hesitantly, not sure I wanted to hear the answer, I asked, "So, how did she do?"

Cougar gave me a tired smile. "It took some tormenting, but we got her talking. She perked up when the nurse gave her an update on her grandma, said she was doing fine. Then the little brat found Angel's comb. She nearly scalped me and Tucker both, playing beauty shop."

I giggled at the image. "I thought you guys looked a little, ah . . . rumpled."

"She asked about you when she started getting sleepy," he added.

"Really?" I felt a twinge of hope. "She was so mad at me."

"Kids are resilient," Tucker said. "She'll come around."

Mrs. Angelino and Tori came in, bearing another carton of Karamel Sutra.

Cougar smiled. "You see what you started? I'll have to run him around the municipal building five times a day to work off that ice-cream gut he's building."

"Speaking of municipal building . . . I'd better get going. I've got an early day tomorrow." Tucker stood and ruffled my hair. "Just wanted to make sure you were all right."

I told him good-bye, then answered a string of anxious questions from Tori. After reassuring her I was fine, I turned to Cougar. "Are you still meeting Massey tomorrow?"

"Yeah. You wanna come with me?"

"I'd better pass. I have to catch up on some paperwork at the office, then I need to see if I can knock off early to check out some after-school care for Abby."

"Necie, we'll watch your little girl," Mrs. Angelino said, and Tori nodded.

I shook my head. "No, you came to Philly to be with Angel, not babysit for me. Besides, I'd better be looking for something permanent. I don't intend to keep Abby from her grandmother, but I figure Elizabeth won't be as willing to help anymore."

"Do you remember Julie Arp?" Cougar asked. "She was a traffic cop downtown—"

"I remember," I said, recalling another of Cougar's old girlfriends. "The one who talked like Fran Drescher."

Angel laughed and I gave him a wink. Cougar ignored us.

"You know she married one of the cops from the sixteenth district, right? They have a little boy. Well, she and a handful of the other policemen's wives started a round-the-clock operation—Cops with Kids, I think they call it—because they couldn't find sitters who would accommodate our weird hours. I've been inside. It's a pretty nice setup . . . beds and everything. Sorta like school. I mean, hopefully you won't have to use it much, but there are cops dropping off and picking up kids at all hours. I can check on it for you, if you like."

"That would be great," I said, though it gave me a pang to think of strangers caring for Abby.

Cougar must've seen through my smile, because he reached over and took my hand. "We're going to help you through this, you know."

I nodded, but he didn't release me. Goose bumps ran up my arm when he stroked the top of my hand with his thumb.

"Barnes's jury selection is in the morning," he said. "I hate to miss it, but Bill said he'd be there." He looked at Angel. "He's going to pay for what he did to you, I swear it."

The fierceness in Cougar's eyes made my throat constrict. My father—my *father*—had done this to Angel. I dreaded the trial, because I was sure Barnes would use our connection to try to save himself. At what point would he show his hand, and what would my lie of omission cost me?

"Necie, you don't look so good," Cougar said, and

I blinked.

"I'm okay. Just tired."

"Let's go. It's time I took you home."

Twenty minutes later, I dropped my purse on the kitchen counter and shrugged out of my coat. "Thanks, Coug, for everything. I would've never gotten her upstairs without you."

"Glad to help." He gave me a long, searching look. "Do you want me to stay?"

A dozen thoughts raced through my mind, none of them pure, but I managed to shake my head. "No, you go get some rest. I'll be all right from here."

He nodded and surprised me by grasping my shoulders. He planted a firm kiss on the center of my forehead before releasing me and walking out the door. I watched him go, resisting the crazy impulse to call him back.

After locking the door, I limped down the hall to the bathroom. While the tub filled, I retrieved some Epsom salts from beneath the sink and dumped half a box into the steaming water. With the exaggerated care of a ninety-year-old, I stripped and climbed into the tub.

For a moment, the sharp zing from all my cuts and abrasions electrified me. I gritted my teeth until the pain faded to a dull throb. The heat seemed to seep into my muscles, drugging me. It took all my efforts to turn the water off a few minutes later. Closing my eyes, I lay there like a dead woman.

I awoke around 2 a.m. to find my water chilly and my neck stiff. Somehow, I dried off, pulled on some clothes, and staggered to bed. I fell asleep as soon as my head hit the pillow, but too soon, my alarm blasted me back awake. I winced at the sunlight streaming through the shades and wondered how I was going to get out of bed, much less get to work. At some point, Abby had crawled in beside me. She raised up on an elbow and squinted at me.

"Oh, Mama, your face . . ."

"Um," I replied, and swung my legs over the side of the bed. My stiffened limbs screamed in protest, and I gripped the edge of the mattress to counter a wave of dizziness. I caught my reflection in the dresser mirror and grimaced.

The bride of Frankenstein had nothing on the soon-to-be ex of Grady Bramhall. Part of it I expected for going to bed with wet hair, but I hadn't anticipated how swollen and discolored my face would be.

"What happened to you?" Abby asked, her voice small and quiet.

I wanted to be straight with her, and after all, God only knew what Elizabeth had said about me, but I could not look my child in the face and tell her that her daddy had done this. I told her I'd fallen in the parking lot and banged my face. Then I tried for a smile and patted the spot next to me. Abby scooted over to sit beside me.

"Honey, can we talk about last night, and why you were mad at me?"

She stared at the floor. "I wanted to see the wedding. I was playing with Trish, and you made me leave. Grandma was upset and crying. She said you were going to take me away from her and Daddy and never let me see them again." She peeked at me from beneath her bangs. "Are you?"

"I know how much you love your grandma and daddy, and how much they love you. I'd never keep you from them, unless I thought you were in danger. I'm not going to lie to you; things will be different. Daddy won't be living here anymore, but no matter what problems he and I have, it doesn't change the fact that we both love you."

"But why can't Daddy live here anymore? Is it because of your job?"

I gritted my teeth and did a ten-count. "No, baby, it has nothing to do with my job. Did Grandma tell you that?"

Abby nodded.

"What else did Grandma tell you?"

"She said for me not to believe the awful things you told me about Daddy, and I told her you hadn't said anything about Daddy. She said you would, and when you did, I should tell you to stop lying about him."

Oooh, that woman. If she weren't already in the

hospital, I'd be tempted to put her there.

"She said you and Daddy would be the death of her. When I saw her lying on the floor, I thought . . ." She frowned and chewed on her thumbnail. "But Cougar said it wasn't your fault, that you'd never hurt her because that would hurt me and you loved me more than anything."

I hugged her and gave Cougar a mental "thank you." "He's right, you know. I love you more than anything. Never forget that."

"I love you, too, Mama."

"So, we're good?"

She smiled and nodded.

"Let's get you ready for school then."

At the office, I felt like a bug in a glass jar. Everyone stared and whispered and stopped by to see if I was okay. After a visit from Ms. Runner-Up New Jersey, Mrs. Run-Down Philadelphia collected her paperwork and fled to an empty conference room for some privacy. I was almost finished when my cell phone rang.

"Are you able to be there?" Bill demanded.

"I'm fine. A little scary looking, but fine. Even managed to get here without the crutches Cougar procured for me last night."

"I'm still at jury selection. I got worried when I tried to call your house and couldn't get you. I thought maybe you were sleeping it off, but then Ubi told me you were there. I can't believe you came in today."

"Ah, you know . . . it's that slave driver I work for . . ."

"Yeah, yeah . . . well, that slave driver wants to buy you lunch. Grab the Willis file and meet me at the courthouse. The Barnes proceeding should be breaking soon, and we'll grab a bite to eat. You can kick around the rest of the afternoon with me."

"Sounds like a plan. See you in fifteen."

Bill pegged it pretty close. By the time I figured out which courtroom he was in, the doors opened and people started streaming out. Bill winced when he saw me and made his way across the hall to join me.

"Ouch, you weren't kidding about the scary thing, huh?"

"Ha, ha. Thank you. Thankyouverymuch."

"Come on." He took my elbow. "Let's get out of here. I'm starving."

We turned to make our way to the exit, and Bill snapped his fingers. "Hang on a sec. I forgot to tell Mac something."

Mac was the prosecutor. Thinking they'd led Barnes away through the back already, I followed Bill into the courtroom.

Barnes still sat at the defense table with his lawyers, and he glanced up when we walked in. A horrified look crossed his face. He placed his palms on the table and tried to stand. I pivoted and hurried back outside.

I leaned against the wall, my heart beating wildly. I

didn't know why the concern on his face affected me so, but I still felt skittish when Bill rejoined me a moment later.

"Linda said the new Chinese place down the block is pretty good. Want to give it a try?"

I managed a squeaky "Sure."

The cold walk cleared my head. By the time we reached the restaurant, I almost felt normal. We watched a couple of teenage boys through the window as we waited to be seated.

"How do they stand that, in this weather?" I asked, gesturing at the jeans belted below their boxer-clad buttocks.

"That's a style?" Bill helped himself to a peppermint beside the cash register and winked. "I figured some rapper died, and they were wearing their pants at half-mast."

I laughed. "You're a funny guy. Almost as funny as my lawyer."

"Two?" our greeter asked, and Bill nodded. "Follow me."

My cell rang and she shot me a disapproving glance before walking away. I flipped the phone open, but didn't recognize the number displayed. I answered it anyway.

"What happened to you?" a gruff voice asked, and I nearly dropped the phone when I recognized Barnes's voice.

I stopped in my tracks in the middle of the crowded restaurant.

"How did you get this number?"

"What happened to you?" he asked again.

Bill glanced back at me, his eyebrows raised. I

placed my hand over the receiver and said, "Go ahead. I need to take this."

I turned and strode back outside. The wind hit me like a slap, but my cheeks were hot with fury. "Look, I don't know how you got this number, but—"

"Denise, please," he said. "I can't talk long. I'm your father. I want to know what happened to you."

I gripped the phone. "Because you're so concerned, right? I'm nearly thirty years old. This doting-daddy stuff is too little too late."

"What can I do?" he asked, and I was taken aback at how defeated he sounded. "Isn't there some way to show you I'm sorry, that I never meant to hurt you . . . that I do love you? Won't you give me a second chance?"

I shoved my fist into my coat pocket and hugged myself against the cold. "A second chance? You've got to be kidding me."

"I'm an old man, Denise. I'm probably going to prison. I don't want to die knowing my firstborn hates me. What can I do to make things better between us?"

"You can start by taking responsibility for your actions."

"I'm sorry I hurt your mother—"

I pinched the bridge of my nose. "I'm not talking about her. I'm talking about Angel, one of the best friends I've ever had. Did you or did you not shoot him and leave him for dead?"

Silence.

"Fine. I see how you've changed. Good-bye, *Daddy*. Don't call this number again."

I snapped the phone shut and stood there for a moment, trying to tamp my fury before I rejoined Bill. Who did Barnes think he was kidding? Did he think I was that stupid?

When I felt like I had myself under control, I went back inside. I brushed off Bill's questions, and we went to check out the buffet.

We were in the middle of our wonton soup when his cell rang. He opened it, squinted at the number, then answered. "Yeah, Tuck. What do you have?"

His eyes widened. "You're kidding me. What? Are you sure? Okay. Yeah, I'll meet you there."

"What?" I demanded as he shut the phone and stared at me.

Maybe Barnes had ratted me out. That was probably his plan all along, and now there were cell phone records proving we'd spoken—

"It's Barnes," Bill said. "He's changed his plea to guilty."

"What?" I gasped.

"He's also requested expedited sentencing. The DA's all over it. The hearing is in half an hour."

CHAPTER 11

My team buzzed with speculation about Barnes's sudden reversal.

Ubi helped me into a seat near the back of the already crowded courtroom. "Man, I wish Cougar was here. He'll die when he finds out he missed this."

I nodded, though I felt sick inside. It wasn't supposed to be like this. My team was jubilant, but I could muster none of their enthusiasm. Even though I knew it was crazy, I felt responsible. Barnes had pointed that gun at Angel and he'd pulled the trigger. I kept telling myself he deserved whatever he got. But what bothered me was the fact that he hadn't pleaded guilty out of remorse.

Barnes had pleaded guilty because it was what I wanted.

I'd turned it over and over in my mind, and that was the only conclusion I could reach. I saw no possible benefit for him to forfeit his right to a trial. I'd asked him for something I was sure he wouldn't give me, and he'd called my bluff. What was I supposed to do now?

Barnes entered the courtroom through a side door, handcuffed and wearing an orange jumpsuit. I expected him to scan the courtroom, maybe even stare me down with a silent "So there," but he never looked around.

Maria hurried into the room a few minutes before the trial was scheduled to begin. She shoved and stumbled past the seated spectators to get to him, and a strange silence fell over the courtroom as people stopped whatever they were doing to watch her.

"Papa!" She leaned over the barricade. "You can't do this!"

Barnes turned toward her. "It's already done. I'm sorry, honey."

"It's because of *her*, isn't it?" she spat, and involuntarily, I slouched lower in my chair. "She did this—"

"Maria!" Barnes barked, and the bailiff placed a hand on his gun. Barnes lowered his voice. "That's enough."

Maria's head dropped. Her bodyguard evicted a couple of onlookers from their chairs and sat in one. He pulled Maria down beside him, and they began an animated, hushed conversation.

"Wonder who she's talking about?" Bill whispered, but I was too rattled to even attempt an answer.

The sentencing lasted only fifteen minutes. Barnes

declined to make a statement on his behalf, though his lawyer pointed out that he had no prior criminal convictions.

The judge sentenced Barnes to fifty-three years in federal prison, twenty years of it suspended, with the stipulation that if Angel died within a year and a day of the shooting as a direct result of his injuries, the charge would be upgraded to capital murder.

Okay, thirty-three years, I thought. *Not bad, since Angel is a federal agent. He'd serve less than half that with good behavior—*

I broke off, horrified by my train of thought. What was I doing, thinking about it from Barnes's point of view? Angel was my friend—one of my best friends. He was doing better, but he might never be the same as he was before. What were sixteen or seventeen years in the face of that? Nothing. Not a damn thing when you were twenty-eight years old and unable to feed yourself.

My stomach churned, and I thought I was going to be sick right there, but somehow I managed to make it out of the courtroom with the rest of my team, pretending that nothing was wrong. In the hallway, I grabbed Ubi's arm. Thankfully, Bill was talking to someone.

"Hey, there's someone I need to speak with," I said. "Tell Bill I'll catch him back at the office."

"Okay, but we'll probably all head to see Angel first, tell him the good news."

"I'll find you."

I wove through the crowd and barely made it to the restroom in time. Holding my hair back with one hand, I threw up until I could do nothing but heave. My legs trembled, and I wiped tears from the corner of my eyes.

When I opened the door, I found Maria waiting for me.

"What's the matter, *mi hermana?*" she said. "Feeling guilty for what you've done, or the aftereffects from Grady kicking the crap out of you?"

"Leave me alone," I said, stumbling toward the sink. I splashed my face with water and cupped my hands to catch enough to rinse out my mouth.

"I'll never leave you alone again. Daddy won't be able to protect you now. You think my taking Grady was bad, wait until I take everything."

"Don't flatter yourself," I snapped. "Grady and I were over long before you came along. And I don't need his protection. I'm not afraid of you." But instantly I thought of Abby and wondered how far Maria would go to hurt me.

"You'd better be afraid. I can get to you anywhere, anytime. You remember that."

She leaned against the sink. I stared at her hands, at the long red nails that tapped against the white porcelain.

"How did you do it?" she asked, when I didn't respond. "How did you talk him into throwing his life away?"

"He did that a long time ago."

"You mean when he left your mother for mine."

I stared up at her. "I don't get why you think this is a competition. I'm not trying to come between you two. In fact, I want nothing to do with either of you. As far as I'm concerned, he's yours."

The pain that flickered across her face caught me off guard. "No," she said quietly. "He isn't."

She turned and walked out.

I washed my face again, wondering what I should do next. I meant what I said to Maria, but I felt like I owed Barnes at least a visit, even though I was scared to death someone would recognize me and ask what I was doing there. I could wait on him to call again, but that felt cowardly. Besides, by rights, the next move was mine.

I took an elevator to the ground floor where he was being held before transfer to the penitentiary. His lawyer waited for me outside the double doors. She smiled and offered her hand. Warily, I shook it.

"I'm glad you came," she said. "I was about to give up on you."

"What is this?" I asked tiredly. "What does he want from me?"

"Just to talk."

She headed toward the doors and I followed.

"You carrying?" she asked, and I shook my head.

"Not in court."

"Your father doesn't want to complicate things for you, so follow my lead."

She strode up to the front desk and addressed a young officer I didn't recognize. "I'm Frank Barnes's legal counsel, and this is my assistant. We'd like a word with him before the transfer."

He shot me a curious look, probably wondering how roadkill had passed the bar. But then he slid a clipboard to her and told her to sign us in. She scrawled Tanya Davis and the name Anita Bennett under it. I hesitated, figuring they'd probably want a copy of our licenses, but she grabbed my arm and dragged me toward the metal detectors.

This was wrong to the nth degree, but I didn't know what else to do. Momentarily, I found myself inside a small windowless room I'd never been in before.

"This is a secure room," she said. "They can't record lawyer-client conversations."

We sat at a small, chipped table, and a deputy led Barnes inside. He looked as tired as I felt, but he managed a smile. I couldn't return it.

"You have ten minutes," the deputy said. "His ride will be here soon."

When he exited, Tanya reached for her briefcase. "Sorry," she said. "I can't leave, since I'm primary counsel and that would look funny, but I'll try to give you what privacy I can."

She pulled a set of headphones out of her briefcase and clamped them over her ears. She touched a button on the side, and 3 Doors Down blared so loud I could identify the song.

She extracted a notebook and walked over to the corner, where she braced the paper against the wall and stood scribbling.

Barnes and I stared at each other across the table. I didn't know what to say.

He smiled. "Now I know how Darth Vader felt."

That surprised a laugh out of me. Some of the tension that held me rigid released. "That was pretty funny. I'll give you props for that."

"I don't know what props are, but I'll take them," he said with a wink. He leaned back in the chair and studied me. "So, have I earned the right to hear what happened to you? Will you tell me who—or what—hurt you?"

I sighed and rubbed my forehead. "Okay, sure. My husband did it. My soon-to-be ex-husband. I served papers on him."

Barnes's smile vanished. He scowled and thumped his fist on the table. "Huh, easier widowed than divorced. One call, and I can make sure he never touches you—"

I jumped up and waved my hands. "Now, see, this is why we can't talk! Can you hear yourself? You're about to go to prison for attempted murder, and you're talking about arranging a hit. What is wrong with you?"

"There's nothing wrong with wanting to protect your family," he said, looking hurt.

"Yes, there is, when you're talking about murder." I

shook my head. "I don't know who's crazier, you or me, for thinking we could actually *communicate*—"

"Okay, okay. Just sit back down. I'll behave." When I didn't smile, he said, "I'll tell you what. We'll play this game I used to play with Maria when she was little and I wanted her to tell me what she'd done in school that day. You get a question, then I do."

That made me cringe, because I had no memories of playing games with my father, but I took a deep breath and sat back down. "Why did you plead guilty?"

"It was the only way I could show you I was serious. Besides, I did it. My turn."

I motioned for him to go ahead.

"Are you in danger from your husband? Don't look at me like that. I won't harm him if you don't want me to, but I can provide security for you and my granddaughter."

"Not necessary. Grady won't bother me again. I'm probably in more danger from Maria that I am anyone else."

Barnes's eyes narrowed. "Maria? Has she threatened you?"

I laughed. "Only every time we speak."

Barnes waved his hand dismissively, though his expression was grave. "She's all talk, a petulant child. She knows better than to hurt you."

"She told me today that you couldn't protect me anymore," I said, feeling vaguely like a tattletale. "I'm only telling you because . . . I'm worried about my daughter, and I don't want this to go any farther."

"I'll take care of it. I don't want either of you hurt any further because of me." He cleared his throat. "I know it's your turn to ask a question, but how is that boy, the agent I shot?"

I stiffened at the reminder of what this was and who I was talking to. "Do you care?"

"I care because you care."

"He's doing better."

"Does he have brain damage?"

I gritted my teeth, feeling like a traitor. "Look, I really don't want to talk about him with you."

"Then what do you want to talk about?"

"Why did you leave us?" I blurted, and was disgusted by how hurt it sounded.

Barnes winced. "I got involved with the wrong people. It was my own fault. I'm not trying to shift blame. Your mother and I grew up in the same neighborhood. Both of our families were dirt-poor. When I went to work for Salvador, I got a taste of the good life and I liked it. I never dreamed it would cost me my family, my baby girl. All the money in the world wasn't worth that."

"You left us for another woman."

Barnes sighed. "No, not really. I met Maria's mother at one of Salvador's parties. I'd had too much to drink." He blinked and stared at the table. "I was unfaithful. The next day, I confessed to Gail and begged her to forgive me. She was hurt, but she agreed to try to work it out if I quit Salvador and promised never to see Ana again. But things were never really the same between us. The resentment grew every day. Then one day Ana showed up on our doorstep, pregnant and demanding support. Gail was so enraged she threw my clothes in the yard and told me to take my whore and go. She refused to let me see you, though there were times when her mother would sneak you out to visit, before Gail found out about it and put an end to it. But I never stopped loving you. I never stopped taking care of you."

I leaned back in my chair, incredulous and angry. "Taking care of me? The day I arrested you was only the second time I remember us being face-to-face."

Barnes gave me a sad smile. "There are other ways of taking care of people. By the time you were of age, your mother had poisoned your mind against me. You told me to leave, so I left, but I couldn't step out of your life completely. You wouldn't take my money for school, so I arranged for a nice scholarship to fall into your lap. I didn't like the neighborhood you lived in, so I had a professor give you a lead on an apartment in a better place. I'm sure you wondered why the rent was so cheap. It was because I was paying half. I even had people pad your tip jar sometimes, until I figured out your boss was stealing most of it. He and I had a little talk about that, too."

I stared at him, awash in surprise and fury. It took me a moment to find my tongue.

"Y-you . . . I can't believe . . . I never would've accepted your money, and I resent you trying to control me like that."

"It wasn't about control. It was about taking care of my daughter. I'm only telling you now because I want you to know I never forgot you. I was there for you, in the only way I knew how."

I paced in front of the table, too upset to process this. "I suppose you think I owe you now?"

He frowned. "No, it is I who owes you, more than I can ever repay."

The guard rapped on the door and opened it. He shot me a curious look. "Time's up, ladies."

Tanya pulled off her headphones and put them back in the briefcase.

"Will you come again?" Barnes asked softly.

I glanced at him and gave him the most honest answer I could. "I don't know."

He nodded, and I walked out the door.

Tanya caught me as I stepped inside the elevator. Before I realized what she was doing, she pressed something in my hand. "He gave me that today. He wants you to have it."

She pulled back and left me staring at the object in my palm. My breath caught at the little black-and-white photo of a much younger Barnes smiling and holding a three-year-old on his lap.

Me.

I didn't realize I was crying until the first tear splattered on the photo.

At the office, the party was in full swing. Most people weren't even pretending to work. A portable CD player belted "I Saw Mama Kissing Santa Claus" while my co-workers scurried around, rearranging tables and carrying in steaming pizza boxes.

Ubi had an elf hat pulled over his massive head. "Hey, Necie! Looks like Christmas came a couple of weeks early, huh?"

"Yeah." I faked a smile. "I figured you guys would be with Angel now."

"He's in physical therapy. They kicked us out, so we thought we'd come back here for awhile and visit again tonight." He eyed another armful of pizzas coming through the door. "Hope you're hungry."

I wondered who'd sprung for it all, and that made me think of Barnes and how he'd paid my way through college when I thought I was earning it myself. I felt like I was going to be sick again.

I excused myself and headed toward the restroom. I hadn't seen Cougar yet and wondered how his meeting with Massey had gone.

When I caught a glimpse of my pale, battered

reflection in the mirror, all I could do was groan. After giving myself a moment to make sure I wasn't going to heave, I ripped a couple of paper towels out of the dispenser and scrubbed my face.

I was so jumpy that when the door swung open, I half-expected to find Maria standing there. Instead, Andrea Jacobs walked in. Her cheerful expression faded when she saw me.

"Geez, Denise. Are you okay?"

Clutching the edge of the sink, I replied, "I'd have to get better to die."

"Anything I can do?"

"Got any gum? I've got an awful taste in my mouth."

She rummaged through her purse and came up with a little silver canister. Grinning, she tossed it to me. "No gum, but here's this. It's either breath spray or Mace. I'd say either one of them will knock the taste out of your mouth."

"Ha, ha," I said, and helped myself to a shot of peppermint so strong it made my eyes water. Coughing, I handed it back to her. "I still don't know which one it was, but thanks."

She edged closer to me. "You know, I'm glad we have a chance to talk . . ." She nudged a stall door with her shoe and peered inside. ". . . alone. I know we don't really know each other that well, but I'm going to tell you this anyhow. What I'm about to say is probably none of my business, but—"

Uh-oh. When anyone began a statement with the phrase *it's probably none of my business, but*—it usually wasn't.

"I want to talk to you about Jason."

My guard went up. I knew she was Kim's best friend. "What about him?"

"You seem like a nice person, and I know you've got a lot to deal with right now. I only wanted to warn you . . ." She hesitated and took another step toward me. "Don't be fooled by that 'Aw, shucks' good ol' boy shtick. Jason is a player. He knows exactly how far that Texas charm can get him."

I couldn't keep the edge out of my voice. "And this has what, exactly, to do with me?"

"Oh, come on, Denise. He's after you. I see it, everyone sees it. He chased Kim, too, in the beginning. Then he got what he wanted and broke her heart."

Everyone sees it?

I leaned against the sink. "She seems awfully friendly with a guy who used her so badly."

Andrea sighed. "Because she's still in love with him. She pretends she isn't, that she's over him, but I know she'd take him back in a heartbeat if he'd ask her. But he's moved on to new prey."

I didn't know whether to be flattered or offended or to laugh in her face. The whole thing seemed ridiculous, and yet . . . I remembered the way he'd kissed me that night. I couldn't deny I was attracted to him, and I knew it wasn't one-sided. Something that seemed so harmless in the beginning felt so intense lately. Now that I was free, how far would he push it? How far would I let him?

Whether this was or wasn't a game to him, Cougar and I were close enough that I didn't feel comfortable having this conversation with a casual acquaintance. "Thanks for the advice," I said, and moved past her to the door. She didn't follow.

Outside, I joined Ubi and Tucker in the conference room. As we jockeyed for an empty table, someone handed me a stack of plastic plates. I counted out three and passed them on while Tucker snagged us a box of pizza. I twisted to grab some paper towels from the table behind me and turned to find a drink sitting beside my plate. Though my wonton soup had pretty much worn off, I wasn't hungry. The smell of onions and pepperoni made my stomach lurch.

"Cougar's on his way," Tucker said. "Should we wait for him?"

Ubi laughed. "Let's just save him a piece. I'm starving."

I took a sip of my drink and nearly spat it out. "What's in this?" I gasped.

"Matthews didn't have enough booze, so he cut it with antifreeze," Tucker said with a wink. He tapped his plastic cup to mine. "To justice."

"To justice," I said, and took another sip.

I picked at a slice of cheese pizza, finished my drink, and shook my head when Ubi offered to refill it. I couldn't concentrate on the conversations around me. I thought about me and Cougar and wondered if Andrea was right, that maybe the only reason he wanted me was because he hadn't had me yet. Even if that were true, was it wrong? We were adults, and I wasn't searching for another husband. If we wanted to have a fling, whose business was it? Fifteen minutes later, my thoughts were turning to obsession and I found myself watching the door. Waiting for him.

Cougar, Cougar, Cougar, I thought. *Where are you?*

Sweat trickled down my back. "Is it hot in here?" I asked Tucker. "Why is it so hot in here?"

He gave me an odd look, so I decided to wander around a bit. Five minutes later, Cougar finally walked in the door. His blue eyes scanned the room, then lit on me. He smiled, and I thought that surely I'd never seen anything so beautiful. Kim and Andrea stood by the water fountain, and I felt them watching as I hurried to him.

You're just jealous, I thought, then turned my attention back to Cougar. Suddenly, everything seemed all right. Better than all right. Fantastic. I was so happy to see him that I threw my arms around his neck and smacked a loud kiss on his cheek. "You're here! You're finally here."

The look he gave me was puzzled, though not displeased. He tweaked my nose. "Are you drunk?"

"I've only had one," I sniffed, trying to act offended, but instead I caught a whiff of his aftershave and shamelessly sniffed again.

"Pitcher or glass?"

"Ha, ha," I said, and tugged on his hand. "Dance with me."

His eyebrow lifted. "To 'Frosty the Snowman'?"

I pressed up against him and brushed my lips against his ear. "Better yet, let's go someplace private. There's something I've been wanting to tell you."

That was the last thing I remembered.

I was lost in some feverish, dark dream world in which Cougar and I were the only inhabitants. Clutching a fistful of his T-shirt in each hand, I slammed him against a wall and kissed him for all I was worth. He tensed beneath me, then kissed me back, giving as much as he took. I pulled away just long enough to yank his shirt over his head.

He breathed my name like a prayer while I rained kisses on his throat and chest. Winding his fingers in my hair, he forced my face up to meet his and delivered another crushing kiss. His body molded against mine, but it wasn't enough.

I was burning, burning, desperate for the feel of skin on skin. Planting my palms on his chest, I shoved him backward and tore off my shirt and bra. He clutched my shoulders like a drowning man and yanked me back in his arms . . .

"Wake up," someone called in the distance. "Please wake up."

I turned to see who it was, and Cougar faded away. I found myself alone in the dark.

"No," I mumbled. "No, come back."

Something icy splashed over me. Suddenly, I was lying in a frigid pool. The freezing water stabbed me like pinpricks all over my body. I tried to sit up, but something kept pushing me back down.

"Cougar!" I cried. "Where are you?"

The blood roaring in my ears drowned out all sound.

The cold gradually faded away, or else my body grew numb. Maybe I didn't even have a body anymore. I felt nothing, nothing except for a strange sense of peace and space. Was this what it was like to be dead?

Someone wiped my forehead with a cool, damp cloth. My skin felt hypersensitive, sunburned. Even the gentle strokes made me want to scream. I tried to slap the cloth away, but I couldn't lift my arms. Maybe if I moved, they would stop. I willed myself to open my eyes.

"Hey, you."

Cougar! I nearly sobbed with relief.

I couldn't hold my eyes open long enough to focus on him.

"How ya feeling?" he asked softly.

"Mmm, thirsty," I rasped.

"Hang on, and I'll get you some water."

I twisted my head in his direction. My eyes rolled like marbles in their sockets, and my jaw ached. Something cold lay against my wrist. I stared down at an IV.

"Hospital?" I croaked. "Why?"

Cougar grimaced. "This isn't a hospital. It's hell, with fluorescent lighting."

My next thought left me breathless. "Abby! I have to pick up Abby!"

I tried to sit up, but Cougar gently pushed me back down. "Shhh. Abby's okay. She's with Grady and his mother. We tried to get her, but the school wouldn't let us have her. Said we weren't on the list or whatever, but Linda called an hour ago and checked on her. She was doing her homework."

I blinked at him. "Elizabeth's out of the hospital?" With a trembling hand, I touched the growth of beard on his cheek. "How long have I been here?"

"Since yesterday." He pressed the cup to my lips. "Drink slow. They said I can't give you much at once."

I tried to obey, but the cool liquid felt like heaven on my parched throat. I drained it, and could've chugged a gallon more. "What happened to me?"

Cougar set the cup on the tray table and shifted on the mattress beside me. "What do you remember?"

I closed my eyes and tried to collect my thoughts. I remembered meeting with Barnes, but I couldn't tell him that. "Pizza. At the office. People were bringing in pizza."

"Someone slipped you something, probably in your drink. Haven't got the tox report yet, but the doctor guesses a hallucinogen like DXM or PMA."

"What? That's cra—" I broke off, remembering Maria's threat.

I can get to you anywhere, anytime.

Cougar gave me a fierce hug. "I know. In the middle of the friggin' DEA building. Nobody knows what the hell happened, but you're the only one that got it." He hesitated. His voice was distraught when he said, "Babe, I can feel your heart pounding."

Babe?

I pulled back and searched his face. Something in his eyes made my heart thump even harder. My gaze dropped to his lips.

Cougar trailed his fingertips down my cheek. I shivered when his hands lightly caught my shoulders and tugged me closer. He lowered his head. I caught the warm, cinnamon scent of Dentyne an instant before he grazed my mouth with a featherlight kiss. My lips parted beneath his, inviting him deeper, but he tormented me with another soft whisper of a kiss. His hands barely skimmed my shoulders, but they burned through the thin hospital gown. The tip of his tongue darted between my lips. This gentle assault was even more maddening than the raging passion of my dream.

His fingers tightened on my shoulders, and he pushed me away.

"Umm, no. I shouldn't do this." He stood and turned his back. "Not until I'm sure it's really you this time, not some drug."

I froze. "*This* time?" Heat flooded my face when I recalled my "dream." "Cougar, please tell me I didn't do something to embarrass myself in front of everyone."

He didn't say anything for a long moment, then he chuckled and shot me a devilish grin over his shoulder. "Not everyone. Just me, but I won't tell anybody."

"What—" I broke off as the door opened and Tucker stuck his head in.

"Hey, whaddaya know. Sleeping Beauty's awake." He walked in and nodded at Cougar. "When you get a sec, Angel wants to see you."

Cougar rubbed his face, and I realized how exhausted he looked. "Something wrong?"

Tucker smiled. "Nope, something's finally right. They're walking him around in the hallway. He's been asking for you and Necie, but we didn't tell him . . ."

"Okay." He looked at me. "I'll be right back."

"Take your time, and tell him I said hello."

Cougar surprised me by striding back to me and

kissing my cheek. Tucker's eyebrows lifted, and the corner of his mouth twitched before he covered it with his hand.

"Hey, Coug," he said. "I'll stay here. You grab something to eat before you come back."

"Not hungry." Cougar winked. "I've been taking hits off Necie's IV when she wasn't looking."

He walked out, shutting the door behind him. Tucker pulled a chair up to my bedside. "He's been here the whole time." He cleared his throat. "So . . . what do you remember?"

"That's what we were just talking about." *Before we started kissing, anyway.* "I remember the pizza, and the conference room. I remember Cougar coming in. What happened after that?"

Tucker smirked. "You mean, before or after you danced on the table?"

"I did not!"

He rolled his eyes. "Okay, so you didn't. To be honest with you, I didn't know anything was going on until Cougar started hollering that something was wrong with you. You were a little quiet while we were eating, kept saying how hot the room was, but you acted normal until Cougar showed up."

He paused, waiting for a reaction, and I said, "C'mon, Tuck. Don't do me this way. Tell me what I did."

He held up his palms. "Okay, okay. No more teasing. You just greeted him a little . . . enthusiastically. A big hug and a kiss on the cheek. Then you guys disappeared into one of the offices. Cougar came out a minute later, dragging you behind him. You were burning up and mumbling. When we got you here, your temp was 105." He frowned. "I didn't see who put the cups on our table. Neither did Ubi. People were passing them around. I don't know if it was random, or—"

"I think Maria had it done," I blurted, and his eyes widened.

"But . . . why? You can't help it if her old man waived his right to a trial. And you've left Grady."

I hesitated, wishing I could tell him the whole story. "I guess you're right. But who else? Why else?"

"What about Grady? Maybe someone he knows has access."

"Grady?"

"He's probably pretty mad about the way your lawyer handled him. Then there's Abby . . . He may not have primary custody, but he's got her right now."

"I have to get out of here. I have to go get her. Elizabeth's not well, and I don't trust him not to drink around Abby."

The door flew open. Bill and Cougar charged in.

"What's wrong?" I asked, panicked by the anxiety on their faces. "Is it Abby? Did something happen—"

They looked at each other, then looked at me.

"It's your house," Bill said. "One of your neighbors called the station looking for you. She said your house is on fire."

CHAPTER 12

"What?"

I could barely process what was happening to me. This wasn't a grudge, it was war.

Wait until I take everything.

I can get to you anywhere, anytime.

Maria's hateful words echoed in my head. I felt like screaming, but I was afraid that if I did, I wouldn't be able to stop. I yanked the IV from my wrist and swung my legs over the side of the bed.

"What are you doing?" Cougar yelled.

My head swam when a bright bead of blood swelled and trickled down my arm. Cougar pushed past Bill into the bathroom. He emerged with a fistful of paper towels. Kneeling in front of me, he pressed them to my wrist.

"Necie, there's nothing you can do. Lie back down,

and I'll—"

"No!"

He paused and stared up at me in frustration.

I struggled to speak over the lump in my throat. "Take me to my house."

"But, honey—"

I silenced him by brushing my fingers against his lips. "Jason, please."

I don't know what made me use his real name, but I could see it affected him. He looked away, and finally he nodded. "I'll get your clothes."

Bill and Tucker slipped outside while Cougar rummaged through the closet. He tossed my clothes on the bed and turned his back.

"Holler if you need help," he said with none of his usual playfulness.

Having him so close should've felt strange, considering I had no idea what had happened between us yesterday, but it didn't. My life had been turned upside down. Everything—absolutely everything—had changed, including my relationship with Cougar, but he was the only thing that felt right anymore. Part of me longed to tell him that, but I didn't know how.

The things I felt for him scared me. I tried to tell myself I could keep it under control, so long as I remembered the rules of the field I was playing on. I couldn't get hurt if I had no expectations. Cougar wasn't about commitment or marriage or kids. But still . . . all my life, there were parts of myself I'd kept guarded, and they didn't concern Barnes or Maria. Those two had "happened" to me, like a car wreck or a disease. They didn't have anything to do with who I was. Grady knew my secrets, but he never knew my soul. With Cougar, it was the opposite. Even in the beginning, I feared I couldn't love Grady enough. With Cougar, I feared I'd love him too much.

"You okay?" he asked, and I jerked my T-shirt over my head.

"Yeah. All dressed except for my shoes."

He walked over and again knelt in front of me to help. Like a kindergartner, I let him put my sneakers on.

After a five-minute argument with the head nurse, I signed myself out against medical advice. The four of us caught an elevator to the parking lot. I grasped the elevator rail to steady myself when we lurched in motion.

"Bill, how long will it take the arson investigators to move on this?" Cougar asked. "I don't want Grady to even *think* he's going to get away with it."

"Grady didn't do it," I murmured, and Tucker shot me a sharp look.

Cougar frowned. "Come on! Surely you don't think this was a coincidence?"

No, I thought. *No coincidence at all.*

"Grady's a lot of things, but he's not an arsonist," I said.

"So, he had it done." Cougar shrugged. "Same difference."

"He wouldn't do that to Abby. All her clothes, all her things . . ."

Bill squeezed my hand, but Cougar scowled. He drummed his fist against the elevator wall. "A guy like that, he thinks he can replace all that stuff. He was mad because you got Abby and you got the house. Now—"

Tucker elbowed Cougar and he fell silent.

"Now he has Abby and I have nothing," I finished softly.

"We don't know how bad the fire is," Tucker said. "Let's not assume the worst."

But it *was* the worst.

Twenty minutes later, I stood in my front lawn, staring in shock at the smoldering remains of my home. Some of the foundation still stood, a weary skeleton of exposed beams being beaten by the relentless blasts from the firefighters' hoses.

Fury roared inside me, as consuming as the flames that had devoured my house. The structure groaned and shifted. I cried out when what was left of the second story hit the ground with a thunderous crash.

Cougar's arms encircled me from behind. "It's only a house," he whispered.

I broke away from him. "No, Cougar, it's not only a house! It's my videotapes of Abby's first steps. Her baby book. It's our clothes, my pictures . . ." I twisted my hands in my hair. "One photo album . . . that's all I had left of my mother."

"I'm sorry." He squeezed my shoulder. "I didn't mean it like that. I'm just glad you and Abby are safe. It could've been worse. So much worse."

He was right, I knew, but what about next time? Would this satisfy Maria's bloodlust, or merely stoke it? I wondered if Barnes had talked to her yet, and if he could even make a difference.

"What about insurance?" I asked. "If it *is* arson, will they still pay?"

I didn't know what I'd do if they didn't.

Bill nodded. "When I lived in San Antonio, my neighbors went through something like this. They were separated, the husband torched the house. The court determined she was entitled to her half of the insurance proceeds as an innocent spouse."

"Court? How long was it tied up?" I asked.

"Two years. There was something about the policy, a clause that—"

"Two years? I can't wait two years!"

I hated the hysterical edge I heard in my voice, but I couldn't help it. Anxiety tightened my chest, and nausea burned my throat. Realizing I was on the verge of another panic attack, I started walking. To where, I wasn't sure. I just needed to move. I heard footsteps crunching behind me in the snow and knew without looking they belonged to Cougar.

I stopped in the middle of a vacant lot and stared up at the sky. "What am I going to do?" I asked brokenly.

"First, you have to calm down."

I hugged myself against the howling wind. "I'm scared of being . . . homeless."

Cougar gave a surprised laugh. "Babe, you're not going to be homeless. Even if the insurance doesn't pay, you have friends. You have a job." He paused. "You have me."

He walked up behind me and grasped my shoulders, pulling me back against him. "You and Abby can stay at my place for as long as you want. No strings. Anything I have is yours."

"I can't stay with you. The divorce—"

"Screw the divorce," he said sharply, then his voice softened. "I know you're scared, but you're not alone."

I laid my head back against his chest, and he wrapped his arms around me.

"I was homeless, once," I said. "Did I ever tell you that?"

He grew still. "No."

"I was ten. My mom hurt her back and lost her factory job. In a couple of weeks, she found another job working as a maid, but we got kicked out of our apartment building in the meantime. For a month, we lived in the backseat of our old Ford. During the day, I went to school and she worked at the hotel. It wasn't bad, except sometimes it was a hassle to sneak me into one of the empty rooms to grab a shower in the mornings. But at night, from eight to four, she worked as a waitress at a bar called Buddy's. I couldn't go in there with her, and there was no one I could stay with, so I sat in the car."

"Alone?" He sounded shocked. "A ten-year-old kid, and you spent the night alone in a bar parking lot?"

"The noises of the city scared me, the people coming and going, the sirens screaming . . . Most nights I would lie in the floorboard with a blanket over me, pretending I was somewhere else, but one afternoon, I went to sleep sitting straight up in the seat. When I woke up, Mama was gone and it was dark. I thought I heard something scratching on the driver's window, but I couldn't see anything. Then I twisted my head to look out *my* window, and found myself nose to nose with a wild-eyed, stringy-haired derelict. I screamed and crawled backward in the seat. He beat the glass between us with his filthy hands and laughed."

Cougar's arms tightened around me, and I was grateful for his warmth. This was the first time I'd allowed myself to think about that night in a long time, but the horror I'd felt never seemed to dissipate.

"He tried for the door handle, and I swear, I thought my heart would explode in terror, though I knew the door was locked. Mama always locked the doors. He yelled at me to let him in, spraying the window with tobacco juice and spit. I screamed louder. I was too scared to look at him, too scared to look away. He fumbled with his pants, and he . . . he exposed himself to me. He stood there, stroking himself while I screamed and screamed. I couldn't open the door for the policemen who took him away. I couldn't even open the door for Mama, but she had the keys."

"*Honey*," Cougar whispered. "What happened then? Did they take you away from her?"

I pulled away and glanced at him. The horror on his face shamed me. This wasn't one of the cases we'd worked. This was my life.

"Uh, no. Mama borrowed some money from her boss for the rent deposit, and we got another place. It wasn't much, but she put a whole row of locks on the door. It felt safer anyway."

He stood there, still as a statue.

I dropped my head, embarrassed. "I'm sorry. I don't know why I told you all that."

"Hey." He caught my chin and made me look at him. "You can tell me anything. I only wish . . . I only wish that had never happened to you."

The pity in his eyes made me feel a little defensive. "It was a long time ago. The point is, I swore that would never happen to my daughter."

"It won't," he said.

Tears burned my eyes. "No, it won't, but not for the same reasons. If I don't have a home, Grady and Elizabeth will take her from me. I have to find a place of my own or I'll lose my daughter. I can't lose her, Cougar. It would kill me."

"I know." He exhaled and ran a hand over his face. "We'll find you a place tomorrow. Tonight you stay with me."

He looked so tired and worried that I didn't argue. Instead, I brushed a kiss on his jaw and thanked him. He smiled and said, "Ready to go back?"

I nodded and he held out his arm. I slid in close to him. deletion Side by side, we walked back to the fire. I realized that the only time I felt safe anymore was when his arm was around me.

Bill was talking to a man in fire gear when we walked up. He motioned me over. Cougar released me and went to stand by Tucker.

Bill handed me a business card with a number scrawled on the back. "Talk to this guy tomorrow."

"He'll be in charge of the investigation," the man said.

"Do you think it was arson?" I asked.

He stared at the still-burning remains. "I'd really rather not comment until you talk to the investigator."

"Come on, Dave," Bill said. "Just give us your opinion."

He sighed. "Well, the neighbor said that she spotted the flames in the living room first, then the whole bottom floor was engulfed within minutes. Rapid lateral fire spreading could be an indication of flammable liquids. But until he gets in there and pokes around, it's anybody's guess." He nodded at me. "Miss, Bill told me you were in the hospital when this happened. I'm sorry for your loss."

"Thank you," I murmured, and looked up to see Tucker walking toward me, holding out my cell phone.

"This thing's been ringing off the hook. I hate to interrupt, but thought it might be important."

Abby, I thought, and took it from him. I flipped it open and said hello. I heard a muffled voice, but couldn't make out the words over the noise at the scene.

I plugged a finger in my other ear and said, "Hang on a sec. I can't hear you."

Excusing myself, I walked down the sidewalk until at least I got away from the sound of the other conversations. I glanced at the caller ID but didn't recognize the number.

"Okay, I'm here. Sorry about that. It's a little noisy here."

A woman laughed. "I bet! I wish I could've hung around, stayed for the show."

My fingers tightened on the phone. "Maria."

"Where will you go tonight? Not to Grady's, I bet." Her voice hardened. "Or maybe you'll go running back to Papa. I can't believe you *tattled* on me!" She gave a barking laugh, then muttered, "I can't believe he threatened me over you, after what you did to him."

I hugged myself and sighed "I'm so sick of this whole thing. Can't we call it even? I hurt you, you hurt me. Let's stop right now before one of us gets killed."

"Do you think—" she hissed, "—if it really came down to the wire . . . that he'd choose you over me?"

Fear coated my heart like a sheet of ice. As insecure as Maria was, how far would she go to find out? My mind raced as I tried desperately to reason with a sociopath.

"Of course, he wouldn't," I snapped. "He's your father, not mine. You're just like him. Obviously, he loves you more. He raised you. He doesn't even know me, and never attempted to know me until I was grown. It's too late for us. I don't want anything to do with him. You have my word, if you'll back off, you'll never have to worry about me contacting him again."

There was a long pause.

"Are you still there?" I asked.

"You swear it? You swear you will never talk to him again?"

I exhaled. That was an easy promise to make in return for my daughter's safety. "I swear."

"Because if you do, I can get to you. You cut your own throat when you had him thrown in prison. We both know he's the only thing that could protect you from me." She hesitated. "If he calls you—"

"If he calls me, I'll hang up. If he writes me letters,

I'll destroy them unopened. You don't want him out of my life any more than I do."

There was another long pause, then she said, "Fine. Good-bye, Denise."

Shaken, I held the phone for a moment even after I heard the click. Then I took a deep breath and called Elizabeth's house. Grady answered.

"Necie!" he said. "Are you okay? Where are you? I tried to call the hospital—"

"I'm standing here watching our house burn."

"What?" he said. "You're joking!"

"I've just spent the past five minutes trying to pacify that psychotic bitch you slept with, and now I'm standing here shivering on the sidewalk and watching it burn. I'm not in a joking mood."

"Necie, slow down. What are you saying?"

"What I'm saying is, it's gone. It's all gone. You'll probably be getting a visit from the arson investigator tomorrow."

"What?" Grady squeaked. "Necie, you have to believe me, I didn't—"

"I know you didn't. It was her." I massaged my throbbing temple. "I hope you have an alibi."

"I do! I was in court today, and I had a meeting with my AA sponsor and the LCL guy right after. I've only been home a few minutes."

"How's that going?" I asked.

"Ah, you know . . . I'm trying. I hope you can believe that." He cleared his throat. "But about the fire . . . how do you know it was her?"

I glanced up and found Dave and a cop staring at me. "I'll tell you later, okay? I only wanted to check on Abby—"

"She's fine. Mom's feeling better, and we're taking care of her."

"I'll start looking for an apartment tomorrow. Can you keep her for another day or two, until I find something?"

"She's my daughter, Necie. Of course, I can." Hurt tinged his voice. "Unless you don't trust me with her."

"You're a good father, Grady, when you're not drinking. I know you love her."

"I do," he said softly. "What about you? Where are you going to stay tonight? You're welcome here."

"Your mother would love that."

I heard the smile in his voice. "She would, wouldn't she? But she'd get over it. Do you need money?"

"I'm okay. But thanks for offering. Can I speak to Abby for a sec?"

"Sure, hang on."

He yelled for Abby and a moment later, she picked up the phone. "Hi, Mama."

"Hi, baby. Are you okay?"

"Yeah. Me and Grandma are making cookies. Are you still sick?"

"I'm okay. There are just some things I need to take

care of—"

"I know, work," she said, and I rolled my eyes.

Thank you, Elizabeth.

"Not work. I'll tell you all about it when I see you tomorrow, okay?"

"Okay, Mama. I love you."

"I love you, too, babe. Bye."

I hung up and went over to answer the policeman's questions. I didn't mention Maria. Now that I'd calmed down a little, I realized that a house was a small price to pay to get her out of my life forever.

Bill invited me to stay with him and his wife, and Tucker said I could stay with him, but I told them I'd crash at Cougar's tonight. We rode back to the hospital with them and retrieved his car.

Cougar had a gorgeous car, a 1964 black Camaro. Sliding into the passenger seat, I felt the first tingle of apprehension.

I was spending the night with Cougar.

I stared at him, thinking that he was one of the few men I knew who looked better when he was scruffy. I remembered the feel of his stubble against my palm and wished I had the nerve to touch it again.

He glanced at me, then snapped his gaze back. "What?" he asked warily.

"What, what?"

He made a face, and I held up my palms. "Okay. I

was thinking that the rugged look works for you."

"Yeah?" He gave me a pleased smile and rubbed his chin. "Itches, though."

I leaned over to scratch his jaw.

"Ahh. If I were a dog, my leg would be twitching right now."

I giggled and pushed his shoulder.

"I'm having a hard time deciding if I'm more tired or hungry," he said. "How about you?"

"Or dirty." I tugged a lock of my hair to my nose and sniffed. "Uggh. Smoke."

Cougar snagged a pack of Dentyne from the console. "Tell you what. Since you are the guest of honor tonight at the Casa de Cougar, I'll make you dinner while you take a nice, hot bath."

"That's sweet, but you don't have to cook. There's a Taco Bell on Fourth Street, and a McDonald's right beside it. We could—" He narrowed his eyes and I laughed. "Ex-cuse me. I forgot who I was talking to."

"Make fun of me if you want. My body can't survive on all that fast food and vending-machine crap like yours can. I was thinking soup. Good, homemade soup like Mama makes. Don't worry, there's hamburger meat in it, so you'll get your daily grease quota, but at least I'll get to slip in a few of those nasty vegetable thingies you seem so afraid of."

"Vegetable thingies . . . you mean French fries?"

He snorted, and I laid my head against the seat. "For real, you know how to make homemade soup?"

Cougar snapped his gum and drawled, "Darlin', I'm from Texas. I can do anything."

We laughed, and lapsed into an easy silence. I reached over and squeezed his hand. "Thanks for letting me stay."

He winked. "You kidding? I've dreamed about taking you home with me for years."

A month ago, a comment like that would've gone in one ear and out the other. Cougar and Angel were notorious flirts. But now I felt my ears burning hot. The space between us seemed to shrink, and I had the irrational fear that he could hear my heart pounding. What was it about him that could make me feel so comfortable one minute and so unnerved the next?

As casually as I could, I slipped my hand out of his. "Can't you drive any faster? I want that soup."

"Good things come to those who wait."

"They come faster to those who don't."

"Is that right?"

"Yeah. Ben Franklin said so." That made me think of Milano. "Oh, crap," I said, fumbling for my phone. "Bill told me to call my lawyer, and I forgot."

Milano answered the phone on the first ring. "Whoever this is, you've got three minutes!" he yelled. "I'm watching the season finale of *Smoke Jumpers*."

"Why don't you swing by my place and watch some real firefighters?"

"Necie, is that you?"

"It's me, with my latest calamity. I'll hurry. My house burned down tonight. They suspect arson. I know signing those papers made me the sole owner, but did it also make me the sole insured?"

"He burned down your house?" Milano shouted. "That miserable piece of lawyer scum!"

"No, no. He's got an alibi. It wasn't him." I ignored the look Cougar shot me. "What about the insured thing?"

"One of those papers you signed removed his name from the insurance policy. You should be getting something in the mail about it."

"Thanks, Milano. I'll let you get back to your TV show."

"It can wait. Are you okay? You weren't home at the time, were you?"

"Actually, I was in the hospital."

"Hospital!"

"It's a long story. I'll fill you in over lunch one day. But, yeah, I'm okay."

"Have you got someplace to go?"

I glanced at Cougar. "I'm staying with a friend."

"Ahhh," Milano said gleefully. "Mr. Tall, Dark, and Goo-Goo Eyes is playing hero, huh?"

I repressed the smile that twitched at my lips. "You

could say that."

"Well, you just let him, okay? I've got a hunch about that one. If I weren't a straight man, I'd marry him myself."

I laughed. "Good night, Milano."

"Good night, doll. Don't do anything I wouldn't do."

"That gives me a lot of leeway."

"Take it and run with it."

He hung up. I laughed and clicked my phone shut. "My lawyer is insane."

Cougar grunted. "He's a little too *friendly*, in my opinion."

I hid a smile, amused by the fact that he seemed jealous of Milano.

Cougar swung into a parking space. "Madame, we've arrived."

The inside of Cougar's apartment was much as I expected it to be, very neat and sparsely decorated, with an open floor plan. When we walked in the front door, I could immediately see his bedroom, living room, and kitchen. A weight bench that looked like it'd seen a lot of use sat in one corner next to a huge stereo system.

"This is nice," I said.

He tossed his keys on an end table and shrugged off his jacket. "Thanks."

It wasn't until I'd started for the shower that I realized I didn't have any clothes.

"Um, hang on a sec," Cougar said, and headed toward his closet. "My brother, Gabe, left some shorts here last time he visited. He's a little smaller than me. They might work."

He tossed me a pair of silver Cowboys drawstring shorts and a T-shirt. "That's the best I can do for now, but I'll run your things downstairs and throw them in a machine while you shower."

The thought of Cougar washing my underwear was a little unnerving, but I managed a smile. "Thanks. You're the bestest."

He winked. "Nice of you to notice. I'll wait by the door, and you can pass your things back out."

I entered the bathroom and quickly stripped down. I stuck my underwear between my shirt and jeans and cracked the door to shove them out, taking care to lean enough so Cougar couldn't see me. It was unsettling enough to see *him*.

"Hey, I'm an excellent back scrubber," he offered. "Hair washer . . . you name it."

"Don't tempt me," I muttered.

"What was that?"

"I'm more interested in the soup-maker part," I said.

He gave a dramatic sigh. "That's what I was afraid of."

Whew, this was going to be a long night. I shut the door behind me and climbed into the shower.

Thankfully, Cougar had great water pressure.

The pounding spray beat some of the tension from my shoulders. He also had more hair products than a beauty supply store, with at least four different types of shampoo and three conditioners. I, on the other hand, sometimes resorted to using lemon-scented Dawn dishwashing liquid when I'd forgotten to buy whatever shampoo was on sale at the grocery store that week.

It was amazing how being clean could make a person feel so much better. I was almost lighthearted when I stepped out of the shower and toweled off. I laughed when I tried on the shorts and T-shirt Cougar had loaned me. I looked like Abby playing dress up. Life could be cruel sometimes when you were five foot two.

The smell of fried hamburger and onions greeted me when I opened the door. An oldies station played on the radio. I found myself humming along to "If Lovin' You Is Wrong (I Don't Want to Be Right)."

Cougar had his back to me, stirring something on the stove. When I drew closer, I realized he was on the phone.

"No," he said. "Not tonight. I've got company. Necie's here."

He paused, and sprinkled salt over the skillet of meat. "It's not what you think. Her house burned down tonight. Yeah, it's gone. Nothing left. So, I told her she could stay here with me until she finds something. Abby? She's with Necie's ex."

I hesitated, feeling like I was eavesdropping, and

the awkwardness was compounded by the fact that he was talking about me. There was nowhere to go in this apartment to give him privacy except back in the bathroom. I turned to do just that when he laughed and said, "You know better than that. You're my best girl."

I froze, wondering if he was talking to Kimberly or someone I didn't know, then I cursed myself for caring. For feeling so betrayed. Men were all the same. Some were simply better liars than others.

Before I could figure out where to retreat to, Cougar spotted me. He turned his startled eyes on me and flushed bright red.

He surprised me by motioning me over. For some reason, I obeyed. He dipped a spoon in the pot of soup, then brought it to my lips.

Are you kidding me?

I simply stared at him. He frowned and lifted his eyebrows. Grudgingly, I tasted it.

It wasn't enough that he was good-looking and smart. He was a good cook, too. It wasn't fair.

"Enough salt?" he whispered, then shifted the phone. "Sorry, I was talking to Necie. Yeah." He glanced at me. "Mom says hi."

I blinked. It was my turn to be embarrassed, but Cougar didn't seem to notice. He set the spoon down and frowned, staring at something over my shoulder.

"Why?" he said suspiciously. "You're not gonna—

don't, okay? All right. Yeah. Hang on."

He pulled the phone from his ear and dropped his head. He held the phone to his chest a moment, then he sighed and gave me a beleaguered smile. "My mother wants to talk to you."

"Me?" I mouthed, and accepted the phone he thrust at me. "Mrs. Stratton, hi!"

Her Southern accent was so thick and honeyed, it took me a moment to translate what she'd said. "Necie, sweetie, I'm so sorry to hear about your house."

"T-thank you," I stammered.

"Do you have homonna's?"

Covering the receiver with my hand, I whispered, "Homonna's?" Then it dawned on me.

Homeowner's!

"Yes, I have homeowner's insurance."

Cougar's anxious expression faded, and he snickered.

"Shh!" I hissed, and tried to concentrate on what she was saying.

"What size clothes do you and Abby wear? My sista owns a consignment shop. Maybe she has some things to tide you ova until the insurance pays off."

Behind me, Cougar launched into a near-perfect *Sling Blade* imitation. "She likes the way I talk, and I like the way she talks, mmm-hmmm."

Nearly choking on my laughter, I stalked out of the kitchen. Cougar shot me a delighted grin and followed.

I plugged my finger in my ear and ran to the bathroom. "That's very sweet of you, Mrs. Stratton, but I don't want you to go to the trouble."

"Nonsense, darlin'. It's no trouble at all. I want to help." She paused. "You're important to Jason, so that makes you important to me."

A sudden lump rose in my throat. "Thank you, Mrs. Stratton," I said, and gave her our sizes.

Outside the door, Cougar said, "I like them French-fried potaters, mmm-hmmm."

Smiling, I sat on the edge of the tub and listened to Cougar's mother. She was so sweet. I liked the way she called me honey and suga and darlin'. She talked to me like we'd known each other forever, sharing funny gossip about people I didn't know and a few tidbits about Cougar's childhood. She had the same openness and friendliness that first attracted me to him. After growing up in the city, I didn't expect that from people. In Philly, we freaked out if someone spoke to us on the subway.

Cougar rapped on the door. "You can come out now. I'll stop."

I put my hand over the receiver and said, "Okay, I'll be out in a sec."

She must've heard me, because she said, "I'm sorry, baby. I didn't mean to rattle on. I imagine Jason's wanting his supper, and his daddy is, too. Keep your shorts on, Charlie," she yelled, and I laughed. "Anyway, I'm glad we had a chance to talk. Tell Jason I love him, and that Gabe and I will be up there to see him as soon as we can."

"I will. It was nice talking to you, too, Mrs. Stratton."

"You take care, hon. I'll get those clothes out to you tomorrow."

We said good-bye, and I wandered back outside. Cougar was getting a couple of bowls down from the cabinet. I walked up to him and punched his shoulder.

"You jerk," I said. "That was your mom you were making fun of."

He pointed a ladle at me. "I would never, *ever* make fun of my mother. My mother is a saint. She's put up with my jackass father for thirty years. I was making fun of *you*, Ms. Homonna." He frowned. "She hung up already?"

"Yeah. She said she loves you and that she and Gabe will visit as soon as they can."

"My mother never hangs up without telling me 'bye' a thousand times. It's a Southern thing. We tell each other 'bye' when we go check the mailbox."

"She said your dad was waiting on his supper. Speaking of which, what can I do to help?"

"You can make peanut-butter sandwiches if you want."

"With soup?"

He sighed and tossed me a jar of Skippy. "Yes, with soup. Must I teach you Yankees everything?"

While I smeared the peanut butter on a slice of

bread, he snickered and said, "You know that guy from personnel I told you about, the one whose kid played against me in high school? He came up to me that first day on the job, and said, 'Son, don't worry that you can't understand anyone. They can't understand you, either.'" He shook his head. "That became apparent when I met Angel. He talked to me for three days before I realized he was speaking English."

I laughed, and he squeezed my waist as he reached around me to open the silverware drawer.

"Seriously, my first week there, he was running around the office yelling that he couldn't find his khakis." Cougar placed a steaming bowl of soup in front of me. "I didn't know how he'd gotten separated from his pants, but I thought, *What the hell*, and helped him look. Then he grabbed this huge Red Sox key chain off the floor and said, 'Found 'em!'"

I covered my mouth with my hand and laughed so hard tears came to my eyes. Cougar grinned.

"What's really a hoot is when he and Mama get together. He was asking her about Texas once, and if they had any bay-uh down there. Meaning 'bear.' My poor, sweet mother looks at him for a moment in absolute confusion, then she winks and says, 'I won't let him keep them in the house, but you can always find a few of them in Charlie's outbuilding.'"

I was howling by this time, having picked up enough

of both Cougar and Angel-speak to see where he was going with this, but Cougar was on a roll. "Angel looks at her, dumbfounded, and says, 'Really? You keep bay-uhs in your outbuilding?' Man, I thought I was going to die. When I picked myself up off the floor, I explained to him that she thought he meant bee-ah instead of bay-uh and to her that he meant bear instead of beer. I felt like a translator at the tower of Babel."

"Please stop!" I gasped. "My sides hurt, and I'm gonna pee on myself."

"You'd better not," he said. "Your clothes are still in the machine downstairs. You'll have to run around here naked as a bay-uh."

I don't know how long I stood there, fanning my face and trying to stop laughing. We were hopeless by this point. Even after we sat down to eat, all it took was a sideways glance or a snicker to get us going again. Cougar finally turned his back to me and shoveled down a few bites of soup.

I ate two bowlfuls and half a sandwich. Cougar polished off the other half, along with another bowlful of soup.

With a contented sigh, I leaned back in the chair. "That was great. You *are* a good cook." I sighed. "How do you do it? Today has been one of the most miserable days of my life, but I feel more relaxed right now than I have in weeks. I can't remember when I've laughed so much."

Cougar gave me a crooked smile. "We've always had

something special between us, huh?"

So much for relaxed. My heart beat like a jackhammer while I stared at him. I felt like he was waiting on my reaction. What would happen if I took his hand? What would happen if I kissed him?

I wimped out. Jumping to my feet, I grabbed our bowls and carried them to the sink. I thought I heard Cougar laugh softly when I turned on the faucets. He came over to help.

"No," I said, nearly panicked by the feel of his arm brushing against mine. "You cooked. I'll get the dishes while you get a shower."

He gave me a funny look. "You okay?"

"I'm fine."

He cupped my shoulders and gave me a brief kiss on the back of the head before he walked over to his closet. "Your clothes are probably ready for the dryer now," he said. "I'll go downstairs and check."

"I'll get them. Just tell me where to go."

He grinned. "You're going downstairs like that?"

"Like what?" I glanced down at the baggy shorts. "Hey, at least they're long enough to cover my scabby knees."

He winked and said, "Just teasing. You look adorable. Laundry room's in the basement. I used the machine near the coin changer. And I brought you a couple of newspapers up. Thought you might find an apartment in the classifieds." He pointed to his stereo. "That cup over there has quarters in it. Help yourself."

"Thanks, Cougar."

He shut the bathroom door and in a few moments, I heard the water come on.

By the time he came out, I was sitting in the floor, going over the newspaper ads.

"Find anything interesting?" he asked, coming to sit on the sofa behind me.

I caught a whiff of Dove soap and dared a peek. He wore a tank top and pair of black shorts.

Be still, my Yankee heart.

"I've got a few marked."

He peered over my shoulder. Taking the pen out of my hand, he crossed off one of them. "Bad neighborhood."

"That neighborhood's okay."

He tweaked my nose. "Not good enough for you. I stopped by the manager's apartment and asked if he had anything open in this building. He said not right now, but he could put you on a waiting list. I told him to go ahead and write your name down."

He stood and walked over to the bed. I watched him pull a box from underneath it and take out a couple of extra blankets.

"I'll take the couch," he said, then gestured at the television at the foot of the bed. "Are you gonna be a few minutes? I thought I'd watch the news if you are."

"Sure," I said.

He grabbed a pillow and the remote and flopped across the foot of the bed.

Somehow, I forced my attention back to the classifieds. Twenty minutes later, I'd circled five possibilities within reasonable distance of Abby's school and my workplace, not counting the one Cougar had crossed out. I looked up to tell him so and realized he was sound asleep.

Quietly, I walked over to the bed and eased the remote from his slack fingers. I turned off the TV, then the light. Moonlight streamed through the window, bathing his face in silvery light. He looked younger. Vulnerable. No way was I going to disturb him. Since he was lying on the bedspread, I picked up one of the extra blankets he'd gotten out and covered him with it.

I looked from the queen-sized bed to the couch, debating what I was going to do. Cougar's couch didn't look very comfortable. I could imagine my skin sticking to that leather all night.

We were adults, right?

I moved the other pillow to the foot of the bed, shook out a blanket, and crawled in beside him.

The next thing I knew, sunlight streamed through the big bay window. I think I'd crashed as soon as my head touched the pillow.

Cougar was gone.

Shielding my eyes against the glare, I crawled out of bed and staggered toward the kitchen before I realized, to my dismay, that I would find no coffee in this place. What I did find was a note propped atop my neatly folded clothes, along with Cougar's car keys, two one-hundred-dollar bills and his Visa. Yawning, I sat down at the table to read.

> *Hey,*
> *Had to run by office. Didn't know what your $$ situation was, so take what you need. Here are my khakis so you won't be stranded (just don't drive my Camaro like you did Grady's Porsche). I've got my cell if you need me, but I shouldn't be long.*
> *Love,*
> *Jason*
> *P.S. There's some Folgers in the cabinet.*

I was so happy to have coffee that I tried not to wonder who he kept it there for. After gulping down a cup, I grabbed the clothes and the keys, left the cash and plastic, and got dressed to go apartment hunting.

The first office I went to was closed, since it was Saturday. It didn't look like the kind of neighborhood I wanted anyway. By the time I got back to the parking lot, three teenage boys were circling the Camaro. The ringleader, a tall blonde who could've been the poster child for the Hitler Youth, wanted to get a little friendly, but he backed off when I flashed my badge. The next three neighborhoods weren't any better, and I couldn't believe how high the rent was.

The last apartment on my list was in a decent neighborhood, and the rent was better, but the place was a disaster—peeling walls, stained carpet, and no furniture save for a scarred kitchen table.

Discouraged, I told the landlady I'd think about it, then I went to visit Abby. When I pulled up the driveway, I found her and Grady playing basketball by the garage.

He looked up, and I felt a rush of apprehension. Although the panic dissipated quickly, the strangeness of the emotion lingered. I never thought I'd fear the father of my child.

"Mama, Mama!" Abby said, and ran over to hug me.

"Hey, baby!" I kissed her cold nose and tightened the drawstring on her hood.

"Whose car is that?" Grady asked.

I smiled at Abby and forced myself to look at him. "A friend's."

He nodded. The muscle in his jaw twitched before he turned and tossed the ball at the net. It sailed through it with a *swish*.

Abby tugged me toward the house. "Mama, come on, you've got to see my new room."

"New room?" I asked, staring at Grady.

He refused to meet my eyes.

A sudden chill raced through me, and it had nothing

to do with the cold December wind. I'd dismissed the idea that Grady was responsible for the fire even before I'd gotten Maria's phone call, but what if he'd known about it? Was he still seeing Maria—maybe still under her influence? He'd taken this all pretty calmly, considering many of his things had been destroyed, too.

"Abby, honey, why don't you run on up to your room, and Mama will be right behind you. I need to talk to Daddy for a minute."

"Okay, Mama," she said, and ran toward the house.

Grady exhaled and violently dribbled the ball against the asphalt. "Don't make a federal case out of this."

I crossed my arms. "I was just thinking it was pretty convenient. A new room already, the day after our house burns down."

Abruptly, Grady slammed the ball against the garage door. I flinched at the metallic clang. He took a step toward me, and I jerked backward, nearly falling into the hedge that bordered the drive. "Don't!" I yelled, angered as much by my fear as from his reaction.

For an instant, he froze. Surprise chased the fierce expression from his face, and he slowly lifted his palms. "I wasn't . . . I . . ."

Grady cursed softly and turned his back. For at least a minute, I watched his shoulders move up and down, and the soft white clouds of his breath rise.

Finally, he looked at me. In a calm voice, he said,

"Convenient? What are you trying to say, Necie? I thought you believed me."

"Tell me you're not still seeing her, Grady. Tell me you didn't know it was going to happen."

Hurt contorted his face. "I already told you it's over with her. It was nothing. A mistake that cost me a million times what it was worth. And as for your second question, I resent like hell that you could even ask me that. The room was Mom's idea. She started on it before the fire, when you kicked me out. Said that since Abby would be spending half her time here, she needed a room that was really her own, not a guest room. You know how she is with Abby."

He rubbed his eyes with the heels of his hands. "I hate this. I hate that you're scared of me now, that you're so suspicious of me, and I don't know how to make it better." He looked me in the eye and pointed at the house. "If you never believe anything else I say to you, believe this: I love that kid in there. I'd never hurt her. Not to get back at you, not to have her to myself."

My vision blurred, and I swiped at the corner of my eye. "I know you love her. I also know you think I'm a rotten mother. Maybe you think she'd be better off without me."

"Shh, Necie, no," he said, and walked over to me. Before I could protest, he wrapped his arms around me and hugged me tight. "You're not a rotten mother.

I'm sorry for the things I've said and done to hurt you, especially where Abby is concerned."

Footsteps clicked on the walkway. I pulled away from Grady and found myself face-to-face with Elizabeth. "What's going on?" she asked. Her voice was pleasant, but the ice in her eyes betrayed her true feelings.

"Nothing, Mom." Grady took my hand and pulled me toward the house. "We were coming inside. Abby wants to show off her room."

"I see." Elizabeth caught my sleeve. "I want you to know, Denise, that we'll take good care of Abby until you get back on your feet."

"Thank you," I murmured, and let Grady lead me to the house.

Even though I was well acquainted with Elizabeth's extravagant taste, the sight of Abby's new bedroom stunned me. It was a room fit for a princess, with pale ivory satin on the walls, a bed with a gossamer canopy and plush baby pink carpet. A white play castle with pink turrets occupied a full quarter of the enormous room. Although it had been many years since I'd been upstairs in Elizabeth's house, I didn't remember any rooms this large. She must've had a wall knocked out and joined two rooms together. My unease was back. I knew my mother-in-law, and I saw what she was trying to do. Taking a deep breath, I tried to calm myself. Abby ran past me and flung herself on the bed.

"Isn't it *beautiful?*" she exclaimed.

"Yes, it is," I managed.

Grady rubbed the small of my back, and I walked away from him, toward Abby. Over my shoulder, I said, "If you don't mind, I'd like a few minutes with Abby."

"Sure," he said, and I heard the click of the bedroom door when he exited.

I sat on the bed beside Abby and swept her up in a fierce hug. "Oooh, I've missed you, Tink!"

She giggled at the old nickname and smacked a kiss on my nose. "I've missed you, too, Mama. And Ralph."

I winced. Ralph was a fat purple bunny Grady had won for her at last year's fall festival. A pang went through me when I remembered how Grady and I had laughed when she'd christened him with the unlikely name, and how she'd carried the ugly, cross-eyed toy everywhere for the next month before he took up permanent residence on her bed.

Old Ralph was gone for good.

Gently, I told her about the fire, and of how I was trying to find us a new place to live. Abby's eyes darkened, and she bit her lower lip. Her next question caught me off guard. "But how will Santa find me now?"

I blinked. My mind whirred, trying to pinpoint the day of the month. With everything that was going on, I was doing good to know what day of the week it was. Monday had been the eighteenth, so today was . . . I paused, counting on my fingers.

Oh, God, today was the twenty-third. Tomorrow was Christmas Eve, and all the presents I'd had stored in the attic for Abby had been cremated along with Ralph. Although I knew Abby wasn't lacking for anything, it made me sick to my stomach to realize I didn't have anything to give her for Christmas.

"He won't find me, will he?"

"Of course, he will," I said, wondering how I was going to make that happen and pay first and last month's rent on an apartment, too. I hadn't worked much in the past week, so my next paycheck would be nonexistent. Maybe Cougar would let me stay with him for a couple of weeks, until . . . but that would mean I wouldn't get to spend Christmas with my daughter, and that wasn't going to happen. I was too proud to accept money from either Grady or Cougar, though they'd both offered. Bleakness settled over me like a heavy blanket. What was I going to do?

"Guess what Grandma's buying me? A portrait doll! She said it will look just like me. And a DVD player for my room, and . . ."

Abby rattled off a list of promises from Elizabeth, and I felt a little disgusted with myself. The last thing Abby needed was more presents, but that didn't keep me from wanting to give them to her. There was just no way I could keep up with the Bramhalls.

We played for about an hour, then I told Abby I had to go. I kissed her, promised to be back soon, and headed for the door. From the top of the stairs, I saw Grady and Elizabeth in the living room, their blond heads bent in conversation. They looked up at the same time, and I felt a rush of resentment that made me feel petty and mean-spirited. Grady stood.

"I've got to go," I said. "I'll be back to get her as soon as I get in my new place. I'm going to put a deposit down today."

"Today!" Elizabeth blanched. "You mean you've found something already?"

"Yeah." I shifted, thinking of the run-down apartment I'd last visited. Maybe Abby was better off with them, after all. But no, I told myself, money didn't mean everything. I was her mother and we'd get by. I thought of my mother and the sacrifices she'd made. I didn't know if that made me feel better or worse, but I suddenly felt closer to her than I had in years.

"But surely you'll let her spend Christmas here, won't you? The family's coming, and we're having a big dinner."

I rubbed my forehead. I didn't even know if I'd have a refrigerator by then, much less anything to put inside it. I wasn't so selfish that I could deprive my daughter of a happy holiday. "Sure. Abby can spend Christmas Day here."

"You're invited, too," Grady said. We both ignored

the poisonous look Elizabeth shot him.

"Thanks, but I have plans," I lied. "But look, I want her with me on Christmas Eve."

"Sure, that's fair," Grady said quickly. He crossed the room and touched my elbow. "I'll walk you to the car. There's something I want to talk to you about."

I tensed, figuring whatever he wanted to say couldn't possibly be a good thing, but Grady surprised me. When we stepped out on the porch, he said, "I got the tickets in the mail yesterday. I wondered what you wanted me to do with them."

"Tickets?"

"*Mickey on Ice*, remember?"

That was so out of left field it startled a laugh out of me. We'd ordered those tickets a lifetime ago, before Angel had been shot, Barnes had been arrested, and my world had been turned upside down.

The tension between us evaporated, and I slouched against my car. "When is it?"

"The twenty-ninth."

"Well, it was your idea. You should go with her."

Grady shrugged. "I was hoping we both could go." He raised his hands, cutting off my protest. "You don't have to say it, I know we're over. This isn't some evil ploy to win you back." He paused. "I was thinking of Abby. She really wants you to go, and I really want you to . . . not hate me."

"I don't hate you, Grady."

His green eyes were clear and serious. "You have every reason to, but I don't want us to be like that, for Abby's sake." He laughed and glanced up at the gray sky. "This sounds so cliché, but I want us to be friends."

"I want that, too."

"So, you'll go? I'll even let you drive."

A smile twitched at my lips. "Talked me into it. The twenty-ninth . . . what time?"

"I figured we'd leave around five, grab something to eat on the way. Is that okay with you?"

I agreed, but while backing out of the drive, I wondered if I was the dumbest woman walking the planet.

Cougar called while I was signing the papers on my new place, so I invited him over to check it out. He met me in the parking lot, and we walked up together. From the look on his face when he walked through the door, he was less than impressed.

"It's . . . ah . . ." He rubbed the back of his neck and squinted. ". . . something."

I laughed. "So don't hold back or anything."

His smile faded. "Are you sure about this? You're welcome to stay with me as long as you like. Ubi lives alone, right? Maybe I could bunk with him a couple weeks—"

"Cougar, I am *not* booting you out of your own apartment."

"—or you could stay with Mrs. Angelino and Tori . . ."

I folded my arms over my chest. "This place will do. It only needs a little fixing up."

He grunted. "Well, we'd better get started then. I need to run home and grab a few things. Be right back."

We traded cars, and I drove down the block to Walgreens to buy cleaning supplies. I was scrubbing the kitchen floor when Cougar returned forty minutes later.

He brought reinforcements.

Ubi, Tucker, Kimberly, Bill . . . I watched in amazement as half the field office filed in the door. They carried paintbrushes, boxes, and even a carpet shampooer.

"Cougar, what—"

He tugged my ponytail. "Don't be mad. Everyone wants to help, so I thought we'd make a party of it." He winked. "I promised pizza and beer for slave labor."

I think the other half of the office workers drifted in and out during the next hour. Oddly enough, Cougar, Kim, and I ended up working together in the kitchen. I scrubbed the floor, she worked on the caked-on crud on the stove hood, and we both snuck glances at Cougar, who looked all sweaty and perfect while he struggled to mend a sagging cabinet.

"Man, I'm dyin' in here," he muttered, and yelled to the living room, "Hey, Tuck, turn on the AC!"

He pulled off his T-shirt and tossed it on the counter. Kim and I looked at him, then looked at each other. She grinned and I nearly laughed. I knew what she was thinking, because I was thinking it, too. She fluttered her hand in front of her face and I winked.

A blond guy I barely knew from the payroll department stuck his head in the doorway. "Hey, Coug. I can't stay. My kid's got a ballet recital, but I brought that couch I told you about. Can you help me unload it?"

"Sure." Cougar hopped down from his perch on the counter and grabbed his shirt. He rolled it up and snapped it at Kim before yanking it back on.

"Hey!" she said, while I thanked the payroll guy.

"No problem," he said. "It's kind of old, but it'll do you until the insurance comes through."

After they left, I glanced at Kim and said, "Yay, I have a couch!"

She raised one perfect eyebrow. "Honey, you have a lot more than a couch. Jason's very efficient. He called around, got other people to calling around. . . I'd say you'll have enough furniture to fill this place with. Not to mention clothes."

I didn't know what to say. I was touched, and maybe a little embarrassed. Unlike Blanche DuBois, I wasn't used to depending upon the kindness of strangers.

"Thank you for coming today, Kim."

She smiled, wrinkling her perfect nose. "Don't mention it. A favor for a friend."

We both knew which friend she was talking about.

Her sociable expression faded, and she tossed the

S.O.S pad she was using into a trash bag. Stripping off her gloves, she approached me. "Necie, I need to talk to you about something."

I stopped scrubbing. "Go ahead."

She glanced toward the doorway. "I don't want Jason to know."

Wiping my hands on my thighs, I stood. "You'd better hurry then."

"It's about the night you were drugged. I feel so bad about what ha—"

She broke off when Tucker entered the kitchen. "Bedroom's looking good," he said, moving toward the sink to refill his water bottle. "Though I'm getting high off paint fumes."

Ubi chased a giggling Linda through the door, threatening her with a paint-spattered rag.

"We'll talk later," Kim whispered. "Too many people."

"No, wait!" I said, but she edged past Bill toward the living room.

I started after her, but Bill intercepted me. "Hey, I pulled a few strings. The fire investigator I know . . . he says he'll give your case top priority. Did you ever talk to your lawyer?"

"Yeah, Milano's on it. He said he'd fixed all the stuff about switching over the insurance."

"Good." Bill wrapped an arm around my shoulder. "You know if you need anything in the meantime, all you have to do is ask, right?"

I hugged him. "I know."

He handed me an envelope. "And because I know you won't ask . . ."

"Bill, I can't take money from you."

"I knew you'd say that, too. So it's not a gift."

"No loans, either."

"Not a loan. Well, not from me, anyway. An advancement on wages. Twenty bucks a week will be held out of your check until it's paid back." He winked. "So, you don't owe your Uncle Bill, you owe your Uncle Sam."

Rolling my eyes, I took the envelope. "You're so sneaky."

"Have to be, because you're so hardheaded."

"Pizza!" someone yelled from the other room.

After washing up in the kitchen sink, Bill and I wandered into the living room, where paper towels and pizza boxes were being passed around.

Cougar sat on the floor, propped against my new couch. He scooted down to make room for us. He handed me a bottled water and offered one to Bill, who declined it and snagged a beer from the cooler instead.

"Where's Kim?" I asked.

"She had to go."

Damn. What did she know about the night I was drugged that she didn't want anyone to hear? So much had happened since then that I hadn't had time to think about it much. She said she was sorry. Could she have been responsible? Or her friend Andrea? Maybe they'd only wanted me to look bad in front of Cougar, and things had gone too far. But that seemed a little far-fetched—and paranoid. It was hardly worth risking their jobs over. But I couldn't stop thinking about it, and that stupid breath spray Andrea had given me.

The afternoon passed quickly. When I opened the door to show Tucker out, I was surprised to find it dark outside. "Wow. Time flies when you're having fun."

He lifted his eyebrows and smiled. "Is *that* what that was?"

I punched his shoulder lightly. "Be careful, Tuck, and thanks for everything. Tell Anne Marie I appreciate the clothes."

"Will do."

I stepped back inside and shut the door. Once again, I found myself alone with Cougar.

"So . . ." He perched on the couch arm. "You going home with me or what?" Shooting me a wicked grin, he said, "I swear I won't go to sleep on you this time."

"Ha! That's what I'm afraid of."

His smile flickered. "You know I'm teasing, right? When I said no strings, I meant it." He held up two fingers. "Scout's honor."

"Like *you* were ever a Boy Scout," I scoffed, but it was too late. We'd flipped the switch again, and the sudden silence felt thick. Oppressive.

Tension coiled in the pit of my stomach. Desperate to regain our light mood, I joked, "You're not the one I'm worried about."

Cougar's smile reappeared. I sucked in a breath when he approached.

"Is that so?" he said, and touched my hair.

I swallowed hard and forced a smile. "I don't do so good with temptation."

"You want to talk about temptation?" he murmured. "Temptation was waking up to find you beside me this morning." He idly twisted a lock of my hair around his finger. "You looked so beautiful, with your hair fanned out on my pillow. I wanted more than anything to kiss you."

His hand slipped to my throat, and I wondered what he thought about the pulse hammering beneath his fingers. I shivered when he stroked my bottom lip with his thumb.

"Would it be such a bad thing . . ." he asked softly, ". . . you and me?"

It would be a dangerous thing, I almost said.

His mouth lingered close to mine, and part of me actually ached to kiss him again, though I knew I should turn and run like hell.

His cell phone jingled to life. Saved by Big and Rich.

Cougar knew what I was thinking, because he laughed and said, "You're gonna have to answer that question sooner or later."

He flipped open the phone. I attempted to duck

under his arm, but he stopped me with a hand on my waist. We stood as close as lovers while he answered.

"Oh, hey, Bill," he said. "What's going on?"

I didn't protest when Cougar hooked his finger in my belt loop and tugged me even closer. I rested my head against his chest while he talked.

"What? Oh, yeah. Sure."

His fingers gently kneaded my back. It should've felt awkward standing there like that, but I felt safe. Lulled.

"I'm glad you reminded me. No, not a problem. I'd just forgotten, with everything else going on. I'll be there."

He clicked the phone shut and shoved it in his back pocket. Then he pushed my hair aside and kissed my throat.

"Please come home with me." The vibration from his whisper caused goose bumps to break out on my arms.

I think I tried to protest when he nuzzled my ear, but it was negated by the way I clutched his shoulders and tugged him closer. The only real protest I managed was when he pulled away.

He frowned and dug his phone from his pocket to check the caller ID. Dimly, I heard his ring tone over my roaring pulse.

"I need to take this," he said, and turned his back. "Hey, Kim. What's up?"

My face felt hot as I ran my hands over it, trying to regain some semblance of composure. Even though Kim's call had saved me from making a big mistake, I couldn't help feeling resentful of her interruption. The fact that Cougar didn't seem to want me to hear this conversation upset me even more. He'd moved clear across the living room.

"That's great!" he was saying. "You're a doll. So, when—"

He paused, and I wondered again what she'd wanted to talk with me about. Maybe she'd simply wanted to tell me "hands off."

"Tonight?" He cast a frowning look over his shoulder at me. "Can't we do it tomorrow?" He sighed. "Okay. Yeah, I understand. I'm on my way."

Bitter disappointment filled me when he disconnected and crossed back over.

"I have to go," he said, and reached for me.

Pretending I didn't notice his outstretched hands, I moved past him to grab his jacket from where it lay on the bookcase. Without looking, I tossed it over my shoulder to him. "See you later."

"That was Kim. I—"

"No explanations necessary." I plastered on a smile and faced him. "Just be careful out there. The roads are probably a mess."

His brow knitted. "Are you sure you don't want to go home and wait for me? I shouldn't be long."

"No, thanks."

He slid into his jacket and adjusted the collar.

"You're mad."

"Nope."

And I wasn't, really. I simply felt like I was getting too old for this junior-high tug-of-war stuff with Kim. Being with Cougar would be complicated, and my life was complicated enough right now.

He caught my hands in his, and I grudgingly looked up at him. The earnestness in his eyes threatened my resolve. "This is really, really important," he said. "But like I said, it shouldn't take long." He paused. "If you don't want to go to my place, I could come back here."

"I'm kinda tired," I said, but inside I was thinking, *Kiss me. Convince me.* But he simply squeezed my hands. "Okay."

I walked him to the door and hugged myself against the blast of frigid air when he opened it. "Be careful," I said again.

He nodded and turned to walk away. More than a little disappointed, I grasped the doorknob.

Before I could close the door, Cougar shouldered his way back inside and seized me in his arms. He kissed me so hard my knees buckled.

When he released me, I had to grab the edge of the bookcase to keep from falling. He winked as we both tried to catch our breath. "I don't do so good with temptation, either, and I've been dying to do that all day."

I didn't know what to say, so I merely stared. Kissed

senseless.

"I'll call you tomorrow."

With a massive effort, I made my head nod.

"Good night," he said, and I gave a little wave.

When he shut the door behind him, I wobbled over to lock it. My lips still tingled from his kiss. Touching my fingers to them, I realized I was grinning like an idiot. I giggled, then giggled some more.

Mercy, what was I getting myself into?

I got up early the next morning to do some shopping before time to pick up Abby. Two hours later, I had a trunk load of *things*, but nothing I was happy with. I couldn't outbuy Elizabeth, and it griped me that I felt like I had to try.

The morning didn't get any better. Elizabeth all but bared her teeth at me when I buckled Abby into the car, and then there was Abby's less-than-enthusiastic reaction to the apartment . . .

"I hate this place," she said without preamble. "I don't want to live here."

"We won't have to live here long," I said. "Just until the insurance company sends us a check."

"I want to live with Grandma. I miss my room."

"You've got a new room here. We'll fix it up, however you like."

Her little Bramhall nose turned up a fraction of an inch. "I won't stay here. I want to call my daddy."

Things deteriorated from there. We argued, and before I knew it, Abby was sobbing in her room and I was on the sofa, fighting back tears of my own.

Merry Christmas and Happy New Year.

My cell phone rang. I dug it out of my purse and checked the caller ID. Flipping it open, I said, "Hey, Cougar."

"Hey. What's going on?"

"Fighting with Abby."

"About what?"

"She hates the apartment. She hates her room." My voice cracked. "She hates me . . ."

"Hey!" he said softly. "She doesn't hate you. It's a big adjustment for her, but she'll get used to it."

"I yelled at her, Cougar. It's Christmas Eve, and I yelled at her. But when she opened her mouth, all I could hear was my mother-in-law talking. I don't want my daughter to be like that. I won't raise a spoiled brat."

He fell silent, and I laughed. "Sorry, didn't mean to unload on you. I bet you'll think twice before calling *me* next time."

"If you can't talk to me, who can you talk to? But that brings me to the reason I called . . . I'm supposed to deliver our Angel Tree presents to the shelter today, and I wondered if you and Abby would like to come along."

"Ah, I don't know. We might not be the best company."

"C'mon. It might be just what Abby needs, to see

that there are others less fortunate than she is."

I glanced at her closed door. "Maybe you're right."

"Of course, I am. Pick you up in an hour?"

"That depends. You dressing up as Santa?"

"Uh . . . no."

"Shoot."

He laughed. "Well, if it means that much to you . . . I'll let you sit on my lap later and tell me what you want for Christmas."

"It wouldn't be the same without the red suit and beard."

"All these years, and I never guessed you had a thing for old, fat guys. No wonder none of my pickup lines worked."

"Your pickup lines suck. Your problem is that you're too good-looking. You've never had to work at it."

He snorted. "As insightful as all this is, I've gotta run. I have a couple of stops to make before I pick you up."

I was smiling when I hung up. Feeling a little more hopeful already, I knocked on Abby's door. When she didn't respond, I went in anyway.

"Hey, baby. You remember my friend Jason? He—"

"No," she said sullenly.

"You know, he went to Fat Daddy's with us."

"You mean Cougar."

"Yeah, sorry. His real name is Jason. Anyway, he's delivering presents to some people today, and he wants us to come with him."

Her eyes lit up. "Are any of the presents mine?"

"No. They're for kids who don't have a home."

She crossed her arms over her chest. "Well, *I* don't have a home."

I did a ten-count, then pasted on a smile. "Get cleaned up, okay? He's coming by to get us."

Surprisingly, she did what I asked and even came into the living room to wait with me.

Cougar arrived ten minutes early in one of the raid vans. We met him in the parking lot.

"Hey, ladies," he said, and gave me a look that made my face heat when I thought about the kiss we'd shared the night before.

He helped Abby into the back and fastened her seat belt.

"I hope you don't regret this," I whispered when I climbed inside.

But I found my tension loosening almost as soon as we were on our way. Cougar and Abby joked and chatted. She seemed like a different kid from the surly one I'd spent the morning with.

At the shelter, Abby immediately took up with a little blond girl named Kaylee. They played together while Cougar and I handed out presents, though Abby insisted on giving Kaylee hers.

Abby walked over to me as Kaylee ripped the bright wrapping paper from her gift. "Okay, Mama," she said. "Give me the rest of hers."

Cougar and I glanced at each other, then I squatted beside Abby. "Sorry, baby. That's it."

"Oh," she said, and looked over her shoulder at her new friend. Resting her head on my shoulder, she said, "Do you think we can bring her back something? One of my presents?"

"I think that would be nice," I said, and kissed her forehead.

Abby smiled and ran back to Kaylee.

"You're a genius," I told Cougar, and he squeezed my shoulder.

"Hey, what are you and Abby doing this evening? I don't want to intrude, but if you didn't have anything going on, I had another idea."

I thought about how lonely he'd seemed at Thanksgiving, and didn't think Abby would mind if we shared our Christmas Eve.

I smiled. "No plans. What do you have in mind?"

"An old-fashioned Christmas," he said with a wink. "Let's get out of here and find ourselves a tree."

When Abby scrambled back into the van, she said, "Hey, you left two boxes in here."

"I know," Cougar said. "Those are for us. No peeking."

We stopped at the deli on the corner to buy ham, potato salad, and bread, then drove nearly forty minutes out of town to a Christmas tree farm. Abby had never had a real tree before, and she clapped her hands in delight when Cougar told her to pick one out.

"Before I get the environmental lecture . . ." He draped an arm around my shoulder and pointed across the yard at the proprietor, who was busy helping a couple of other last-minute customers. "That guy recycles. I just have to bring it back here when we're done. They make mulch and stuff out of them."

"Okay," I said. "But I don't have any decorations."

"You let me handle that."

Back at the apartment, Cougar wrestled the fat tree through the door while Abby and I carried the boxes and groceries in. After we got the tree upright in front of the window, I left them prowling through the boxes while I went to make sandwiches.

Upon reentering the living room, I gaped at the odd assortment of supplies spread across the living room floor. "What are you doing?" I asked.

Cougar smiled up at me. "We're going to make our own decorations. I promise, I'll clean up the mess. Mama never bought any of that stuff at the store, except for lights."

He seemed as excited as Abby, and that was saying something. They devoured their food in record time. Cougar was showing Abby how to cut snowflakes out of typing paper before I was even halfway finished with my sandwich.

I stood and brushed my hands on my pants. "What can I do?"

Cougar reached into the box and tossed me a couple

of packs of microwave popcorn. "Would you?"

"Sure."

By the time I returned with the popcorn, Cougar was helping Abby glue sequin eyes on cut-out gingerbread men. I sat on the floor beside him and munched a handful of popcorn.

Cougar nodded at the box. "Mom sent a package of peanut-butter candy and fudge."

"Oooh, I love your mother!" I set the popcorn aside and dug the Christmas tin out of the box. Jerking the lid off, I inhaled deeply. "Oh, man . . ."

I abandoned the popcorn while we still had enough to string and stuffed my face with chocolate. We spent the afternoon laughing, eating, and decorating. Cotton-ball snowmen, toothpick-and-pipe-cleaner reindeer. . .I couldn't believe all the things Cougar could make out of *nothing*. I was seeing a whole new side of him, and Abby seemed as dazzled and charmed as I was.

"Ta da!" Cougar yelled.

Abby and I clapped when he plugged in the lights.

"We've never had a more beautiful tree," I said.

The dingy little apartment suddenly seemed like a home. It even smelled like one. Pine, chocolate, Elmer's glue . . . the occasional whiff of Cougar's cologne.

"Now what, Martha Stewart?" I asked while Cougar swept the floor.

He mimed swatting me with the broom. "Now we

color. Wanna color, Abby?"

"Yes!"

"I'm going to fix hot chocolate," I said, while he pulled a stack of Christmas coloring books out of the box.

In the kitchen, I smiled and hugged myself. I couldn't remember the last time I'd felt so content. It was scary to feel optimistic about anything, but I couldn't help it. I didn't want to help it.

I stirred the chocolate in the cups, then wandered back to the living room. "Now, be careful," I said. "It's—"

"Shhhh," Cougar said.

I glanced at him and he winked. Abby's cheek lay on her coloring page, a red crayon dangling from her fingers. She was fast asleep.

"Oh!" I said with a laugh.

"One minute she was talking, the next . . . she just fell over." He shrugged and pushed himself up. "Want me to carry her to her room?"

"Yeah."

Abby mumbled, but didn't wake when he lifted her. I ran ahead of them to turn down her blankets.

"She's a doll," Cougar said, and gently brushed a kiss on her forehead.

I pulled the blankets up under her chin and did the same.

He wrapped his arm around my shoulders, and I leaned into him. Like an old married couple, we walked back to the living room.

I looked at the tree, then smiled up at him. "You are just full of surprises, aren't you?"

"Got one more."

He pulled away from me and reached into the box to pull out two presents. One bore Abby's name in bold letters, the other mine. He put it in my hands.

"Oh, Cougar. You really shouldn't have. I didn't—"

He silenced me with a finger to my lips. "Open it."

I tore back the paper to reveal a slim ivory photo album. A lump rose in my throat when I thought about what I'd said to him the night of the fire, and that he'd remembered.

"It's beautiful," I whispered. "I can't wait to fill it with new memories."

He smiled. "We'll have to get you another one for that. This one's already full."

I stared at him, then flipped open the first page. An eight-by-ten of my mother stared back at me. I gasped. "Wh-how did you get this?"

He rubbed the back of his neck and gave me a rueful grin. "That was the Kim favor from last night. She's got a friend who works with the DMV. That's an old license photo that we blew up."

A tear slipped down my cheek, followed by another. I swiped them away with the back of my hand and kept flipping. Pictures of Abby filled the pages.

"I got most of those from Bill, but we all had a few.

I spent half the night at the CVS making copies."

The back section was filled with pictures of our team. With a shaking hand, I touched one of me sandwiched between Cougar and Angel at last year's New Year's Eve party.

I snapped the book shut harder than I intended to and threw myself into Cougar's arms, hugging him fiercely. "Thank you!"

He hugged me back, then tilted my chin up and wiped away my tears.

"I didn't mean to make you cry."

"I'm sorry. It's the best present I've ever gotten. I just feel guilty, because I don't have anything to give you."

"You've given me today," he said quietly. "This is the first time I've felt at home in ten years."

Wrapping my arms around his neck, I tugged him to me and kissed him. His arms closed around my waist, pulling me up tight against him as the kiss deepened.

This kiss was different. I felt more than just the terrifying passion of our other kisses. When he held me in his arms like that, I felt I belonged there.

I backed him to the couch, and he sat down, pulling me into his lap.

"You're so beautiful," he whispered, pushing a wave of hair from my face. "With the Christmas lights dancing on your face."

Then he enveloped me in another hungry kiss.

So intoxicated by everything I was feeling for him, I didn't hear Abby until she called out my name.

Mortified, I scrambled out of Cougar's lap. "Honey, I—what are you doing up?"

I ran a hand over my disheveled hair. "Um, why don't you go get a drink of water, and I'll be right there to tuck you back in."

She nodded and shuffled toward the bathroom. I glanced at Cougar. He looked embarrassed.

"Sorry," he said. "I'll go so you can take care of her."

He retrieved his jacket, and I walked him to the door.

"Hey." He took my hands in his, looking as reluctant to leave as I was to let him. "Abby's going to her grandmother's tomorrow, right? If you don't have plans, give me a call. I'll either be at the apartment or at the hospital. I'll take you out to eat."

"Okay." I straightened his collar and pressed a soft kiss to the corner of his mouth.

He smiled and stepped outside. Even though it was bitterly cold, I stood in the doorway for a moment, simply watching him. From the bottom of the stairwell, he glanced up and waved. I waved back and shut the door.

After locking it and unplugging the Christmas tree, I went to Abby's room and crawled in bed beside her. She scooted to make room for me, then snuggled back against my chest. I didn't know if I should try to explain, or keep my mouth shut. Silence was easier. I closed my eyes and slipped into a drowsy daydream about Cougar.

"Mama, are you going to marry Jason?"

Abby's soft question jarred me like a scream, and for a moment, I simply froze.

"It's okay if you do," she said with a yawn. "I like him a lot."

Instead of making me feel better, her statement troubled me. My "making out in front of the Christmas tree" daydream vanished. I tried to imagine Cougar taking out the trash, taking Abby to ballet practice, and all the other little, mundane husbandly tasks Grady had performed, and I just couldn't. It didn't fit.

Who was I kidding? Cougar and I weren't working on forever. Deep down, I knew that. I'd seen him go through enough women to know I wasn't anything special. I knew he cared for me, but he cared for Kim, too. Our friendship might sustain, but the thrill was in the chase. How long would it be before the novelty wore off and he needed someone new to spark his passion? I had wrestled with this so many times, and had even come to accept it, but Abby's simple question sent me into a tailspin. I could take the chance of his breaking my heart, but not his breaking hers.

I had to call things off before she got too attached to him.

CHAPTER 13

The next morning, Abby opened her gifts and we played with her new toys on the living room floor. She was most impressed with the Barbie Salon. I felt a burden lift off me while I watched her laboriously styling her dolls' hair. I couldn't match Elizabeth's spending, but apparently I still knew what interested my daughter.

Around noon, I took Abby to her father. I kissed her good-bye and declined Grady's invitation to stay for Christmas dinner. I needed to call Cougar, but I didn't have the guts. Instead, I drove aimlessly around the city for the next two hours, wondering how I was going to handle it.

Finally, I pulled into a parking lot and took out my phone. Maybe his phone would be off since he was at the hospital. I breathed a sigh of relief when I got his voice mail, and left a slightly incoherent message that I couldn't make it today and I'd catch up with him tomorrow at work. I contemplated turning off my phone, but then I worried that Abby might need me. If he called back, I just wouldn't answer.

Dammit. Being a coward sucked . . .

My temporary reprieve was extended when, due to a case he was working on, I didn't see Cougar for the next couple of days. Finally, he caught up with me in the break room at work.

"Hey, stranger!" He looked worried as he leaned against the gray locker beside mine. "You avoiding me or something?"

I swallowed over the lump in my throat and forced a smile. "Of course not."

He favored me with a killer grin. "Good, because I've missed you like crazy. What are you doing tonight? I thought I'd take you and Abby out to eat. Maybe I'll survive another trip to Fat Daddy's—"

"Girl Scout meeting."

"Oh." He looked disappointed. "What about to-morrow, then?"

I shut my locker. "*Mickey on Ice.*"

"No worse than that damn eagle at Fat Daddy's, I guess. Have I got time to pick up a ticket?"

I made myself look at him. "Actually, Grady's going, too."

His smile faltered. "What?"

"We bought the tickets a long time ago. Abby wants him to go."

His smile died completely, chased away by his scowl. Then he laughed, a short, dry bark. When he spoke, there was an edge to his voice. "You're kidding me, right?"

Andrea Jacobs was coming through the doorway, and I didn't want her to overhear. I headed for the elevator, and Cougar chased after me.

"After what he did to you, you're seriously going out with him?"

"No, I'm going with Abby. So is he. We're not *together*."

He caught my shoulder and spun me around. "You're riding together? Sitting together?"

Reluctantly, I nodded.

"Sure sounds like *together* to me."

People stopped in the hallway to stare. I grabbed Cougar's arm, dragged him into one of the conference rooms, and slammed the door. "I çan't change the fact that he's Abby's father. Whether you like it or not, he's always going to be part of her life."

"You're right. I don't like it. But I get it. What I don't get is why you won't look me in the eye." He grabbed my chin and forced me to look at him. In a softer voice, he said, "We didn't leave it like this. What's *happened* in the past few days?"

Self-pitying tears burned my eyes. "What's happened

is, I realized I can't do this. Cougar, you're a great guy, but this is a mistake. It'd be different if it was just me, but I have Abby to consider. She really likes you—"

"I like her, too."

"—and I can't let her get too attached—"

"Why not?" he demanded. "Is Grady so insecure he's afraid she'll love someone else? Why are you even listening to him?"

I blinked at him, confused. "This isn't about Grady."

"Then what's it about? Because I'm not following." His blue eyes searched my face. "Are you saying you don't have feelings for me?"

"No, I do! You're my best friend—"

He grimaced. "But you're not attracted to me?"

"Of course, I am. It's crazy how much I want you. I wake up thinking about you, and I go to sleep thinking about you . . ."

He seized my hands. "I feel that way, too. So, what's the problem?"

I pulled away. "The problem is, it's not enough. I'm not like Kim, and those other women you date. I have a little girl. I have responsibilities. When I get involved with somebody, it can't be just about sex. I can't have a fling."

"A fling?" He cursed under his breath, then shook his head. "A fling. So, that's what this is?"

"Isn't it?"

"Necie, I—" He shook his head. "You know what,

never mind. You're right. This is a huge mistake. Thanks for pointing it out to me. I'll see you around."

He stalked out the door.

The next morning, someone stole my parking space, so I had to take one at the end of the row and trek through the freezing rain. Cougar's Camaro was already on the lot.

When I drew closer, I noticed the windows were fogged over. A female palm slapped the glass from the inside, startling me. Horrified, I averted my eyes and walked faster.

A car door slammed when I reached the building. I couldn't resist a look back at the giggling woman who emerged from the passenger side. Simone, one of the girls from the secretarial pool, adjusted her skirt and beamed at a rumpled Cougar as he climbed from the car. My gaze connected with his. For an instant, he looked conflicted. Almost apologetic. Then he glanced away. I yanked the door open and ran inside.

I had no right to compare this to Grady's betrayal, but the pain was just as sharp. I barely managed to hold my tears in check until I made it to the restroom.

After allowing myself a good cry—all I was apparently good for these days—I washed my face and caught the elevator to my floor. I said hello to a couple of people and thought I had it under control until I made it back to my desk and found Cougar waiting for me. I dropped my head and pretended to organize a stack of papers. "What do you want?" I asked abruptly.

"I got the clothes Mom sent. Do you want me to put them in your car, or bring them—are you crying?"

I swiped my eyes and turned my back. "Does it matter?"

"Of course, it matters. I care about you." He touched my shoulder and I jerked away.

"Yeah, I saw that. You looked very broken up."

He spun me around. "So, that was a test?"

"No test needed. You're exactly what I thought you were."

His jaw clenched. For a moment, he said nothing. Then he muttered, "I'll put the clothes in your car," and walked away.

I felt someone watching and looked up to find Kim gazing at me from her office. She pecked on the glass and mouthed, "Lunch?"

I nodded, though I doubted we had anything left to discuss. Four hours later, we sat in a booth at the little café across the street. It had been a miserable morning, and the sight of the waiter tripping all over himself to talk to Kim didn't improve my mood. We ordered, and finally he left us alone.

Kim took a deep breath and grabbed a napkin from the dispenser. "I wanted to talk to you about Jason."

"There's really nothing—"

"He'd kill me if he knew I was doing this." Her eyes brimmed with tears, and she gave a shaky laugh as her fingers twisted the napkin. "But what can I say? I love the guy."

The pain in her voice caused a rush of compassion. Awkwardly, I patted her hand. "Kim, we're not seeing each other—"

"I know, and I feel like that's my fault. Andrea told me what she said to you, about him being a player. It's not true, Necie. He was always straight up with me about what he felt . . ." she ducked her head as a tear streaked down her cheek, ". . . and what he didn't. I held on for awhile, hoping I could make him fall in love with me, but it wasn't happening." She paused. "He was already in love with you."

A startled laugh escaped me. "Cougar doesn't love me. Whatever this *thing* is that's been happening between us lately . . . it's not love."

"It is. And it's not just lately. He's been in love with you for a long time. I think I knew it even before he did. We'd be together, and it was always 'Necie this' or 'Necie that' . . ." She laughed. "I got so sick of hearing your name."

"You're confusing friendship with love. We were tight—me, him, and Angel. But all this crazy stuff only started happening lately."

"Because you were finally available."

"That may have been part of it," I admitted. "A new challenge for him, another notch on his bedpost, whatever. But it's not love. I was just the one who was there at the time."

"You sound like Andrea." She leaned back and studied me. "I hope you're only saying that because you're still getting over your divorce and everything else that's happened lately, because if you really believe that, you don't deserve him anyway."

Ouch.

She frowned. "You need to open your eyes, Necie. Jason craves love, real love, more than any man I've ever known, and he thinks you're the one. I'd give anything I had to be in your shoes."

"Maybe you should try Simone Walker's shoes. She's the one he was making out with in his car this morning."

Her lovely face paled. "What?"

I dug some money out of my purse and tossed it on the table. Standing, I forced a smile. "What's that they say on that trashy talk show, don't hate the player, hate the game? Looks like we've already struck out, Kim, and the next batter is already up."

Back at the office, I tried not to think about him, but it was hard to do, especially when he was so close. I watched his shoulders hunched over his desk and wished we could go back to the way we were before, wished that Kim had been right, wished I'd handled it differently. Then I ran out of wishes and felt sorry for myself some more.

That night while we were getting ready for the ice show, I got a collect call from Lewisburg Penitentiary and declined the charges. It made me feel somehow guilty, but I couldn't risk getting Maria on my back again.

Grady acted stiff and formal when he picked us up. I was so stressed out by that time I just wanted to scream "What's wrong?" but I got my answer when we were standing in line to buy Abby a Mickey Mouse doll. While Abby sat on a bench a few feet away eating a hot dog, Grady stared straight ahead and asked, "Who's Jason?"

"Jason is . . . nobody," I said.

"Abby said you're going to marry him."

With a mortified laugh, I said, "That is *not* true. He's a friend, from work."

"Must be a pretty good friend. She said you spent Christmas Eve with him." He cleared his throat. "She said she saw you kissing him."

"It's none of your business."

"Abby's my business. You're always telling me to act appropriately in front of her. I expect you to do the same."

"Fine."

"Fine."

The rest of the night we ignored each other, saying what we needed to through Abby. It was just like old times.

But then she went to sleep, and we resorted to a stony silence. He gave in first, after we pulled into my parking lot.

"Mom sent some of Abby's clothes over, so she'd have them to wear to school."

"I'll carry her up, then come back to get them."

"I'll carry them. It's a big box. You get her."

My phone rang. I handed him my keys. "Four-B," I told Grady, and answered it. It was Bill, with a new case for me. I hoped Cougar wouldn't be working it, too, but I didn't ask. I'd find out soon enough in the morning.

Through the windshield, I watched Grady struggle up the stairs with the box. Bracing myself against the blast of cold wind, I opened the door and climbed out of the car while I listened to Bill's briefing.

Despite the bitter cold, a teenager coasted up and down the pavement on a skateboard. He didn't even have a coat on. I shivered and hugged myself, watching him execute a jump, before I retrieved Abby from the backseat.

I heard a crash, and turned to see the skateboard flying in one direction, the boy in another. He smacked the ground hard and cried out, clutching his knee.

"Let me call you back, Bill," I said. "A kid on a skateboard's just killed himself." Hanging up, I shoved the phone in my pocket and set Abby down. "Go upstairs. Daddy's up there already. I need to check on this boy."

She nodded and headed up the sidewalk, clutching her Mickey doll. I ran over to check on the teenager.

"Are you okay?" I asked, squatting beside him.

"I think . . . so . . . ahhh." He groaned when he tried to straighten out his leg.

"Where do you live? Do you want me to call your parents?"

"No, I . . . agggh. Could you help me up?"

I wrapped my arms around his chest and tried to tug him up. After a couple of tries, we got it. "Thanks, lady," he said.

"Necie!" I turned my head when I heard Grady shout.

"Over here!" I yelled, figuring Abby had told him about the kid. When I glanced back at the kid, I was surprised to see him running around the corner of the nearest apartment. I looked down to see if he'd taken my purse, but realized I'd left it in Grady's car.

"What are you doing?" Grady asked, stepping around a snow-covered car. "Where's Abby?"

"I sent her upstairs to meet you. Some kid wrecked on a skateboard, and I was trying to see if he was all right."

"In this cold? What kid?"

I shrugged, and he frowned. "I didn't pass Abby on the stairs . . ."

We looked at each other, and I felt that first burst of fear. Grady spun on his heel and took off running back to the apartment. With my heart thudding in my chest, I raced for his car.

No Abby.

"Abby!" I yelled. "Abby, where are you?"

Grady stuck his head out the apartment door and shook his head. "Abby!" he shouted.

I ran to the spot where I'd set her down. Her small footsteps were still visible in the muddy snow. They went on for a few feet, heading toward the building. Then. . . My stomach clenched when I saw another set. A bigger set. Abby's footprints stopped abruptly, joined with the bigger ones. Then the big ones reversed, heading back the other way. They were spaced farther apart, and I realized whoever had left them had been running.

I raced around the corner of the building, following them. The buildings were U-shaped, and the footsteps stopped at the pavement of the next parking lot. Something red caught my eye.

Lying in the muddy snow was Abby's Mickey Mouse doll.

CHAPTER 14

I wasn't sure who called the police. Maybe it was Grady, or maybe it was one of the neighbors, calling to report me. Although I saw the footsteps and what they suggested, I couldn't comprehend it. This wasn't happening.

Not my daughter. Not my baby.

I ran down the sidewalk, screaming her name. I darted between buildings, scanning the shadows for her like we were playing hide-and-seek. Splashing through a puddle, I ignored the icy water that soaked through my shoes.

"Ma'am," someone said. "Ma'am!"

The officer ran alongside me and caught my arm, stopping my frantic pacing. "Ma'am, you have to calm down."

I don't think it really hit me until I watched the blue

lights play on his face.

Abby was gone. I didn't know who'd taken her or if I'd ever see her again.

I swayed on my feet. The young cop made a grab for my waist, and I shoved him away. He grabbed me again, and I barely got my head turned in time to keep from vomiting on his shoes.

When I finished, he wrapped his arm around me and led me to his car. Opening the driver's side door, he gently pushed me into the seat. He was speaking, but I couldn't focus on what he was saying. He motioned for me to stay and jogged over to speak to his partner, who stood with Grady.

My cell phone rang, and I fumbled in my coat pocket until I found it. For some insane reason, I half-expected to hear Abby on the other end, but it was Tucker who said hello.

Choking on my sobs, I tried to answer him.

"Necie? Necie, what's wrong? Where are you?"

The young officer reappeared so quickly I jumped. He gently pried the phone from my fingers.

"Hello," he said, and turned his back. I couldn't hear most of his muffled conversation, but I didn't care. I hugged myself and rocked against the seat. The oily smell of Armor All made my stomach lurch.

I wiped my face and spent the next several minutes trying to calm myself. I wasn't doing Abby any good like this.

Just when I thought I could hold it together, Tucker's car roared into the parking lot. On shaking legs, I stood to meet him. One look at his pale face, and I lost it again.

He ran over and took me in his arms. I buried my face against his shoulder and sobbed.

"We'll find her. We'll find her, I swear," he said.

An angry-looking Grady stalked over with the other officer on his heels. Tucker released me and turned to face them. He shifted slightly, and I realized he was putting himself between us.

"What happened?" Tucker asked.

"Who are you?" the cop said.

"A friend. Do you know for sure she was kidnapped?"

When no one spoke, Tucker reached into his back pocket and extracted his wallet. He flashed it at the officers. Even though the DEA had absolutely no jurisdiction here, they seemed to relax. One of them handed Grady's statement to Tucker. He read it, ignoring Grady's stony gaze.

The other cop quickly pulled me aside to get my statement. I realized he was trying to make sure we didn't compare stories. By the time we'd finished, two more units had arrived, and people had gathered in the parking lot to watch. The officers went door to door, asking if anyone had seen anything. For a moment, Grady, Tucker, and I stood there alone.

Grady ran his hand through his hair. "I can't believe . . . how could you just leave her alone like that? In this crappy neighborhood? She's six years old, Necie."

"It was only for a minute," I said, hugging myself. "I saw that skateboarder fall. All she had to go was up the stairs. I didn't think—"

"Damn straight, you didn't," he snapped, and Tucker moved in front of me.

Holding out his palms, Tucker said, "Please, just calm down. I know you're upset. Necie is, too. This won't help th—"

"Jason, is it?" Grady said, and threw a lightning-fast punch before either of us could respond.

It caught Tucker square in the chin. Horrified, I watched him fly backward onto the hood of the police cruiser.

"Don't tell me what to do!" Grady said, and lunged for him. I jumped between them, but Grady shoved me aside like a rag doll. I tripped over the sidewalk and fell to my hands and knees in the dirty snow, but at least I'd given Tucker a moment to recover. He launched himself off the police car and tackled Grady like a linebacker. They went down in a pile, rolling in the slush.

A car door slammed, and a couple of men ran past me. It took me a moment to realize it was Cougar and Bill. Bill grabbed Tucker and yanked him off Grady, while Cougar planted a boot in Grady's chest to keep him down.

"Give me a reason," Cougar snarled.

Looking over his shoulder, he said, "Tuck, are you okay?"

Tucker nodded, but blood streamed from his nose and he nearly slipped as Bill helped him to his feet. Cougar's gaze darted past them and seemed to find me for the first time. His eyes narrowed, then blazed while I feebly grasped the cop's side mirror and pulled myself up.

"What did he do?" Cougar yelled. "What did he do to you?"

"Cougar, no!" I shouted, but he ignored me.

Seizing a fistful of Grady's shirt, Cougar jerked him to his feet and slung him across the narrow yard into the side of the building. Grady smacked against the brick wall with a dull thwack and slumped there, dazed.

Cougar yanked off his coat and threw it on the ground. "Come on!" he said. "You wanna hit somebody? Hit me. I'm ready for it. Man, I'm *aching* for it!"

"Stop right there!"

The cops had finally realized what was happening. They ran toward us, guns drawn.

"He's armed!" one of them said, and my gaze fell to Cougar's ankle holster.

"Raise your hands and don't move, Cougar," Bill said calmly. "Let me handle this."

Bill approached the officers, his hands held wide at his sides. "It's okay. It's over. I'm William Davidson,

DEA supervisor. My badge is in my back left pocket. This man is one of my agents."

The cops moved forward. One of them seized Cougar's gun as another checked their IDs. Bill did some fast talking. After making sure no one wanted to press charges, they finally stood down, though they didn't give Cougar's gun back yet. Grady followed one of them to the manager's office to get some ice for the rapidly swelling lump on his head. Some of the tension followed with him, like air rushing out of a balloon. I sagged against the police car, and Cougar hurried to my side.

"Are you okay?" he asked softly, placing his hands on my shoulders. "Did he hurt you?"

"She's *gone*, Cougar," I whispered. "Somebody took Abby."

"Tell me exactly what happened," Bill said, and for what seemed like the thousandth time that night, I told them my story.

Bill and Tucker looked shocked that I'd gone to the ice show with Grady. Cougar merely grimaced. I'd never felt more stupid in my life, but I plunged on. ". . . so, Grady was going on up to the apartment—"

"What was he doing up there?" Cougar asked, his eyes suddenly icy.

I frowned. "I'm stupid, but I'm not that stupid. He was carrying up a box of Abby's clothes. I was carrying Abby. At least until I saw that skateboarder kid fall."

They listened to the rest without comment.

"It sounds like a setup," Cougar said finally. "We need to find that skateboarder."

Bill nodded. "I'll go make sure they're asking around."

We watched him walk away, then Cougar glanced at Tucker. "What happened here, with you and Grady?"

Tucker's eyes widened as if it were just dawning on him. "He called me *Jason*, then he slugged me."

Cougar blinked. "He did what?"

Tucker's mouth twitched, and he almost smiled. "This knot . . . it was supposed to be yours! He was yelling at Necie, and I stepped between them. He said, 'Jason, is it?' and he sucker punched me."

Cougar exhaled and smacked his fist against his palm. "He wants a go at me, all he has to do is step up. I'll be happy to oblige."

"Poor Tuck," I murmured, and touched his chin. "How many punches are you going to have to take for me?"

Tucker wrapped an arm around my neck. "Ah, it's okay. He and Cougar both hit like girls."

Cougar chuckled, but I couldn't manage a smile. All I could think about was Abby.

Restlessly, I shoved my hands in my pockets. "I can't stand this. I should be doing something."

"Hold on," Tucker said. "Let me see what Bill's found out."

He walked away, leaving me alone with Cougar.

"Babe," he said, his face pained. The bleakness in his eyes scared me. I put my hands over my face.

He wrapped his arms around me, pulling me against his chest and hugging me tight. "It's going to be okay. We'll find her, I swear it."

In the safety of his arms, I could almost believe it. But then I thought of Maria—

Wait until I take everything . . .

If Maria had Abby, the police couldn't help me. Even Barnes

. . . Daddy won't be able to help you now.

might not be able to stop her. But he was my only hope.

"I need to make a phone call," I told Cougar and took a few steps away from him while I fished my cell phone out of my pocket. He stayed back, trying to give me privacy, though I knew he could still hear me. I didn't care anymore.

I retrieved the number Barnes had phoned me from before the arraignment and called it. His lawyer answered on the second ring.

"This is Denise Bramhall. I need to speak to my father," I said, and sensed Cougar look up.

"Denise! I'll be glad to give him the message, but you know visiting hours—"

"Look, I know you can get to him. I don't care how. I have to speak to him tonight."

After a long pause, she said, "Okay," and hung up.

I closed my eyes and prayed that she would do it. I wasn't worried about his ability to contact me. People like Barnes didn't play by the rules, and I'd be surprised if he didn't have free access to a phone.

"You're calling your old man?" Cougar said, when I shut my phone.

I exhaled. "He has money, and power. He can move through channels quicker than we can."

"You make him sound like the Godfather," Cougar joked.

Shoving the phone back in my pocket, I had to force myself to meet his eyes. "There's something I need to tell you. Something I couldn't—"

Cougar's cell rang. He glanced at it, then held up an index finger. "Bill."

He answered, then nodded briskly. "Yeah, we'll be right up."

Closing the phone, he said, "They want you to come up to the apartment."

We hurried up, hoping for news, but all they wanted was a current photo of Abby.

I searched for my purse, then belatedly realized it was still in Grady's car. I headed after it and met Grady coming up the stairs.

"Do you have Abby's last school photo, the one with the purple jumper? The police need it."

"Yeah, I think so." He fumbled for his wallet.

From my pocket came the muffled ring of my cell phone. My heart raced, and I said, "Grady, could you take the photo up to Bill?"

"Yeah," he said, and moved past me.

I didn't recognize the number on the caller ID. "Hello?"

"Denise," Barnes said. "What's wrong?"

Quickly, I filled him in on Abby's kidnapping. For a long moment, he said nothing.

"Hello? Are you still there?"

"I'm here," he said. "But, Denise . . . I don't think Maria would do this. The thing with your husband, the threats—"

"She drugged me and nearly killed me. She burned down my house. Don't tell me she's not capable of it."

I related my last conversation with Maria and was again greeted with heavy silence.

"Will you help me or not?" I demanded.

"All my resources, anything I have is yours."

"I don't want your *resources*. I want my daughter."

"I promise you, Denise . . . if Maria has done this . . . if she has harmed that child—I will kill her."

"If Maria's hurt Abby, you won't have to kill her. I'll do it myself," I replied, then clicked the phone shut.

While I climbed the stairs, I contemplated what a murderous, cannibalistic little family we were.

Grady sat on the landing, his face in his hands. I didn't speak as I went by. Reentering the apartment, I found Bill and Cougar huddled behind one of the cops, who was typing furiously on a laptop.

"Okay, now I'll take off the threes and fours," he told them. "They're spousal rapes, indecent exposure, pornography charges. Not high risk."

"What are you looking at?" I asked, and Cougar shot me a guilty look.

No one answered, so I turned the screen around.

I didn't know what I was looking at. Numbers one through four littered the map of the city. I frowned at Cougar, but he wouldn't meet my eyes.

Bill cleared his throat. "Registered sex offenders. We thought maybe—"

"Okay," I interrupted, forcing back the bile rising in my throat. "So what do you have?"

I moved beside Cougar, who gave my shoulder a squeeze. He nodded at the cop, who resumed clicking.

Dozens of numbers disappeared from the screen, but still dozens remained.

"Can we weed out the rest by age of victims?" Bill asked.

The officer held down Ctrl + F. A menu popped up, and he quickly typed in the search parameters. When the screen flashed back to the map, a one and a trio of twos remained.

"What do those mean?" I asked, my heart lurching when I saw how close two of those numbers were to my apartment building.

"Ones are high risk, most likely to reoffend," he replied. "They've been convicted of multiple violent offenses, at least one sexual. Twos are sexual felony offense or misdemeanor child molestation."

Tears burned my eyes. Number one was only a block away. By moving here, had I made Abby a target?

He clicked on the number one, and a mug shot filled the screen.

Barry Green was a tall, skinny blonde with a pockmarked face and hard brown eyes. He smiled for the camera like a tourist at Disneyland. The room spun as I imagined this man with Abby, touching her, hurting her . . .

Cougar grabbed me when I swayed on my feet. "Hey!" he cried. "Easy." In one smooth motion, he hooked his arm around my waist and pivoted me around. I let him herd me to the couch.

"Try to be calm, Necie. We don't know anything yet. We're looking at everything."

I nodded, but I was about to hyperventilate. Barry Green or my half sister, Maria . . . either one would be my fault and either one could be deadly.

"Okay." Bill wiped a hand down his face and sat on the other side of me. I thought I was going to lose it when he hugged me. "They're going to question Green, give the other ones a shake, too."

"I want to do it," Cougar said, and Bill shook his head.

"You take care of Necie. You know how the state

guys are. If they think we're trying to butt in, they won't do a damn thing for us."

I barely heard them, unable to erase Barry Green's smiling mug shot from my mind. Even knowing what Maria was capable of, I almost hoped Abby was with her.

I knew the statistics. Of the thousands of children taken and murdered by sexual predators every day, 76 percent were killed within the first three hours.

Nearly two hours had already passed.

Stop it, stop it, stop it! my mind screamed.

A commotion at the door drew my attention. Everyone stared at the harried-looking woman, who was yelling at someone behind her. I watched an officer drag a teenage boy through the doorway. My heart stalled when I recognized the skateboarder.

"Where is she?" I demanded, jumping off the couch and running toward him. "Did you have something to do with this?"

The boy looked at me and began to cry.

"Tell her!" his mother said sharply. "Tell her what you told me."

"I thought it was a joke! He gave me a twenty to act like I was hurt. I didn't know—" He gulped. "I didn't know he was going to take that kid."

Someone behind me started firing questions.

"What did he look like?"

"He was a white guy. Big. Maybe six foot four, 250

315

pounds."

"Hair? Eyes?"

"Red hair. I think his eyes were brown. They were kind of droopy."

"Any scars, tattoos that you noticed?"

"No, I . . . I don't remember."

"What was he wearing?"

"Dark jeans, a Bears jacket."

"Somebody call in a sketch artist and add the information to the Amber Alert."

He repeated his story of how the man had approached him when we'd pulled up.

"He came out of nowhere," the kid said.

"Did he give you the money?"

The boy nodded and pulled out his wallet. An officer stopped him before he could extract it.

"Maybe we can get a print off it. We'll need to take yours for comparison."

The room buzzed with activity, and I felt a burst of hope.

But those hopes dimmed when hours passed with no new leads. Grady and I talked to the reporters, pleading for any information. At some point, he went back to Elizabeth's.

I watched the sun rise, wondering where Abby was and if she was okay.

I hadn't heard from Barnes, and I didn't know if that

was a good or bad sign. In my hands, I held the sketch of Abby's abductor. I didn't recognize him, but Barnes might. I'd tried to call him to make sure he'd seen it on the news, but no one answered the phone. Tanya Davis didn't answer, either.

The only prints on the bill belonged to the kid. A neighbor reported a black Suburban in the area right before the kidnapping. They canvassed the neighborhood, asking questions. Then they asked them again.

Cougar and I sat at the kitchen table for hours, pouring over DMV records in an attempt to find it.

Before I realized it, it was almost sunset.

Cougar noticed it, too. He rubbed his neck and stood. "C'mon. We're going to get something to eat."

"Just a few more—"

"We're going to eat," he said firmly. "And then you're going to get some sleep. You can only go on adrenaline so long."

I knew he was right, but it felt wrong to eat, when I didn't know if Abby had been fed. It felt wrong to sleep, when I didn't even know if

Hush! Don't you say it. Don't even think it!

Abby was okay.

We were pulling out of the parking lot when I realized I didn't have my purse. The last time I remembered seeing it was in Grady's car. Hesitantly, I asked Cougar if he'd mind taking me by Elizabeth's to retrieve it.

"I'll buy," he said. "You don't have to worry about it."

"It's not just my money. My badge . . . everything's in there."

"Okay. We'll get it after we eat."

Later, I would remember going into the restaurant, and knowing that I ate, but I couldn't have said where we'd gone or what I'd ordered. I had to force myself to concentrate enough to tell Cougar how to get to Elizabeth's house.

Cougar didn't speak for awhile, then he mused, "So Grady's living with Mommy, huh? How's she doing?"

"I don't know," I admitted.

When Cougar pulled up to the curb in front of Elizabeth's, I said, "Be right back," and bailed out of the car.

Grady sat on the mansion's front steps, smoking a cigarette. I had talked him into giving up the habit when I was pregnant with Abby. He knew I hated cigarettes, but apparently, my opinion didn't mean much anymore.

"Any news?" he asked, punctuating the question with a puff of smoke.

"No. I left my purse in your car." A drop of rain splattered on my nose when I climbed the steps. His green eyes were bloodshot, and his blond hair was uncombed. His rumpled gray suit looked slept in. For an instant, my heart went out to him. Then I smelled the liquor.

"How could you be drinking at a time like this?"

"What better time is there?" he asked. "My daughter is missing, and I don't have a clue where she is. The FBI just left, and they don't have a clue, either. I'd say it's a perfect time to drink." He stared at another drop of rain that splattered across the top of his expensive Italian shoes. "Do you really want to get into this now?"

I took a deep breath. "No. I didn't come here to fight."

Grady glanced beyond me, and I could tell by the way his eyes narrowed that Cougar had followed me.

"My purse?" I said, hoping to diffuse the situation before it got out of control. "If you'll let me into the garage, I'll be out of your way."

Grady took another quick puff from his cigarette. "It's in the house. I saw it, brought it in. I was going to bring it to you, but—" He shrugged and stared at Cougar. "I figured you had company." Staring up at the darkening sky, he said, "Come on, and we'll get it. You might as well come, too, Jason."

He snubbed out his cigarette and tossed it in Elizabeth's rosebushes. Then he walked into the house.

I glanced back at Cougar. "You don't have to come," I said. "I'll be okay."

"I've seen what he's done to you when he's drinking. That shit will never happen again."

When we walked inside, we found Grady and Elizabeth waiting in the foyer. He leaned to whisper something to her. She shot him a dark look, then came forward to greet me.

"Denise. How are you holding up?"

"Not so good. Grady, could I speak with you?" I glanced at Cougar and Elizabeth. "Alone?"

"In the kitchen," he said, and resumed walking.

"I'll only be a second," I told Cougar.

I could tell he didn't like it much, but he let me go. I heard Elizabeth offer him a drink as she led him into her sitting room.

There were a few things I needed to talk about with Grady that I didn't want to mention in front of Cougar. Not yet.

After pulling out a chair at the kitchen table for me, Grady grabbed my purse off the counter, handed it to me, then reversed a chair and straddled it. He shook another cigarette out of the pack, but didn't light it. "So what's up?" he asked, rolling it absently between his fingers.

"I'll get to the point," I said.

He snorted. "You always do."

"I might have to tell the police about your affair with Maria."

"What? Why?"

"You know why. I think she has Abby. I just wanted to give you a heads-up, so you'd know I'm doing this for Abby, not to hurt you."

He frowned. "Are you going to tell them the rest, about her being your sister?"

"If I have to."

Grady raked a hand over his mouth and stared at the

wall. "It's not her, Necie. Why would she want Abby?"

I cleared my throat. "The same reason she wanted you—to hurt me."

He gave me a long look, then shook his head. "It's always about you, isn't it?"

"When it comes to her . . . yeah, it is. Grady, she burned down our house!"

"So you said."

"Yeah, so I said. Since when is that not good enough anymore? She told me she'd done it. She *laughed* about it."

Grady cocked his head and stared at me. The doubt in his eyes infuriated me. What, did he think I was jealous? Making the whole thing up?

"Don't look at me like that," he pleaded. "I don't want to fight. We didn't mean to hurt you. I'm sorry you found out about us like that."

Something about his plural pronouns set off warning bells in my head. "You swear you're not still seeing her?"

Grady cursed. "No. I've told you that. I was with her one time. One lousy time. Since when is *my* word not good enough? Do you want me to take a lie-detector test? The police said we'd probably be asked to anyway." Agitated, Grady stood and paced in front of the table. "I could scratch out an apology in blood and it wouldn't matter to you. I'm sorry I slept with your sister."

Anger flashed inside me. "You think it would've been easier if it had been a stranger? But yeah, it sucks that you'd be with her, knowing who she is and everything she's done . . . Not that it matters now, but was she even the first?"

He was quiet for a long time. Too long.

"No," he said.

The word hung between us for a moment. I was too stunned to move. Too hurt to breathe. Even though I'd been angry at Grady, some part of me had shifted most of the blame onto Maria. She was gorgeous, cunning . . . It was easier to believe she'd led him astray than to believe he would seek to betray me.

"When?" I demanded.

Grady stared at the saltshaker. "That time I went to San Francisco . . . when Abby was little and we were fighting about you going back to work. There was this girl, Judge Milton's assistant. We had too much to drink, and . . ." He lapsed into silence, which was okay, because I could figure out the rest.

Four years ago. I'd never even suspected.

"You bastard."

"Hey, what did you expect from me?" he asked, as I lurched to my feet and turned to go.

He grabbed my arm and jerked me up close. The stench of Jack Daniels made my eyes water when he said, "I loved you for years, but I never knew you. You never knew yourself. What did you live for? It wasn't me. It wasn't Abby. It was revenge, and look what it's gotten you."

"Let go of me," I growled, but Grady wouldn't be denied this confrontation. Like a genie freed from a whiskey bottle, his anger swirled all around me.

"Something's wrong with you, Denise. Something is missing inside. You talk about my affair with Maria being empty and cold, but empty and cold was what I felt every night in bed with my own wife."

My palm cracked against his cheek like a gunshot. Grady released me and staggered backward, bumping against the refrigerator. Throwing my purse strap over my shoulder, I stalked down the hall. When Grady didn't follow, I pressed my back against the wall and tried to calm myself. If Cougar saw me cry, he'd kill Grady.

I took a couple of deep breaths before I stuck my head through the living room entranceway. Cougar shot me a relieved look from the sofa.

"You ready?" I asked, as steadily as I could manage.

I walked away without waiting on a reply. Cougar caught up with me when I started down the steps.

"Are you okay?" he asked, and I nodded.

"Man, it's like the White House in there. And Grady's mother . . . that dame's a piece of work."

In spite of my mood—in spite of everything—I smiled. Cougar had to be the only man under seventy who said words like "dame."

Encouraged, Cougar jogged beside me down the walkway. "I haven't had my grammar corrected since sophomore English. High so-ci-e-ty. No wonder Grady's such a tool." He jostled my shoulder and grinned. "I can see why you were the black sheep of the family."

He tried to make me laugh on the way back, but I kept replaying Grady's words in my head.

His words about our cold, empty marriage knifed me. If that was true, why hadn't I felt it?

Something's wrong with you, he'd said.

I couldn't deny that. But he couldn't tell me I didn't feel. Every time I looked at my daughter, I felt love.

No squad cars sat in the parking lot. No one hung around the apartment. It made me feel like they'd given up hope. As I unlocked the door, that stupid voice was in my head again, telling me how dismal Abby's chances were now.

We're closing in on the twenty-four-hour mark now, and we know what that means, don't we, boys and girls . . . The odds are now 88 percent (or was it 89?) against Abby ever coming home.

I clamped my hand over my mouth as I staggered through the door, trying to muffle my sob, but there it was, and there was another . . .

I fell to my knees on the living room floor. Cougar dropped beside me, taking me in his arms. I clung to him.

"Baby, don't," he begged. "It's okay. We're going to find her, I swear."

Though I knew that wasn't what he intended, I cried

harder when I realized he was no longer promising me we'd find her alive.

I'm not sure how long we sat there like that, but when Cougar tried to stand, I clutched his hand and begged him not to leave me.

"I'm not going anywhere."

He scooped me up and carried me to the bedroom. Placing me on the bed, he removed our shoes and coats and crawled in beside me. I rested my head on his chest and cried until I felt as cold and empty as Grady had accused me of being.

But that wasn't exactly true. I was filled with rage, filled with frustration . . . filled with pain and desperation. I don't know why I started kissing Cougar, other than maybe—just for a little while—I didn't want to think. I didn't want to feel so alone.

I turned my face into his neck, brushing feverish little kisses against his skin. He groaned, and his arm tightened around me. Brazenly, I crawled on top of him and kissed his mouth in earnest. It was a kiss of desperation, need, and maybe even anger, but he responded to it. As my hands wound in his thick hair, tugging him closer, deeper, his fingers dug into my hips, practically lifting me off the ground. His tongue met mine thrust for thrust, feeding the dark feverish desire that had taken possession of me.

But then he grabbed my shoulders and pushed me back.

"Um, no, Necie," he gasped. "What are you doing?"

"Make love to me," I begged. "I need you."

"What? He sounded shocked. "Baby, no. This isn't what you need."

"It's exactly what I need. Please. Don't you want me?"

"Of course, I want you, but—"

"Then stop talking," I said, and leaned to kiss him again.

I felt him fighting himself, and knowing that he wanted me made me more desperate for him than ever. He turned his face away again, and I kissed his throat.

"Necie, stop," he said forcefully, his breath ragged. "I won't hurt you. I won't take advantage of you. You're tired, scared—"

I felt absurdly near tears and unjustifiably angry when I said, "You're right. I *am* tired, and I *am* scared and I can't sleep and I can't breathe. I'm not asking for commitment. It doesn't have to mean anything. All I'm asking you for is tonight, for you to help me shut out all these voices in my head. Just for a little while, let me feel something besides fear."

He didn't say anything. I felt the tension humming from his body.

I slipped off my shirt and reached behind me to unfasten my bra. After tossing it onto the floor, I took his hand and brought it to my mouth.

"Please," I said, and sucked gently on his finger. "Please, Jason, don't deny me this. I'm not drugged this time. I know what I want."

He groaned, and I knew I'd won. I took his hands and placed them on my bare breasts.

He growled my name as he stroked them. I leaned to brush one hard nipple across his mouth. He nuzzled it, licked it . . . then he took it in his mouth and sucked hard. I cried out, my back arching as he devoured me. He flipped me onto my back and rained kisses on my chest. His knee slid between my legs, forcing my thighs open. His erection throbbed through the thin denim of my pants. His tongue invaded my mouth while he tugged at my zipper. Hot with anticipation, I had my first orgasm before he'd even gotten me out of my jeans.

He left a trail of fiery kisses from my breasts down my stomach. I lifted my hips to help him slide off my jeans. His fingers slipped inside the edge of my panties, and he groaned when he found me wet. Wanting.

I nearly ripped his shirt off him and tore at his zipper. Never had I felt anything so primal, so powerful. I craved his body like a drug, resenting even the few seconds it took him to put on protection.

Then we were both naked, our bodies hot and slick as they slid against each other.

"Necie, are you sure?" he gasped, and in response, I guided him inside me.

He pounded into me, knowing somehow that's what I needed. Then he rolled me over.

Sweat sheened our bodies, and my headboard banged against the wall as I rode him. He begged me to slow down, but I couldn't as I careened toward the most explosive orgasm of my life.

"Say my name," he begged hoarsely.

"Jason," I murmured. "Jason." I nearly sobbed as the tension inside me wound tighter and tighter. Suddenly, white light exploded behind my eyes like a migraine, blinding me as my insides seemed to shatter in a liquid release. "Jason!" I screamed.

Delicious waves of sensation slammed into me. I was so dazed I barely felt it as he pumped faster and faster beneath me. Then he cried out and rose halfway off the bed with his climax.

For several minutes, I couldn't move. I rested my head in my arms, holding myself up with the help of the headboard. I was sucking wind like a dying fish, and Cougar didn't sound much better beneath me.

My legs trembled so badly I barely had the strength to climb off him. Exhausted, I rolled onto my side away from him. Cougar rolled onto his side, too, and pulled me against him. His heart beat against my back like a jackhammer.

His lovemaking accomplished what I'd hoped it would. I slumped against him, too tired and too spent to think about anything. Just before I drifted off, I noticed that my breathing matched the rhythm of his.

I jolted awake a few hours later, my mouth open wide in a soundless scream. Caught up in the remnants of a nightmare I couldn't remember, I pushed Cougar away and sat up. He never stirred. Moonlight glowed silver though the window, and I felt a stir of panic while I gazed at his handsome face.

What had I done?

I felt so ashamed. My daughter was out there some-where—needing me, and where was I? I was so weak. So weak and stupid.

I jumped up and quietly grabbed a change of clothes out of my closet. Moving down the hall, I shut the bathroom door behind me and snatched a towel from the rack to wedge in the crack between the door and the floor to muffle the sound of my shower.

Hot water beat against my back, and tears streamed down my face while I wondered what I was going to do next. I was tired of waiting for someone else to find Abby. I was going to have to do it myself.

After locking the apartment door behind me, I called a cab and waited in the parking lot. When it got there, I wasn't sure where I wanted to go. I contemplated visiting Barnes, or visiting his lawyer, but I figured that anything he was going to do, he'd be doing it already. I only wished he would call and tell me if he knew any-thing.

I asked the cabbie to drop me at headquarters. I

killed some time in the cafeteria, eating breakfast out of a vending machine and drinking bitter coffee, then I went to find Bill.

He was a notorious early bird, but I still had to wait around another hour before he arrived. His eyebrows shot up when he stepped off the elevator and saw me sitting in the reception area.

"Necie! Any word on Abby?"

"No. Can I talk to you in your office?"

"Sure," he said. He held the door for me and pulled out a chair with his foot as he passed by.

"There's been no news. That's why I'm here. I need your help."

"Anything."

"I need to see the Barnes surveillance tapes."

Bill frowned. "Why?"

Steeling myself, I said, "I have reason to believe that Maria Barnes is involved in Abby's kidnapping."

Instead of the surprise I expected, Bill merely grimaced.

"Because of the affair?" he asked.

I almost asked how he knew, but then I realized . . . Bill had been in charge of the surveillance operation. Of course, he knew.

"I wanted to tell you," he said.

Ignoring the stab of betrayal, I said, "She's out to get me. She's the one who drugged me, and she's the person who burned down my house."

My cell rang, and I glanced at the caller ID. It was Cougar. I shut the phone off.

"I know the tapes better than anyone, Necie. I haven't seen the guy."

"Are you sure?"

"I'm sure."

The phone rang, and he motioned for me to wait.

"Daniels, how—" His eyes widened. "You're kidding! What happened? You're sure it's him?" He scribbled something on a Post-it. "When you get a positive ID, I want to know."

He hung up and stared into space for a moment. Then he looked at me.

"There's been an explosion at the prison. Frank Barnes is dead."

CHAPTER 15

My vision swam, and it took effort to focus on him. "What?"

"Some crude explosive device in his cell, rigged to the light switch."

I pressed my hand to my mouth, a dizzying wave of emotions flashing over me.

"He said the bodies were burned pretty badly, but they seem confident that it's Barnes and his cell mate."

The news left me reeling, unsure of what to feel, other than scared. How would Maria react? Now nothing stood between us.

I sat in Bill's office for a few more minutes, struggling to compose myself while simultaneously trying to look normal.

This time it was Bill's phone that rang. When he glanced at it and said, "The wife," I excused myself and walked into the hall.

I took a detour to the ladies room and splashed my face, trying to clear my head.

I'd been counting on Barnes' help, his ability to influence Maria . . .

Now what was I going to do?

Moving toward the elevator, a familiar, husky laugh stopped me in my tracks. I turned my head in slow motion to see Cougar standing in Kim's office. He hugged her, then smacked a kiss on her cheek.

Wow. At least it had taken Grady four years to cheat on me.

A lump rose in my throat, and I hated myself for caring. Dropping my head, I hurried for the elevator.

My heart sank when he called out my name. I jabbed the elevator button, pretending I didn't hear him.

"Necie!" he called again, closer this time. I didn't turn around.

Damn, damn, damn. I punctuated each curse with a jab of the down arrow. Maybe I should just throw myself out the nearest window.

"Hey." He caught my arm and forced me to look at him. Everything about him looked a little sharper in the fluorescent light—the damp brown hair darkened almost black from his shower, the shadows in his eyes . . . I could smell my soap on his skin, and the sensual rush I felt at the sight of him horrified me. Sleeping with him had been a mistake. Letting this go any farther would be a disaster.

"What?" I asked briskly.

His tentative smile dissolved into a frown. He tucked a sheaf of papers under his left arm, and hooked his right through mine. "Let's talk," he said, and dragged me down the hall without waiting on a reply.

"Hey!" I said, yanking free. "I've got to go. Why don't you go talk to Kim?"

Cougar pushed me into an empty office and shut the door behind him. He regarded me quizzically. "Is that what this is about? You're *jealous?*"

"Don't be stupid. I am not," I snapped.

He grinned. "Are, too."

I wasn't about to get into a schoolyard argument with him. Poking my finger at his chest, I said, "Look, my daughter's missing. You're not even a blip on my radar right now. Is that clear?"

His smile faded, and his eyes glittered like blue diamonds. "Crystal. I guess I should've gotten that message when I woke up and found you gone." He yanked the papers from beneath his arm and slapped them on the desk. "For the record, since I'm not a bastard like Grady, all I was getting from Kim were more DMV records."

I felt stupid, and sorry for being so short-tempered with him. I caught his arm when he grabbed the doorknob.

"Cougar . . ."

He grimaced. "So we're back to Cougar now?"

"What?"

He stroked the scar on his forehead and stared over my shoulder. "Did I . . . did I do something wrong last night?"

The pain in his eyes stunned me when his gaze slid to mine. "No," I whispered.

"Then what is it? You asked me to stay at your apartment last night. You begged me to stay. But now you're pushing me away. I thought it was good between us. Was I wrong?"

"No, I—" Turning away, I rubbed my eyes. I couldn't do this right now.

He touched my shoulders, and his big hands felt so good that I had to resist the silly urge to lean into him. "I thought this was something real."

Something real?

I whirled to face him. "I don't understand. Why are you acting like this? It *was* good. It was great—"

"I'm not looking for an ego massage here," he said, his voice rising. I tried to shush him, and when that didn't work, I talked over him. Probably the whole office was listening, but I didn't care. I had more important things to worry about.

"Why are you acting like this?" I repeated.

He threw his arms wide. "Me? You want to know why *I'm* acting like this? You couldn't have made me feel more used if you'd thrown a couple of twenties on the dresser—"

"Used? What are you talking about? I told you I wasn't asking for a commitment. It was just sex—"

"It wasn't just sex to me," he said.

His statement stole the words from my lips. We stood nose to nose, so close his breath moved my hair.

"I love you," he said.

I blinked once. Twice. Waiting for him to deliver the punch line. When he didn't, I laughed anyway. "What? You *love* me?"

"Is that so hard to believe?" he demanded, his face reddening.

"Coming from you—yeah, it is."

"What the fuck is that supposed to mean?"

A sharp rap on the door made us both turn. The door cracked open, and Luke Jacobi, another agent, peered in.

"What?" we both yelled, and Luke flushed. "Necie, I need to talk to you. It's really important, so when you're finished—"

"Oh, we're finished," Cougar said, shouldering past me. "We're beyond finished."

He pushed past Luke, who stared at me open-mouthed. I turned my back to him and grabbed the phone records off the desk. Folding them, I stuffed them in my purse.

"What is it?" I asked, when Luke didn't speak.

"There are some men on the way. Feds. They want to talk to you, said they couldn't get you on the phone."

The phone. Damn it. I'd forgotten to turn it back on.

"Did they say what it was about? Have they found Abby?"

Luke blanched. "Necie, I think you'd better wait—"

Fear washed over me in a cold, breathtaking wave. I staggered against the desk. "Luke, I can tell you know something. Talk to me!"

He stared down at the floor. His Adam's apple bobbed when he swallowed. "There's . . . ah . . . a little girl, in the morgue at County General. They're checking dental records now—"

Whatever Luke was saying was lost in the roaring of my pulse in my ears. With a trembling hand, I yanked my cell phone out of my purse and punched in Cougar's number.

When I heard his "hello," all I could say was his name. I grabbed the edge of the desk to keep from falling.

"You called me," he said pointedly, when I said nothing else.

"Abby," I gasped. My teeth chattered so hard I thought they'd break. "It's Abby. They think . . . they think . . . There's a girl, at the morgue . . ."

Instantly, his voice changed. "Babe, is Luke still there with you?"

Numbly, I nodded, before I realized he couldn't see me.

"Y-y-yesss," I stuttered.

"Put him on the phone. I'm on my way. Don't move until I get there."

I handed the phone to Luke and sank to my knees on the thin gray carpet, hugging myself.

Not my baby. Not Abby. Oh, please, God, not Abby.

Time blurred while I prayed. Someone's child was dead. Someone's little girl. And all I could do was pray that it wasn't mine.

A pair of strong arms slipped around me, and I turned my head against Cougar's neck when he hugged me.

"Baby, it's okay," he soothed, his voice raspy and hoarse. "We don't know anything for sure."

"Take me to the hospital. Please."

"We're going right now." A sea of concerned co-workers parted as Cougar led me to the elevator.

He kept talking to me, and somehow I drew strength from him.

We made it to County General in record time.

"Hold the elevator!" Cougar yelled, sticking his hand out to stop the sliding door.

Grady's frantic eyes met mine. Tears streamed down his cheeks, and wordlessly, he held out his arms. I let go of Cougar's hand long enough to hug him.

My stomach lurched as the elevator descended to the basement.

Grady charged ahead when the doors opened, following the arrows to the morgue. I noticed the restrooms directly across and remembered a cop joking about the bathrooms being directly outside the morgue so the rookies wouldn't have so far to run.

When Grady touched the swinging doors, Cougar grabbed his arm. "Hey, man, let me go in. If it *is* her—"

"If it is her, I need to see for myself," Grady said, and shouldered past him. Cougar turned to me, placing both hands on my shoulders.

"Necie, you don't need to go in there. Not yet. Let me go."

Bile rose in my throat, and I felt myself nodding. I didn't think I could see Abby stretched out on one of those slabs. I couldn't do it.

Cougar kissed the top of my head and pushed through the doors.

Time seemed to stand still while I waited for them to emerge. The only sound I heard was the buzz of the fluorescent light over my head.

Then Grady burst through the doors with his hand over his mouth.

He barreled past me into the men's room, and I heard him gagging. My heart clenched in my chest like a fist.

Cougar burst through the morgue doors and seized me in his arms. "It's not her," he said. "It's not her."

My knees sagged, but I was safely pinned in Cougar's arms. "Are you sure?" I asked.

"I'm positive. Fucking feds should've never called until

they were sure. I'm gonna ream somebody over this."

I was about to ask Cougar to check on Grady when I heard the roar of a water faucet. He stepped out of the bathroom a moment later, his blond hair dripping water, his face the same shade of gray as his jacket.

"Are you okay?" I asked, and he nodded.

His eyes flitted wildly around the hall. He looked like a junkie in withdrawal.

"Man, can I give you a ride?" Cougar asked, loosening his death grip on me. Grady shook his head violently. His whole body was shaking.

"You can't drive like this," Cougar said. "At least let me call you a cab."

Grady patted his pocket and cursed when he didn't find a phone. "Okay," he said, "but let's get out of this friggin' basement."

We took the elevator to the first floor, and Cougar walked outside to make the call. Grady and I sat side by side in the padded waiting room chairs.

"I don't know what I would've done . . ." he said softly, and rubbed his hand across his mouth.

"I know."

He took my hand and squeezed my fingers. "It's going to be all right. We're going to find her."

"We have to," I agreed.

Cougar walked back in. I saw him glance at us, then purposely look away. I let go of Grady's hand and walked over to join him.

"Cab's on its way," he told Grady, then led me outside.

"We're parked a million miles away," he said. "Do you want me to go get the car?"

"No. I want to walk." Somehow the warm sun on my face lifted my spirits. I slipped my fingers in Cougar's and he squeezed them.

"Cougar . . . about this morning . . . I'm sorry. I'm sorry for everything. I'm so crazy right now—"

He sighed. "It's okay. You were up-front with me about what it was. It wasn't your fault that I wanted to make something more out of it."

He stopped and we faced each other in the middle of the parking lot. He tucked a lock of hair behind my ear and gave me a crooked grin that made my heart stumble. "Now's not the time or the place. First, we find Abby. Then we talk."

"Cougar . . ."

He held up his hand. "No, no. It's okay. I was thinking about your reaction. It wasn't exactly what I'd hoped for, but I can see why you laughed at me. I know I haven't been exactly settled in the past, but that was before I realized what I wanted. What I needed. It's you, Necie. I've wanted to tell you for so long."

"How long?" I asked, surprised.

He grimaced. "Long enough. Probably ever since we started working undercover assignments together.

Working with you made me a little nuts—Angel used to torment me about you—but I tried to leave you alone. You were married, Abby was small . . . I figured that eventually I'd get you out of my head. Then all this happened with Angel, and Grady . . . All that stuff got stirred up inside me again. But, anyway, like I said . . . Abby is our only priority now, but once we get her home . . . I'd really like to sit down and talk with you."

"Okay," I said, my head spinning. I squeezed his hand and brushed a soft kiss on his mouth.

On the way home, my shock from the morgue experience dissolved into a gnawing anxiety. I told Cougar about Barnes's death. I wondered if Maria knew yet. Was Abby in even greater danger? I weighed the options and decided I had to take a chance.

"Cougar," I said. "If I asked you to trust me with something, without asking questions, would you do it? There are a lot of things I need to tell you, things I should've told you a long time ago, but I was scared, and I didn't know how—"

"Necie, relax," he said, offering me a puzzled smile that made me feel ashamed. "I trust you. Whatever it is, I trust you."

"I need to go see Maria Barnes."

He stared at me for a long moment, then focused his attention back on the road. "Okay. Are you going to try to arrange a meeting at the station—"

"I want to go to her house."

Cougar wiped his hand over his mouth. "Honey . . . are you sure that's such a good idea? Her father just died. She's not the most stable person under any circumstances—"

"I think she might have Abby."

He blinked at me. "Why would she have Abby?"

"She has a . . . vendetta against me. She had an affair with Grady. She . . ." I paused, unsure of how much I should say.

He frowned, and shook his head. "Maria Barnes had an affair with Grady?"

"Yes, but . . . You just have to trust me. She's out to get me. Out to ruin my life."

"Over Grady? But you're divorcing him. I think you're exhausted, and I'm not sure you're thinking too clearly—"

"There's more—a lot more—but don't make me go into it now. I know it's a lot to ask, but please trust me. Now might be the best time to see her. She's angry. She wouldn't be able to hide it if she's guilty."

"Then let's call the police—"

"We don't have time to go through the proper channels. I have no proof. I don't have anything. But if she did it, she'll boast about it. At least then I'll know."

"Okay," he said again.

We pulled up to the gates of the Barnes estate fifteen minutes later. A burly blonde approached the car.

"I'm here to see Maria," I said, with as much authority as I could muster.

"She's not here."

"Please tell her Necie wants to talk to her."

"I would, if she were here, but I already told you she isn't."

"Can we go in and wait for her?"

He laughed. "Not without a search warrant, Officer."

So he knew who I was. I don't know why that surprised me, but it did.

"Will you tell her I stopped by?"

He smirked. "I'm sure she'll be in touch."

I rolled the window up and chewed my thumbnail. "I have to get in there. I have to see her."

Cougar snapped his gum and shrugged. "So, we'll get in there."

He pulled out, drove about a quarter of a mile, then wheeled the car into the driveway of a home with a realtor's sign staked in the yard. He pulled the car all the way behind the house, hiding it from the road.

"We're hoofing it from here," he said, and killed the motor.

We crossed the road and reentered the woods, walking until we encountered the imposing fence.

"Probably wired," he said. "We get too close, set off an alarm."

"So what are we going to do?"

"Keep walking."

We'd traveled another hundred yards, and he touched my shoulder. "Aha."

He pointed at a sprawling oak ahead. Looking at its long, overhanging limbs, I knew immediately what he had in mind.

I sighed. "Let's go, Tarzan."

He scaled the tree first, then stretched down a hand to help me up. We moved up a few more feet.

"Me first," he said, and edged out onto the limb.

It creaked and dipped under his weight, but he managed to clear the fence. Then, he locked his hands, lowered his body, and swung for a moment before dropping to the ground.

Closing my eyes, I tried to mimic his actions, but somehow I didn't manage to land as gracefully.

"You okay?" he asked, and I could tell he was trying not to smile.

"Fine," I muttered, dusting off my behind.

The huge pines nearly blocked the sun. Cougar didn't seem to have any problem navigating the woods, but I kept sliding in the snow.

"What's the matter, city girl?" he asked. "Can't walk if it's not on asphalt or concrete?"

"Ha, ha . . . Very—" I gasped when a man shot out from behind a tree in front of us.

We went for our guns.

"Denise!" the man cried. "Don't shoot!"

My arm faltered when I recognized his voice.

Frank Barnes took another step toward us, holding up his hands.

"I'm here to help."

CHAPTER 16

D umbfounded, I stared at him, but Cougar harbored no such indecision. He pointed his gun at Barnes's head.

"What . . . how . . ." I stammered.

"You were right," Barnes said. "After I talked with Maria, I knew you were right. This is the only way I knew to help."

"What's going on here?" Cougar demanded.

Barnes ignored him. "If you walk in there, she'll kill you. I failed her, like I failed you."

"Necie, what's he talking about?" Cougar asked.

I took a deep breath. "Don't shoot him, Cougar. He's my father."

"What?" Cougar laughed, but his eyes were hard. "You're joking, right?"

"I wanted to tell you. I tried—"

"When?" he snapped. "All these years we've been working together, and . . ." He paused, and his face went stony. "You're the mole! All this time, you've been saving his ass."

"That's not true! I wanted to put him away more than anyone."

"And what about Angel? Even after your father shot him, you tried to help him destroy evidence."

"I love Angel. I would never do anything to hurt him."

"All that time at the hospital . . . it was guilt, wasn't it? You didn't expect it to go down like that."

"How can you say that?" I said. "You know me better than that."

"I don't know you at all." Cougar cast a baleful look at Barnes, then spun and stalked back the way we'd come.

"Cougar, wait!"

"Stay away from me!" he yelled.

"Wait here!" I commanded Barnes, and chased after him.

He strode purposefully, his long legs widening the distance between us until he was little more than a shadow up ahead.

Suddenly, a group of men jumped out from behind the trees and wrestled him to the ground. I pulled my gun, but I couldn't discern his shadow from theirs.

My heart raced. I had to do something.

Someone clamped a hand over my mouth. I struggled and bucked against him.

"Denise, stop it," Barnes hissed. "If you run out there, you'll both die."

"Check around!" one of the men yelled. "There was a girl with him earlier."

"Come!" Barnes said urgently. The hand that clamped my wrist was surprisingly strong.

I struggled again while he dragged me into the forest. "Where are we going? I have to help Cougar."

"They'll take him to the house."

"You don't know that. They could just shoot him and leave him there, like you did Angel."

"Maria will want information. She'll want to talk to him. I know a way in. Please, Denise, trust me."

Trust him? I'd spent my whole life not trusting him. But with Abby and Cougar's lives at stake, I had no choice.

I wasn't sure how long we walked, but it seemed like forever. I was cold, tired, and terrified of what might be happening to Cougar while we tromped around the woods.

"Here," Barnes said. "This is how we get in."

I stared down at the drainage ditch poking out of the hillside.

He pulled a flashlight out of his pocket and said, "I'll go first."

On his hands and knees, he entered the small tube,

leaving me little choice except to follow. The smell of rotting leaves and stagnant water gagged me.

"It gets better in a minute," he said.

A few seconds later, he added, "Watch your step, there's a drop-off."

The little tube spilled out into a cavernous room.

"What is this?" I asked, following the beam of his flashlight as it played on the stone walls.

"The house was built by bootleggers in the twenties. This is an escape route. The house itself has a few tricks, as well."

He led me into a larger tunnel. We wandered around for nearly an hour, so long that I'd half-convinced myself Barnes was stalling, when he said, "There's the ladder."

The flashlight beam jerked crazily, flying from the ladder to the wall to his feet.

"Are you okay?"

"I'm . . . fine," he gasped. "Just a little . . . winded."

"Maybe you should rest a minute."

In response, he began to climb.

"Where does it come out?"

"Basement."

We climbed a few more feet, and he snapped off the light. I heard a long, scraping sound as he pushed away the section of flooring.

Once inside, we paused, listening. Then we split up to search.

The house was eerily quiet. Damn it, she was gone again.

I went through room after room, thinking of the day we'd found Angel in the snow.

Then I opened a door and entered a bedroom with pale blue carpet and walls. A pile of clothing lay on the floor at the foot of the bed.

I edged forward, my heart pounding in my ears.

A low, soft groan came from the other side of the bed. I ran around the corner, and what I saw knocked the breath out of me.

Cougar lay facedown on the carpet, naked and bleeding. Blood smeared the powder blue carpet around him, streaked his skin like war paint. He groaned again, and I realized he was regaining consciousness.

I scrambled over, falling on my hands and knees beside him.

"No!" he yelled—a low, guttural cry filled with fear and pain.

I realized he couldn't see me through his swollen left eye. "Cougar, it's me, Necie," I said, and touched his shoulder. He jerked violently at my touch.

"No!" he yelled. "No!"

"Cougar, it's me. It's only me. Necie."

"Necie?" he whispered.

"Yeah, baby. It's me. What did they do? Where are you hurt?"

"I'm okay," he said, shaking his head and struggling to sit up.

"You're not okay. I have to call an ambulance."

"No! Just . . . get my clothes."

"But—"

"Get my clothes!"

While I helped him dress, he asked, "Where's Barnes?"

"Looking for Maria."

Cougar leaned back, resting his head against the wall. A thin line of blood and spittle trickled down his chin. "So I didn't dream it?" he asked softly.

"No," I said. "But it's not what you think."

I talked to him while I finished buttoning his shirt and helped him to his feet, but I wasn't sure whether he heard me or not.

"Does Grady's mother smoke?" he asked abruptly.

"No. Why?"

He picked a cigarette butt off the floor, examined it, and shoved it in his pocket. "Let's go."

"Wait!" I grabbed him and he flinched. "Where are we going?"

"Your mother-in-law's. She knows where Abby is."

"How—"

"We'll talk on the way," he said. "I want to get out of this fucking house."

We collected Barnes and left out the front door. No one manned the gate this time. Cougar maintained an angry silence until we reached the highway.

"The cigarettes," he said. "When we went to Grady's mother's house, you remember how he put his out before going inside? When we went into her parlor, it smelled like smoke in there, too, only different. She sprayed air freshener and coughed. On the end table was one of those little rock and marble displays. There were a couple of cigarette butts in it. She noticed, and it pissed her off. She used a tissue to pick them out, and I noticed they had lipstick stains. They're the same brand Maria smokes, and they're some fancy kind—"

"From France," Barnes said.

"—not the kind you buy at the 7-Eleven."

"So she and Grady . . ." I said numbly.

Cougar shook his head. "I don't think so. You saw him at the morgue. He wasn't faking. That leaves—"

"Elizabeth," I finished.

At first, I simply felt relief. If Elizabeth had Abby, she was safe. But the more I thought about it, the angrier I grew. "How could she do this, to Abby or Grady?"

Her accusations rang in my ears. Did she really think I was such a horrible mother she had to steal my child? And who better to help her than the woman bent on destroying me?

I don't remember what else—if anything—was said on the rest of the trip to Elizabeth's. All I could think was, "Find Elizabeth, find Abby."

By the time we pulled up at her house, my nerves were singing. I slammed the car in park and was running up the lawn before Cougar could even open his door. The front door was locked, so I pounded on it with both fists.

"Hang on!" Grady yelled.

He threw open the door, and I saw the fear in his eyes. "Necie, what is it?"

"Where's Elizabeth?" I demanded, pushing past him. I screamed her name up the stairs.

"She's not here," Grady said. "She drove to Lansdale. There's a private detective there who's supposed to be really good."

"Have you got the address?"

"Are you going to tell me what's going on?"

Cougar walked in. Grady blinked at his bloody, battered face, but Cougar didn't acknowledge him at all. He stalked past him to Elizabeth's parlor.

"Hey," Grady yelled. "Hey!"

Cougar dumped the wastebasket and picked a cigarette butt off the floor. With his free hand, he retrieved the one from his pocket and held them out to me. The butts were identical.

"Will somebody tell me what's going on?" Grady asked.

I spun to face him. "Your mother paid Maria Barnes to take Abby."

"Is this some kind of joke?"

"Why else would Maria's cigarette butts be in the

trash can? Has she been here, with you?"

Grady stared at the butts. "No! I told you—"

He looked at me, and I'm sure my eyes mirrored the desperation I saw in his. He ran from the room and returned, clutching a piece of paper. "I'm going with you."

We ran for the car. Grady jumped in the backseat and yelped, "Who the hell is this?"

I'd almost forgotten Barnes was with us. "Grady—"

"Grady! The man who hit my daughter?"

"Your father!" Grady shouted. "The drug dealer?"

Ignoring them, I peeled tires pulling away from the curb.

"What coward hits a woman?" Barnes asked.

"You *killed* people, and you're judging me?"

"Should've had *you* killed."

I glanced at Cougar. He gazed out the window like he didn't even hear them.

"Shut up!" I yelled, and mercifully, they did. For awhile, at least. I gave up trying to referee and instead tried to explain to Cougar why I hadn't told him the truth. Who knew whether he believed me or not? He merely stared straight ahead.

"Please don't hate me," I begged, and put my hand over his.

No response.

Thirty minutes later, we pulled up to a neat, cream-colored house.

Grady sighed. "Necie, if you're wrong—"

But we both knew I wasn't. We ran to the door, and Grady knocked. He motioned me over, so that if she glanced out, she wouldn't see me. Cougar caught my gaze and motioned that he was going around back, in case she tried to get out that way.

The shade fluttered, then Elizabeth opened the door, looking pale and tense. Then she spotted me and tried to shut the door. I shoved hard and barreled my way inside.

"Where is she?" I cried. "Where's Abby?"

"Shhh," Elizabeth said. "Please . . . she's sleeping."

"Mother!" Grady said, his mouth tight with rage. "How could you? You know we've been going crazy—"

"I know, and I'm sorry, but I was only trying to protect Abby. The two of you were tearing her apart!"

I took the stairs two at a time, with Grady on my heels. I opened doors, searching for her. In the last room, I found an empty bed with a bear propped up on it. The curtains billowed in the open window. The bear held a note written in red marker.

It read, *Too Late.*

CHAPTER 17

Elizabeth appeared in the doorway. I grabbed the note and thrust it in her face. "Do you know what you've done?" I screamed.

Her pale face grew even chalkier. "But . . . she was just here. I checked on her half an hour ago."

Barnes tugged at my sleeve. "Let's go, Denise," he whispered. "I know where she's going."

Grady yelled after us. I told him to call the police and let them know Maria was in the area.

We left him there with his mother. Back on the road, Barnes said, "Her grandmother's old place. Maria might take her there to avoid the roadblocks."

"We need to call Bill," Cougar said.

"No," Barnes said. "We go in there with guns blazing and they'll both die."

"Why don't you call her?" Cougar asked. "You taught her everything she knows. Call her off."

"I don't know if I can." He stared at his hands. "Maria is very angry at me. When I asked her about Abby, she was enraged. Accused me of choosing Denise over her. A couple hours after we talked, someone tried to shiv me in the prison yard."

"You think Maria tried to have you killed?"

"I called her, asked for help. I was moved to a new cell, with a man who said Maria was paying him to protect me. He tried to kill me."

"So you escaped not to save Abby, but to save your own skin?" Cougar asked.

"No! I realized how out of control she was, what she might do."

"Who was the other body?" I asked. "I assume one of them was your cell mate?"

Barnes shook his head. "Don't ask questions you don't want the answers to."

"Murdering bastard," Cougar said, then looked at me. "Is this the kind of help you want?"

I met his gaze. "I want any help that gets Abby back." To Barnes, I said, "So, what do we do?"

Barnes had a plan in motion, an operative he trusted on the inside. When he asked us to wait until nightfall, Cougar was enraged and I was frustrated, but we had to do as he asked. We rented a cheap motel room with double beds to catch a little rest until we could meet with his man.

Cougar immediately entered the bathroom, and I heard the shower come on a moment later. Barnes squeezed my shoulder and stood. "Get some sleep. I'll wake you when it's time."

"Where are you going?"

"To stand watch." He gave me a tired smile. "Never trust anyone completely, Denise."

He went outside, shutting the door behind him.

Cougar emerged from the bathroom shortly afterward, fully clothed and toweling his hair. He merely nodded when I told him where Barnes had gone. Then he walked over to the other bed and lay down with his back to me, facing the wall.

I rose and pulled the shades. Hesitantly, I approached the bed. Cougar didn't speak when I slipped in beside him, but he flinched when I wrapped my arms around his waist. I wanted to tell him so many things—

Thank you . . .

I'm sorry . . .

—but I didn't know how. Would he ever forgive me?

He covered my hands with his, and I felt a tear slide down my nose.

Barnes was wrong. I did have someone I could trust completely.

I couldn't breathe. Hands locked around my throat. Someone straddled me, crushing me. I beat at the hands, scratched at the hard forearms. I frantically reached for the light on the nightstand. Spots danced before my eyes, and consciousness began to ebb away.

In my efforts to grab the lamp, I managed to knock it over and turn it on. A brilliant beam of light shone right in Cougar's face.

He blinked, but his eyes remained vacant. Unfocused. His grip relaxed the slightest bit. I dug my fingernails in his forearms again. He cried out and looked down at me. Then he finally saw me.

He rolled off me and yanked me to a sitting position.

"Necie, are you okay?" he cried. "I didn't know—I wasn't awake!"

I couldn't answer him. Every breath I took felt like I was breathing in shards of glass. His fingers roamed my throat, searching for damage, desperate to erase it.

"What . . ." I croaked, ". . . did they do to you?"

He froze, and something horrible, something dark passed over his face. He ran from the room.

Stumbling to the bathroom, I flipped on the rest of the lights and inspected the ugly red welts on my throat. The door clicked open, and I hurried back, thinking it was Cougar, but it was Barnes. His eyes narrowed when he looked at me, then widened with rage.

"What did he do?" he bellowed.

Tears welled in my eyes, and he mistook the reason. He stalked toward the door.

"Wait! He didn't mean to."

"Didn't mean to? How could he not mean to?"

"This wasn't Cougar. He was asleep. He didn't know what he was doing." I sat on the edge of the bed. "He's . . . damaged. What did they do to him? He won't talk to me."

Barnes stared, then he sighed. "There is a bodyguard of Maria's . . . He . . . he takes a certain perverse pleasure in breaking men like Cougar, by taking from them the thing they value most—their self-respect."

"What do you—" I broke off when I saw his face flush. He refused to meet my eyes. Horrified, I realized he was implying a sexual attack.

"You horrible, horrible people!" I cried. "How can you employ monsters like that?"

I couldn't stand to look at him. All I could think about was Cougar, and what he'd suffered because of me.

I found him by the chipped, cloudy-looking pool. He glanced at me with red-rimmed eyes, then came over to look at my throat.

He cursed loudly, violently, and turned his back. "I'm sorry," he said. "I'm so sorry."

It killed me to see him so broken. He'd always been

there for me, and despite everything, he was still there.

"I love you," I blurted.

Though I hadn't known I was going to say it, I knew it was true.

"You love me?" he repeated, shooting me an incredulous look. "Necie, I nearly killed you!"

"I love you," I said again, and held out my hand to him.

For a split second, his face was open. I saw hope. Fear. Then it was gone.

"We've got to move," he said, and brushed past me.

⌐ ⌐ ⌐

Barnes's man got us in without incident, transporting us in the back of a rattling black van. A Trojan horse with bad shocks. But once we entered the garage, he told us we were on our own.

Barnes thanked him, and we moved to the connecting door. As promised, we found it unlocked. We slipped into the spacious kitchen. From upstairs came the muffled sound of music and a woman's laughter.

A door slammed nearby, and quick steps approached from the hallway. Barnes and I crouched behind a kitchen island, and Cougar slid behind the refrigerator.

A large man with brown hair and a tattoo on his forehead sauntered past me, heading for the fridge.

He never made it.

Cougar sprang from the shadows and seized him. With one quick, savage motion, he snapped the man's neck.

Stunned, I watched the body fall to the floor.

"Cougar!" I hissed. "What—"

Barnes grabbed my arm and whispered, "Let him alone, Denise. This is the man I told you about."

Looking at Cougar's wild, angry face, I felt my heart break.

Maria yelled from upstairs, "Hey, Granger! Make yourself useful and bring up that tray of sandwiches. The brat's getting hungry."

My hopes surged. Abby was still alive!

Cougar and I moved for the stairs, but Barnes cut in front of us. We were halfway up when Maria appeared at the top of the stairs.

"Hurry up, will—" She gaped at her father. "Papa!" she gasped, her hand fluttering to her throat. "You're alive!"

Then her gaze found me. Her face contorted with pain. "You lied to me, did this to me because of *her?*"

"Maria, honey . . ." Barnes held out his hands. "Please, come. Let me explain."

"I loved you!" she screamed. "I would've done anything for you."

"Mija, please. I did this for both of you. You are my flesh and blood, my—"

"She despises you! Are you too stupid to see that?"

"I couldn't let you harm that child, because of my failures as a father."

"Hurt her?" Maria shouted, her eyes black with rage. "I'm going to kill her."

With that, she turned and ran.

"No!" I screamed and nearly knocked Barnes down as I raced past him. I launched myself at her, snagging her ankle. She went sprawling on the white carpet and slipped from my grasp. I clawed after her on my hands and knees.

"Cougar!" I shouted. "Find Abby."

Suddenly, Maria rolled onto her back and kicked me in the face. The blow snapped my head back. Blood spurted from my nose and filled my mouth. I couldn't see, couldn't hear for the ringing in my ears. When I could focus again, there was a gun pointing at my face.

"No, Maria, no!" Barnes barked. "Don't!"

She swung the gun around and shot him. He fell backward against the wall.

"Papa!" she screamed, and I threw myself at her legs.

She crashed into a table, knocking it over. I guess that's where the fire came from, an overturned candle that caught the curtains, because the next thing I knew, that side of the room was engulfed in flames.

CHAPTER 18

Maria and I grappled for the gun. She smacked me across the face with it, cutting my cheek as she tried to bring it around to shoot me in the face.

She fought like a demon—biting, clawing, kicking, and punching. Dimly, I heard Cougar yelling for Abby, but I didn't dare take my eyes off Maria.

The house was old—large, but inexpensively made. The flames spread quickly, and the floor creaked and moaned beneath us.

I jerked Maria's arm, banging it against a coffee table. The gun clattered away. With a shriek, she went for my eyes, and I sank my teeth into her hand.

The floor gave another long, shuddering groan, then it buckled.

Maria's eyes met mine. We realized at the same moment that the floor was collapsing, but it was too late to do anything. The room seemed to fold in half. We slid toward a yawning, crumbling hole.

Maria cried out something in Spanish and dug her fingers in the carpet, trying to gain purchase. I grabbed at a table and nearly bashed myself in the head when it toppled.

"Hold on!" Barnes cried. Blood flowered his left shoulder, and that arm hung limply by his side. He lay on his stomach and edged toward us.

"Papa, help me!" Maria screamed.

We were side by side now. She darted her eyes at me, then cried, "Papa, don't let me die!"

Barnes's face contorted and—in the midst of everything—I saw a tear slip down his cheek.

He stretched out his good arm to me.

Maria gave one last, horrible scream before she fell. Barnes gave me a mighty yank and pulled me out of the worst section.

"The stairs," he gasped. "We have to get to the stairs."

Gagging and choking on the heavy smoke, we crawled toward the staircase, then half-ran, half-fell down the steps.

"There!" Barnes said, and I spotted Cougar with Abby in his arms. He saw us and motioned for us to follow him. Momentarily setting Abby down, he picked up a chair and smashed the French doors. Grabbing

Abby, he swung her through the opening and set her on the grass.

"Come on!" I yelled, and reached for Barnes.

He wasn't there.

Coughing, I turned back, trying to find him in the smoke.

Then Cougar appeared, seizing my arm. "Necie, we've got to go. This place is going to collapse."

"I have to find him!" I cried. "He saved me."

The house shrieked and swayed. I saw Abby through the broken door. She was screaming for me.

I took Cougar's hand, and we ran for the door. A man stepped out, blocking our way. At first I was confused, wondering how Barnes had gotten in front of me, then I was even more confused to discover it was Bill.

He pointed a gun at us.

"I'm sorry," he said. "I never meant for it to come to this, but I don't know what the old man's told you."

"You?" Cougar asked. "It was you?"

"I'm sorry," Bill said again, and steadied his arm.

Frank Barnes came charging out of the flames. He launched himself at Bill, and they tumbled out of sight. I heard him shout, "Get her out of here!" and Cougar did.

He seized Abby with one arm and we ran.

With a loud rumble, the house caved in.

I stared at it in shocked silence, then Cougar held me while I cried.

CHAPTER 19

Later, Cougar told me that he'd called Bill from the motel, because he feared we were walking into a trap. I still couldn't believe Bill had tried to kill us, and that ultimately, Frank Barnes had died for us.

Elizabeth was sentenced to ten years for her role in the kidnapping, but would probably only serve a third of that.

The things we do for love . . .

I wish I could say things were perfect after we got back, that Cougar and I finally found the "happily ever after" we knew we could have with one another, but if anything, life grew harder.

With Maria and Granger both dead, I'd hoped Cougar could come to terms with whatever they'd done to him, but he had changed. Maybe irrevocably. I knew he loved me, but there was a wall between us that I couldn't crack. I would give anything if he could only talk to me, and it killed me to know he felt the same way.

His eyes were empty, and he seldom smiled, or even talked. Though he spent every night that Abby wasn't there in my bed, and every night when she was on my couch, we didn't make love. He would hold me and tell me everything was going to be all right. When he woke up screaming, I would hold him and say the same.

One day, he left work early before I got out of court. He didn't tell anyone where he was going and left his car in the parking garage at work. Grady wanted to take Abby to a movie that night, so I dropped her off at his place and went home to wait. Minutes turned to hours, and my anxiety grew. Cougar stumbled in around two, soaking wet from the freezing rain and smelling of tequila. That scared me as much as anything, because in all the years I'd known him, I'd never seen him drink.

"Where have you been?" I asked, as calmly as I could.

He wouldn't meet my eyes while he stripped off his shirt. "With Angel."

"I called the hospital. They said they hadn't seen you."

"With Tucker, then."

"Tucker's the one who told me he hadn't seen you."

"Those are your only two choices." He forced a smile and stumbled toward the bathroom. "Shhh, or you'll wake Abby."

"It's Friday. Abby's with her father. I want to talk about you, and where you've been for the past fourteen hours."

He nearly fell when he twisted to face me. His eyes narrowed. "If I wanted a curfew, I'd still be at home with my mother."

"Yeah, and if I wanted a drunk, I'd still be with Grady." I threw the pillow I'd been hugging on the couch and stood. He flinched like he'd been slapped, and I lowered my voice. "Please, Jason. Don't shut me out."

He hesitated, staring at me for a long moment as he swayed on his feet. Then he brushed my words away with a wave of his hand and turned back toward the bathroom.

"Nothing they could've done to you is worse than what I've already imagined," I blurted.

He froze.

I didn't want to hurt him, but I was desperate for something—*anything*—to make him open up to me.

"Whatever they did, it wasn't your fault."

I touched his back and he startled me when he gave a great, heaving sob. He pivoted and—in doing so—lost his balance. I tried to grab him, but he was too heavy. We crashed to the floor. He pulled me into his lap and hugged me so hard I could barely breathe.

"Don't give up on me," he begged. "If there's one thing I hang onto . . . that gets me through the night . . . it's you."

His tears burned hot against my neck as he rocked me, but the rest of him was icy cold. "Never." I stroked his damp hair. "Never."

He pulled back and looked at me. The anguish in his reddened eyes seared me to the bone. "I-I can't. There are some things . . ." He squeezed his eyes shut. "God help me, I can't even say it out loud. I'm s-sorry, but I can't. Not now. Maybe not ever."

Tears coursed down his face. Down mine.

"I know you l-love me, that you believe those things you said," he said. "But there are things I can't talk about—not with you, not with anybody. It doesn't mean . . ." He slipped his hand behind my head and wound his fingers in my hair. Pressing his forehead to mine, he said, "I love you with all my heart. Can't that be enough?"

Tearfully, I nodded. We shared a desperate kiss, and sometime later, I helped him to bed. I wanted to be strong for him, but I felt so weak in the face of all the things he could never tell me.

r r r

A week later, we were in his kitchen making a late breakfast when the phone rang. I had my hands in dishwater and Cougar was flipping eggs. I wiped my hands on a towel and hurried to answer it. The machine clicked on before I got there.

A cheerful female voice said, "Mr. Stratton, this is Dr. Hargrove's office. Your test results are in—"

I heard a clatter as Cougar yanked the skillet off the stove. He nearly knocked me down in his haste to get to the phone. "This is Jason Stratton."

He cast a guilty glance in my direction. I quickly walked back toward the kitchen, but I heard him say, "Yes. When can I—as soon as possible. Today would be great. Thank you."

He hung up and I busied myself wiping down the stove. I felt him approach, but I didn't turn around.

"That was my doctor's office," he said in a "no big deal" kind of way. "I had a physical last week, my semi-annual HIV test . . ."

"Oh?" I said with deliberate casualness, though my stomach knotted. Would this suffering never end? One glance at his face confirmed the underlying tension I heard in his tone. His eyes looked suddenly hollow, his face tight, though he was trying so desperately to act normal. I couldn't hold his gaze long for fear that I'd bawl like a baby.

"Yeah," he said and gave me a smile that was so wrong it looked grotesque. He must've realized it, too, because it quickly disappeared, though he tried to keep his tone light. "Now that I'm off the market, I won't have to fool with those damn things much longer. I guess I'll run by there now so I won't be late for work. Okay with you?"

I nodded, unable to speak. He couldn't even kiss me. He smacked a kiss in the general vicinity of my ear and left.

I waited until he left, then picked up the skillet and hurled it at the wall.

🔫 🔫 🔫

I went on to work, but I couldn't concentrate on the file in front of me. I should've followed him. What if it was bad news? What if he needed me right now? I made myself wait another twenty minutes before snatching up a phone book to search for Dr. Hargrove's number. My hand was on the receiver when Cougar strode through the door.

He flashed me such a wide, happy smile that my knees nearly buckled with relief. It was a real smile, and it didn't fade when he walked over to me.

I stood and he came around the desk to plant an enthusiastic kiss on my lips. "Hey, babe."

"Everything's okay?"

"Everything's great."

For awhile, we simply stood there. I knew I was grinning like an idiot, but I couldn't help myself, not when I saw a glint of happiness in his eyes again. A spark of hope. It was crazy, but his irises even looked

373

lighter, like someone had flipped a switch inside of him and chased the shadows away. They were the most beautiful blue I'd ever seen. Impulsively, I hugged him. He laughed and squeezed me back.

"Hey," he said, when I could finally bear to let him go. "What do you say we knock off early, grab Abby, and go someplace? I'd like to take my girls to an early dinner."

I smiled. "I'd love to . . . but, oh, wait . . . today's Friday, and Grady's supposed to pick Abby up at four."

Cougar folded a piece of gum and shoved it in his mouth. "I called him and asked if we could drop her off around seven. He's cool with it."

That made me pause. He'd *called* him? We all got along pretty well these days—crazy relatives notwithstanding—but I figured that was mainly because Cougar and Grady didn't do more than exchange greetings when Grady dropped by the apartment for Abby. The thought of them having an actual conversation was somewhat unnerving.

Abby's kidnapping had made us remember what was important, and I don't think Grady had touched a drop of alcohol since that day at the morgue nearly two months ago. I was proud of his regular AA attendance and knew he loved his daughter. That was enough for me. The past was the past, and I held no grudges. I hoped he felt the same.

"An early dinner sounds great," I managed. "Where are you taking us?"

Cougar made a face. "Well, I'd take you to Le-Bec Fin, but I doubt they serve hamburgers or pizza, so I know you and Abby would hate it. We'll resort to the second swankiest place in town . . . Fat Daddy's!" I giggled, and he slung his arm around my shoulders. "But I'm warning you, if that bird gives me any beak this time . . ." He thumped his fist in his palm.

The rest of the day passed quickly. Cougar laughed and joked with the others, flirted with me. He seemed almost like his old self. I dared to think that maybe we could get past this.

I'd worried at first that my relationship with Cougar would hurt Abby, that she'd resent him for taking her father's place in our home, but those fears had proved unfounded. He was so careful with her. I'd never asked him to sleep on the couch when she was home, but he'd done that out of respect for her. He played with her and helped with schoolwork, not because I asked him to, but because he wanted to. He loved her, and she knew that. She loved him, too.

That night, even Abby seemed to notice the change in his mood. She clung to his side and laughed a little too hard at all his jokes, even the goofy ones. I guess I did, too. I wanted us to stay that way forever.

We spent five dollars' worth of quarters playing games while we waited on our pizza. We'd skipped lunch, and I was starving by the time the waitress set it in front of us. I don't know if I'd ever eaten anything that tasted so good. I even caught Cougar licking his fingers. He'd lost nearly ten pounds, and I was happy to see his appetite back.

The eagle walked by and ruffled Cougar's hair. Cougar gave him a dirty look that dissolved into a reluctant smile when Abby and I giggled. This just encouraged the eagle, who launched into an impromptu dance at our table. He kept trying to pull Cougar up with him.

Cougar laughed and tried to shoo him away. "C'mon, man, cluck off."

"Jason!" I said.

He gave me a sheepish smile and rolled his eyes. Then he reached into his back pocket and motioned the eagle forward. Flashing his badge, he said, "Hey, man. You see the initials DEA?"

The eagle nodded vigorously and ruffled Cougar's hair again.

"They stand for Designated Eagle Assassin. I get paid to shoot birds."

The eagle waved him off with a "pshaw" gesture and grasped my arm. He pulled me out of the booth and motioned for Abby. She crawled out from behind Cougar and took his wing. He led us in a conga line that grew to around twenty people before we made it back to our table. Breathless and laughing, it took me a moment to notice the ring boxes on the table, one pink and one blue. The eagle saluted Cougar and led the line away from us.

"What are these?" I asked when Cougar slid the pink one toward Abby.

Cougar gave me an odd smile and stirred his ice water with his straw. "Open them and see."

I did as he said, and my heart thumped in my ears as relentlessly as the conga music when I saw the square-cut diamond ring inside. I twisted to look at Abby, who stared down at a tiny diamond eternity band.

Cougar's eyes shone when he said, "So much has happened in the past few months, things that I never thought could happen to me. I never thought I'd fall in love with my best friend." He winked at Abby. "And her daughter. I never thought I wanted to be a husband or a father." He gave me a crooked smile. "And for sure, I never thought I'd end up proposing in some dive called Fat Daddy's with the help of a giant bird, but here we are."

I laughed and swiped at my eyes. He slid out of the booth and took a knee in front of us. "So, I don't know a lot of things, but one thing I know for sure is that I want both of you in my life forever. What do you say?"

"We say yes!" Abby blurted. She tugged on my hand. "We do, don't we, Mama? We say yes!"

I nodded happily. "We say yes."

Cougar put her ring on first, then took my hand. "You're shaking," he said with a tremulous smile. He slid the ring on my finger, and suddenly the music stopped. I glanced over my shoulder to see the eagle hold his wings out in a "well?" gesture.

Abby and I looked at each other and held up our hands. The crowd roared. The eagle strutted over to give Cougar a sorrowful pat on the back before cuing the teenager by the jukebox. The walls shook with the opening strains of "Another One Bites the Dust."

The eagle fell to the floor and proceeded to twitch and kick before throwing his feet up in the air and playing dead. With a mortified laugh, Cougar grabbed mine and Abby's hands and dragged us toward the door. He tried to pay the cashier, but she grinned and yelled, "On the house!"

Cougar thanked her and gave the eagle a bow. The eagle bowed back and gave him a thumbs-up. When he acted like he was going to follow us, Cougar practically shoved us outside. We stumbled into the cold evening, laughing and gasping for breath.

After dropping Abby off at Grady's, we went back to my apartment. Cougar helped me out of my coat, then shrugged off his own. With a smile, he hung them up and strode over to turn on the radio.

"Let's dance," he said, and scanned the stations until he found a song he liked, "Shameless" by Garth Brooks. "Oh, that's perfect." He held out his hand and grinned. "May I?"

Giggling, I tucked my hand in his and let him pull

me close. He glanced at our entwined fingers, at the sparkling engagement ring, and said, "I love you. I love you so much."

"I love you, too," I whispered, and his other arm tightened on my waist.

He sang along with the radio as we swayed and I laughed.

He smiled. "What's so funny?"

"I think that's the first time you've sung anything to me that wasn't X-rated."

"Oh, now you're just confusing me with Angel," he said, and dipped his head to kiss me.

The kiss, gentle at first, grew more urgent. He fumbled at the buttons on my sweater, pausing only to let me skin his shirt over his head. We left a haphazard trail of clothing before he picked me up and carried me the rest of the way to the bedroom.

He made love to me with a quiet desperation that left us both exhausted and satiated. We fell asleep tangled in each other's arms and, for one night at least, the nightmares didn't find him.

Things seemed to settle down after that. We were happy, especially when Angel's condition improved enough that he was released from the hospital. If everything wasn't just right, at least it was getting better. Cougar and I eased into a comfortable routine while we planned for the wedding. Although I knew the storm inside Cougar was still there, it had subsided enough to give him some peace. At least, until the night of his bachelor party.

The phone jarred me awake. I woke wild, my heart thumping painfully against my rib cage, and automatically felt for Cougar beside me. His side of the bed was cold and empty. I squinted at the clock. Two a.m.

I fumbled for the phone and pressed it to my ear. "Hello?"

"Hello, Necie?"

The tone of Ubi's voice shook off the last spider webs of sleep.

I sat up straight. "What is it? Is it Jason? Where is he?"

Ubi paused. "I don't know."

"You don't know?"

"He freaked out, and he left."

"What do you mean, he freaked out? Tell me what happened."

"We were just having fun. Cutting up and drinking, then. . ." Ubi hesitated again, and I grew impatient.

"Damn it, Ubi, what?"

"We had a stripper come in."

"Oh, thanks a lot."

"It was just for fun. Cougar didn't know, I swear. Before she came in, a couple of guys grabbed him, cuffed him to the chair. She came in and danced over him . . . Necie, he lost it. He nearly tore the place apart, yelling and cussing until somebody let him loose. Then he left. We thought you should know."

I hung up without replying and threw on some clothes. I thought I knew where I'd find him.

Fifteen minutes later, I knocked softly on the door of Mrs. Angelino's apartment. She answered the door in her robe, her dark eyes worried. "He's here," she said. "Said he had to talk to John. Is something wrong?"

"I don't know, Mrs. Angelino," I said honestly. "How long has he been in there?"

"About half an hour, I suppose."

"Can I—"

She gestured to the closed door of Angel's bedroom. "Sure."

I knocked, and Angel yelled, "Come in!"

Cougar sighed when I let myself in and gently shut the door behind me. He leaned back in the chair, looking wild and more than a little angry. "Which one of those sons of bitches called you?" he asked.

"They were worried." When I drew closer, I noted both his and Angel's red-rimmed eyes and felt a sense of relief. If he couldn't talk to me, I was glad he could talk to someone.

"It pissed me off." Cougar pushed a hand through his hair. "I kept telling them to let me up, then that woman wouldn't stop crawling on me . . . I told them no strippers. Hey, when I asked you to marry me, that meant you were the only woman I wanted to be with."

"I know," I said lightly, and moved around the bed to sit in his lap.

He held himself rigid for a moment, then relaxed. He draped an arm across my knees and kissed my forehead.

I glanced at Angel, and he gave me a reassuring wink, though his handsome face was creased with worry. "Besides, no fair having strippers there when I can't be there," he joked.

Cougar laughed and drew me up closer. "But the doc cleared you for the wedding. That's the important thing. I don't know what I'd do without my best man."

"Yeah, it's a good thing you didn't ask me to give Necie away," he said with a grin. "Because I'd just keep her." He cleared his throat. "It's good that you're marrying a friend, Coug. Somebody you can talk to. Somebody you can tell anything."

Cougar dropped his head. "I-I know."

We sat in awkward silence for a moment, then Cougar gently slapped my knee. "Well, we'd better get going, babe. Let this guy get some beauty sleep. God knows, he needs it."

I stood and hugged Angel, then Cougar did the same. Angel held him for a moment too long, and whispered something.

It'll be okay. Just talk to her, man.

Back at the apartment, I hoped he would, but he

had other things on his mind. He was kissing me before I ever got the keys out of the door. Everything felt off, however, as if he were being so aggressive merely to prove to me that nothing was wrong. The wildness I felt in his kiss . . . the distress . . . frightened me. I didn't want to go back to the way we were following the attack. It was as if all the progress we'd made had been wiped away by this one stupid incident. An idea occurred to me, but I was hesitant to speak it aloud because—although I knew it had the potential to make things better—it also might make things a thousand times worse. Still, as Cougar ravaged my throat, I decided to trust my instincts.

"I want to tie you up," I whispered huskily.

He froze, absolutely froze. When he looked at me, I saw a flash of anger. Fear.

"What?" he asked thickly. "Why the hell would you want to do that?"

"Because . . ." I stroked his cheek, ". . . when you go to sleep tonight, I don't want you dreaming about some stripper. I want you dreaming about me."

We both knew I wasn't worried about "some stripper" invading his dreams. There were worse things that came for him when he slept, and I thought maybe—just maybe—we could banish them by recreating another memory. A good one.

"I don't know," he said, looking pale and shaken.

I kissed his neck. "If you decide you don't like it, I'll

untie you. You just have to say the word."

He stared at me for a long moment, then walked to the bedroom.

Wordlessly, we undressed, and he allowed me to tie his wrists to the headboard. For an instant, I saw the terror in his eyes, bright and stark.

"Leave the light on," he commanded.

For a long time, I simply kissed him, touched him . . . murmured a thousand I love yous. He finally relaxed, the fear in his eyes turning to desire. I made love to him slowly, gently, praying that somehow all the love we had for each other would prove stronger than the memories that haunted him.

EPILOGUE

"Wake up, lazy bones." I leaned over the side of the bed to kiss Cougar's neck. He smiled and mumbled something incomprehensible before covering his face with a pillow.

Putting my hands on my hips, I said, "Are you going to get up and run with me or not?"

He tossed the pillow and seized me, pulling me on top of him and regarding me with one sleepy blue eye.

"With all due respect, Mrs. Stratton . . . I am still recovering from the workout you gave me last night."

"But it's the ocean . . . the sun, the salt . . ."

"I like the ocean better after dark. See, I have this idea, for later on tonight . . ."

Rolling my eyes, I crawled off him. "You can tell me all about it when I get back. Call and check on Abby. They might try to call us at the other hotel. I'll order us

385

some breakfast when I get back."

He gave me a sleepy salute and rolled on his side.

I was still smiling when I made my way past the vendors and tourists and ran down the sandy white beach. We were taking a short honeymoon. Neither of us wanted to leave Abby for very long, though we'd left her in the capable and loving hands of Cougar's mother, who seemed quite determined to spoil her new granddaughter. She'd volunteered to stay in Philly to babysit until we got back.

I tried to estimate three miles on my run, then headed back to the hotel. A bike messenger intercepted me under the sprawling red awning.

"Mrs. Stratton?" he asked.

When I said that I was, he presented me with a bouquet of flowers and a card.

Oh, Jason, I thought, pressing my face to the wildflowers. I patted my pockets, realizing I had no money with me to tip him.

"That's okay, ma'am," he said with a smile. "Have a nice day."

I waved good-bye, then gave the flowers another appreciative sniff before opening the envelope. Extracting the card, I frowned when I saw the silver script on the front of it.

Congratulations to Both of You on Your Wedding.

Only a handful of people knew where we were going and—due to a hotel mix-up—none of them even knew where we were staying. I opened the card and nearly dropped the photo and plastic sleeve that was inside.

My heart stalled when I examined the picture.

Maria smiled at me, one side of her lovely face marred by burn scars. In her arms, she held a dark-haired baby. In the plastic sleeve, I found a lock of hair tied with a baby blue ribbon. The graceful handwriting inside the card read simply, "He has his father's eyes, doesn't he?"

With a lump in my throat, I realized he did, indeed.

Numbly, I shoved it back in the envelope, caught the elevator back to our room, and let myself in.

Cougar emerged from the bathroom with a towel swathed around his narrow hips. He grinned. "Hey, I was about to come looking for you."

Wordlessly, I handed him the card. His smile faded when he glanced from me to it. He opened it, then dropped it like it had burned him.

He sat heavily on the bed and buried his face in his hands. When he finally looked at me, his eyes were dark with anguish and fury.

"I am not like Grady," he said vehemently. "I didn't give her anything. She took it."

He paused, as if waiting on me to say something, but I couldn't. I could barely breathe.

Apparently, he mistook my silence for condemnation. He jumped to his feet. Agitated, he paced beside the bed. "Her goons were punching me. The last thing I heard before I blacked out was her telling them to take off my clothes. When I came to, I was naked, and she was . . ."

He grimaced, and wiped his hand down his face, unwilling or unable to say it even now.

"Granger?" I whispered.

I felt dizzy, sick. Still, I needed to hear everything.

"No." Cougar shook his head violently. "No. He and the others . . . they held me down. Laughed. Taunted me. Granger told me he was next, but they ran out of time, or she called him off, or . . . hell, I don't know." He raked his hand through his hair, then glanced at me, his face stark.

I was crying now, and my tears only seemed to stoke his desperation.

"You have to believe me, Necie. I didn't want her. I was scared to death. She was . . ." He squeezed his eyes shut. "She was stimulating me with a knife. I thought she was going to castrate me, or cut my throat, but still my body . . . my own body . . ."

"An erection, and even ejaculation are involuntary, physiological reactions. You couldn't help it. It doesn't imply consent." Words from my training spilled out of my mouth, but they felt hollow, useless, as I stared into the tormented face of the man I loved.

He waved his hand and scowled. "Yeah, yeah, and rape isn't about sex, it's about power . . ." He froze, then gave a mortified laugh. "Rape," he repeated. Then he cursed.

Not knowing what else to do, I wrapped my arms around him and held on tight.

I don't know how long we stood there like that,

but finally he pulled away. He stooped to retrieve the photograph from the floor, then sat on the edge of the bed, studying it.

"Maybe it's not mine. Maybe she's only doing this to hurt us."

I stood beside him, laying my hand on the back of his neck. "There's a . . . a lock of hair. I don't know if you saw it, but I'm sure she did that knowing we'd take a DNA sample."

His shoulders slumped in defeat. "So, what do we do now?"

I knelt in front of him and met his gaze. "The only thing we can do. We're going to get your son."

"My son," he repeated, sounding weary. Resigned. His blue eyes were troubled when he said, "But what if I can't . . . what if I can't love him? How can I look at him and not . . ."

"You will love him, for the same reason I will. Because he's yours."

I held up my hand, palm facing him. He laced his fingers in mine.

We were going to be okay. We would make it through this.

Maria Barnes was going to pay with her life.

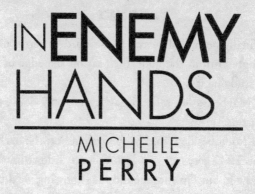

IN ENEMY HANDS

MICHELLE PERRY

How hard could it be to kidnap a pampered little rich girl?

Especially if you're bounty hunter extraordinaire Dante Giovanni, who normally prowls the underworld in search of the most vicious criminals. Piece of cake, Dante thinks, when reclusive businessman Gary Vandergriff offers him a cool half million to bring home his estranged daughter, Nadia.

Enter Nadia.

His first meeting with her is stunning; both literally and figuratively. He foils an attempt on her life, and falls immediately under her spell. It's not gonna be hard duty, Dante thinks, keeping her safe from the Mexican drug lord infuriated by her stepfather's expanding meth operation. He'll take her out of harm's way, no problem, get her back to her father, and enjoy the ride along the way. Everything is great.

Until he delivers her into Enemy Hands.

ISBN#9781932815474
Jewel Imprint: Emerald
US $6.99 / CDN $9.99
Available Now
www.michelleperry.com

michelle perry

The Three Motives *for* Murder

The small town of Coalmont, Tennessee is shattered when a car crash on graduation night leaves three of its teenagers dead and another three fighting for their lives. Four years later, the aftershocks still ripple through the town, and no one feels them more than Natasha Hawthorne, the young driver.

When someone targets the survivors of the horrific crash for murder, the obvious motive is revenge. But things aren't always what they seem, and the notion of revenge served cold doesn't ring true with Brady Simms, newly appointed police chief. To make things even more difficult, Brady ultimately finds himself standing squarely between the killer and his next victim, the woman who broke his heart four years ago.

As the killer escalates his attacks, Brady's only hope of saving the intended victims is to get into the mind of a sociopath. When the relative of the first victim makes a startling revelation, Brady reopens the investigation and what he finds will change all of their lives forever.

ISBN#9781932815801
Jewel Imprint: Emerald
US $6.99 / CDN $8.99
Available Now
www.michelleperry.com